HACKED LIVES

The Intricate-Web of True-Self

ABRAHAM (aka Yemane) GIRMAY MERESSA

&

Asmerom Weldegiorgs Weldegebreal

DISCLAIMER

This is a work of fiction. Names, characters, places, events and incidents are either the products of the author's imagination or used in a fictitious manner. Any resemblance to actual persons, living or dead, or actual events is purely coincidental.

TABLE OF CONTENT

Chapter One

"For how long?" Saba asked. Both Saba and her husband, Million were in their backyard. Their children, Mica and Rui were playing carelessly a few feet from them. Million's heart panged, but he knew he had to stand firm. He had dreamed of such news long before it came. He believed that it was what was best for their family. And he was sure that even his love for his family would not come in the way of him accepting such an opportunity—then, Saba confronted him.

"A year, I think," he said, noting that those two little words added more stress onto his wife's face. He didn't like seeing her disappointed. Leaving his wife and his two children devastated him, but how could he turn down such a magnificent chance? "Maybe two?" He said it cautiously, hoping she would show restraint. He wished, if she was going to yell or curse, she did it in the privacy of their bedroom. "That long? What about your children? They could forget what you look like, you know," she spat. She spoke the words, fighting herself to stay calm, but there was much wrath in her tone. "Saba, please," he begged. "I must do what I must do." But even as he spoke the words, he wasn't sure if he believed them. How could he leave someone he loved as much as he loved her for such a long time? How could he commit to the idea of not seeing her beautiful face? She had played on his weaknesses, making the conversation even harder than it had to be, spending a little extra time styling her jet-black hair. Though thin and silky, she had strategically left curls dripping down the sides of her roasted chestnut skin. Her eyes pouted at him, some of that look was natural, but not all of it. She wore her heartbreak openly, and it only made her more beautiful than she was naturally. To look at Saba was to commit to looking at her. Once a man … any man looked at Saba, it was virtually impossible to look away. She was exotically beautiful. Everyone said so, and Million considered himself the luckiest man in the country to have been the one to get her to say yes to his proposal eight years before.

“I don’t know what I or our children would do without you for that long,” she said, fighting back her tears. She was a strong woman. Firm when she needed to be, but firm in the softest way possible. “What if we become strangers? What if we forget what it is that we love about each other?”

“Saba, please,” he begged again. “Nothing in the world could ever make me forget what I love about you.” Million went to her as he spoke, and her arms automatically embraced him, her hands reaching up to nab the back of his neck. Her eyes traced the outline of his lips, letting him know which part of him she needed for reassurance. He leaned in, bringing his lips to hers, desperately wanting to comfort her. Their lips lingered, but only momentarily. As he kissed her, he felt a warm teardrop trickling against his nose.

"I didn't accept this scholarship to get a break from my family," he said to her softly. She nodded, reaching up to wipe a tear from her cheek.

"I know," she said. "I'm just a little scared." She squeezed the back of his neck with the hand that remained there and then turned her attention to their children.

"How come you're crying?" Mica asked her mother, looking up at them both, showing genuine concern for her. Million felt a sense of pride swelling in him. So young, and yet, already beginning to display such an admirable quality to want to protect her mother from feeling bad. Rui was sitting on the ground, using a stick to trace trenches in the sand. Million noticed the anthill there.

"Rui, those ants will bite you if you anger them," said Million, breaking away from his wife. He went to his son.

"I'm teaching them how to write," he said to his father, his gaze going back to what he was doing. Now that he was learning how to make them, Rui was infatuated with letters.

Will he become a writer someday? he wondered as he crouched next to the kid. He reached up, ruffling his hair and then rubbing his shoulder.

"And what word are you teaching them now?" he asked.

"I was gonna write loop," Rui said proudly. "But I don't remember how to spell it." Rui had drawn the letter 'L' in the sand, separating one band of ants from the other. Already, the ants seemed irritated and a little confused. He'd disrupted their scent trail, and they were wandering around trying to find it again.

"Sound it out," said Million. "What comes after the 'L'?"

"Lu, lu, lup," Rui said as he thought about it. "U?" He looked up at him, waiting for him to either confirm or deny his guess, one eyebrow slightly elevated.

"Close enough. Do you remember the other way to make the *oo* sound that we talked about?" Million said, nodding toward the sand. His son used the stick to trace the letter.

"You mean the one like in the word 'book?' Okay, I remember now."

Million became aware of the things he was going to miss in his absence. If everything went according to schedule, he would be gone for two years. When he returned, it wouldn't be spelling lessons that he'd be teaching Rui. He'd already have a firm grip on that. Rui would grow as well. He'd be taller and his hair would be longer. Rui might not forget his face. At least he hoped not, but there would be other things he would. In his absence, Rui would cling to others. He might come to accept that he didn't need him so much. There was a good side to that. Independence isn't all bad, but at his son's age? Five? Depending on his father wasn't such a bad thing. Role models are important.

"Very good," Million said. Rui smiled, got up, and then hugged him, planting himself onto his bent knee.

"How come you made Mom cry?" Rui asked him sincerely. "Is it because you're going to Merica?"

"America, yes," he replied gently, emphasizing the 'A.' "How did you know that I'm going to America?"

Rui turned, looking over at his big sister. Mica was clearly listening intently to the conversation but had her back turned to them. She was sitting on the ground, her favorite doll cradled in her arms, and she was crying. She sniffled, letting the doll go with one hand, reaching up, she wiped her cheek with the back of her hand. Million choked back his own tears as he got up. Settling Rui back onto his feet, he went to his daughter.

"What's the matter, princess?" Million asked as he crouched behind her. He reached up with one hand, hoping to console her, but she shied from him, swaying his hand away.

"Leave me alone," she grumbled resentfully.

"Mica, why do you shun me?" Million asked, feeling alarmed by her reaction of scooching further away from him.

"Because you're leaving!" she bellowed angrily. "You're going away, and you aren't coming back!"

"Mica, of course, I'm coming back! I would never abandon you," he said, keeping his tone calm.

"You're lying!" she screamed at the top of her lungs. Immediately, Million worried about what their neighbors would think if they heard his daughter screaming like that, and his first instinct was to scold her. He hid that instinct back. The last thing his daughter needed at that moment was her father yelling at her.

"I heard what you said!" she added, her brown face getting darker with anger. She got up, backing away from him, ripping his soul in two. She folded her arms over her chest, challenging him, tears streaking down through the dust on her face. He so desperately wanted to console her, to let her know how much he loved her and that he was trying to do his best for her. For everyone in the family. "You're going to leave us for a year!" There was so much anger and hurt in her tearful eyes. He stared into them, seeing nothing but betrayal.

"Mica, please," he begged, unsure how to reach her. She stood there only meters in front of him, but her heart felt an immeasurable distance away from him at that moment. "This is something I must do."

"Because you don't love us anymore. You don't care!"

"Mica, how could you think something like that about me?" he asked. "You mean everything to me."

"If that is true, you wouldn't want to leave," she spat. In so many ways, Mica could be like her mother. So passionate. So, determined. Changing her mind on this wouldn't be easy.

"I must further my education, my darling," he said. "I'm doing this for you. So, you can be like Sayat Demisie. That is what you want, isn't it?" Mica shrugged. His daughter admired the Ethiopian model, singer, actress, and youth ambassador so much, that she spent most of her weekends listening and singing Sayat's songs and reading magazines and newspaper articles and creating a memory book with them. Million had been helping her with that project.

"Not if it means you have to leave us," she said. "I'll tear down all of her posters, and I won't sing anymore."

"And what will you do instead?" Million asked her.

"Hug you every day, because you'll still be here," she replied swiftly.

"I will always be with you, Mica. No matter how far away I am, and when I return, I will return with that dress you've been begging me for. The one that looks just like Sayat's."

"You said we can't afford to buy it," Mica replied.

"Which is why I must do this, my darling," he said desperately. "This will bring us a better life. This will help us be able to afford a better life."

"Please don't go, baba," she begged, breaking into a run. She clashed into his chest, just as he reached his arms forward to receive her. She pressed her head against his chest, wrapping her arms around his shoulder and squeezing his back. "I'm scared without you!"

"I will always protect you. You believe me, right?" he said. "I have an idea. Before I leave, I will give you and Rui special presents, and when you miss me or feel scared, I will show you what to do with those gifts."

He squeezed her back as she cried into his chest. Doubts about his choice lingered in his mind, adding weight to his heart, but he knew he couldn't change his mind.

A few days prior to leaving for America, Million bought two toys for the kids. Considering his budget, he paid heftily to get the toys modified to have animations of himself, Saba, and the kids. Especially his animation, with him saying things that were familiar to his son and daughter, it looked real. Both Mica and Rui liked the toy they each got. They even took them to bed the first few nights. Then, their attention shifted to other toys and threw away those. Seeing the kids didn't play with them as long as he hoped, Million almost regretted that he spent the amount of money he did on them.

***

"So, what do you think?" Ava said, standing behind her daughter, Teena, hands-on both of her shoulders as they both stared into the mirror of Ava's vanity. After shaving her daughter's scalp, she had wrapped her head with a colorful bandana to both keep her head warm and to adorn it.

"I kind of like the way my head looks bald, Mommy," Teena said, smiling and looking up at her mom in their reflected image. "I look like an alien." She giggled, and her smile brightened even more.

"That isn't funny," Ava said, her heart sinking. Mostly, because the same idea had crept into her own mind. Her daughter's hair was so beautiful. Shaving it off had been so hard for her to do, but doing so was the necessary evil. She couldn't stand the idea of watching her daughter's hair slowly thinning to the point of falling out in splotches. And the chemo would have that effect on her. Silently, Ava prayed the chemo treatments would work. She prayed and then prayed some more.

To kill her brain cancer, the most effective treatment was to poison her system, so thoroughly that it virtually risked killing her daughter.

"Can I rest for a while?"

"Yes, sweetie," Ava said, leaning down to kiss her daughter's head.

"You still think I'm beautiful, don't you?" she asked gently.

"Of course, I do," Ava replied.

"Even if I never become a beauty contestant like you were?" Teena asked, slipping from her chair. She started walking away, heading toward her own room. Ava followed her.

"You'll be a contestant someday, Teena," her mother said to reassure her.

"I don't care if I'm not pretty enough," Teena said.

"Teena, you take after me, sweetie. Of course, you're pretty enough."

"I'm just saying," Teena said, leaving her slipper feet padding down the hall. "My teacher said that being pretty isn't everything."

"No, no," Ava said. "It isn't everything." Teena entered her room and headed for her bed. She turned, lowering herself onto it and then laid back. Ava pulled the covers over her daughter's fragile body and began tucking her in. She leaned down, kissing Teena's forehead, fighting back the tears that threatened to spill out.

"Are you going to be okay, Mommy?" Teena asked her.

"Of course," she said. "I'm just a little tired too."

"No, I mean, after I die," Teena said. Ever since she overheard the doctor telling her mom that she could die from the treatment regimen she was on, she had been asking their chauffer, Angel, and the nurses what it meant to die.

"Teena!" Ava blurted harshly. "Don't say such things! You are *not* going to die!"

"I don't want to," Teena said. "But I want you and Daddy to be okay if it happens."

"You aren't going to die, Teena," Ava insisted firmly.

"I can feel it happening," Teena informed her mother. She looked so serene as she laid in her bed. Ava's knees weakened, and she had to brace herself not to collapse to the floor.

"You just need to rest, honey," Ava said, kissing her daughter's forehead again. "When you wake up, you'll feel stronger again. I promise."

"Okay," said Teena, letting her eyes slip closed.

Please, God, Ava begged silently. *Let them open again.*

Ava straightened into a standing position, noting that her daughter had drifted into sleep already. Just like that—she'd closed her eyes and slipped into the dream world as easily as a mouse would escape into its hole.

Ava backed out of her daughter's plush room and quietly closed the door behind her. She was able to remain in an upright position until she made it back into her own bedroom, but she didn't make it into her own bed. Her knees gave out before she could reach it, and she dropped onto her knees, falling against the side of her bed.

“Oh, please, God!” Ava begged, the dam holding back her tears breaking as she spoke. “Please don’t let my baby die!” She sobbed into her hands, her voice hitching as her mind went blank. Teena was her only chance to have a child. The doctors had convinced her of that after having an extremely difficult delivery. She had accepted that fact and had clung even harder to her one and only daughter up to that point. Now, death was threatening to take away the one true thing that gave her meaning in life. Up until Teena’s birth, success was her driving force. Success and popularity. Those had been the only things that mattered to her.

Was this punishment for that? Had she somehow done something to offend the spirit world? Had her vanity somehow cocked some hidden trigger and directed the barrel of a gun at her head?

She wasn’t sure, but the one thing she was sure of was that she wasn’t going to just sit down and accept that fate as her daughter seemed to be willing to do.

"Doctor, Woods," Ava said, almost as if his name had been ushered into her mind by some unseen force. "He has a solution." Saying this aloud somehow made that conclusion seem more real. It was a thought she had every time she sat with the man. Something in his gaze said it to her. "Why aren't you telling me about it?" she asked herself, still speaking as if the man was with her in the room. "Why aren't you suggesting it?" She was sure she was right. She *knew* it as surely as she knew she was kneeling before her bed. "Is it money?" she continued on. "Do you need more money?"

To Ava, that was the solution to everything. It always had been, anyway. Her life was so different now from the way she had grown up. Poverty no longer afflicted her. It no longer plagued her days and nights, because she'd struggled her way out of it, first with her looks, then with her tenacity. She wasn't the kind of person who gave in easily. She wasn't the kind of person who took "no" for an answer. The doctor had a solution to the biggest problem that she'd ever faced, and Ava vowed to herself at that moment that she'd drag the answer out of him. One way or the other, he'd tell her the idea that she had been seeing in his expressions. She'd find out how the man could help her daughter.

One way or the other.

***

"There it is, Daddy!" Sandra said excitedly as she peered through her window in the backseat. She was strapped into her safety seat. Deric and Lesha Johns still insisted that their daughter use a safety seat. Not just because it was the law, but because it was safe. Sandra didn't like it. She'd much rather sit in the front next to her father.

Sandra pointed toward the private school. The very same one that Mr. Johns had spent the last several months freelancing on the side to pay for.

"I see it," Deric said. He'd taken the long route on their way to visit Sandra's grandmother, just so he could hear and see her excitement over the school. One thing Mr. Johns knew for sure was that her childhood would be better than his. He geared his entire life around that idea. Married a woman who he knew would stick by him through thick and thin, knowing that the best way to ensure a better life for his offspring was to make sure any children he sired had two parents.

"Daddy, that's where I want to go to school," Sandra said. "I like their uniforms. Do you like it too?"

The children who were playing next to the building all dressed the same. The girls wore long checkered skirts and the boys wore slacks, but each student had on white shirts and ties, regardless if they were boys or girls. The children all laughed and played, and the playground had brightly painted jungle gyms, a merry-go-round, and swing set. There was no rust anywhere. Just the way he'd always imagined it. Yes, Sandra's life would be better than his, and dammit if he'd give into the idea that being black automatically meant being impoverished. Dammit if he'd permit his daughter being limited from attending the college of her choice when she got older. Dammit, if he'd let any of the things that had made his life so challenging from keeping her away from an ivy league school if that's what she wanted.

"Sounds like you'd love to go to school there," Mr. Johns said.

"Please, please, please," Sandra begged, cupping both of her hands together. "Two of my friends said they are going there." She sounded so hopeful.

"I don't know," Mr. Johns said. "I heard that school is awfully expensive." He didn't want to spoil the surprise. Her birthday was coming up soon.

"Please, Daddy," she begged him. "You always say everything is too expensive."

He smiled internally. She had a point. He often did say that the lesser important things were too expensive, but that was more because they were the lesser important things. Where his daughter went to school was the most important thing. He worked hard. Very hard. Worked on his education and his way up the ladder to sit in front of the camera as a newsman from the assistant cameraman he was when he and Lesha first married. All for this. Finally, that day was coming. The day when he could genuinely feel like all his sacrifices were starting to mean something.

"I suppose I could sit down with your mother and we could look over our budget," Mr. Johns said.

"Oh, boy!" Sandra said, her shoulders deflating. "Mom always says everything's too expensive too."

This was true. Both Mr. and Mrs. Johns did share the same priorities.

***

"Hi, Mimi," Sandra said as she filed into her grandmother's living room, heading immediately over to her grandmother for their traditional greeting. Sandra hugged her grandma, laying her head against her Mimi's bosom and her grandmother cradled it, kissing the top of her head.

"Bless the world, honey child," Mimi gushed proudly, taking her head in both hands so she could look at her as Mr. Johns settled in, leaning against the wall next to the door. "Lemme have a good look at that pretty little face of yours!"

Sandra beamed up at her grandmother, smiling broadly. "Did you miss me, Mimi?"

"Oh, I always miss my grandbabies. Why, the moment they walk out of the room, I already start wishing they were here again."

"Is Charlotte still singing the blues, Mimi?" Sandra asked her, pulling away and walking over to Mimi's birdcages. They were all lined up in a neat row, each cage containing a bird of a different array of colors. Mimi had cockatiels, a parrot, and several finches, making her living room sound like an aviary.

"Oh, she doin' much better now," Mimi suggested.

"Hey, pretty bird," Sandra said, peering in at the bright blue cockatiel. Charlotte cocked her head back and forth, tweeting a barrage of things at her visitor. Sandra reached into the bag sitting on the table beneath the cages, pulling out some birdfeed. Immediately, Charlotte hopped forward as Sandra brought her hand up to the cage, and the bird pecked some food from Sandra's tiny little hand.

"You do seem fond of those birds, don't you, baby girl," Mimi said.

"Mmhmm," Sandra said. "I love them, Mimi. They're so beautiful, and I love listening to them sing."

"Sing, Sing," Captain Stark chirped in the cage next to Charlotte's.

"Mimi! You got him to talk?" Sandra said excitedly. "You finally got him to talk!"

"Well, now, not exactly," Mimi said. "'parrently, Captain Stark likes you better than he cares for me. I ain't been able to get that bird to utter a single thing!"

"Say it again, Captain Stark," Sandra said, moving over to his cage. "Sing, sing!"

"Sing, sing!" Captain Stark said, dancing back and forth on his perch. "Sing, sing! Squawk. Sing, sing!"

"He really can talk, Mimi! He really can!" Sandra giggled with glee and fed Captain Stark a little treat. The bird thanked her by bobbing his head up and down, repeating his new phrase a few more times and squawking incessantly.

"Well, now, isn't that somethin' else!" Mimi said. "Seems to me, since your birthday is coming up, that old Mimi should bring the stubborn old Captain to its new rightful owner."

"Mom!" Mr. Johns barked. "Don't you even consider such a foolhardy thing! I'll never get an ounce of sleep with that bird squawking all night long."

"Oh, nonsense," Mimi said, disregarding him completely. "It's a grandmother's prerogative to spoil her grandbabies."

"I can really have him!" Sandra chirped excitedly, hopping up and down, clapping. "Can we take him now, Daddy? Please, Daddy, can we?" Sandra asked her dad, looking up at him with enthusiasm.

Mr. Johns stood there, unsure what to say about this new development. He was stuck between wanting to make his daughter as happy as possible, regardless of how much sleep having such a loud bird in the house would mean. There wasn't much he could do about it now. Mimi had already locked the decision in place.

"Honey baby, the captain is your birthday gift. Grandma gets him a brand-new cage and brings him to you wrapped," Said Mimi, looking at Deric, then at Sandra.

***

A week later, the Johns family, along with all of their friends were gathered in their backyard to celebrate what Mr. and Mrs. Johns considered to be a momentous occasion. They'd gone all out for their daughter's sixth birthday, and the entire yard was decorated with a *Disney Pixar* theme. This year, Sandra would be starting what they considered to be a new life, going to the school they'd worked so hard to get her into. Sandra was sitting on a blanket in the middle of their backyard, tearing open all of the wonderful presents that her friends and family had brought. Already, she'd torn open the wrapper Mimi had surrounded his cage with, starting there because she already knew what was in the birdcage. The bird made sure everybody knew.

"Just a birthday card?" Sandra said, looking up at both of her parents, Lesha and Deric, looking a little surprised and confused. She was used to her parents spoiling her a little with at least one large present. In a sense, that's exactly what this present was, only, sometimes, large gifts came in small packages.

"Open it," Lesha said, barely able to contain her enthusiasm. Sandra shrugged, still looking a little disappointed, but her demeanor changed the moment she saw what it was.

"The school registration!" she gasped, jumping up. Her eyes were wide and filled with joy. Gleefully, she ran up, arms extended, holding the registration card to St. Augustine's school for the bright and gifted. Sandra slammed into both of her parents, who were standing tightly next to each other, trying to wrap both of her arms around them both at the same time. "You got me in! You really got me in!"

"Yes, we did, sweetie!" Lesha said. Mr. Johns patted his daughter's shoulder proudly. It wasn't only paying the tuition that was a challenge. It was also dependent on Sandra's capabilities, but the school had reviewed her application and was impressed with the aptitude test that they'd had her take a few weeks before.

"I can't believe it! I actually get to go to school there!" Mr. and Mrs. Johns both crouched before their daughter as their friends and family clapped in the background.

"Now, you have to work really, really hard in this school, Sandra," Lesha said. "Otherwise, they won't let you keep going there."

"I know," Sandra said. "I'll do my homework every single day, I promise!"

"We know you will, sweetheart," Deric said proudly. "You'll make us both very proud."

"Uh, huh," she said. "Because I wanna go to college when I get old enough. Like Mamma did."

"That's my girl," Mr. Johns said, rubbing her head. He stood up again.

"Let's celebrate!" he announced.

"Here, here," Mimi replied. "Finally got rid of that silly bird!"

"Yeah, about that, Mom," Mr. Johns said.

"Oh, no," Mimi said back to him, raising one finger into the air and waggling it in front of her. "I don't wanna hear nothin' about takin' the old captain back."

"It's fine, Deric," Lesha said. "Your daughter needs something to be responsible for."

Mr. Johns knew when to give up on an argument. He was outnumbered, three to one. Sandra was standing there, both fists on her waist, staring him down menacingly.

"All right, all right. I give."

"You better, Daddy," she said. "I love my captain!"

"Better Daddy, better Daddy," the bird cried out. "Love my captain. Love my captain. Squawk!"

***

"How long do you think, until we'll be ready for human trials?" Doctor Ross Emmanuel asked his mentor, Professor Marg Woods, standing before his desk. Doctor Woods thought for a moment.

"How is Charli responding to the treatments?" he inquired.

"Charli's new brain is performing its functions, but the complications still persist," Dr. Emanuel replied.

The University Hospital where Professor Woods directed the surgery department was extremely advanced and equipped with highly sophisticated high-tech systems. The scientific community knew it well for its contribution to advanced research and outcomes. Its modernization and goodwill had made the hospital the most acclaimed medical center on the planet. The medical school and the research centers of the university hospital had published countless peer-reviewed articles and had well-accepted medical breakthroughs.

In addition to its celebrated medical advancements, the hospital was known for accomplishing seemingly impossible transplants and implants of human anatomical components. As with all research and development of such complicated procedures, the first few attempts were more of a disaster than a success. However, they were the best learning moments and discovering new technology always came with those challenges.

Their most recent medical foray was brain transplants. Their goal was seemingly impossible, and yet, they were getting closer and closer to success, almost daily, now that they had finally mastered the basics of the procedure. They had worked hard to develop reliable technology that made their idea real.

The survival of a brain out of its natural environment was limited to very few minutes. To tackle this issue, Professor Woods and his team developed a medical device called THE SYSTEM. This device could keep a brain alive for hours and in some cases up to a few days. THE SYSTEM incorporated multiple devices; including a robotic body, an artificial heart and lung, and a very sophisticated ventilator.

THE SYSTEM's efficacy was proven in multiple animal trials. The robotic bodies to which the animal brains were implanted had programs to send and receive signals with nerve impulses. In fact, the professor and his team credit the success of some of their laboratory trials to THE SYSTEM.

After over fifty trials of brain transplants on different animals, they proceeded to twelve primates. Charli happened to be the lucky thirteenth primates whose trial became the defining one. Though, with each trial, victory grew closer, Charli's sealed assurance.

Success was almost within Dr. Woods' grasp now, and he could almost feel it. Almost smelt the vindication he would get over his peers, some of whom believed that he was trying to play God. But what did they know about such things? If a man was capable of saving a life, that was all that mattered. Dr. Woods refused to stand idly by, letting the helpless pass away. Not when there was something that he could do about it.

Charli was proving that it could be done. That a brain, in fact, could be transplanted successfully.

Sure, there were sacrifices. He barely had time even for his thirteen-year-old daughter. Luckily, she understood why he was married to his work. After the death of her mom, other than the occasional visit to her dad, all her afterschool time was spent in her reading room or the community library.

Even though other well-known researchers worked side by side with the professor, his assiduity and creativeness had earned him more recognition, which gave him more confidence and determination to do the thing many scientists said could never be done.

He would show them. His quietness, added to his tall and slender body with a graying beard and full head of hair made him look either shy or confident, depending on how well the person who was judging knew him. With the new success under his belt, however, he felt everyone was sensing his confidence.

***

The university hospital had five centers, each with a specific research specialty. It was in Sub Center Delta (SCD as the researchers called it) where Professor Woods and his associates conducted the most complicated trial they had ever attempted before. The brain transplant trial on primates.

Researchers in SCD were reporting great progress and improvements in the procedures and outcomes of the brain transplant trials on human's closest ancestors. The first transplant into a monkey was barely a success. The donor's brain was able to trigger action in only a few body parts, but the subject died quickly.

On the twelfth trial, over half of a monkey named Job's body was activated by the donor's brain. The result of this trial was not only encouraging, but also had the answer to the fundamental question of the research, 'can a donor brain and recipient body live in harmony, doing their parts correctly?' The answer to that question seemed to be "yes!" But they still had details to work out.

***

Equipped with the new knowledge and skills they learned from the trial on Monkey Job, the team took a thirteenth primate named Charli to the table. A few days later, though disappointed with the result of the procedure being similar to that of Job's, they celebrated that they were able to extend Charli's life.

Without wasting a minute, they went back to investigate why the other half of Charli's body wouldn't receive instructions from the brain. They started comparing it to Jobs. Looking meticulously deep into each nerve connection, the firing of the nerves, and the strength of conductivity using the fibrotic camera that relayed live pictures and videos to the sophisticated system.

***

It took multiple weeks of countless tweaking of every part of each nerve fiber and changing the tools and techniques to see activity in the parts of the monkey which were not receiving instruction from the donor's brain.

Then, one evening, sighs of relief and smiling faces filled the procedure room. The unflagging and steadfastness of the team paid off, the donor brain instructed Charli's whole body, head to toes!

***

Charli, however, started to get sick with high fever, seizures, and nonstop violent shaking. The standard antibodies that she received before and during the procedure were not enough or were not working. In addition to other medications, more doses of the standard antibody could not help Charli.

As a precaution, the team had been preparing new antibodies with DNA both from the donors and recipients of each trial. The plan was not to be used unless absolutely necessary. Charli's case became that absolute. After receiving a small dose of the new antibody, Charli started to show improvement. After a couple of high dose treatments of the antibody, Charli woke up and started observing its surroundings.

Seeing the outcome, Dr. Woods laughed and cried with happiness. Apparently, half success had no value on the professor's measurement.

"I thought the antibody solution was working," Dr. Woods said, giving Dr. Emanuel a frustrated look after returning to the present from his thoughts.

"It is working, yes," Dr. Emanuel said. "But the subject still drifts in and out of remission."

"Give her another dose," Dr. Woods said.

"Sir, I..."

"Give her another dose," he insisted.

"Won't that put the permit at risk?"

"I didn't say log it," Dr. Woods growled, slamming his fist on the desk. "We will do whatever we have to do!"

"Yes, sir," Dr. Emanuel said. "Whatever it takes."

"We cannot afford to fail with Charli," Dr. Woods reminded him. "We're not the only ones doing these trials. We must succeed first."

"Yes, sir!"

"*I* will be the first to successfully transplant a brain, do you understand?"

"Yes, sir!"

"Good. Now, do what must be done."

Dr. Emanuel turned and left Dr. Woods' office, committed to cutting yet another corner.

***

The next day, "How's our favorite subject," Dr. Woods asked his associate, Dr. Emanuel.

"Flooding her system turned out to be the right approach, Doctor," Dr. Emanuel replied with a smile. Charli was sitting up at the time. She still looked a little groggy, but with every passing day, she was showing more and more signs of recovery. As Dr. Woods stood there staring at her, Charli lifted a hand, bumping it to her chin several times. Her signal that she was hungry.

"You see that?" Dr. Emanuel said proudly. "This will be the second time she's asked for food today."

"You think she's ready to start eating solid foods?" Dr. Woods asked.

"I think her system can handle it, yes," Dr. Emanuel said. "Do you want us to give her?"

"A small portion. Let's start her off easy and see how it goes."

"Right away, sir," Dr. Emanuel said, heading for her food supply. He peeled a banana and broke off a small piece. He brought it to the cage and lifted the door latch. He opened it and handed Charli the banana piece. Charli ate it tentatively, as if unsure of the taste, but after eating it, she quickly tapped her chin again.

"That's a girl," Dr. Woods said. "You'll be back to normal in no time."

"What do you think this means as far as human trials go?"

"I think it means we're ready," he said. "As soon as we can get the government to sanction it."

"Any word on that?"

"No, we should have heard something by now. I'm starting to lose patience with the red tape."

"Too bad we don't have a choice," said Dr. Emanuel with the intention of picking on his mentor's mind.

"Don't we?" Dr. Woods said, turning and heading for the door.

"What did that mean?" one of the other assistants asked Dr. Emanuel as soon as their boss was out of the room.

"It means that he does whatever he wants."

***

On the evening of his flight to America, Million's whole family accompanied him to the airport. His mom and his wife were crying inconsolably. Though heartbroken, he tried to act tough—and he managed to hide his poignancy until his wife whispered, "I will always love you!" into his ear. Right then, he forgot that he was supposed to control his emotions for the sake of his family, especially his kids. He held his kids tight and began weeping. Then everyone started to sob. He tried to avoid this kind of goodbye, but some things are never meant to go as planned.

His brother who worked at the airport had seen many travelers arrive late to their flights due to impassioned goodbyes. So, he helped him to give everyone a quick hug and dragged him toward the main security check line.

Soon, as they went inside and said bye to his brother, he made a conscious decision to collect his composure and joined his fellow passengers on board. He excused himself and sat by the window. The person sitting by the aisle was a gentleman of his age.

"Hello, my name is Million, and this is my first international flight," said Million with a smile on his face, inviting the gentleman sitting beside him for a handshake.

"Same here, my name is Amin," he said while shaking Million's hand.

"What State are you heading to?" asked Million.

"Massachusetts," Amin replied.

Million's face lit up with a smile and said, "Brother, we are going to the same State, how interesting is this? I'm going there for school."

"Me too, I finally received a scholarship into Reach School of Medicine after three years of corresponding with the university. I paid a load of money, and I have to pay more. Nevertheless, I feel like I hit the jackpot. I'm a medical doctor in general practice. I desire to specialize in Ear, Nose, and Throat."

"This is funny! I'm not kidding if I tell you that I received a scholarship from Reach School of Medicine too. I guess it is not unusual that two guys, who never met before would sit side by side in an airplane and they both happen to be going to the same school," said Million with excitement, then continued, "I received this scholarship through work. It was something I wished to get for a long time. I'm a pharmacist, and I'm going to earn my Ph.D. in pharmacology. As you can tell, I'm very excited about this opportunity," he concluded with a big smile on his face.

Just like Million, Amin was married and had two boys, ages three and five.

***

The university had a contract with a city guide agency to introduce the new students to Boston. The agency's tour bus was parked in front of the library.

Numerous new students from various parts of the world were sitting in the campus' orientation building waiting patiently for whoever was supposed to come and speak to them.

Two men came into the hall and stood by the podium. One of them said, "Hello, ladies and gentlemen, first I'd like to welcome all of you! We called you here to introduce you to the tour company who will guide you in your orientation to the city of Boston. Mr. Peter is the representative of the agency, and he will tell you more about Boston and today's tour, so let me hand the mic and the stage to him."

"Welcome to Boston! Before we get you into the tour bus and start showing you around, let me give you the intro. Boston is a harbor city of Massachusetts, a North-Eastern State of America. People of all races live in Boston, the majorities, however, are of African, Irish, and Italian origin.

"Among the sons and daughters of the city who are well known in politics was John F. Kennedy. There are countless in the entertainment industry and other works of life. In the literary circle, Boston was nicknamed The Athens of America because it was full of intellectual and educational resources.

"As you know, the city has universities and colleges that are well known around the world, and you lucky bunches have joined one of them—congratulations! As you will notice or learn throughout the tour today, the city once was the cradle of liberty, now it is the cradle of civilization."

The tour guide's speech about Boston not only made the new students eager to tour the city, but also invigorated a sense of gratitude because they felt lucky to be there.

Mr. Peter continued, "The first public school in America was opened here in Boston. Now, there are a lot of public schools in the city. They all are different for various reasons, such as the qualification of the teachers and reputations of the schools. There are also very expensive private schools. These schools are left for the rich. There is a lot to talk about Boston. While touring, I and the other guide will describe places and explain their historical value and perspective. Now, let's head out to the bus waiting by the library."

Million and Amin were sitting toward the middle on the right side of the bus. Everything on the campus had started to wow them. They were fascinated by the architectural beauty of the University's Library and other buildings on the campus. They also talked about how the landscape of the campus was meticulously taken care of. Then the city guide took them around Boston.

"This city is beautiful and full of history," Million said after they got back to the bus from the Freedom Trail.

***

Putting himself on call for a temporary team in SCD, Professor Woods gave the permanent team of the unit a week off to relax and celebrate the successful transplantation of a brain on Charli.

He spent three days with his daughter. Then he went back to the university to discuss his plan and strategies of starting the clinical trial with Professor Tylor, the university's president.

"I understand your frustration, but we can't take a risk," said the president with a calm voice, noticing the professor's impatience with the government red tape.

"Are you telling me to sit and wait for a freaking permit even if it takes another two years?"

"You can polish your methods and techniques with a few more Charli like trials," said Professor Tyler with half-smile on his face.

"Or we can set up a new lab in a trial-friendly country. I don't think you understand how tightly we are racing to the finish line with other research groups that are conducting similar studies," said Marg, sitting erect and staring the president intensely.

"Come on, Marg! Give it another six months to a year. You know how the permitting process works."

"Actually, I don't. I don't know how you bureaucrats think," he said and stormed out of the office, slamming the door behind.

After the unsatisfactory meeting, he decided to take his mind off the whole clinical trial. While walking to his car, the smell of cigar filled his nostrils and the familiar sound of laughter came into his ears. As if he just discovered a new way of living, he smiled ear to ear.

When he arrived at David's place, everything was as he imagined. The living room was pitch dark, and the smell of whiskeys and cigars had created a unique aroma. Belay was laughing at something silly David had said. *This is where life is*, Marg thought while group hugging with Belay and David.

***

Five days later, Marg came back to the center and started coding a new computer program that he thought would help determine the perfect match of donor and recipient.

He knew even if they received a permit in the near or far future, finding candidates for the trial would be the very first obstacle in the road to their success. For when, somehow, the opportunity surfaced, the program that he was coding would come handy.

The rest of his team members were still drunk on their successful work on Charli, and hungry to conduct the human trial. A few of them, as long as it remained classified, didn't care about waiting for the permit to get approved. But the majority, reasoning having the permit would enable them to freely recruit volunteers, decided to wait patiently for approval. In the meantime, they were dedicated to perfecting the procedure on the common ancestors.

However, with each passing day, the never promising news about the permit and lack of human subjects started weakening most team members' enthusiasm. Some of them joked about getting two professors to voluntarily exchange their brains.

***

It had been a year since Million and Amin made Boston their adopted city. Though they didn't have enough time to enjoy the majority of what the city had to offer, they were impressed by its beauty from the few places they abled to tour.

On occasional mornings, they enjoyed the sunshine in Charles Park, went on a duck ride, and a couple of weekends they drove around the suburbs in a rental car. They also dined in a couple of fine restaurants in the Back-Bay area.

The university was closed for one week during spring break. Despite the load of papers that they would be working on for their research thesis, Amin and Million decided to hang out in New York for the first four days of the week. They rented a car and bought things that they might need on the way there. They filled their tank and joined the morning commute on route I-90 west at around ten o'clock.

Even though it was Saturday morning, there were lots of cars and trucks on the freeway. Million was driving in the right lane at about the speed limit.

They both seemed to be thinking about their families back home when Million said, "I wish this visit to New York was with our wives and kids." And, he took memory lane and galloped to the town where he was born. Effortlessly, he arrived at his parent's back yard, opened the gate, then the front door, and went inside the house.

***

As if they had nothing else to speak about, silence had taken over in the car. They both had gone back to thinking of good times with their families. Million was deep in thought that he didn't even realize he was driving faster than he needed to. They were on I-84 west, and the traffic was light.

Despite their physical presence in the car, Amin and Million were still darting horses of thought. They had gone their separate ways. They were at each one's city, neighborhood, and house with family. They seemed to have forgotten their reality.

***

Million, who did not realize the road was starting to curve, failed to slow down and started to lose control. He startled and pressed the gas pedal harder, thinking he was stepping on the brake. The road being wet made things more complicated—the car sideswiped a metal pole and began rolling end to end and hitting the ditch on the other side of the road. Amin, who was back home with his family, came back to the present. In seconds, he fell into a deep sleep that he might not wake up from.

"Oh, my God! Oh, my God! Oh, my Goaaaad!" a young man yelled, witnessing the accident with his girlfriend from their stalled car on the side of the road. They both got out of their car and tried to live feed a video of the accident on Instagram. However, the rainstorm made it impossible to even stand outside for a minute.

They went back into their car.

The girl dialed 911 and said in a hurry, "Hello, a car filliped into the other side of the freeway. Can you please send help?"

"What is your location?" asked the dispatcher.

"The accident is on I-84 by exit 6," replied the girl.

"You are the fifth caller about that accident, and help is on the way," confirmed the dispatcher.

The guy thought, *Accidents like this make people wish life was like in the movies where you could rewind time and prevent such things from happening*. And he said, "A research on time manipulation could be the king of all researches."

"But someone is controlling the clock," said the girl.

"Time is life. So, whoever controls time, controls life," said the guy looking deep into his girlfriend's eyes.

***

Seconds before the accident, Million was reliving the interaction he'd had with his wife and daughter earlier that morning. Saba had told him that she missed him so much and could hardly wait until he came home. His heart sank thinking what his daughter said, “Baba, please come home…” and she’d started crying

***

Seven thousand and thirty-eight miles away from their families who adored them, the two earnest, badly missed, and highly anticipated gentlemen were fighting between life and death. Would their families know how badly they had missed home? Would they know that homesickness was partly to blame for the accident? They may intuitively know, or they may not.

***

Chapter Two

At the ER, a team of doctors assessed the two men. The driver, Million, was found squeezed between the dashboard and the seat, and they established that he was badly hurt. Though it might not be for long, he was still breathing.

Amin, who was not wearing a seatbelt, had smashed into the windshield, and his head was split open in the front. He was bleeding internally from where he'd hit the roof multiple times. When he arrived at the ER, he was dying. The team concluded that the two men had very little time left. Other than reducing their pain and suffering, there was no medical intervention that could be done. The ER doctor was planning to transfer them to the intensive care unit (ICU) where they would remain until nature took its course. In the midst of the transfer process, another doctor suggested the surgery department evaluate them.

***

Professor Woods was busy working on the new program of matching donor to the recipient when he received a call to the emergency department. Annoyed by the call, he arrived in a grumpy mood. When the ER doctor finished his report, the professor could hardly contain his elation.

He advised that they get transferred to the Intensive Care Unit (ICU). There, they were to receive some life-sustaining care until he discussed their case with his team. When he returned to the center with the excitement of a hunter who just scored game, his team was setting up a new trial on a Chimp named Holly. He summoned everyone to a small conference room and spilled the proposal. Not only surprised, but his suggestion also put the majority of the members in a dilemma. They had made up their mind on the importance and validity of securing the permit before starting the human trial, but the professor's idea seemed to make sense to some of them.

Especially when he said, "We have been waiting for the permit, but for how long? What if this kind of opportunity never surfaces again? These two men are dying as we speak, however, our procedure could save one of them. Why not save one life instead of losing two. Elsewhere, where a permit is not the issue, some researchers might be closing to the finish line. This is our chance to at least try to sprint to that line.

"If we think about our permit status, time-sensitive opportunities like the one we have on hand can't wait. Also, it is not news to you that we sometimes have to make quick decisions about whether to perform a lifesaving procedure that we know is legally questionable. There are times that we put rules aside so as not to forego golden opportunities such as the one we have now. All in all, I don't have to remind you that a great deal of research is conducted in secret."

"I agree, this is a terrific opportunity for us to do our human trial, and if successful, it could save one life. But, is it worth taking the risk of shutting down the center?" said Professor Emanuel Ross.

"Ross is absolutely right, we have been taking risks, maybe not as serious as this one, to save lives. Let's look at this in terms of saving a life. That is what we are here for," said Professor Jackson Art who Marg had discussed his plan with while heading back from the ER. He continued, "If we are going to undertake this risky endeavor, we all need to come to terms and be on the same page."

After considering all the comments and opinions, Dr. Woods said, "Everyone's opinion on the subject boils down to the fact that we are ready to do the procedure, except we don't have the permit. But I have to be honest with you, they might not grant us the charter. Even if they do, it won't be for a while. Remember how excited they were to talk about the subject when we first submitted the application? Now, whenever I call to check on its status, it takes them over twenty minutes just to locate the application. "I learned that there are a few applications waiting for the first review committee, and two other committees will scrutinize each application before it gets to the board for a final decision. Since they review applications according to their order of submission, our application is the last one in the list. Recall how long it took them to approve our permit for the trial on uterus transplant?

"The one sure thing is that we are close to the finish line and so are other research groups. It is a matter of who sprints ahead and gets there first. We all have put in precious hours, and too much energy and money has been invested in this research, so we owe it to ourselves to move it ahead to its successful completion." He took another sip of water. "We don't have time to discuss the matter any further. If you all agree on the plan that I will present to you, we will do it. If not, forget that we have had this conversation. Here is the plan: the men will be brought to our center under the guise of further evaluation. We will place Million's brain into Amin's body. Within a few hours, we will know whether the transplant is a success or not. If we bring our techniques from Charli to human biology, we should see positive results. If for some reason the transplant is not a success, we will check every video, audio, and written procedural data of the system, as we did for Job. Then we will go back and try to amend every error report. If we still have no positive results, we will step back and evaluate what went wrong. In the meantime, we will email the social services and the hospital administration to say that both men have passed, and the corpses will be sent to the morgue."

He stopped, got up, and walked to the computer screens on his left and glanced at Million's chart. "If the procedure is a success, we will run into a slight problem, we will have only Million's deceased body that donated a brain. The closest we could come to accounting for Amin's body would be the African American man's body from the unidentified decedents that we had in the small lab. Now, if you all agree, we should get to work."

"Among the things that I learned from checking both men's registration profiles, Million came on a scholarship that he received from this university," said Professor Art noticing Professor Woods had stopped speaking, "Amin, on the other hand, came on his own and was paying out of pocket.

Therefore, while the university has a responsibility to notify Million's family and send his body to them. There is no immediate need to notify Amin's family or anybody outside the university."

"Well, sooner or later, Amin's family will need to be notified too. In case they ask for his body, we should 3D his face and his other prominent features to graft them onto the unidentified African-American decedent that Marg mentioned," added Professor Hun Kim.

"Good points. The secretory of this center will notify Million's family immediately after the procedure and will work with social service for his body to be sent without delay. As for Amin's family, we will wait to see how long the subject lives," said Dr. Woods.

***

The professor called the meeting for formality and to make the team feel that they had input on the decision, otherwise, he had already made up his mind. The trial was going to be conducted even if he had to fire all the professors for insubordination.

The fact that the men were foreigners and that their immediate family members were not around to question the details of the accident and their whereabouts, seemed to make the undecided professors less apprehensive about agreeing to the procedure. They also discussed that the men were dying, therefore the trial would only either delay their death by a few hours or save one life out of the two. After some discussion about the actual procedure and what seemed to be an optimistic view on its result, they all agreed to conduct the trial and to maintain its secrecy at all costs until an appropriate time to reveal came.

It was exactly how the professor wanted their meeting to adjourn.

***

When it came to the sophistication of its tools, infection prevention, and control system, there was no place in the world that came close to the transplant and recovery units of Sub Center Delta, or SCD. Even the door-handles of the unit were tested for infectious organisms pre and post-procedure. The robots that assisted with all the surgeries and transplants had extendable fingers that became smaller and smaller with the nerves or vessels to be disentangled or connected.

The Nerve Connection System of the unit was proven to be the most precise of any similar system around the globe. It had fibers that served as temporary synapses between neurons. And it detected the activities and functions of each nerve.

The two dying men were situated in different rooms, in beds that were set up close to the robots which were to assist with the operation of removing their brains. Multiple tubes were dangling from Amin's body. IV antibiotics, immunosuppressants, and sedatives running through some of the tubes. Before being removed, a sophisticated ventilator was conducting the exchange of oxygen and air to Million's brain via a bigger tube that was inserted into his throat and secured on his mouth. After removal, the brain would be placed into a robot, called the Transition-Body. This robot, with its avatar sculpture of a person's looks, was designed to mimic the human body, complete with artificial organs, vessels, and arteries.

The researchers worked in two groups; each group separated the brain from each man's body. One team removed Million's brain and placed it into the Transition-Body, while the recipient was prepared. After carefully evacuated from its body, Amin's brain was sent to the group who were working on Million. That brain then was interpolated in Million's body. After stitching the head, Million's corpse was sent to the morgue.

Following a short break, both groups began orienting themselves with the body and brain that they prepared to assimilate into one complete person. The group who worked on Amin shared their observations about his body, especially the areas where Million's brain was to be installed. In turn, the group who amputated Million's brain apprised the other group, all needed information before both groups could come together to complete the operation.

Amin's body was sterilized and taken to a new procedure-room that was bigger in size and equipped with more surgical and emergency tools. The Transit-Body with Million's brain in it was brought to that same room from the holding area. Both teams donned their gowns and steeled themselves for the delicate operation.

***

As in almost all complicated trials, Dr. Woods led the team to commence this most intricate, intensive, and trying of all the trials they had conducted so far. With each passing moment, the complexity and intensity of the procedure escalated. Seconds changed to minutes, minutes to hours, hours to a day, and a day to a day and a half.

Finally, the donor and the recipient were one. The procedure proved that in order to awake a sleeping brain, other minds must toil scrupulously. After long hours of tiresome work, the researchers discovered the person they named Million/Amin. He was transferred to the observation room and attached to multiple treatments and monitoring devices.

In the room next to his, the care team's eyes watched the screen, anxiously awaiting any movement from his body. The care team from the day shift left, wishing luck to the night shift. The next morning, the care team from the previous day arrived, awake and fresh. The person, however, was still asleep.

A few minutes after the completion of the transplant, the system had detected clear nerve signals throughout the man's body. The electromyogram, however, continued to trace faint-to-no response.

Despite that, the care team couldn't say that Million/Amin was legally dead because his brain was alive. He breathed, although through a ventilator, and his heart continued to beat.

Before Dr. Woods and his team left to catch a few hours of sleep, he told the leaders of the care team, with conviction, that the patient would wake up. They remained committed to waiting as long as it would take. It was not like they had a choice. It would be up to Doctor Woods to pull or not to pull the plug.

***

Two and half days later, the anxious care team noticed a series of activities traced on the electromyogram. When they looked at the camera monitors, they saw two arms moving haltingly. Still staring on the monitor, before any of them could say anything, they noticed his whole body shaking violently and his bed began moving erratically, the normally strong brakes of the wheels of the bed seemed weak and loose. Different alarms from multiple devices went crazy. The body and the bed restrained to each other kept circling the room, hitting everything along the way.

All available staff in the unit and security personnel frantically run into the room. While some tried to stop the bed from moving, others held the patient's head down to the bed, and others began to restrain him from his chest down to his legs with a sheet tied to the frames of the bed. Gowned up nurses pushed anticonvulsants and sedatives through his IV. Slowly, his convulsions subsided. Twenty minutes later, Dr. Woods and a few members of his team conferenced with the care team. Million/Amin was asleep, but his lips moved as if he was trying to speak. The sleep monitor traced deep sleep.

Everyone in the room wondered what he might be dreaming about.

***

"Million's case is easy. I'm more concerned with Amin's. How are we going to tell his family?" said one of the two men tasked with notifying the passing of the men to their respective families.

The second person thought he had a pretty good handle on the case. "His situation isn't as concerning as you think. We will convey a condolence letter along with money and his items to his family. In the letter, we'll indicate that he had been buried here. We'll tell them that they could recover his body at any time, at their own expense. They will be reminded that they would be expected to pay the cost of his hospital stay, burial, exhuming and transporting of his body. When they see that the sums of money are unreasonable, they will forget about it. If they are well-off enough to pay for all that and take his body, we will give them any decomposing black man's body. I don't believe that they do DNA tests in their country."

The first man felt relieved. "I like your idea. It will work."

***

Million's family had high hopes for him. Upon his return from higher education, they hoped that he would support his elderly parents and his family more than ever. Now he would come home in a box. It was incomprehensible to all of them. When his wife was first told about his death, she thought she was having a nightmare. When they brought his body in a box and showed her, she was waiting for them to say that they made a mistake, that the person in the box was not her husband and her husband was alive.

The sorrow and calamity that his wife and family felt were indescribable. Hearing them cry made even people who never met Million shed tears. His funeral looked like that of a celebrity's.

***

In the northern part of Addis Ababa, Amin's family was devastated by the news that death had taken away their loved one. They howled and wept. Seeing his belongings, they wanted to believe the truth, but they couldn't accept his death as a fact. His wife cried uncontrollably, holding close to her chest his shirt and a family album that she took out from his bag. Could seeing his body in a box give her comfort? Not having his body in front of them turned the family's anguish to melancholy. Amin's father believed that he would never have peace of mind until he saw his son's resting place.

Both Million and Amin's wives and children lost the comfortable lives they'd had. The adults lost hope and felt that they had embarked on a painful, strange, and incomplete journey into the future.

***

The next day after her birthday, Sandra woke up before her parents and went to the bird. Taking a handful of birdfeed close to the cage, she cheered, "Good morning, Captain!"

The bird nodded a couple of times and twitted, "good morning Capitan, good morning, Capitan."

Smiling big, she poured water into the bird's water feeder and tip toed to her playroom. The room was next to her parents' bedroom. She opened the door quietly, so not make too much noise. Inside, she began playing with her new toys; trying one, then another, she could hardly contain her excitement.

Hearing her talking to her new doll, Deric went to Sandra and said, "Sandy, you are up early."

"Ya, Daddy, I'm still excited about my birthday presents. I fed the bird and I got him to say, "good morning captain."

"Guess what, after breakfast, we are goin' go to check out your new school, isn't that exciting?"

Sandra hopped with exaltation and opened her arms to hug her dad. "Is Mommy going with us?" she asked.

"No, she has to go to work."

She felt a slight sadness but forgot it right away. Giggling, she sprinted to her room to get ready for the big day.

Around eight am, Lesha left to work after hugging and kissing her daughter and her husband. An hour or so later, Sandra and Deric headed out.

Sandra's excitement seemed over the roof. Hanging out with her dad and going to her new school were thrilling to her.

When she saw the school, she could hardly wait to get out of the car. Looking out through the window, she noticed that two of her friends from preschool were standing with their parents on the sidewalk. Her smile got bigger, her eyes widened, and her face glowed more.

Deric pulled to the entrance of the school, before he could proceed, a man in uniform approached him and told him that the school parking lot was full.

Sandra was anxious to join her friends. "Daddy, what did the man say? My friends are over there, can I go now? Please, Daddy."

"Sandy, come down, we have to park by the curb. Your friends might be here when we come back, if not, you will see them when school starts."

While pulling out, he eyed a spot across the street from the school. He rushed for it. Unfortunately, it was tight, so he decided to look for another one. But then, looking through the rare view mirror, he noticed Sandra stretching her neck to see if her friends were still there. He decided to give spot a try. After a few tries, he secured the site. He didn't want to think about how hard it would be to get out.

He got out of the car and went to the other side and helped Sandy out. Leaving her by the curb, he went to the driver's side to grab his phone. He didn't know it, but Sandy had followed, and she was standing in front of the car.

By the school, Sandy's friends were giggling and running around their parents. She yelled their names and started running toward them. She didn't see the car heading south at 40 miles per hour.

"Oh, no! it's Sandy, she is my friend from school. The car hit her. She is hurt, Daddy, please go help her!" said the older of the girls, shaking nervously.

Deric, emptying his hands to hold his daughter's, inserted his phone and keys into his pockets. When he heard a screech of tires as a car halted, he was walking toward where he left Sandy. It startled him. He stopped and turned to see what was happening in the middle of the street.

"Come here Sandy," he said, without taking his eyes off the scene of the accident.

A crowd, including the girls' father, was circling the scene. Deric had stretched his left arm out for her to grab his left hand. His plan was to tell his daughter to stand where he could see her while he went to see if he could help. When Sandra didn't come and hold his left hand, he started calling her name and walking toward where he thought she should be standing. She was neither around the back of the car nor the front. He began to panic. Then he got upset, thinking that she had joined the crowd.

Shouting her name, he headed toward the circle. “I’m sorry, sir! Come this way. She is still breathing. I called 911, an ambulance is on the way,” said the girls’ dad, looking at Deric with tearful eyes. They knew each other through their daughters and had chatted more than a couple of times at the preschool while waiting for the kids.

Deric didn’t comprehend what the man was saying. He smiled and stood there searching with his eyes. Then, his eyes landed on the bloody fender of the car, under the fender, a small girl in a shirt that looked like Sandy’s, except blood-soaked.

Deric got nervous. as if in rewind, he heard what the man said and understood it. The girl on the ground was Sandy. His heart began to pound hard; he didn’t know what to think or say. His legs gave out on him.

Somehow, he found himself kneeling and trying to hold his barely breathing daughter. Holding her, he wept uncontrollably. He tried to open her eyes with his bloody hands. When she finally started to move her mouth, it seemed that she was trying to say “Daddy,” but no sound escaped her lips.

Deric, hoping that she would say something or at least move her lips, started whispering into her ear. “Sandy, I love you so much. Please, talk to Daddy. Sweetheart, please say something.” Sandy, however, didn’t give him any sign of recognition. *What am I to do now?* he thought. He felt lost, weak, small, and helpless. He bent his head to her chest and cried.

He heaved his head and noticed a lot of people are watching him with sad faces. “She is my only child,” he said in agony. The crowd joined him in sobbing.

For a second, he thought that he was dreaming. He couldn’t believe that something could happen in the blink of an eye and affect him for a lifetime. Minutes ago, she was a beautiful child, full of excitement and exaltation. Now, she was lifeless and covered with blood. Nature was mockingly cruel, Deric thought—the legs that were designed to help her run from danger carried her straight into it.

Holding his blood-drenched dying daughter, Deric struggled to his feet and began to walk aimlessly. As if to wake her up from her sleep, he started to shake her and yell her name. But she made him doubt that she could hear him. Though he had heard the saying, “seeing is believing,” he couldn’t believe what he was seeing.

Because of the accident, the street was closed, and vehicles were lined up bumper to bumper. The drivers who couldn’t tell why the traffic wasn’t moving started honking aggressively.

An ambulance and the local fire department arrived with a couple of police cars. The Emergency Medical Technicians took Sandy from her dad's arms and laid her on a stretcher. They immediately started her on oxygen and attached her to monitors. They listened to her lungs and noticed that there wasn't very good air exchange, they put a breathing tube in through her mouth and attached it to a breathing machine.

Then the ambulance sped up to the university hospital with her disheartened father at her side.

***

Lesha was at work when she received a call from the hospital nurse.

"Hello, am I speaking with Mrs. Johns?" asked the nurse.

"Yes, can I help you?" Lesha felt nervous. No one except her husband ever called her at work.

"My name is Amy, I'm one of the trauma nurses at Reach University Hospital, your daughter, Sandra, is with us because she suffered a serious injury from a car accident. Mr. Johns is in the waiting area."

Nurse Amy paused to hear if Lesha had a question. However, Lesha said nothing.

"Hello, Mrs. Johns?" wondered Nurse Amy.

"... bang ..."

The nurse, suspected Lesha had fainted and fallen. She hoped that someone was around to help her. She hung up and called back wishing that someone would answer.

"Hello," answered one of Lesha's coworkers who'd run to Lesha's rescue, noticing her fainting.

"Sorry, this is Nurse Amy from the hospital. Is Mrs. Johns ok? Did she faint? Is she breathing alright? I was just telling her that her daughter is with us because she was hit by a car."

"Yes, she fainted. Luckily, she fell into a chair. She is trying to get up. I will bring her to the hospital."

"Come to the ER, it's on the first floor. Mr. Johns is in the waiting area."

Lesha got up and began to walk aimlessly toward the exit. Two of her coworkers walked beside her, one of them carrying her purse and set of keys. They went to her car. One of them offered to drive and the other one sat with her in the backseat. When they arrived at the hospital, Lesha, began sobbing.

When she saw her husband crying, she fell on her knees. Her coworkers helped her up and tried to get her to sit next to Deric. But she held her husband's arm tight and started dragging him toward the entrance of the ER, saying, "Deric, where is my daughter? Where is my Sandy? I want to see and hold her."

Deric embraced Lesha and held her tight and wept. She fought herself from his grasp, looking into his eyes. "Is my Sandy dead? I can't believe it. No, I don't. It's impossible."

Deric didn't say a word. He couldn't stop sobbing, even if he wanted to.

Death had destroyed their life by stealing their only daughter from them.

Two nurses came and took Lesha to see her daughter. Sandra was stitched up, bandaged, and wearing a clean hospital gown, but was seemingly lifeless, hooked up to intricate medical devices and monitors. Lesha knelt down on the side of the bed and laid her head on the edge and continued weeping. The nurses helped her up and led her outside toward her husband. The couple hugged one another tightly and kept on crying. There was nothing more they could do.

***

Participants of the annual medical researchers' conference were presenting their research topics and associated outcomes of the year. When Professor Woods took the stage, he discussed brain transplantation. He spoke in great detail about the problems the researchers had been facing and how advanced technological systems were contributing to the success of the research.

The majority of the participants had never heard of such research being conducted—the report came out of the blue to them. They were not sure what to think of it. They thought that such research required further scrutiny. But to those familiar with Dr. Woods and his previous research topics, him conducting such groundbreaking research was not a surprise.

They suspected that he may present a final report of the research soon. There were also those who thought that it would be a while before research on brain transplants could be conducted thoroughly. However, no one had the guts to question Professor Woods' report.

One scientist, who was seated near the middle of the conference room, had a question, "If a brain transplant becomes practical, wouldn't it lead to a human identity crisis?"

"Our work is more on the biological nature of the subject. Extending human life by transplanting one organ at a time. As for the possible issue of an identity crisis, a team of professionals on the subject is working on it."

Another participant added with a smirk, "I guess you are saying we will address the issues with the hardware, while concerns about the software will be studied by others."

To some of them, it felt as if the idea was similar to mixing real life with a dream. They thought brain transplantation was an impossible and impractical fantasy. The discussion was growing much deeper and more heated when Dr. Woods received an urgent call from the emergency department.

***

At the ER, the attending physician gave Dr. Woods a detailed report on the little African-American girl who was in a car accident. She had suffered a bleak chest injury and many other complications throughout her body.

He went to her room and made his own assessment. He noticed that she had endured multiple injuries that were beyond medical and surgical repair—even those that could be attempted wouldn't save her life. He concluded that she was dying and that there wasn't anything that could be done for her. While heading to his office, he asked the attending physician, "Can you get me her parents?"

The Johns were close by, so it didn't take them long to get to his office. Deric seemed to be losing his youthful appearance with each passing second. Lesha looked lost, and she was sobbing. Professor Woods got up from his seat and invited them to sit on two of the closet chairs to his table.

He addressed them in a subdued voice. "I'm very, very sorry about what happened to your daughter. She has suffered a hard blow to the chest and multiple severe fractures. I'm sorry, but your daughter will never wake up. So far, everything that can medically be done has been done for her.

"Now, she is on comfort measures. It is only because her brain is still alive, at least for the next thirty-six to forty-eight hours, that we, legally and medically, are unable to pronounce her dead. If you have any questions, please don't hesitate to ask me or her care team."

Hearing the worst news that they could bear, Sandy's parents froze. They didn't know what to say or do. They got up and walked out of the office, holding hands and crying quietly.

***

After a few hours of a meaningless stay in the hospital, families, and friends who were visiting with them suggested that they go home.

But going to their house was torture. Sandy's toys were spread everywhere, they seemed to yell her name. Deric tried to imagine that the day was Saturday, and like most weekends, Sandy was at her grandmother's house. However, his mind began to mock him by bringing scenes of his daughter soaked in blood.

Sobbing, Lesha stood in front of the playroom door, holding the knob, as if someone or something was daring her to enter. Deric put his left arm on her shoulder and his right hand over hers and helped her turn the knob. Both went in and stood on one side of the room then slid down to the floor. She threw her head on his shoulder and continue to cry quietly.

"Lesha, I'm partly to blame for what has happened to Sandy," said Deric weeping.

Lesha sat up and gave him a look that seemed to say, "What do you mean?"

He got up and sat across from her, and between his wailing, he said, "She begged me to stay with her friends while I go park across the street, but I told her that we would come back together. You know, I was being protective but didn't protect her from the real danger."

She went to where he was sitting and hugged him tight and whispered to his ear, "Baby, don't blame yourself. You were doing what a loving father would do. Some things are meant to be and could never be avoided no matter what anyone did or didn't."

His wife's words were a comfort to his broken heart but couldn't mend his broken soul.

They sat in the room for a few more minutes, dealing with their internal dialog. Then, Deric got up and gave his wife a hand to do the same. Holding hands, they walked to the living room and sat on the couch quietly.

Lesha felt hope spreading into her soul and said, "Deric, what if Sandy beat the odds and surprise the doctors with her recovery? That is possible, right? After all, they said that she is still alive."

"That would be a great miracle," said Deric admiring his wife's positivity.

Then he thought to himself, *A person is considered alive until his or her brain is dead.*

As he had been doing every night for the past seven and half years, he sprang from the sofa and helped his wife to get up. Holding hands, they went to the bathroom to brush their teeth, before they retired to bed.

***

As soon as Sandra's parents left his office, Professor Woods reviewed her chart for the second time. He assured himself that there was nothing left to be done for her. Since the moment he saw the child in the ER, in the back of his head, the figure of Ava and her daughter was illuminating more and more.

He sprang from his chair, then he sat back as if someone pressed on his shoulders. He took out his cellphone and dialed Professor Art. "Hey, Jack. Are you busy?" he asked his trusted assistant.

"I always have a few minutes to spare with my boss and my friend," Jack said.

"Remember how we were lost on what to do for Teena, Ava's daughter?"

"How could I forget her? I saw Ava on TV yesterday in one of her commercials and thought about the ideal solution for Teena. But, since we don't have a donor, I didn't mention it to you."

"Jack, I love that you always think ahead of the crowd. Your wish might have come true. There is a six-year-old possible donor. I did the transplant match analysis and it came out to 80%. I'm sure Ava will be more than happy for us to try the procedure as the last resort. Do we have a newer update on Teena?"

"No, not since last month. Here, it says her cancer is spreading but at a slower rate. This report is after she was placed on the second experimental treatment. I will call her oncologist for any recent update."

"What do you think about harvesting the possible donor's brain and replacing it with Teena's cancerous one? They both are dying, except one is from the accident and the other from cancer."

"Do we have some kind of consent from the donor family?"

"Sort of, after giving them the bad news of nothing left to do for her, we had them sign the organ donation form. I know what you are going to say, that form needs to be updated to include the brain. But the brain is an organ."

"Well, there are at least three issues that we have to address before considering this proposal. We have the no permit, Million/Amin hasn't shown any countable progress, and how are we going to convince Ava to give up or donate her daughter's body?"

"Leave the last one to me. The other two, discuss with the rest of the team because I don't see them as concerning. Can you please check with Ross and Hun to see if they acquiesce to conducting a trial on a child? Don't go into detail. Not yet. This is another opportunity that we should take advantage of. Million/Amin seems heading in the right direction. The permit, I don't know—we may not even get it."

***

Professor Woods, after reviewing Teena's recent oncology report, dialed to her mom.

Seeing the caller ID, Ava felt anxious and panicky. "Professor, is my daughter dead?" she cried.

"No, no, no! Is she still in the children's hospital? I'm not calling from there. I actually have sort of good news."

Trying to straighten herself out, she said, "So, my daughter is okay? Please, tell me, what is the good news?"

"I have a plan that could save your daughter's life. You need to come to my office as soon as possible. I will explain the plan in detail. I need to go; my daughter is on the other line."

"Hi, baby girl!"

"Hello, Dad!"

"Are you checking on me?"

"Yes, also, are we going to hang out this weekend?"

"Yes, I will see you Saturday afternoon. I love you!"

"I love you too!"

***

Ava was in a studio making a commercial video. She dropped everything and left without saying anything to anyone. Though it felt like an eternity to her, it took her only fifteen minutes to arrive at the professor's office.

She said hello, and didn't sit down before asking, "What is the plan? What do you need me to do?"

"Please, take a seat. The plan is more complicated than you think. To get to the point, in our research center we have been conducting trials on brain transplantation. We placed a healthy donor brain of one animal into a healthy body of another animal, and we have seen satisfactory results. Our trial on humans, however, is too far in the early phases to talk about results.

"Also, not only that, we don't have a permit, yet, we have to have a donor's brain, and a recipient body and consent from each party to conduct trials on humans. If you are still willing to do what it takes to let me try to save your daughter's life, I need your consent. The donor is a six-year-old African American girl. Her name is Sandra. A serious car accident has left her on life support. Her parents, Mr. and Mrs. John are a young couple who, understandably, are having hard time accepting their daughter's death." Noticing, she was crying, he paused. Waiting for her to say something.

Then he continued, "If I have your permission, we will immediately perform the trial of replacing Teena's cancerous brain with the healthy donor brain. The procedure will keep Teena's physical look intact, and if successful, she will have a better life.

"Despite the outcome, you could be sure that the last possible thing on Earth that could be done to save your daughter's life has been done. That may give you peace of mind and comfort upon her passing."

"Oh my God! I can't believe what I'm hearing. Other organs, I expected, but I've never heard of a brain being transplanted. Doctor, how confident are you that you could do this transplant?"

"If your question is my confidence level on the success of the result, I'm seventy percent confident. If that is plenty enough assurance for you, let's try."

"I'm aware that even simple medical procedures don't have a hundred percent certainty. Your confidence level tells me that the procedure is as easy for you as one of the kidney transplants that you do. Okay, what do I do now? You guys do your absolute best, okay? There is nothing I won't do to see my daughter having a chance of living as a healthy person," she talked fast, then got up in a hurry. She believed she needed to go get her checkbook from her car quickly before the professor changed his mind.

"There is one important thing that you need to be aware of," said the professor, getting up slowly. "I don't have a permit to do the procedure. Until they issue me, I have to have you sign a confidentiality contract. I'm hoping that we will have our permit by the time your daughter wakes up."

"Sure! I will sign," she said, reaching out to give him a hug.

Ava felt the best feeling she'd ever had about her daughter's future. She left the professor's office with the highest hope she'd felt in a long time.

***

Even though the girl was still unconscious, the system had detected that all nerve connections were established, and the brain was receiving all its life needs from the body. At this stage, compared to the Million to Amin's operation, Sandra to Teena's had a quick response. Some of the body parts were seen as quivering sporadically. Dr. Woods knew that some form of communication between the brain and the body was taking place.

The flourishing of life in the lab didn't look real. Rather, it seemed a scene from a movie. It was an exciting and hopeful marvel to everyone involved in the process. Death gave way to life. The researchers congratulated, chests puffed, and high-fived each other. Nobody seemed to be concerned, or was not aware of, or didn't want to think about any of the significant social and personal issues hanging around the procedure and its outcomes. In the heat of the moment, those concerns were secondary to the matter of life and death.

The new girl, whom they named ST Harvard was having frequent convulsions. At first, they were limited to non-muscular areas of her body. As time went by, however, the effect began to spread to her fingers and toes.

Thinking about the current success of his work, Professor woods felt a happy sensation spreading through his body. But all he did to express that elation was a smile. If there was a contest on how much people could limit expressing their happiness or sadness, this professor would have won hands down. He simply smiled in the supposedly most joyful event of his life. Compared to the level of his achievement, the degree of pleasure and satisfaction he felt was minuscule.

When he sank into moments of self-reflection, he thought, *there is a serious discrepancy between some people's attainment and how happy they felt about it.*

That reminded him of what his professor in medical school said.

"We humans, despite our relentless attempts, couldn't go deeper than the accumulation of material riches to affect the level of happiness we feel. There are better sensations of happiness and wonder in the dream world than in the real one. Even our fears are more clear and vivid in dreams.

Though bliss, love, peace, satisfaction, and relaxation are the most important and precious riches, humans couldn't scratch their surfaces. Maybe they don't exist in the material world—they are just illusions. So, which is true? Is what is called reality real, or is illusion real?"

He added, "I don't question the need for material riches, but some people prioritize material things over human love and pure bonding. Hence, marriage and social life are losing their value. This is the same as replacing the emotion and awareness, the core of being human, with objective reality. In fact, the ceaseless pursuit to accumulate material riches is responsible for some of the distractions of social lives, and loss of love and respect among members of families, and society at large that we see nowadays. Perhaps, because it takes more time from family and social bonding than it could give back."

He once asked the whole class, "Where does human emotion reside? If known, instead of trying to create happiness by amassing material things, would you be amused by shepherding it? is emotion an ordinary thing? Why can't being human be construed?"

Professor Woods thought his college professor's questions were not meant to be easily understood.

The college professor had also asked all his students, "Why did William Shakespeare think that the world is a stage? Did he, himself, understand what he meant by that? I like to think he did. He wouldn't have said it otherwise.

However, I'm more curious about those who quote him—do they understand what he meant? If the world is a stage, then we are the actors.

"Hence, the rich, the poor, the educator, the student, the authority, the retainer, the one with great life, and the one with a miserable life are all actors of this theatrical world. Then, who is the spectator? Since the show has to go on, the one who is on the stage, the King or the Servant, remains on the stage and doesn't go beyond. What if getting off the stage is a must? Where would the actor go?

"So, how could I confidently accept that the life I'm living is the only, and the absolute thing? I'm not crazy enough to surrender myself to this unreliable and contradictory world. After all, I don't have proof that this world actually exists. I'd rather wake up and try to understand the truth instead of remaining asleep believing that the full of chatter, illusion world is real. What about you? Are you driven by unclear emotional complications, accepting you're being an actor in this staged world as living? You should rather think more deeply about how to get off the stage and try to reach the real world. It is always better to live than to pretend or act as if you are living."

***

Chapter Three

Noticing Teena's speedy recovery coupled with Million/Amin's satisfactory progress, Professor Woods' team was drunk with elation.

Teena was half asleep. Her body movements had advanced from just toes to arms and legs. She constantly blinked her eyes. However, she needed to wake up to be able to see. Her lips were no longer shivering, rather, they were moving in a regular rhythm.

The incision on her head had healed quickly, and the sutures were absorbed, the issue of infection on and around the area was no longer a concern.

Because Ava kept asking if she could see her daughter, they brought her into the surveillance room where the care team watched and recorded Teena's every move.

Except for its ceiling, everything else in the observation-room was made out of one-way glass. Looking through the glass window, Ava saw her daughter laying in a bed that was huddled with bells and whistles. Teena was attached to multiple medical devices. The robot nurse that everyone called RRN was standing on the left side of her bed to report any unusual occurrences that were not picked up by the cameras or naked eyes of the care team.

The RRN was also awaiting patient care instructions from the team members in the surveillance room. Ava, observing the complexity of the patient care system and erudition of the care team, felt high hope.

A couple of minutes later, the supervising doctor and a couple of members of the care team who had been with Teena since she was transferred to that unit joined both Ava and the nurse. Taking turns, they explained how Teena's recovery was progressing.

Ava's excitement grew more when the lead nurse pulled her to the other side of the room and had her sit in front of a computer that was recording live data. A monitor displayed live feeds of the video recorders in Teena's room.

Then the nurse showed Ava previously collected data and compared that with the current readings. After all that, it seemed to her that Teena was asleep but trying to wake up.

"What you are looking at is a complete circuit that is awaiting energy to start giving light or heat. In other words, all the nerve connections from the brain to the body are complete, and messages are being exchanged between them.

All parts of the brain are up and running. There is only

one important thing missing, Teena's awareness. As soon as she wakes up, everything will start to follow its rhythm," explained the lead nurse.

Ava was thrilled about her daughter's promising outlook. She was very impressed by Professor Woods and his teams' miraculous workmanship.

***

Five days after Ava's visit, two members of the care team were seated in the observation room, one surfing the web and the other one, newly hired to the team, blankly staring at the live video monitors. The new staff, startled by what she saw on the monitor, jumped from her seat with her eyes open wide, one hand covering her mouth and the other hand pointing at the screen. The web-surfer turned her attention to the monitors and started staring with her mouth wide open.

"Hey everyone, the child just woke up!" the web-surfer screamed. The lead nurse and others came in running. Teena had her eyes open wide, looking around the room with intense curiosity, her eyebrows raised.

The observation room filled with happy bunches who were laughing, clapping, yelling, and screaming with excitement.

One member of the team later told a friend, "The excitement in the unit was similar to that of NASA's control center when Neil Armstrong first landed on the moon."

When Professor Woods heard the news, he asked whether she'd spoke. The answer was negative. He told the caller to call him with her first word or sound.

That evening, she made a short humming sound and continued to make other sounds. The next day, she pointed to a multicolor balloon that some of the nurses brought for her. She attended the movements of people and objects with curiosity.

When Ava heard the news of her daughter waking up, she couldn't wait to go see for herself. In the observation room, she couldn't believe what she was seeing on the monitors. Her Teena's beautiful eyes were open and looking around as if to find someone or something. The half-smile on her face made her look like she was mocking someone. Thinking as such, Ava smiled big. She begged the nurses to go kiss her daughter. They helped her put on a hospital gown that covered her from head-to-toe and took her to the room.

She kissed, kissed and kissed the little girl in the forehead. The girl stared at her with raised eyebrows. Then, as if she remembered something, she smiled. Ava's eyes and mouth kept opening wider and wider. She kissed her for the fourth time and left the room, wiping tears of joy from her face.

***

The attending physician of the observation and treatment unit was in the midst of developing a plan to transfer ST Harvard to a less intensive unit where she would start receiving physical and speech therapy, when he received the call that scared the bejesus out of him and had him running to her room, leaving the receiver of the phone dangling from the table.

Without any form of warning, her body looked like a circuit board that had lost connection to power. Her eyes shut closed, her lips turned blue and purple, her skin became cold and clammy to touch.

The care team ran franticly to gate oxygen to her brain. They put a breathing tube into her throat and blasted a mandatory mode of ventilation.

When Doctor Woods learned the situation, he told them to rush her to SCD. A few hours later, the research team put the child's lifeless body on the table and began exploratory surgery. They took out the brain and placed it in the SYSTEM. Noticing that it was still alive, they smiled and sighed relief. Then they flew back to figuring out what went wrong. But that seemed to take more out of them than they went through when they put Sandra's brain and Teena's body together.

***

Ava was calling nonstop, wanting to pop in and see her daughter. The first day, they told her that Teena was not feeling well and had been moved back to the surgery unit. Hearing that, she was curious rather than nervous. Her faith in Dr. Woods and his team was intact. On the third day, Dr. Woods had her come to his office. As soon as she sat down, he said, "Ava, I'm really sorry to say this, but we lost Teena," with a nervous voice but a serious face.

She looked at him with shock, her hands on her mouth, she gasped for air. "How could it be. I saw her, was it three days ago, yes—I kissed her! She gave me this huge smile," she cried.

"Yes, it happened a few hours after your visit. All her systems shut down. We are still trying to figure out what happened."

"What am I to tell her dad, and our entire family and friends whom I had told that she made it through, and we're expecting to see a healthy Teena?"

"I'm really sorry!" he said and paused. Then continued, "You never know, we might…" he stopped, because doubt surged into him, *what if we never find out what happened and we put the brain and the body together again; and she dies for the second time? No false hopes!*

"You might what? Is there any hope?" she inquired, she never lost faith in the professor.

"No, never mind! We are working hard to figure out what went wrong, but that is where it will stop. Again, I'm sorry for your loss!"

Deep inside, the professor had high hopes and some confidence that they would solve the problem and the child could be in the recovery room the next day, but he wanted to show, not tell of it.

***

Million/Amin resurrected a few weeks after ST Harvard's death. His revival was slow and challenging. A week and a half after he woke up, he recognized that he was in a hospital, and was able to ask for food and drink. Going forward, he needed around the clock medical attention.

His care team watched him with great anticipation that he might crash just like the child. However, he was getting stronger by the day. He surprised the team with his slow but consistent progress to recovery.

A few days after he was able to form some sentences, he asked his caregiver how he was doing.

"You're doing great. If you want to, I can help you get out of bed, then you could try to take a few steps using that walker. You'll need to go slowly, though," said the caregiver, pulling out the walker from the head of the bed.

When Million/Amin talked, he stuttered. He constantly felt certain sensations throughout his body, but could not explain them. He was having a demanding time caring for his own body, it felt to him as if he was dragging a box full of a hundred-eighty-pounds of meat. He could read but was having difficulty vocalizing words.

"Doctor, am I going to remain like this for the rest of my life?" stutteringly, he asked his attending physician, Abigail Muzik.

"No, this is your transition to full recovery. You will slowly get better each day. Also, you are now on a schedule for physical therapy. Do not worry too much. Before you know it, you will be good as new," she said smiling.

"Okay, but why do I feel like I'm carrying something very heavy?"

"All that sensation will go away soon. The primary thing is that you are aware of your condition."

After he started physical therapy, he began to sense a heavy pressure in his head and detected some strangeness about his body. He noticed most of his body parts were slow to react. He couldn't grip objects or walk well and felt his skin rubbing each other.

It was easier for him to simply think than to do or apply his thoughts—easier than seeing, hearing, tasting, and talking.

He felt as if his body was cracking from dryness and pieces were falling off.

One evening, after his physical therapist left his room, he pulled himself up using the bedrails and sat on the side of the bed. Then, he cautiously stepped on the floor, one foot at a time. His legs were partially numb. His body didn't cooperate with his desire to move. He tried to walk, but his feet delayed several seconds after his brain prompted them to move. He sat back on the bed, fearing he might fall.

***

Though Million felt bad about his situation, motivations from his primary physician, Doctor Muzik, fueled by the goal of seeing his wife and kids one day, started to give him hope and strength.

Noticing Doctor Muzik's patience with him and her attentiveness, he wished that she was his sister. On the days she was on shift, she would come to his room and chat for a few minutes. She also stopped by before leaving to go home. On one of those occasions, using every ounce of the skill of speaking he had learned, he asked her about his friend Amin. She told him the unfortunate news of his friend's passing. He felt sad and miserable.

That day, after Doctor Muzik left, he sat in his bed with his knee bent to his chest and began sobbing uncontrollably. While crying, pictures of Amin began to form in his mind. Memories of their first meeting in the airplane, time together in Boston talking about back-home and laughing at silly jokes, bloomed in his head.

As if his brain was protecting him from more anguish and sorrow, he didn't remember the day of the accident.

The next evening, Doctor Muzik came over, as she had been doing for a few days previously, to say goodbye for the day. They chatted about different topics for an hour. When it was time for her to leave, loneliness began to creep on him. After she left, the feeling of sadness tramped into his mind.

Deciding not to give power to sadness, he tried to think happy thoughts. He pictured himself sitting in the living room of his house, talking to his wife about his time in the US. He might have chosen the wrong topic to talk to his wife about—it brought him the memory of Amin. That took him back to feeling sad. To make matters worse, the memory of the day of the accident surfaced. "O-h m-y Gosh! Oh-my-gosh! I killed Amin!" He screamed. "I was driving when that happened. How and why did I survive? I wish I'd died too," he began wailing. Then, guilt, sorrow, and anguish ganged up on him.

***

The next morning, Million/Amin woke up on a wet pillow, feeling crabby, sad, and hopeless. However, his biggest surprise didn't come until he struggled into the bathroom, leaning on his walker. He caught a glimpse of himself in the mirror on the bathroom wall and saw a strange, scary figure. He didn't dare to look at the terrifying figure in the mirror again. Instead, he dragged his heavy, slow body, moving like a zombie who uses a walker, back to bed and pressed the emergency call button many times with his shaky hands.

All available personnel, including Doctor Muzik, came running to his room. They found him sitting fearfully on the floor next to his bed breathing too fast and drenched in sweat. When they tried to learn what happened, he couldn't say a single word. He kept pointing to the bathroom.

Doctor Muzik told all responders that she had the situation under control, and they left. She had him stretch his legs out and sat him back into the bed, placing a pillow behind him. She kneeled on one knee at forty-five degrees to him, "Million, what happened?" she asked looking into his eyes.

"Please, go look at the bathroom mirror and tell me what you see," he said, stuttering worse than he had been. He pointed to the restroom still whimpering with a terrified look on his face.

She entered the bathroom and looked around but didn't see anything different. So, she yelled from the restroom that all she saw in the mirror was her reflection and there was nothing else around."

"You don't see somebody else's figure?" he asked, still stammering more.

"No, I don't see," she said walking back to him.

"I guess it just vanished. I saw it in front of me. It was an angel of death."

"What did it look like?" she asked with curiosity, she was thinking of referring him for a mental health evaluation until she heard him explain who the figure on the mirror was.

"My dead friend, Amin. I saw him in the mirror and immediately felt a horror going throughout my body and I didn't look back to verify what I saw. Instead, I ran to the alarm to get help," he said with a shaky voice.

The situation was clear to Abigail. She knew better than to leave him by himself, so, she walked to the far corner of the room and dialed to Professor Woods.

"Try to help him to calm down and relax, but tell him," said the professor from the other line.

Abigail returned to Million. He was in his bed.

Rubbing his hand, she began "Million, in a minute we

will talk about what you saw in the mirror. If you can, try not to think about that for now, and answer me this. Have you ever felt lucky that you survived the accident?" without waiting for his reply, she continued.

"Now, you are in a position where you only need a few weeks' worth treatments to be your old self, at least for the most part. You could go back to finishing your education, and pursuing other goals you have or had."

"Now, I'm not worried so much about my health. I'm more worried and terrified of the strange thing that I saw in the mirror. I don't feel safe here. Please find me another room," he said with a nervous voice.

"Million, your friend's body that you saw in the mirror is not some creepy thing. It is your instrument that has contributed for you to be alive," said looking into his eyes. She noticed that he was getting upset.

"Doctor, what are you talking about? I saw an angel of death with my naked eyes. And it terrified me. If you leave me here by myself, it will come and take my spirit. You have to believe me! Please, get me out of here. I'm really scared, I don't want to be alone," he said.

"Okay, I understand. You won't be left alone. Also, I want you to understand me—I'm not saying you didn't see your friend's frame in the mirror. But it was not a spirit as you thought. It is your friend's physical body that your brain is installed into. It is what has enabled you to hear me, see me, and believe it or not, for us to have this conversation."

What Doctor Muzik was telling him, Million thought was the strangest, bizarre, difficult and complicated concept for him to accept.

Beginning the day, he became aware of his surroundings, he had felt that there was something aberrant about his torso. Now, learning the strange body that he was put together with was that of his friend's, it creeped him out. The more he thought about the fact that his physique had once belonged to his dead friend, the faster his depression escalated.

He wished he could escape and disappear from that body. He believed he would have been the happiest man, if he took it off as if it were a cloth. He didn't want to think about the irony that the legs to escape from it with, and the hands to take it off, if it was a cloth as he wished, were the tools that were part of that body.

He considered his life an ugly and hopeless phenomenon. He felt contrived to live in solitary confinement for the rest of his life. He couldn't leave things to faith and accept what had happened. "So, now I'm a different person," he said, tears rolling down his face.

"Million, it goes without saying that it is because of this body that I met you and that you and I could have those personal conversations we have had and the one we are having now. Therefore, this physique is another factor that makes you a human being. Think about that for a moment. Convincing yourself is wise. Do you think your friend benefited, in any way, from dying? He is gone, never to return. On the other hand, you are still alive in his body. In a few days, you will be just like everyone else, and you will be a person who is capable of doing anything he pleases.

"Million, I spoke with you about my late fiancé. I wish there were opportunities like yours at the time of his accident. He was in a coma for several days, if procedures like the one you had were discovered back then, I would have paid anything to see him in a donor body.

"All I'm saying is you have bitten death, so enjoy your victory. You are very special, not only to those who brought you to this position, but also to humankind in general."

He understood what the doctor was saying. But all he could think was how he got cheated into something he could never change. His fear changed to anger. His respect and admiration toward the doctors instantly diminished and he hated their guts. He started to get tense and upset.

"Doctor, please leave, I want to be alone," he said, looking at her fiercely.

She was surprised to hear him say that with such a look on his face because normally, he was nice and polite toward her. In her office, she got upset thinking about him. She seemed to have taken it personally. It could be because she had been trying to help him at a personal level. She thought Million was a special gift of both nature and science. She was caring for him not only as a doctor but also as a friend. Caring for Million, she thought may somehow honor her late fiancé, because she believed if he'd had a similar opportunity, he would have survived.

Along the way, she mixed her professional and personal believes and vowed to herself to do anything in her power to see Million succeed.

A few minutes later, she went to his room to see how he was doing.

Apparently, he was kicking himself for including her in his reaction to the other doctors earlier. He was happy to see her, he hugged her and apologized. "You have been more than my doctor, I think of you as my sister, I can never be mad at you. After all, you are not one of the doctors who conspired to put me in this mess," he said, smiling.

"To be honest, I was taken back, but it is my weakness to take it personally. I understand your frustration. And I never meant to ignore your feeling. There are going to be many more ups and downs. They come with being alive. Welcome to life. Anyway, how you feeling right now?"

"Stressed out, and I have a bad headache."

"I will order medications to help you with that. But the best medicine is in you," she said, preparing to leave.

His nurse gave him a relaxant, anti-pain, and anti-anxiety medications, and stayed with him, chatting until he fell asleep.

***

Doctor Kevin Paul was a little superstitious when writing the "New" ST Harvard's discharge from the recovery unit. He remembered the shocking phone call of her crashing that he'd received while he was writing her transfer plan to a less critical unit. However, this time, she didn't crash or fall, rather, her progress was much quicker, and two hours after he gave the order to the charge nurse of the unit, New-ST Harvard had settled in another unit comfortably and received her first speech therapy.

***

When the professor called a few weeks after the bad news, Ava was still mourning the loss of her daughter. She was depressed and sad to speak to anyone. Her chauffeur, Angel and his wife Sabrina were the only people she felt comfortable to talk to. It could be because a month prior, the couple was in grief for their son who'd drowned while they were vacationing in Hawaii.

The professor left a message, "Ms. Murphy, this is Marg, call me when you have a minute. I have great news for you! In fact, you can go to the rehabilitation center and meet your renewed daughter."

The couple was with her when she listened to the voicemail on speaker phone. "What is this? A joke! One minute he tells me my daughter is gone, another minute he …"

"Do you know the caller? Some degenerates do not know what to joke about. You should call and tell him to never call you ever again," Sabrina fumed.

Angel knew the caller was not anyone but the professor, who Ava used to worship until a few weeks ago. Thus, he told his wife to calm down.

Ava called the professor back, but she received his voice mail. “Angel, can you take me to the hospital? Sabrina, you can come with us. Unless he is insane, Marg would NOT joke around.”

“Sorry, I didn’t know who the caller was. I just thought he was some lowlife who gets satisfaction from the suffering of others,” said Sabrina while they were heading to the car.

“Believe it or not, I had a feeling that he would call and tell me that they have fixed my daughter. Let me tell you something, if God was replaceable, this guy would have taken his place in no time,” said Ava, smiling corner to corner.

***

When the nurse ushered Ava and the couple to her room, Teena was walking toward the entrance slowly with the help of a physical therapist. The nurse knocked once while opening the door, she said, “Hey, beautiful, you have visitors who would like to say hi.”

The child looked at Ava, smiled, then tilted her head to see who else was behind her.

Ava stood frozen in the middle of the entrance, her mouth open and the hairs on her skin erecting. Drops of tears rolling down her face, she walked to her daughter and touched her shoulder as if to confirm if what she was seeing was real. Then, she gently kissed her forehead.

The child looked at Ava with a blank face and peered to who the other visitors were.

Angel and Sabrina couldn't believe their eyes. They both sensed their skins tingling. Angel couldn't control the urge to go and hug the child, he went and hugged her tight. The child, however, looked at him nonchalantly. Then, as if she just remembered who he was, she smiled big. Ava and Sabrina, who were focused on the interaction, seeing her smiling at him, pumped another set of goosebumps into them.

While the elated Ava and her friends were leaving Teena to her therapy with the plan to come back in a couple of hours, the nurse told them that the child was learning everything, including how to walk, talk, eat, and toilet all over again. "Her brain is still foggy, yet it is clearing more and more by the day," she added.

***

It seemed that there was something that the child wanted to say. She would make an unintelligible word or sound, and her caregivers could not understand her, and that made her cry. Her physical and speech therapists thought they knew what they were dealing with and what to recommend for treatment. But it wasn't as easy as they thought it was.

When she was not in therapy, Ava was visiting and playing with her. She would bring her different toys and surprises that she thought would make her happy. She brought toys from home that her daughter used to like. The girl, however, didn't like most of them, so, she threw them toward Ava. This situation was a little concerning to Ava. Among the toys that the child threw away was a custom-made Barbie doll that Teena loved so much and never slept without. Ostensibly, Ava had secretly hoped and wished that the girl not just looked like her daughter but that she would think like her as well.

Even though she couldn't express her needs with words, her direct care staff recognized that there was something that she was eagerly awaiting to see or have. They brought different things that they thought might interest her, but she expressed her disinterest by getting upset and throwing the things away.

They felt bad for her and sometimes frustrated that they couldn't figure out what she needed. Physical and speech therapists were having difficulty providing her with therapy because she was refusing and crying when they asked her to do something.

When Doctor Charles, the most experienced psychologist of the hospital, learned about her refusal of therapy and her behavioral issue with her caregivers, he decided to interview her team of caregivers and spend more time with her to observe her moments of happiness and sadness.

All the doctors who were involved in her care suspected the source of her frustration could be the desire to see Sandra's parents. However, they knew bringing them into the picture would loosen the bond that they hoped would be formed between her and Ava.

One day, while Doctor Charles was working with her, Ava showed up. After hugging and kissing, she started to unwrap and hand her fancy toys. The psychologist knew such toys could excite and elicit happiness in an ordinary child's brain of her age. The girl, however, gave only minor attention to the toys. The psychologist thought that he had found one point that supported his hypothesis that all the girl wanted to see was Sandra's parents.

Sitting far enough not to disturb their time together, he started to observe the interaction between Ava and the girl. The girl barely noticed that Ava was there. She made it seem like they had almost never met before. The only reason that she gave her some attention was because of the multiple presents that she brought her. Ava's approach to the child, the psychologist noticed, was authentically motherly—she loved her, she worried about her, and she tried to make her happy.

As the psychologist was forming his observational analysis, Ava left in a hurry after kissing and telling the child and her caregivers that she would return the next morning.

Doctor Charles explained his observation to her care team saying, "The girl doesn't have any problem other than loneliness and the feeling of solitude. She wants to go home and be with her family. Perhaps she has siblings that she loves and misses playing with. Children behave and act the way she is doing if they are separated from their parents, siblings, or are taken away far from their homes."

Until he read Dr. Charles's official report, Professor More didn't realize that he was getting into a deep predicament that he couldn't reverse.

Teat, one of the girl's fulltime caregivers, seemed to have a better rapport with her. She would scream and yell with her. Slowly, she showed her how to open her mouth, move her jaw, and where to place her tongue to make different sounds. The girl started to improve in making sounds. She was walking on her own, but very slowly. Interestingly, it took her less effort and time to learn and use her hands.

One morning, Teat was sitting with the girl when the later said, "Mama, mama." stuttering. At the same time, she was pointing toward the gate of the facility. At first, Teat didn't make anything out of what the girl was saying. However, when she kept saying it, again and again, Teat asked her, "Are you trying to say mammy?" and she nodded.

It was around the time when Ava had been coming to visit; "mammy will be here soon," Teat told her.

When the girl heard her mom would be coming, she jumped and giggled. Teat was astonished that she missed her mom because she had never seen her react positively whenever Ava came to see her. Lo and behold, Ava showed up. The girl was looking different directions, so Teat said, "Your mommy is here."

She turned around with a huge smile on her face,

immediately her smile hid like the sun on a cloudy day. She frowned at Ava and Teat. She shunned Ava and ran to the window. Ava beseeched multiple times and tried to wheedle her, but she refused to look at her, staring out the window.

Ava, handing the toys she brought to Teat, asked, "Why is she mad?"

Teat didn't want to describe what she understood of the situation, so she said, "I'm not sure, maybe she didn't get enough sleep."

The girl was resentful toward Teat because she lied to her about the coming of her mom and tried to tell her so. However, except Teat, no one could understand what she was saying.

Ava didn't even attempt to figure out what ST was saying. She simply stood behind her and began caressing her growing blond hair, and said, "My beautiful, Teena, it's okay! The doctor told me that I could take you out for a ride around town and stop by at home. We will do all that tomorrow."

***

The next day, Ava took her girl out for a ride. She wanted to strike up a conversation, but she noticed her daughter's attention was elsewhere.

Outside, the wind blowing east seemed to hasten the arrival of the ice-rain broadcasted for the next day. The child, rolled the window down and filled her lungs with the cold but fresh air, then rubbing her right shoulder, closed it back.

However, her eyes remained locked on the outside.

Hadn't the nurses told her that the child had been doing the same every time they left the facility on outing, and they reasoned that it could be part of the relearning process of her new brain. Ava, would have thought that she was avoiding her. She moved and sat close to her daughter and whispered into her left ear, "I know you think you are someone else, but to me, you are my beautiful Teena." Then she thought, *I guess it will be awhile before she gets to know me.*

When they arrived at the house, Ava said, "My beautiful Teena, did you miss home? You probably missed the most a nice bedroom with a comfortable bed. I have some surprises for you in there. Come on, let me help you down," she said, approaching to get her out of the car. But the girl shunned her and resisted every attempt. She told Angel, "Please, take her for a ride and come back when you see her getting tired. In the meantime, I will prepare us some food."

***

Meanwhile, Lesha and Deric were desperately trying to fill some part of the vacuum left by Sandra. Lesha was scared to try again after suffering two miscarriages in a row. Their family, even their doctor reminded them that adoption could be another option, but Lesha decided to give it one last try before sitting to discuss the idea of adoption. "I know, having another child is not going to wipe out the pain that Deric and I are enduring from losing Sandy, but it might be comforting," said Lesha, on one of her heart-to-hearts with

Deric's mom, Mimi

Her medical provider referred her to a physician who she said was experienced in helping patients with similar cases. After a couple of visits with the new physician, she was diagnosed with Cervical Weakness. When the doctor told her that the issue was treatable, she jumped from her seat with excitement.

The next time she saw the doctor was while prepping for the surgery and in the recovery unit, after her anesthesia wore off. "Going forward," the physician told her, "You won't have a miscarriage."

Sitting alone in the room, an image of herself in a maternity dress with a popped-up belly began floating in her mind's eyes. She smiled and leaped into another train of thought. While completely submerging to the new thought, she startled by a knock on the door. It was Deric, "Hey, sweetie! How are you holding up? Are you hurting?" he said, walking to the bed. He put a bouquet of roses and a newspaper on the bedside table and went and kissed her on the lips.

"My pain is tolerable. I guess my brain is busy processing excitement to register any pain that otherwise I could have been sensing. The doctor was here a couple of minutes ago and told me that my disappointment days are over! No more miscarriage! Isn't that exciting, honey?"

"I'm so happy for us, baby! I'm sorry you went through a lot, though."

"It is okay, honey, I'm sure it all happened for a good reason. I just wish we had known that the problem had an easy fix."

"I agree, mama! I'm with you on that. However, this "easy fix" might be one of the new miracles of medical technology."

"I guess so, otherwise, my primary physician would have known about it."

"Before I forget, Jerrys said hi and told me to pass on his best wishes."

"Jerry who? Our next-door neighbor?"

"Yes, the frontpage story in today's paper is a piece by his daughter-in-law, Molly. I called him as soon as I saw her name. Apparently, he was not aware of the article. Anyway, I have been reading her reports both online and in papers, she is an incredible investigative reporter. If I'm going to be successful in IR, I need to learn from the pros such as her."

"What is the article about"

"It is about an organ exchange market that the government was not even aware existed. Last year, she unearthed a couple of drug and weapon network cases from the Dark Web. I wonder how she gets her tips."

"Honey, what she is doing is dangerous. The criminals can make her a target. Is that really what you want to do? What is wrong with being the local news anchor?"

"Yes, it's very dangerous, but it comes with the job. Investigative reporters are the soldiers of the profession.

Speaking of soldiers, remember the story I told you about how my professor talked me out from becoming a war correspondent? He said that, despite being a press person, just because I'm black, I would be a target. I always kick myself for listening to that. Baby, to be honest, I have no passion for sitting behind a desk and reading the news that someone wrote for me. I want to go get it myself. IR is the adrenaline drip of reporters."

"Honey, I want to you to be happy! I really, really do! But, if whatever makes you happy is going to consume you, I want you to think twice about your decision."

"Baby, you are talking as if I already left my rather boring job. I have the passion, but I need courage like Molly's to do what she is doing. Maybe if she let me shadow her, I will have the confidence to realize the courage I have in me. The courageous me is pushing me to leave my comfortable position in commercial media and become an independent reporter. The coward in me is pulling me to sit back and watch others do what I could have done. One second—Jerry is calling."

"Jerry, what's up, brother? Did you talk to Molly? "

"Yes, and she said that she is happy to meet you on Wednesday afternoon. I told her that I would ask you and get back to her."

"Thank you, Jerry! That is thoughtful of you! Yes, I'm available Wednesday afternoon."

"How is Lesha? Are you guys still in the hospital?"

"She is doing great! She just got out of surgery; we are in a recovery room."

"Good to know. I will see you when you guys come home. I will let Molly know about your availability and give her your number, in fact, I'm texting it to her, as we speak."

"Thanks, Jerry! We will talk soon."

***

Chapter Four

When Molly and Deric met, she told him about an article she was working on. "Is this a follow up to the one you published on Monday?" asked Deric.

"It seems so, but from what I know so far, they are not related. To be sure, we have to wait and see who is involved in it. You never know what might be discovered as we dive deeper."

"Yes, because the research center could have been shopping for organs in the market you just exposed."

"You are already thinking like an IR, all you need to do now is put the hat on and build a case out of a prompt, and differentiate facts from opinions."

"Prompt is what I was going to ask you about—where do you get your tips? Before social media era, the only sources used to be witnesses and agitators. However, yours, because they are so strong, they seem insider sourced."

"Not all my cases are insider prompted. In fact, most of them are outside sourced. This new case, for instance, is suggested by my good friend. She knows the mom and child, but no details of how supposedly the dead child is alive."

“So, if you were to brief the case to an editor or publisher, how do you describe it in a nutshell? Because it seems big and complicated to me.”

“Good question! You reminded me of what I forgot to tell you. When you see cases that have multi investigable parties, you start with the direct ones. In this case, we have the child, who was supposedly dead, and the mom, but we know nothing about the research center. What you do in situations like this is to get your facts about the directly available party and publish about it, then you will start to get tips about the bigger one. I had a couple of tips about the organ market, and I published those tips in a blog post. That is when people began to inbox me more and more ideas that led me to the bigger fish.”

“I like your method of subtle collaborative reporting. You tell the public what you know and they tell you more. What if they don’t?”

“Then, you go deep on your own. If we don’t get information about the research center after we publish the story about the girl who they brought back from the dead, then we have to dig deep into the center itself. I’m hoping that we get insider sources that either condemn or praise what the center is doing.”

“I can’t wait to see how this investigation will turn out. Thanks for letting me tag along!”

“It is my pleasure! In fact, I can use your help. There is nothing fun about working alone.”

"If nothing else, I will help you with reviewing and editing your drafts, I'm very good at that."

***

"Hello, Lesha, is Deric alright? Molly just called and told me that he didn't answer his phone. I guess, they were supposed to meet up for lunch. I called a few times, and his phone was going to voicemail."

"Sorry, Jerry, I just got ahold of his phone. Deric has been in the hospital for the last three days."

"What happened? I wasn't in town myself."

"After I was discharged, he went to the pharmacy to pick up my pain meds. They are telling me that a drunk driver hit him and ran. A couple of nurses found him unconscious in the parking lot. Doctors are sure that he is not brain dead, but not sure if and when he will wake up from a coma," she said and started crying. She continued, "All that time, I was sitting there waiting patiently. I thought he was collecting discharge papers and getting my pain medication from the pharmacy."

"Did they catch the driver?"

"I believe so, but it has no use for me. I just want my Deric to wake up. How unlucky am I to lose the only two people I love, back to back? I'm still sore from the loss of my Sandy, now I'm about to lose my only strength and comforter. I'm sorry, Jerry, I don't mean to unfold the pages of my misfortune on you."

"It is okay, Lesha, you don't have to apologize. Is it okay if I visit him? are you there now?"

"Yes. I will be here until they kick me out. His mom and his sister were here too, they just left."

***

"Lesha, though I'm not a doctor, I can tell you with confidence that Deric will wake up. One of the skills I learned from dealing with cases where the patient is comatose is how to predict whether he or she would wake up or not," said Jerry, when talking to Lesha and one of Deric's nurses.

The nurse said, "I like your certainty! What is that you do, if you don't mind me asking?"

"I'm a retired investigator. You can tell by how the person covers his or her eyes and the expression on his or her face when different visitors come to their room," he replied.

"Interesting! They don't teach that at nursing schools. The only way we know that he will wake up soon is because he is not deeply comatose, his brainstem is not affected and that he has a very good respiratory drive," said the nurse, and hurried to her other patient's room.

"Lesha, have you called his boss or someone from his work? They probably want to report about him."

“Yes, I told his supervisor. As far as airing his condition, no, I wouldn’t let them. Deric and I had talked about it when our daughter died. We don’t want our personal life to be part of the news. There is no benefit in reporting about our personal life. It has no use to the public or to us.”

“I guess you are right. If he was needing an organ donation or money to help with his medical bills, having the media exposure would have helped greatly. Since he has no need for both of those, and like you said, since his condition has no educational value to the public, reporting it is not necessary.”

“That is what I mean.”

“I have to leave now, if you need anything, don’t hesitate to call me,” he said, and walked to Deric and whispered into his ear, “Hey pal, I know you can hear me, hurry and wake up—Molly is waiting for you before she publishes the case you two were working on. Don’t take too long!” he said and headed to the door.

“Jerry, thank you for the visit. I will keep you updated.”

***

“Good morning, Million, today’s rain feels like a waterfall—you should be glad you stayed in,” said Abigail, trying to find a room for her coffee mug on the table covered by the paper he was reading.

“Like I made a choice to stay in a hospital. Or a choice to live or die naturally,” said Million, his head down and his eyes on the paper.

"What's wrong, Million?" she asked, glancing at the title of the section he was reading.

"How many other short-changed, and unfortunate individuals like me are here, in this facility? Are you guys sick in the head? How can you mess with innocent people's lives? You didn't even think twice before screwing with a six-year-old child's brain? Shame on you!" he bawled out, looking at her with squinting eyes.

She only heard a bit of what he said. "Oh, wow! How did this come out ...?" she mumbled. "I'm really sorry, Million—you shouldn't have seen this. I mean, yours and this child's case is slightly different, nevertheless, seeing this might have made you think that the researchers do that on a daily basis. We will talk about it later. I have to go," she got up quickly, grabbed a copy of the paper and walked briskly to Professor Wood's office, leaving her coffee mug by the paper rack.

***

Ava, who had taken her daughter home, canceled all her previously scheduled commitments and stayed at home. The two of them were watching videos of Teena from birth until she got sick, and a few from after. Watching those videos, she believed were strengthening their mother-daughter bond.

One evening, both girls were sitting on the couch and watching children's music video. The child had laid her head on her mom's lap. "Ava, when are we going to see my real parents?" asked Teena, still her eyes on the TV and without moving her head.

Ava quickly stopped caressing her daughter's blond hair and looked at the child with shock. She had hoped difficult questions, such as that one wouldn't come forever or at least until she was able to explain and the child was able to understand what a brain transplant was.

"Sweet child, there is something that I can't explain to you now, but I'm your real mom and Marc is your real dad. We love you, and you are our princess. If you don't mind, please don't say something like that again because it hurts my feeling," she said choking with tears.

Then she looked at the child's big blue eyes with anticipation of hearing her say, "Okay, I won't say it again." However, right when the child opened her mouth to say something, Ava's phone rang. She was more interested in what the child was about to say than answering the phone, but when she noticed that the call was from the professor, she quickly picked up and said, "Hello, Professor, I was thinking about you because Teena asked me a question that is both complex and untimely."

"Ms. Murphy, are you happy with the way things are turning out? I told you that everything about the transplant, including the incidence, should remain confidential, why did you tell anyone, especially a reporter?"

"Professor, I don't know what you are talking about. I didn't tell anyone other than my immediate family and her dad. I haven't been out of the house since Teena came home. Marc doesn't have time to talk to a reporter either. What is going on, anyway?"

"Haven't you read the local newspaper? The reporter couldn't have gotten her lead from anyone in the center. I believe her sources are outside. Who was the couple that came with you to meet Teena after the second procedure? You shouldn't have brought anyone."

"They are my friends who were by my side when I was dealing with the loss of my daughter. When I told them that you had brought her from the dead, they came to see the miracle. I had forgotten all about the confidentiality thing. I'm Sorry! But I don't think any of them would have talked to the reporter."

"I will figure out who did it. In the meantime, tell all the people whom you told about it, to shut their pie-holes," he said and hung up.

Ava stood frozen, staring at the Charles River from her bedroom window. Then, thought after thought began to bounce in her head. "He should have his facts straight before calling me. What the heck is wrong with him? What exactly is in the paper, anyway? Angel should get it for me. Could he or his wife have something to do with the report? I don't remember telling them to keep it a secret," she grumbled. Then she picked up her phone and dialed a number from her recent-call-list.

"Hello, Angel, can you please bring me a current copy of Mass News? Also, if you haven't already told anyone, keep the news of Teena's coming home confidential. At least for a little while."

"Sure! Despite my excitement, I haven't told anyone. You should tell Sabrina though; she loves to talk to anyone about unbelievable things like Teena's miraculous recovery."

"Oh, man! It might be too late. Let me call her anyways."

"Okay, I'm leaving to bring you the paper. Is there anything that you want me to pick up while I'm there?"

"Yes, bring me a couple of bottles of wines, please. You know my favorite. And bring one bottle of Sabrina's favorite too."

"Sure thing, boss!"

***

"Do any of you have a suspect in mind who could have met the reporter?" asked Professor Woods to his team of six professors and three doctors at the urgent meeting regarding the report.

"Obviously, the source is outside the center, if not Ava herself, it could be her friends. The paper talks about her and her supposedly dead daughter, the rest of the story is speculation deduced from the transplant," said Professor Kim.

"Guys, I know it is important to figure out who did it and prevent them from giving up more info, but that is only one of our concerns now. We need to talk about investigations that are being brewed as we speak and about the hungry media that will not hesitate from invading the center," said Doctor Muzik.

They all talked amongst each other about what was coming and what to do about it.

"Listen up, guys, this is a serious matter. Our secrets that we had safeguarded for so long are endangered. Which means, our profession, our names, our lives, and our families' lives are threatened. There is no time to mumble amongst each other, let alone to giggle. Now, bring your ideas to the table and let's discuss them," said the professor, with a clear expression of disappointment.

"I can think of at least three major concerns that we should find solutions for before we step out of this room. We have to prepare for a response about the who and how of the child's donor, we have to decide to block the case of Million-Amin from becoming another news topic, and we need to figure out who leaked to avert further damage," said Professor Art.

The professor listened to everyone's inputs impatiently. Then he said, "Ladies and gentlemen, all your ideas about the donor are great if we weren't dealing with paper flipping and mouse clicking highly trained investigators. My suggestion, therefore, is to give them what they want, documentation. They will want to see proper documentation of who and how we got the brain. And how we did the procedure that they didn't give us permission to do.

"Guys, if they want to be nasty, they can make a criminal case out of this alone and take us to court immediately. Dealing with this by itself is too big for us. Thus, we have to find ways to deter any other cases from becoming part of the investigation, let alone the news. So, how do we evade Million-Amin's case? Any suggestions?"

“I believe, dealing with that case prompts us to really find how it leaked and learn how much the reporter knows about our work, such as this case. Here is what I mean, if they know nothing more than what is in the paper, then we can move the guy and all traces of the procedure that created him to an undisclosed location. However, if we learn that they have a hint, then we should prepare documentation with “proper signatures” of consent both from the donor and the recipient,” said Professor Emanuel.

“To be honest, we don’t have the luxury of time to play wait and see. His case is a hot mess. Therefore, I agree with the first point, the only thing we should do is undo our work and destroy all his traces. Otherwise, they will throw us all in prison without a trial,” said the professor.

“I hope you are not suggesting that we should kill the poor man?” asked Doctor Ted.

“No, we are not going to kill anyone. All I’m suggesting is that we undo our doing. As in taking apart what we put together. That person has no identity, other than what we gave him. Thusly, he has never existed. We put him together to see if it works, now that we know, we should disassemble him. As far as our research is concerned, both subjects are end products of the purpose of what they were created.

"We have no choice, otherwise our and our families' lives are on the line. If any of you are considering the wait and see a game, count me out of it. If you have a suggestion other than what I have bluntly presented, spit it out now. And it better be one where the investigators will not learn that there was a human study in this center other than that of the girl's," said the professor, and sat back in his chair with his arms crossed and his eyes covered.

***

"Hello, Ms. Murphy, sorry, I need to leave before I can bring you the paper and wine. Sabrina is hurt and they are taking her to the hospital."

"Oh, my gosh! what happened?"

"They just called me from the Yoga place where she goes and said that an old lady drove into the building and ended up on top of Sabrina and a bunch of other ladies."

"Sorry to hear that—please go and let me know if I can be any help."

"I will, thank you!"

***

"Marc, do you have a minute?" texted Ava.

"I will call you in a minute. Is everything okay?"

"Everything is alright, I just want to talk to you about something."

"We are putting the twins to bed and I will call you soon after."

"Okay, thank you!"

***

“Hey, Marc, thanks for calling me, I’m not as bad now but I was upset earlier.”

“Well, I’m glad you are calmer now. What is up?”

“Have you read today’s Mass News?”

“No. Should I have?”

“While I was dealing with the most difficult and scary question from Teena, the professor called and screamed at me about a story out in the paper. Apparently, someone has talked to a reporter, telling the story about Teena. Do you have any idea who could it be? I knew it couldn’t be you or Caitlin because you guys are too busy with the twins. I was just curious if you have told anyone who has access to the media.”

“Well, I told my parents, and I highly doubt that they would talk to a reporter about it. Have you asked Angel and his wife? Especially his wife … Wait for a second, Caitlin told me that Sabrina and Molly, the well-known reporter, are friends. They go to the same yoga place. Hold on, let me grab my key from the house and go get the paper.”

“Do you have time to bring me a copy?”

“Is Angel off today, or something”

"That is another thing that I was going to tell you about. He went out to get the paper, a few minutes later, he called and told me that an old lady drove into the yoga place and ran over Sabrina and other ladies. To say the least, my afternoon has been full of bad news! I hope something good comes out of all that."

"Oh, my gosh! Did he say how bad she got hurt?"

"No, he has no idea. They told him that she was taken to the hospital. He said he would call me and tell me how she is doing."

"This is crazy! You know, if she didn't give birth, Caitlin would have been there too. Except the maternity-yoga room is further back in the building."

"I feel bad for everyone involved. Are you on your way? I've got to warn you, we have a hot potato here too. Ms. Teena wants to know who and where her real parents are. Like I told you the other day, I still haven't been out of the house since she came home. We were watching all her videos and lots of kids' movies, we saw all her childhood photo albums. I felt we were bonding really well until she hit me with that question."

"That is a bummer! and really complicated! Obviously, her brain is still full of old memories. I wonder what kind of child they got the brain from. She was smart and eloquent for her age. Her parents must have taught her well. What did you say, when she asked?"

"I told her that you and I are her real parents. And I was begging her not to ask me that question again. In the middle of it, the professor called. Even though I was waiting for her reply to my plea, I was glad that he called because I was dying to talk to someone about what she said. However, as soon as I said hi, he began yelling. He didn't ask, he simply accused me of talking to a reporter. Man, was I upset! I was going to have him hear it from me, but I realized I still need his help with her."

"He is supposed to be wiser than to call people without facts in his hand. Anyway, you did well. Wait, I'm looking at the paper now. Wow! It is front-page news! Yes, the author is Molly. At least, we have a hint to say that Sabrina could have told her. We can't do anything about what is already out, but that should be the last one."

"Believe it or not, I was going to have Sabrina and Angel over for dinner and find out if she had shared the news with anyone. I guarantee it, every news media will want to talk to us. We should never give them a chance. We don't want to make enemies out of the people who saved our daughter's life."

"I agree! I'm a couple of minutes away from your place. I want to come in for a little bit and say hi to Teena."

"Okay, I will let her know that you are on your way."

***

Sabrina was seriously hurt. A broken glass plunged into her neck, and some sort of metal into her back, and her jaw was broken. She was unconscious when the paramedics arrived. They knew that their every move with her would have to be a very-careful-one because they believed the metal might be resting on her carotid artery. In the hospital, she began to wake up and started reaching for the metal and the glass. They immediately sedated and took her for surgery and began working on taking out the foreign objects.

When Angel arrived, she was still in surgery. When Ava called for the third time, Angel said, "We are heading to the recovery unit, they said that she is out from surgery and taken there. I will call you after seeing what has happened to her."

Sabrina, with wired jaw shut, and bandaged everywhere was still loopy from leftover sedation. Seeing Angel, she tried to smile and realized that her jaw was wired, and her lips had swollen like small balloons.

***

A few days after the Yoga place accident, Mass News published a special report on Molly Yemoo's death. The entire paper was about her. It started with her life history, and her biggest breaks in investigative reporting, including the one that was on the front page a couple of days back.

Then turned to the accident that killed her and three other women and one man, and injured eight. There were fifteen people in the Yoga center doing their guided deep meditation when the mother of three and grandmother of ten drove her

BMW straight into the glass wall panels.

According to the paper, the eighty-six-years old grandma was diagnosed with Early Stage Dementia and had surrendered her driver's license and the key to her BMW 2 Series Convertible. It was her eldest son's 4 Series that she drove after finding the key on the kitchen counter. Her son told reporters that she was staying with him and they were getting ready to go see their family doctor.

***

"Hello, Lesha, how are you guys doing? How is Deric?"

"Hey, Jerry, I'm really sorry about Molly. I texted because I didn't want to disturb you with a call."

"Yes, it is heartbreaking. She was a very good person and great daughter in-law. Apparently, she was three and half months pregnant. My son and her family are devastated. We all are."

"It is terrible! How unfortunate!"

"How is Deric?"

"Okay, I guess. The doctor was here a few minutes ago and said that he is responding to pain stimulus. That is something good, right?"

"Yes, that is good! I really want him to wake up and take over where Molly left off. My son gave me the notes she was working on and it has a list of contacts in it."

"He would be trilled if he knew what is waiting for him."

"Hey, please keep me updated. I will come and visit next week."

"Of course, I will! Thank you! And again, I'm sorry for your loss!"

***

With passing days, despite catching national attention, the story about the supposedly dead child changed its theme and became about the first person who received a successful brain transplant. News agencies and paparazzi began flocking to Boston and camped by the research center to have a glimpse of the child who they reported had beaten death twice.

As Ava suspected, she and Marc began getting nonstop phone calls from media agencies and movie directors and producers asking for an interview. The two of them remained firm with their decision not to sit for any conference.

Some reporters who deduced the whereabouts of the child from the original report began to hang around Ava's house. However, as soon as CNN aired the news that the research center was sealed by the Office of Human Research Protection (OHRP) aiming investigation, almost all of those who had camped by the center relocated to driveways a block from Ava's residence.

***

"Marc, Teena is dying to get out of the house, what do I do? Honestly, I'm tired of sitting here too."

"Are the damn paparazzi still around your house?"

"Yes, they are. To make things worse, Angel is not able to come. He said that Sabrina's condition is worsening so he wants to be with her. Which is understandable. My dad offered to take us to his vacation house in Hawaii and stay with us there. But with his fragile health, I don't want to take him far from his regular doctor."

"So, what are you going to do?"

"I don't know. Maybe I will drive there in the morning. Hopefully no one will be out there to harass us."

"I'm sorry, I couldn't be any help."

"I know, I understand your situation. What I need is a husband. I need to find me one! You know, since our divorce, even all that time we were separated, I never went out on a date. Well, with Teena being sick, I didn't have the luxury of time or the enthusiasm to say yes to those who were asking me out. Nowadays, no man has the courage to ask me out."

"Don't you have girlfriends with whom you could talk about that kind of stuff? Where are all those girls that you were partying with when we were married? Do you not understand, all this reminds me of how bad you played me? The only thing you and I have in common is Teena. If it wasn't for her, I would never want to talk to you. Now again, if you want me to be involved in Teena's life, I'm happy to stay tuned—everything else is not my business. Bye!"

Ava couldn't believe what she just heard. "What the fuck!?" she blared. She went to her bar and sat down, staring at a bottle of Madeira she had opened earlier that evening and had a glass from. She threw the glass to the sink and watched it shatter. Then she took a sip out of the bottle and said to herself, "He was the one who was married to his work. He could have been fooling around for all I know. I was struggling to juggle my life at work, and at home with a sick child and still trying to keep our marriage together. Now he's talking as if he was the victim. I had moved on and was trying to be friends. Apparently, he's kept his grudge all along. Whatever!"

She stood by the counter and quaffed three quarters of the bottle of wine and fell back to the couch. She pushed on the armrest of the couch and got up. After picking up her phone off the floor, she walked upstairs slowly. "Teena, my dear, let's go. We have to go to my parents' place."

"I wish we could go to my real parents place instead."

"What did you say, you stupid brat? Didn't I tell you to never say such things again? You have no other parents. I'm all you got. Get over it!" Ava screamed at Teena and slapped her on the face.

Teena rubbed her reddened face, ran to her bedroom crying, and locked the door.

Ava sat in the living room and began sobbing. When she woke up three hours later and found herself on the living room sofa, she realized what she had done.

"Teena, honey, are you sleeping? I'm so sorry! I didn't mean to hit you. I was upset, that is all. I will make it up to you. You tell me where you want to go, I will take you anywhere in the world." She whispered through Teena's bedroom door.

"You promise?" said Teena, opening the door.

"Yes! Baby, yes! Do you forgive me?"

"Yeah. Can we go to Boston? That is where my real parents live."

"Yes! We can go to Boston. It is across the river. The only thing is, I don't know what real parents you are talking about. Come here, baby, let's both stand in front of the mirror. You see who you look like? We both have big blue eyes, straight noses, even our upper lips are shaped the same. Go ahead smile. Look, we look the same even when we smile. Except, you are prettier. Now look at your hair and mine, we both have long blonde hair. So, you see, you are my daughter, and I'm your real mom. All those videos from your childhood didn't make sense to you?"

"No. But if just one time I see my dad and he tells me that he doesn't want me because I look like Teena not Sandra, I will never ask you to take me to them ever again."

“Sandra? Is that what you think your name is? I know, it is all confusing. You had a big surgery. Don’t ask me about it though, because I don’t know much. All I know is that it takes time for everything to make sense to you. To me it is simple, there you are, my Teena. Anyway, I love you! And when you don’t say my real parents, as if I’m your fake mom, I love you more! Can I sleep with you? We have to wake up early and head to my parent’s place.”

“Okay!”

***

The professor and his associates were prepared for the worst. However, the reporter’s death, they believed, was a blessing in disguise. If that wasn’t enough, to their surprise, the Office of Human Research Protection (OHRP) red tagged them only for five weeks and sanctioned them with ten thousand dollars and left them with a warning to never conduct human trial without a permit. That, they thought was a slap on the wrist.

Even though, they were allowed to reopen specific labs, they kept the whole center closed and sent all staff on payed leave, aimed at avoiding employees being harassed by reporters. A few days later, the team noticed that the plan was working as they’d hoped it would, because less and less reporters and paparazzi frequented the surroundings.

***

Media began to report about the scientific breakthrough that the girl was the result of. Then the controversy around the research skyrocketed immediately.

While some people were impressed by the scientific geniuses and technology behind it, others thought that it was a work of evil. Despite its negative connotations, others saw its potential outcomes. Some thought it might help those who suffered from muscular dystrophy and neuromuscular diseases, and those who were blind or deaf, or both since birth or later in life. People with certain mental health problems and their families might also benefit from the outcomes of the research.

And there were those who began to entertain the possibility of implanting their brains in bodies or frames of their liking.

There were also those who were concerned about criminals and terrorists taking new identities to camouflage and that the research might lead to a rise in senseless activities of killing people for their brain or their body. Therefore, they believed that government should intervene to prevent the realization of such potentials.

Unfortunately, the discussion of the research as a controversial social issue outweighed any positive perception of the scientific breakthrough that some scholars considered it as.

***

The research center and its lawyers began preparing to respond to multiple lawsuits and legal actions that were both foreseen and unexpected. The thought of Million/Amin's case leak enhanced Professor Woods' anxiety. He was aware of that its innate religious and foreign policy issues had made it a hot potato. Therefore, if it leaked out, both the center and the researchers would find themselves in dire straits. No one wanted to take that risk. Thus, it was determined that he should be erased from the history of the center, forgotten that he ever was created.

Professor Woods had to convince the research team why the trigger had to be pulled. And this was how he presented his point on their second meeting about the subject, "You all know, when we decided to conduct the trial on what has now become Million/Amin, we set out with two goals in mind. The first and primary goal was to try to break the presumed impossibility of brain transplant on humans, and if it didn't work, to learn why. We did it on all kinds of animals, so, it was time to apply it to humans—and the opportunity surfaced. The secondary goal was to try to save one life out of the two dying individuals. And each of us worked tirelessly day and night to accomplish both goals. So, we all should be proud of what we have done.

"However, due to government bureaucracy, we are unable to apply the unique and advanced knowledge that we have learned, nor could we reproduce our work. Rather, our work is considered a crime in the eyes of the law of the country. So, we are forced to make a choice between leaving things the way they are and take the risk of losing our license-to-practice and closing our center, or taking apart what we put together and forget that it ever has been done, and reproduce similar but legitimate works as soon as our permit is approved."

He took a sip of water and continued, "It may seem inhuman to say that he has to go back to unliving, however, we all should remember that it was always the majority over the minority. In other words, the few must be sacrificed for the majority to live. If we are going to do more research and save more lives, we need to make sure that we all don't go to prison, and our research center remains open."

He stopped and tried to sense the mood in the room, then continued, "For those of you who have not thought about the significance of Million/Amin's case, I'd like to draw your attention to the religious and foreign affair issues that are intrinsic to Million/Amin. Not only to prevent such dire straits but also for the sake of the multiple lives we would be saving, we must find a better place for Million/Amin."

After the professor finished his speech of call for action, a heated discussion and argument went on for over two hours.

There were those who argued, "Killing Million/Amin is the same as destroying history and art. Considering his scientific, historical, and educational value, he is worth keeping alive."

The majority of them, however, argued that, "Keeping him alive could kill the research that made him who he is." And concluded that it was too much a risk and too complicated to keep him alive than letting him go.

Based on majority rules, a decision was made. And the coming Sunday was determined to be his last day on Earth.

***

Since the first day of his transfer to recovery floor, Dr. Abigail Muzik had been Million's attending physician. She knew him more than those who put him together. She had been giving him both medical and emotional support. She was in the meeting where his death sentence was sealed, except she was among the minority.

Looking out the window of her office, she shivered, imagining walking to his room and finding his lifeless body covered with a white sheet. She felt sick. She thought, *The person who has come a long way, who has chosen to live for the prospect of seeing his family one day, a very intelligent and genuine person is going to perish? He was led to believe that he was saved from death because he has something to offer to the world. Now, he is going to be killed by those who saved him*. She began sobbing.

She understood the root of the researchers' concern and its legitimacy. However, she didn't agree that killing him to stop the possible reveal of his case was the only solution, and she didn't believe that it would void their legal responsibility.

She sat down and started weighing a few ideas she considered could prevent the leak of his case. And she calculated the risk of trying to save him, "This could cost me more than my career," spoke out loud.

***

Even though Million's life was bestowed through the scientific breakthrough, and medical interventions then after, his new torso was giving him emotional pain, and he didn't think he would find relief for it. He was worried that people who knew him before would not recognize him now. The thought of explaining himself, especially to his wife, began to give him a headache. But somehow, he curbed and endured his emotional tremor and decided to call his wife.

He picked up the phone and dialed the number and brought it close to his right ear. It was ringing. He missed his wife and kids badly. He was sure that either his wife, or his daughter, or his son would answer the phone, and he was dying to hear their voices.

His wife answered it. "Hello, who is this?" she asked.

In his familiar way, he said, "It's me, Million. How are you, beautiful?"

She was confused about why a man she didn't know was calling her by a pet name.

"Sorry, I'm not sure who you are. Who are you trying to reach?" she asked.

He realized his voice had changed. "Sorry, if my voice doesn't sound familiar, but I'm your husband, Million, calling you from America," he said.

She said, "I don't understand, what you are talking about? Are you insane?" and hung upon him.

Million was sure that he was speaking to his wife, Saba. He knew that she didn't recognize his voice.

"Oh, my dear, Sab! You have no idea! Do you think I'm a stranger just from hearing my voice? I wonder what you would think if you saw me!" tears rolled down his face.

He decided to explain himself to her, so, he cleaned up his tears and straightened himself and redialed the number.

"Hello, who is this?" his wife answered the phone again.

"Sab, it's me, your husband, Million. My voice is strange to you because I had a car accident and the doctors changed my body parts to save my life," he said, hoping she would believe him.

"Why won't you leave me alone?" she said irately.

"Sab, It's me, Million. I'm calling you from the hospital."

"I don't think you understand people's sorrow. I doubt you have a heart and soul," she said and hung up on him again.

He waited for a little while and called for the third time. It rang a few times and went to voice mail. He dialed for the fourth time.

She answered on the first ring and said, "What did I do to you? Please stop disturbing my peace," she sounded confused and frustrated.

Hoping that she would try to understand him, he mentioned their kids' names and inquired how they were doing. Confused and annoyed, she said, "They are fine!"

"Sab, what about you? How are you doing? The reason why you didn't hear from me for so long was that I had a car accident and I was in the hospital. I'm still there but doing a lot better."

"You are adding sorrow to my heartbreak by disturbing my peace. Don't you have other things to do?" she said bitterly and hung up on him.

It was not clear to Million why Saba didn't want to listen to his explanation.

While he was sitting consumed by melancholy, Dr. Muzik came into his room.

She said, "Million, you look sad, what's up?"

She thought that he heard about what they determined at the meeting.

"Doctor, I'm sad because I tried to talk to my wife, but she was not willing to listen. She hung up on me four times."

"Did she say why?" asked Abigail.

"She didn't, but I'm guessing that it is because she couldn't recognize my voice. I tried to explain to her why I sound strange, but she kept saying, don't add sorrow to my heartache. I don't know why she wouldn't let me explain myself? How long have I been in the hospital? Has it been that long for her to forget about me and be with someone else?" he said, getting very upset.

"Oh, I remember one thing. You know what, Million?" said Abigail, hesitating whether to tell him or not.

"I'm very sorry I didn't tell you, but your wife was told you were dead. Your body was sent to your family. So, they all believe you passed away."

He dropped his head in shock. He locked in position for a while, then asked, "What possibly can I do now?" he said, sounding choked up.

"I understand your concern, but there is another issue that requires priority. I'm here to tell you about that," said Abigail.

"What else could demand priority more than this?" he asked her, still looking down.

"Staying alive takes priority over everything else. That being said, the people who saved your life have decided to get rid of you. As in to kill you. So, you need to get out of here. It is very risky for you to stay here any longer," she said, feeling a sense of urgency.

"Wha—t?" he asked stretching his word, perplexed. "How could it be? Why? What did I do?" he asked, muddled more than ever.

After walking to the door and locking it, she said, "Listen! When they decided to do the research that saved your life, they didn't have a permit to conduct such an experiment. They did it anyway. They still don't have one. So, your being alive has become a risk factor to them. That is why they want to get rid of you, and they will—unless you disappear to somewhere where they won't find you.

"You know I'm off today, and I shouldn't be here. Especially, in here with you. Thus, nobody should know that I was here, otherwise, I will be in deep trouble. I was very careful when I came in and I will be when I leave."

"What problems have I caused?" he asked. The issue with his wife was still nagging him in the back of his head, if that was not enough, he was forced to think whether he will stay alive or not.

"You didn't cause any problem. The news you read the other day has terrorized the researchers. They think that it is a matter of time before your cases become public, and the thought of it has terrified them. They believe both the center and the researchers will sink into an impasse that they could never get out of," explained Abigail.

"By all means! They should go ahead kill me and save themselves from any predicament. Along the way, they will put me out of my misery. My life has become the steepest mountain for me to climb, so, I'm better off dead. I don't want to disturb my families' peace by telling them I'm alive when they have already buried me. My death is the best solution for all of us," he said, feeling hated and forlorn.

Abigail sensed his hopelessness from his voice and posture. She said, "Million, your resolute determination is a paramount weapon in this struggle. What is great is that you won't be alone in the combat. I will put my life and career in jeopardy to help you with everything you need until you get to your wife and kids or you no longer need my help. I'm your best friend for life," said Abigail, looking at the back of his head.

Million said nothing. Sitting on the edge of the bed, his tears ran down his face to the floor. He felt lost and helpless. He felt his arms and legs giving up on him—everything went black on him.

Dr. Muzik noticed that he was fainting and was about to fall from the bed. She gently lifted his legs onto the bed. She had him lay on his right side and raised the leg of the bed to lower the top part of the bed just so more blood could flow to his head.

"Million, I understand what you are going through. Problems that are new and you were never prepared for are overwhelming you. Loneliness worsens and complicates the issue. So, from here on, you shouldn't, and you won't be alone. I will be with you until you get to your homeland."

***

Remembering her late fiancé who died from a motorcycle accident, she felt emotional, and her eyes filled with tears. "I wish the current medical innovations were discovered a year ago. My late fiancé's life would have been spared. I would have been happy to see him even in someone else's body. I love him and miss him so much," she said dispiritedly.

Abigail was a thirty-two-year-old beautiful and attractive young woman. It had been only two years since she finished her residency. She was a gold medal athlete both in high school and college. She still ran for fun and to maintain her beautiful shape. She was kind, goal-oriented, and wise.

"Doc, you have been very kind to me. Whenever I start to believe I'm the only living thing on this planet, I remember you. You are the only human being who knows that I'm Million. Those who put me together have given me a new identity. They call me Million/Amin. Anyway, I wish my family back-home would understand me half as much as you," he said, seeing his family in his mind's eyes.

"No worries! Soon, things will take shape. Meanwhile, some prices may have to be paid. Be strong and resolute. Bravery is not fighting just with someone else. It is also grappling with one's self to endure the things that couldn't be changed and to surmount the ones that could be."

"Abigail, I have come to realize that life and death have an equal value to me. Strangely, I'm both alive and dead, my status leans more toward death, though. However, two things are keeping me going, the hope of seeing my family and your kindness.

"We humans are aware that life and death are the head and tail of a coin. But I think hope makes us forget that death exists. You see, my wife and my family believe that I'm dead. But the hope that they will understand my situation is making me choose to live."

"Let me tell you a story about an insane man. This man thought he was wheat. So, he was always running away from a chicken. After seeking professional help for a long time, he recovered from the illness. He understood that he was not wheat but a human being. After evaluating, his doctor discharged him.

"A few days later the man returned to the doctor. The doctor wondered why the man came back and asked him so. The man replied, 'Doctor, I know I'm a man, not wheat—but does the chicken know that?' The moral of the story is that first know who you are. In your case, it is easier to explain and convince your family and friends to accept you as you, only after you know and accept yourself."

"Dr. Muzik, I thank you so much for your wise words of advice. And I do not doubt that I will always have your support. I won't forget until my last breath that you have been my strength and motivation throughout my darkest days, and now you are sacrificing a lot, including your life for me to live. I will use your advice to get through all my struggles in life. Only you understand that, let alone my family, I'm still getting to know me."

She stared into his eyes for a second and said, "The time that you will change things around through your struggle is around the corner. Your wife, children, and parents will be joyous that you are alive. The medical procedure you underwent has never been seen and done anywhere in the world.

"It is strange, even to you because you and the little girl are the only people on Earth who received that treatment. So, no one will understand you at first and possibly for a while.

But, not for very long. Soon enough, there will be a long waiting list of powerful and rich people to receive the benefit of the medical intervention that has changed your life. Therefore, the time, when society will know and admire that you are Million, whose life was saved through a quantum leap in medical research is not too far."

For a few seconds, they both sat quietly. Then Abigail said, "I have to go and take care of a few things. I will call you in a few minutes." She got up and left.

As soon as she left, Million sunk back to his depression. Everything was becoming strange and difficult for him. He remained seated, confused about the what, when, and whys of his life.

The countless things he's had to deal with kept piling up in his head. First, he has to escape from the deathtrap the researchers were preparing for him, introduce himself and convince his family that he was himself whilst looking like someone they never met. What would he do if Amin's family found him? How would he use his identification, school, immigration, and employment documents? He couldn't go back to his previous employment because they wouldn't know him, so, what was he to do for a living? In his mind's eyes, all these issues were forming steep mountains that felt he had to climb. He picked and dropped, and picked and dropped the thought of imagining about these issues. While he was deep in thought, his other attending physician came in.

"Wow! You were elsewhere—what are you thinking about? You didn't even hear me when I came in?" asked the doctor. He continued, "Healthwise, you are doing well. According to Professor Woods, in a few days, you will be able to go back to doing the things that you did before the accident. There is one more thing left, though—you are going throw us a party, to congratulate you on your new fame. Where is the party going to be?" he said with half smile on his face.

"Doc, the chapter of my life where I need the professor, and you good people's help might be coming to an end. The most arduous, craggy, and contemplational, part of my life is just beginning. And the thought of facing it is annoying me bitterly. I wish I was dead. How can a disclaimed man live a fulfilled life? For you, since you never knew me before, my current identity makes no difference. To my family, especially my wife, who already buried my body, it is hard to imagine how they believe what they hear and ignore what they see, and accept the familiar person that is inside. Especially, when I reflect on that, I lose a grip on everything."

"The entirety of what you are saying is undoubtedly a fact. Even if I don't endure the weight of the matter as much as you do, I could imagine the difficulty and complexity behind it. All I can tell you is this, try to deal with life one day and one issue at a time. And be grateful to the smaller things that being alive has given you," said the physician.

"Doc, my issues are not as simple as that. They are like diseases that will cross the ocean back home with me."

The doctor tried to take Million off his depressing thoughts by shifting the conversation to other unrelated topics. At the same time, without saying, he was saying, "In a few days, you will be gone. You will never have to worry about anything—in the meantime relax and enjoy the ride."

A few minutes later, his pager went off. Waving his hand goodbye, he left Million's room.

***

CHAPTER FIVE

After he woke up from his coma and rehabilitated back to his normal self, Deric told his wife that his priorities in life have changed. He said, “Baby, the incident has changed my perspective in life. You might witness me making heathy but unusual decisions that I wouldn’t have made before the accident,” he continued, “Baby, can I see the note Jerry gave you?”

“What note?”

“The note that Molly was working on?”

“How do you know that there was one?”

“Baby, did you think I wasn’t hearing what was being said around me? I did hear every word and understood them more than I would have if I was awake. The disturbing part was that every word had weight. When someone said something bad it landed in my brain as a piece of rock. If something scary was said, it made a sharp and poking sensation. Don’t worry, mama, every word you uttered was comforting.

“When I heard of Molly’s death, I was devastated. I cried

inside. The fact that I couldn't ask how and why worsened my sorrow. It was endless torture, to say the least. Everything was as if I was having one bad dream after another."

"I'm a really sorry that you had endured all that, baby!"

"It is okay! Maybe it happened for a good reason."

"Jerry has the notes. He texted me earlier saying that he will come to see you and he will bring them with him. Speaking of the… There he is."

"Jerry, am I glad to see you! We were just talking about you. Did you bring me Molly's notes?"

"Yes, I have. Here it is. I think you will find it interesting and refreshing, if not handy."

"Great! Let me see. Wow! look at this one, it has my name. At one of our meetings, I asked her, could the research center had shopped for organs from the black market that she had exposed. She circled and connected that question with this one, "Who is the donor of this child's brain?" You see how she linked the two questions! She was brilliant. Why did she have to die? She was one of the best truth seekers I have ever met."

"I know, she was a great person too! My son told me that when they were dating, he didn't know she was a well-established reporter. He liked her thoughtfulness, bubbly personality, and the respect she had for others. Anyway, despite how good they are, people don't live forever; their works do. She has done her part in shining light into hidden corners and therefore contributed to the safety and wellbeing of society. Now, you, my friend, can take the torch and illuminate the deep and undiscovered truths."

"Wow! That is a huge responsibility to bestow on me. I will do my best to follow her footstep, hopefully, her spirit will guide me on my lost days."

"Have you seen this queue of sources? Do any of these names sound familiar to you? I know two of those myself. You see, Sabrina was Molly's friend, and Angel is her husband. Now, I don't know how the sequence works, but if you need help getting in touch with these people, let me know."

"Wonderful! I know two, possibly three from these people. My coworker interviewed Ms. Murphy when she won the Ms. Mass contest. He might still have her contact. Marc is her ex-husband. I have an idea who Jamul is, but I don't know his whereabouts. The only reason I was going to go to the station was to quit my job. Now, I might need to stick around and find ways to get an assignment to interview Ava."

"Were you seriously going to quit your job? Then do what?" Asked Lesha, Joining Jerry and her husband at the dining table.

"Yes, Lesha, I hope you don't mind. I need to do things that I'm passionate about. Anyways, Jerry, even if they don't give me an assignment, as I said, I will find her contact from the guy who interviewed her."

"Well, I will introduce you to both Sabrina and her husband. I guess you are off with a good start. I got to go now, but let me know if I can be of any help."

"Thank you, Jerry! I will call you."

Ever since the decision to get rid of Million was made, Abigail had been planning on how to help him escape from the center to somewhere safe. From a seemingly casual conversation she had with one of the security guys in the cafeteria, she gathered info about the downtimes of the security workers.

In addition to Abigail's blueprint, Million was laying out tactics that could enable him to vanish from the medical center once for all. The next day being Christmas, he wanted to take advantage of the low traffic in the center. He secured his belongings and money that Abigail sneaked to him.

The afternoon before Million's escape day, Abigail rented a car, put a temporary tint on all the windows and removed the license plate. About 4:30 am on the planned day, Million entered into the back seat of a black SUV.

After driving a couple of miles from the center, Million said, "You disguised yourself very well. If you didn't smile, I wouldn't have recognized you."

"You look like an experienced chef yourself. Where did you find the hat?"

"Do you like it? I made it out of paper."

"What? You are creative!"

An hour and forty-five minutes later, they arrived at a gated property. Inside, Million, his mouth opened, his eyes flickering a smile, kept staring at a picture of Abigail with her parents. While he was still looking around, wowed by the beauty of her parents' house, Abigail had him walk his back to the kitchen. When they arrived by the dining table, she left him alone and said, "Tada!" revealing an omelet and fresh mango juice. She made the same for herself, and they sat down to eat.

"Abigail, how do you know that I like over-easy-omelet and mango juice for breakfast?"

"You told me a while back when I asked you about your favorite meals."

While enjoying their breakfast, she said, "Here is the plan for the day, at 1PM we are going to have lunch with a pilot friend of my dad. He flies his own charter airplane. Around 5 PM, he will fly you to DC. Your flight from DC to Ethiopia is tomorrow at 7 Am. He will arrange a hotel close to the airport for you, then he will meet you in the morning and stay with you until you board the airplane.

"Until we meet in your homeland, today is our last time together. Around 3 PM, we could sit for coffee at my favorite café. There, we will talk about Ethiopia. By the way, my flight to Egypt is after midnight tonight. I will spend a couple of hours in Egypt. Then I will get a visa to Ethiopia.

If I make it in time, I will rent a car and wait for you at the airport. If not, a rental car will pick you up. Either way, call me as soon as you land."

"Abigail, you have been my doctor—the best doctor anyone could ever imagine of having. Now, you are my best friend. A friend who is sacrificing a lot and putting herself at risk for me to make it to my family safely. First, you saved me from my misery of loneliness, and today, if it weren't for you, I wouldn't have been out of the center alive. Even if I somehow did, I would have died of loneliness, anxiety, and fear. Abigail, you are my divine messenger!"

"Thank you, Million! You know I'm not doing all this for nothing. I'm expecting one thing in return from you."

"What is it? Anything, including my life, is yours."

"No! It is that you withstand all the adversity that you will be facing along the way to getting accepted by your family and friends. I hope that is not too much to ask. You are both the divine and science's work, so you are special to me. I will help you to the best of my ability, and you keep beating the odds."

After eating lunch with the pilot, Million and Abigail went to her favorite café.

Sitting there, they chatted about different topics. They were putting a plan B together just in case something happened and either of their flights was cancelled, when she suddenly said, "Can you promise me one thing?"

"Sure! what is it?" he asked, leaning forward with his eyes opening wide.

"It is a little complicated." She stopped and began pulling her earlobes down.

"Abigail, please say it. No matter how complicated, there is nothing that I wouldn't do for you—including giving my life away."

She looked around, and people were sitting within hearing distance from them. She said, "I will tell you when we leave here."

They enjoyed their time at the café. The thought of having Abigail beside him here and in Ethiopia made Million smile ear to ear.

She remembered that the ancient country was among her to visit lists, and said, "I have heard that there are many things to see in your country. I'm sure you will show me some of them as time permits. Right?"

"What would you like to see the most?"

"What is the unique thing that you consider deserves time to see?"

"There are obelisks and buildings of long time in history. And you might like to see different wild animals and birds that do not exist anywhere else but in Ethiopia. You may also like to see natural waterfalls, rivers, and cultural life, such as eating habits, clothing styles, and the like."

"Until now, my knowledge of Ethiopia had to do with running. I was a runner, so, I used to keep up with the news about Ethiopian runners in the Olympics, Marathons and different distances. I thought running was one of the country's riches. I didn't know anything about the historical places you mentioned. I believe ancient treasures take you back in time and help you realize or imagine how the people of that period lived. That is something that gets me excited."

"Let me tell you the things that I think are unique to our country. In Ethiopia, you will find traditional clothes that never went through a factory. Planting cotton, harvesting, threading, and weaving are all done by hand. Ethiopia and Eritrea are the only two African countries that have their alphabet. However, these two countries, until recently were one country, Ethiopia.

"There is a unique bread called Injera. It is made from the tiniest grain called Teff. This grain, until recently, was unknown elsewhere. Nowadays, however, I read in one article that it is being harvested in Idaho, California, Nevada, and Texas. I'd like to tell you more about Injera—while it is fresh, you could fold it into multiple sections, just like a towel, without breaking it. To get a bite-size form a big portion, you either have to take a bite with your teeth as you would do with other bread, or press and tear. There are more things that I love to tell you about, but I'd rather witness your reaction when you see them."

"Wow! I can't wait to see all that!" she said, smiling big, then looked to see who was around them. The people who were sitting within hearing distance had left.

"Now that nobody is close by, let's get back to the

discussion that I had suspended earlier. Let me ask you this, how resentful are you of what is done for or to you? Before you answer, let me tell you this. As far as I know, the researchers didn't decide to conduct the trial to save you and the little girl's lives out of a selfish desire to gain some profit.

"They did it to save lives and for purely scientific reasons. However, due to their excitement with the positive results on the animal trials, they didn't consider every possible consequence when they did the clinical trial. To be honest, their ego might have gotten in their way too. I hope you understand."

"I do understand! They did it either to satisfy their ego or out of goodness. I prefer to believe the later—even now, after I learned that they planned to kill me. That being said, aside from me who never consented to go under their knife, even someone who knew what he or she was getting into and had paid a lot of money could have what you call, buyers' remorse. Similarly, I have my bad days when I wish that they had let me go."

"Thank you for consciously choosing to have the right attitude! That means a lot to me. Also, can you make me these two promises? The first one is that no matter what happens, you will never report your situation to the law and that you will not reveal yourself to anyone until the research receives the recognition it deserves?" said Abigail looking up at him with her head tilted to the side.

"I promise, Abigail! After all, I owe my life to you! And I could never envisage myself doing such things, especially not with the intent of hurting anyone," he said with noticeable sincerity, looking directly in her eyes.

***

"Honey, have a good day at work."

"Ha, ha, funny! Just wait, you will see how productive I can be when I'm working from home."

"Just don't sleep too much when you are supposed to be working."

"Don't worry, I didn't wake up at four am to go back to sleep."

"Please, don't make that a habit. I love waking up with you by my side. Remember when we used to horse play first thing in the morning and Sandy would come and help me beat you up? I missed those days! We can still be silly. I'm sure Sandy would want us to be happy and enjoy life—not bury our love and friendship with her."

"Trust me, baby, the most important lesson I learned when I awoke from the coma is to live life to the fullest—despite losses and heart aches. There is nothing more that makes me feel alive than being with you. I'm waking up early because it is the quietest time, therefore, I get engaged better with writing the book I have started. But, if you need me to stay in bed and start work after you leave, I'm all yours."

"Today, when I get off work, unless you have another commitment, can we take flowers and light a candle on Sandy's tomb and chat with her for a little?"

"Sure! That sounds great. I have nothing on the schedule, even if anything comes up, it can wait."

"Okay, I love you, my handsome stud!"

"I love you, my beautiful babe!"

***

After getting a couple of suitcases into her car, Ava went to Teena's room, and said, "Baby let's go. We need to leave early before the guys with the cameras come and block our driveway. You can finish your sleep in the car."

"But I'm tiered. Can we just go later?"

"We can't go later because those guys won't leave us alone. You can sleep in the car, and sleep as long as you want when we get there, but we have to go now. Just brush your teeth, and that is it."

Ava was backing out of her driveway, when the sensor of her car started beeping. She looked at the back up camera and noticed that someone or something was coming toward her. She immediately braked. But it was too late. The person or object had slammed into the fender and had fallen.

Startled and nervous, she reversed the gear to drive and the car started going forward. "Ava, Ava, the wall…" said Teena, but Ava didn't hear. When she meant pressing the break, her foot was on the gas pedal. The car hit the beam of the lower floor of her house and bounced back. Then a smoke started appearing from under the hood.

Ava, who didn't have her seatbelt on, flew forward and her forehead hit the hard edge of the steering wheel and bounced back when the airbag slammed her face. Teena, who was sitting in the back on a booster chair, went forward to the back of the passenger's seat, hit her forehead and bounced back.

For a couple of seconds, everything went quiet, then, Teena looked at Ava's face squeezed between the airbag and the seat. She panicked, and said "Ava, are you okay?" And started crying.

Two men, recording a video with their phones, each approached the driver and passenger doors and started knocking on the windows. The one by the driver side, said, "Hello Ma'am, are you okay? Oh, no, she is bleeding, let me call for an ambulance." He tried to open the door—it wouldn't open. The guy by the passenger side went to Teena's door and tried to open it, Teena pressed the unlock key and exited with the help of the man. At that time, the other guy was speaking to a 911 despatcher.

Teena went running to the driver's side and tried to open the door. She ran back into the car and unlocked the door. Then both guys helped Ava out of the car and carried her close to the gate.

About ten minutes later, the ambulance arrived. The emergency responders assessed both Ava and Teena. While they were checking her blood pressure. Ava woke up and began looking around. Teena, went to her mom and hugged her and started crying. The EMT told Ava that she had a concussion and that they need to take her and her daughter to the hospital for further checkup.

"No, I'm, okay now." She resisted.

"Your blood pressure is low. You heart rate is high. Your daughter's heart rate is high too, So, it is better if you get evaluated further," said one of the EMTs.

Ava reluctantly agreed. And told them that her daughter should stay with her at all times.

"What did I hit when I was backing out? Was that a person? Are they alright?" Ava asked to no one in particular.

"That was a photographing robot. I think its sensor was not working and ended up slamming into your car," answered the guy who made the 911 call.

"The operator of that robot is responsible for all this. My daughter and I almost got killed," she said. Then the ambulance's doors closed.

***

"Hey, Deric, tomorrow, Todd and I are heading to Chicago, he got a job offer there. I have family and friends that I want introduce him to. Anyway, Sabrina, Molly's friend is still in the hospital, and I don't think she is doing great. Do you want to go and meet her?"

"Oh, man! I would love too, but... Wait, how long are you going to Chicago for?"

"A couple of weeks, at least."

"No! man! I can't wait that long before meeting Sabrina. You never know what may happen between now and then. I really need to go meet her. The only issue is that I promised Lesha after she get off work, we were going to go to our daughter's burial place and light up a candle. You know what, I should be able to get back in time. I won't stay long—if you introduce me today, I will go there tomorrow."

"You are taking your own car, then? Do you still know how to drive?"

"Ha, ha, funny! I don't think I would forget how to drive, even if I had come back from the dead."

"Okay, I will watch you in the rearview mirror."

***

The tabloid news website, Thirty-Miles Zone (TMZ) was the first to report that Ava and her daughter were in an Accident. In one of their videos, they showed Ava being rescued from a car that had smoke coming from the hood and taken to the hospital with her daughter. Another video focused on the child who had a brain transplant. They showed how she got out of the car and went to the driver's side, opened the door and begged the reporters to get her mom out of the car to safety. The last scene was her hugging her mom, crying on her shoulder and the mom saying something.

Then CNN aired the accident as one of their breaking

news. Their main focus was on showing what the first and only person in the world with a brain transplant did after the accident.

CNN aimed at analyzing the applicability of the unique medical procedure and how great the child who received the treatment was doing.

Then they pondered whether a person with a new brain would easily accept who they had become.

***

"What is he doing here?" Ava thought aloud, seeing Marc talking to her dad by the hospital elevators. She was getting upset remembering what he said to her the previous evening. However, because Angel exited from one of the elevators, she didn't dwell on the angry thought longer. Instead, she said to herself, *Oh, my gosh! This is the hospital where Sabrina is*. She continued, *This is a great opportunity to visit her. When would have I come otherwise?*

She looked at Teena, who was playing a game on her phone and said, "Teena, can you just hold on to my phone and play later. Walk a little faster, would you?" then she tightened the hold of her daughter's hand and began walking faster.

***

"Ava, Teena, thank God you two are okay! I just saw it in the news. One of the nurses told me you were in the ER, and I was coming from the fourth floor to see you," said Angel, looking for any sign of injury on both ladies.

"We are okay, thank you! It wasn't even newsworthy, but the media don't seem to have any better things to report. Anyways, how is Sabrina? Can we go see her now?"

"She seems a little better today. They took out the wires from her jaw, and she was able to say a couple of words that made sense. Anyway, let's go see her. She is in the ICU."

Ava was chatting with her dad and Teena with Marc, they marched to the ICU with Angel leading the way.

Because only two visitors were allowed at a time, Ava went in with Angel, while Mr. Murphy, Marc, and Teena stayed in the waiting area. The adults were whispering about the child. And the child was playing the game "Monkey-See" on her mom's phone.

Eight minutes into that, three well-dressed men, Deric, Jerry, and Todd, came out of the elevator and headed to the ICU. After being told about the two visitors' rules, they joined the others in the waiting area.

Deric, seeing Marc, his heart started beating fast. He knew him, not only as Ava's ex-husband but also as the voters' coordinator for the governor of the State. He had done extensive reading on him and Ava while preparing to call them for an interview. Looking around for no one, in particular, he noticed a child sitting beside Marc, watching something on her phone attentively.

Oh my Gosh! That is her! he thought, after determining that she looked like Ava. *This is the special child whom*

Molly wrote about, he thought again. He wanted to strike up a conversation with Marc. But he felt his chest tightening. He got up, looking through the window, he took a few relaxing breaths. He sat back and began gathering his thoughts.

Mr. Murphy looked at Deric and said, "I Haven't seen you on TV reading the news for ages, what happened? Did you make a career change?"

That seemed to draw Teena's attention, she threw the phone on the couch and leaped to Deric and hugged him, and began kissing him on the forehead and the cheeks. Though startled, and out-of-breath, and out-of-place, he tried to pretend he was calm. He said, "Young lady, have you mistaken me for someone?" and helped her to sit beside him. His hands visibly trembling, he said to the adults, who had their mouths and eyes open wide, "A few adults have thought they knew me and approached me with close familiarity only because they see me on TV five days a week. But this one is the first of its kind."

Teena, seemed to know what she was doing. Without saying a word, she stood behind Deric and started caressing his head. She leaned to the side and had him look at her by pulling his chin and said, "Daddy, are you here to take me home to Mommy? Ava gets mad when I ask her to bring me to you. I asked her, can we go to my real parents please, many times. But every time I said that, she gets upset. But I was polite, right? That is how you said I should ask for things that I want. How come Ava wasn't nice?"

What is this child talking about? Deric thought, staring at her with a lump in his throat.

"Daddy why are you looking at me funny. I'm Sandy! Okay, okay, now I know why you look at me like that. Ava and I always look in the mirror and she tells me that I look like her. And she says I'm Teena. Daddy, do you hate me because now I look Teena?" she cried forcing herself to his chest.

He carried the child to the floor and had her stand in the middle. He kneeled down and held both her shoulders, looking at her beautiful blue eyes, he said, "Are you telling me that you are Sandra? My Sandy?" Then, he felt ashamed for saying that. He looked at the adults, as if afraid of creating the impression of being insane, "I'm just playing with her, but you never know, Sandy could be incarnated to this white child," and giggled back to his seat.

Before anyone said anything, especially Marc, who was prepared to say something, Teena said, "Yes, silly!"

Marc whispered to Mr. Murphy to summon Ava from Sabrina's room. He then gently pulled the child from Deric's chest and said, "Come here, Teena, your mom will come in a minute." Then, looking at Deric, and the other two adults, he said, "She might be suffering whiplash from the accident. Are you guys here to see Sabrina?"

Deric wanted to agree with Marc, but what the child said kept echoing in his ear. Then, he thought, *Could have I suggested the name Sandra to her? No, this child knows what she is talking about. There is no such complex coincidence.*

He wanted to help Marc take the child from him, but not only did she hold him tight, she started crying saying, "Daddy, you don't love me anymore? But Meme loves me. She gave me the Captain for my birthday. Also, Mommy loves me."

"Okay, little girl, can you tell me what your mom and dad's names are?" asked Deric bringing the girl to eye level.

"You're my dad. Your name is Deric Johns, you said you are Deric Monk at work. My mom is Lesha Johns."

"Okay, Okay, when did I tell you that I'm Deric Monk?"

"I don't know, when I was five, I think. Mommy ..."

***

Ava came—her face red and her lips dry. Her dad was trying to tell her that the man, whom the child was claiming as her dad was Deric Monk, the news anchor, but anything he said seemed to enforce the fear that someone had come to take her daughter.

When she saw Deric smiling, she felt at ease. She stood, her left hand holding her right arm, and smiling big. She said, "Sir, excuse my daughter, she has been through a lot." She thought, she knew him somewhere, but couldn't think of where.

"I understand! I'm aware of how special your daughter is. I just never imagined that who she is would pertain me."

"How do you mean?"

"I'm a reporter, and I'm working on a follow up story to the one Molly wrote about you and your daughter. And I meant to call you and Mr. Soprano for an interview. Now the whole thing is becoming personal to me."

"I guess you're here to see Sabrina. Do you know her somewhere?"

"Actually, I don't, Jerry and Todd are about to introduce me to her. Toddy is Molly's widow, and Jerry is his dad," he said, looking at Todd. Then he looked at Jerry and said, "You guys go ahead, when you come back, I can go with you. Todd can wait here or he can head home, and you ride with me."

"It sounds good," said Jerry.

***

Seeing Marc and Mr. Murphy returning, Jerry and Todd headed to the ICU.

After checking that they were at a comfortable distance from the waiting area, Jerry said, "They are beating around the bush. The child seems to know what she is doing. She obviously has the Johns' daughter's brain."

"This is the most intense identity crisis I have ever witnessed." Said Todd.

***

"Anyway, we need to get moving, my dad probably has something he needs to do, he usually does."

"Sure! Ms. Murphy, and Mr. Soprano, do I have your permission to call you for an interview?"

"If it is something that has to do with the transplant, I can't say a word. The center had me sign confidentiality agreement," said Ava.

"Same here," uttered Marc, barely taking his eyes from his phone.

"No problem, thank you!" he said. Then, he asked Ava with subdued voice, "Can we talk in private, please?"

"Sure!" She whispered equally.

He said, "Beautiful child, please stay with Mr. Soprano. I need to speak with your mom, in private," and lowered her from his shoulder. She was sound asleep. He gently transferred her to Marc's arms and started walking toward the elevators.

At a safe distance, he said, "About your daughter, don't ask me how, but I believe she has my daughter's brain. All I knew until today was that a few hours after her accident, she passed away at the children's hospital. They gave us her body the next day. I do remember us signing a consent for organ donation, which they said was for her heart and lungs.

"I don't remember brain being a part of the list. Now, obviously, they took it out before they released her body to the funeral home. Either way, I need you to be aware that Teena has Sandy's brain. Believe me, I'm very happy that it happened to be your daughter in whom they transplanted my Sandy's brain. It could have been some family from nowhere and wouldn't have known what has happened. But still, the hospital is responsible for stealing my daughter's brain."

"Wow! You are convinced! What sort of things did she say that made you believe that she in fact has your daughter's brain?"

"Many things—and they are all accurate. She even told me that I'm known by Deric Monk at the TV station, where I work. One that broke my heart the most was her talk about her bird. His name is Captain, my mom gave her for her birthday, which was a couple of days before the accident."

"I don't know what to say, sir, except thank you for understanding the situation! The brain that has saved my daughter's life, whether it is your daughter's or not, it is safe in Teena's head. We need to leave now though, before she wakes up and starts bothering you."

"One final request, can my wife meet your daughter?"

"Sure, let us set it up. Definitely, give me a call for that."

Teena was still sleeping on Marc's shoulder, when the family left quietly—seemingly for loss of words.

***

Deric stood outside the waiting lounge, and his eyes accompanied Teena's head all the way to the elevator. His mind wandered restlessly; his heart ached for Sandra. He thought about how to approach the hospital that stole his daughter's brain. While he was selecting words through which to explain Sandy's new existence to his wife, Jerry and Todd came.

Jerrys aid, "Deric, let's go quickly, the waiting took the time that we could have used for visiting. Todd is going to wait here while I introduce you to Angel and Sabrina. Then he and I will leave, we still have more packing to do. Just so you know, Sabrina doesn't seem to have the strength or the comfort to talk. Anyway, you can check with Angel and come back when she is able to talk. I told both of them that you have taken over Molly's unfinished investigative project."

"Yes, I can come back anytime. The important thing is that they know who I am and what I need to talk to them about. Funny as it seems, the case has become more personal to me. In fact, at this moment, I'm at a loss for the processing power to produce questions that I could have asked Sabrina."

"I understand, the child's situation is complex. If I was in your position, I wouldn't have known what to do. I guess you will need to take things one step at a time."

"I'm still lost on coming up with my first step."

***

When Deric arrived home, Lesha wasn't there, he called her cell, she didn't answer. On his way to the hospital, he had texted to let her know that he was going to meet Sabrina. He realized now that she hadn't replied to that either.

He started to worry. *Just in case*, he thought, and dialed her office. "I know no one will be there at this time of the day, but desperation," he thought aloud. He dialed her cellphone—no answer. His worry changed to fear.

He wanted to call someone, but wasn't sure who. Aimlessly, he hopped into his car. He dialed to her cellphone three times in a row. The third time, it went straight to voicemail.

"Baby, where are you? I'm worried to death about you. I love you!" He left a message. He started driving toward the burial place. While driving, he called five times, but each time, her voicemail answered it.

When he arrived at the grave site, he noticed a person sitting by Sandy's tomb. He felt a wave of relief, then immediately a sense of anger started rub him.

"Baby, what is wrong? You couldn't at least answer your phone?" he said, working his nerves to stay calm.

"Why? I thought you had to go to conduct an interview?"

"I'm deeply sorry that I upset you! I went just so Jerry would introduce me to Sabrina and her husband. He and Tod are leaving to Chicago in the morning, and he won't be back until about two weeks. At the hospital, I ran into a bizarre but lovely thing that interests you. I was excited and couldn't wait to get home and tell you about it. Obviously, you weren't there."

"You chose your work over your family, so I didn't want to be in the way. First you quit your secure job for some hopeful fame, without even talking to me. Then, today, after promising that you would visit our daughter's resting place no matter what, you disappeared."

"I don't know what your problem is, but you need to relax about the choices I'm making. If it is about money, I have signed a freelance project, and I will bring home as much as I did before, if not more. Either way, you need to calm down. We have more serious issue that I need to tell you about."

"Don't tell me to calm down."

"I don't know what has gotten to my supportive, caring, and patient Lesha, but I need her now more than ever. Can we at least go home now and discuss whatever you want to?"

"You can go! We didn't come together—remember?"

"Sarcasm? it's alright! I said I'm sorry, what else do you want me to say? Can I at least walk you to your car?"

"Don't act like you care, okay? Your priorities have changed, and I or the family we discussed having is not part of it."

"Baby, I can sense that there's something else that is bothering you. Either you tell me straight up, or give me time to figure it out. One thing that I beg you to consider is this, everything I'm doing is to create a better life for us."

At home, after more begging and beseeching from Deric, they made up.

***

The next morning, Deric woke up at four past ten. He quietly got out of the bed, and went to his office. He sat and tried to gather his thoughts to jot down some ideas for his book. But he couldn't stop thinking about Teena. Every attempt to center his attention toward his writing seemed in vain.

Remembering what his wife had said about being with her when she wakes up, he went back to bed. He tossed and rolled with Teena's voice echoing in his head. He glanced at his wife, sleeping peacefully. She didn't seem to have a worry in the world. *I don't blame her, if I wasn't there, I wouldn't have believed it either,* he thought picturing her reaction when he told her about Sandra in Teena.

Even though he didn't doubt that Teena was someone special to him and his wife, he wanted to start his math at the hospital. When Lesha woke up, he was sitting with his back to the headboard of their bed.

"Baby, I want to go to the hospital and ask about Sandy's final moments, especially about why they took out her brain, do you remember the name of the doctor whom we spoke to?"

"No, let alone now, not even after a cup of coffee would I ever remember that man. I wasn't thinking straight at the time. Honey, though I don't doubt your judgment, we should take things slow. There are multiple things that don't add up, so peel a layer at a time."

"Where are you suggesting we start? Hearing the child talk is almost getting to the nucleus of the matter. Now, you want to begin outside. Where?"

"First, let's make sure that there is such thing called a brain transplant. Very rarely does science fiction become real world theory, let alone, practical. Next ..."

"Let me stop you there. There is no question about whether Teena had a brain transplant or not. The only question we have to ask is who did the brain belonged to? Her mom, When I told her that I believe Teena has Sandy's brain, she didn't deny or confirm. She simply changed the topic. What should be the first step now? Between you meeting the girl or checking with the hospital, which one should we start with?"

"I have a slightly different idea—why don't we begin at the funeral home? Ask them if they had noticed any changes in Sandy's head."

"Though that is a great idea, what if they say no. That may confirm your suspicion, but where would it leave me? Most importantly, where would it leave the child who is a hundred percent sure that we are her parents. Even if they say yes, we are going to need more details about why her head was opened.

"So, instead of the funeral home, we should start at the office where they had us sign for the release of her body. Just a reminder, I will be recording every conversation we may have with the people who try to answer our questions about it. Therefore, we both need to be careful about what we say or how we react."

"Either way, this is right up your alley. So, I will leave it to you. However, I don't mind meeting the child to form my own impression."

"Sure, I will call Ava today. I was going start on the "outside layers" of the matter as you put it."

***

CHAPTER SIX

"May I see your passport or ID please?" asked the TSA employee, when Million handed him only his pass.

He took out his passport from the pocket of his backpack and handed it to the agent.

Million noticed a confused look on the employee's face.

"Whose passport is this?" the TSA asked.

He confidently replied, "It is mine."

"How come the picture on the passport doesn't look like yours?"

This time, he was alarmed! It hit him like a ton of bricks that, instead of Amin's, he gave the passport with the picture of his old look and profile.

"I'm sorry, does that say Million?" he asked, his voice getting slightly shaky.

"Yes, who is Million?" inquired the TSA.

"He is my roommate. We are attending the same university. We share a closet, so I picked up that passport and put in this bag, I didn't even care to look. How silly of me!" he chuckled nervously.

"Who are you, then?"

"I'm Amin. Let me run over and bring my passport," he said trying to hide his nervousness. He took Million's passport from the TSA with his shaking hand, turned around, and walked fast as if to bring the right passport from home.

Though he could have produced the right document from the bag, he decided to run out to avoid further questioning.

For some reason, the TSA guy didn't pull him for interrogation.

***

The pilot had already gone through security and was waiting by the gate. He noticed boarding had started but Million was not there.

He thought, "By now, he should have been done with TSA." And walked back to the area where security check was conducted and began looking for Million among the people in line. He stood as close as he was allowed behind the TSA area and kept seeking for Million.

Million was annoyed by what just happened and he thought, *If this identity thing gets me in trouble from the beginning, what will be next?* He walked slightly farther away from the TSA area and began searching for Amin's passport in the bag.

He returned to the TSA point and approached a TSA lady, holding Amin's passport and his pass in his hand. He told her that he was already in line but had to leave because he forgot his passport and that boarding has started on his flight.

After verifying the boarding time on his pass, the TSA lady sent him to the front of an otherwise very long line.

The pilot was talking to Abigail when he saw Million hurriedly rambling up to the conveyor table. He told her that he saw him and hung up with her.

Million passed the security and joined the pilot. Both of them walked fast to the gate, and he barely made it just as the doors were about to be closed.

Apparently, his name was announced as the boarding time was winding down. But he didn't hear or paid no attention.

As soon as he sat down in the airplane, he remembered he didn't properly thank the pilot. He took his phone out to dial Abigail's number, but she beat him to it.

"Hey, it is funny! I just took my phone out to call you, but you were ahead of me. I'm sitting on the airplane that I almost missed. I will tell you my incident at the TSA point when we meet. Abigail, can you please tell the pilot that I said thank you for all his help. I rushed into the plane before I could thank him properly."

"Okay, I will tell him. Enjoy your flight!"

***

A few days after Jerry introduced them, Deric called Angel to learn how Sabrina was doing. Angel informed him of the unfortunate news of her passing the previous evening.

"I'm sorry for your loss, brother! I don't mean to bother you," said Deric.

"You're welcome to attend the celebration of her life; it will be held this Saturday at the Greek Church close to the hospital."

"Thank you! My wife and I will be there."

***

Lesha stopped what she was doing in the kitchen and went to the bathroom where Deric was brushing his teeth. She said, "Deric, when are we going to meet the child who speaks like my Sandy?"

"I don't know, I have been trying to reach her mom, but her phone is going straight to voice mail. I have left a message, hopefully, she will call me back."

"I have a confession to make, I called the funeral home, and the owner told me that they didn't notice anything out of the ordinary."

"That doesn't mean Teena doesn't have Sandy's brain."

"A brain doesn't have a birthmark—at least not one we can see. Even if they open it and let you look at it, how exactly are you going to identify that particular brain is Sandy's? This Teena girl could have learned the story that Sandra had known before she died. More importantly, they might be playing you as part of their research."

"I know you are conspiracist, however, this is the worst of all your theories. We obviously are not on the same page on this one, so let's talk about something else."

***

When Ava called back, Deric was still collecting information from the hospital and was trying to get his wife on board about the idea of seeking legal advice.

"Hello, Mr. Johns,"

"Hello Ms. Murphy, I was wondering what happened to you guys."

"Sorry, we were on vacation, and it was one of those electronic free ones. So, your wife still wants to meet Teena?"

"Yes, Lesha has been nagging me to meet her."

"Okay, we will get back to Boston tomorrow, then on Thursday, we will be heading to Paris for another vacation. We can meet up on Wednesday around noon at my place. Does that time work for you guys?"

"Sure! We will make it work. If there is any change, I will call you. Thanks!"

"Yea, no problem—see you soon."

***

As soon as she hung up with Deric, Ava told her dad the dilemma she was in. "Dad, what is your take on this? I don't know these people, what if they are some advantageous who would take Teena up on her words? What if she refuses to come to me?"

"I'm more concerned about the child than them. That day, the guy didn't know what to say to her. Even if they believe what she tells them, there is no way that they would want to take her from you. They can't be that dumb and blind. As a black couple, there is no way that they would entertain the idea of Teena being their daughter."

"So, you think I should let his wife meet her?"

"If you don't feel comfortable, don't do it. Children do not know what is good for them. She won't die because she never saw those people again."

"I'm sure, she will give me a hard time. She is anxiously waiting to see the woman whom she calls her real mom. I guess I will tell her that they didn't answer the phone and that we will try again when we come back from Paris."

"Good idea! Such white lies won't hurt a child."

***

"Hello, professor, do you have a minute?"

"Hi, Ms. Murphy, I heard that you ladies were in an accident. How are you two doing?"

"Well, nothing is broken, except my confidence. My daughter ran into the father of the donor. She was already driving me crazy, saying, "Take me to my real parents." She told me that I'm her pretend mom. Now, things seem to be getting worse."

"What are you talking about? How did she run into him? And how do you know who he is?"

"I didn't know him, she did. According to Marc and my dad, as soon as she saw him, she ran and hugged and kissed him. She asked him if he came to take her home. At first, he was confused and he thought she was crazy. Even though she kept telling him that she was Sandra, not Teena, he didn't take her seriously. It was after he cross examined her about his family, and she answered with accuracy, including about Sandra's bird named Capitan, that he believed her."

"Where did all that happened?"

"At the hospital. After we were discharged, we stopped by the ICU to visit a friend. Apparently, he came there to visit the mutual friend."

"This is disturbing! ... What exactly did he say? Last time we talked, you told me that you would be moving elsewhere to give the child a fresh start, why haven't you?"

"I have been in the process of leaving. I just have too many things to just pack and escape. Unfortunately, things keep happening sooner than we can avoid them. In a couple of days, we will travel to Paris, just to arrange things there before we move for good. That being said, the man is threatening to sue the hospital for organ theft."

"It is okay, our lawyers are well equipped to deal with that."

"Also, I mentioned to him that we are going on vacation, he beseeched me that Teena meet his wife before we leave."

"Ignore him, don't give him any more clues. Just leave the country quickly. Don't tell anyone your whereabouts, at least for a little while. One way that would help the child phase-out sooner is avoiding exposing her to triggers. Doing so adds to the therapy and are the best treatments for fading her older memories. As I told you, give her new and more of Teena related stimulus, but nothing that enforces her old memories."

"Okay, sir, thank you!"

***

"Angel, Angel, stop the car, my mom and dad are here. That is mom's car, my dad bought her for Christmas," said Teena, and jumped out and ran as soon as the car stopped.

Ava didn't pay attention to what Teena was saying because she was on the phone with her sister who lived in Paris. Despite realizing that they had arrived home, her heart jumped to her throat seeing Teena jump out of the car. She ran after her saying, "Teena, wait, where are you going?" But it was too late.

"Mommy, you finally came to take me home. I'm mad at Daddy, he didn't bring me home from the hospital," said Teena, jumping on to Lesha.

Deric was sitting in the passenger side and recording a video of the interaction. When he saw Ava running toward them, he set up the camera to capture everything, and joined his wife and Teena.

Seeing Deric, “Oh, it is you guys. Teena you scared me,” said Ava.

“Daddy!” said Teena and left Lesha and slipped to Deric. “I’m mad at you, how come you didn’t take me home?”

“Hello, Ms. Murphy, it is nice to meet you! We arrived here on time, but Deric didn’t want to bother you with a phone call. He said that you might be running late getting stuff for your trip.”

“The plan was for us to meet downtown, at my office. We waited there until a few minutes ago,” she said, hoping that Teena wouldn’t expose her lie. She continued, “Mr. Johns, I don’t remember giving you my address here, how did you find it?”

“I’m sorry, I must have misunderstood you when you said that we should meet at noon at your place. About your address, I found it on google.”

“So, that’s how all the paparazzi found it. I need to get it removed. Please, don’t come here unless I specifically invite you.”

“Sorry, we won’t,” said Lesha, without taking her eyes from Teena, who had laid her head on Deric’s shoulder and was caressing the back of his head. She walked closer to peer at the child’s head and noticed a scar on her crown.

“Teena, let’s go. We forgot to pick up your prescriptions. Say goodbye and let’s get moving,” said Ava.

“No! I’m not going with you. Daddy, tell her, we have to go home. Mommy, I want you to read me my book, The Flying Girl, before I go to bed. Is my Captain okay? Meme said that you guys will get me a brother. Is he at home? I want to go see him.”

“When did Meme tell you that?” asked Lesha, supporting the child while she was trying to leap from Deric to her.

“Before my birthday, silly. I told her about your belly getting big every day, and she told me that you have a surprise for me.”

Lesha looked at Deric with teary eyes.

“Can you guys say goodbye to her? We have to get back to the pharmacy before it closes,” said Ava, grabbing Teena’s arm.

“My dear child, go with your mom now. We will arrange a visit again,” said Lesha trying to lower her to the ground.

“No! She is not my mom. You are my mommy. You don’t like me because I no longer look Sandy? But it is the doctor who made me look like Teena,” said the child wrapping her arms around Lesha’s neck and her legs around her waist.

“This is exactly what I was afraid of,” said Ava squinting her eyes.

“Is it okay, if I take her to your car?” asked Lesha.

“Please do that!” said Ava clenching her teeth.

"My sweet child, you need to go the pharmacy. You don't want to run out of your medication. I heard you are going to Paris. I'm jealous! I wish Ms. Murphy was my mom. When you come back from your vacation, Ms. Murphy will bring you to our house. Right now, Deric and I will go home and prepare for you to come. Okay? Make sure not to take too long," said Lesha putting the seatbelt around the child.

"But I want to go home right now Ava is not going to bring me. Please, mommy! Be nice!" she cried.

"Honey, you're making me cry. Can you at least go to the pharmacy?"

"Okay, don't cry! We will be right back. Wait here, okay?"

"Okay, sweetheart, we will see you later," said Lesha and went back to her car sobbing. "Honey, I'm so sorry that I doubted you!" she said, hugging her husband. He started crying.

When Angel drove the car past them, they were peering with their teary eyes into the tinted back window.

***

"Hello, Angel, how are you holding up? Are you fully back to work, yet?"

"Hey Deric, yeah, I have no choice than living day by day. Yes, the day that you and your wife came was my second day back."

"Man, that was some crazy day. I swear she told me that we would meet up at her place. She didn't say at her office. Do you know when they are coming back from Paris?"

"Well, they were supposed to be back four days ago, but I haven't heard from her for a couple of weeks. Maybe this is part of what Sabrina said."

"What did Sabrina say?"

"There were two facts that she learned about the story after it was published. One of them you already know about. That Teena's brain used to be an African American girl's. The second one is that Ms. Murphy was planning on moving out of State."

"So, you think she has moved to Paris for good? If I tell my wife this, she will go crazy. She hasn't stopped crying since she met Teena."

"I don't know for sure. I'm still on the payroll—she would have told me to find a job."

"Can you please keep me updated? Just so you know, my quest in this case is personal. Thus, I cannot publish an article on it. But I will write a memoir or something similar."

"I will do my best without compromising my employment."

"I completely understand! Thanks, Angel!"

***

Meanwhile, in Paris, Ava was setting up conditions that would make her move there as easy as possible. She rented an apartment at an exclusive community in

16th Arrondissement, enrolled her daughter at a private school where children of high profile individuals attend, and secured a modeling gig for herself.

The mother and daughter spent most of their time visiting Paris and hanging out with Ava's sister Jen, her husband, and their twin daughters.

Jen moved to Paris when she was sixteen to pursue a career in modeling. After working on small gigs for three years, she married a local personality and had twin girls and began working from home designing children's clothing.

When Teena met the twins, they were a month shy of their sixth birthday, however, despite their closeness in age to her and their fluency both in English and French, she didn't immediately befriend them as the parents hoped. It was after her mom told her that they have come to live in Paris and, "Yes, Deric and Lesha will be moving too. In fact, it is their idea that we all move here."

While still in Paris, she signed a contract with a real-estate company specializing in selling luxury homes in silent bidding, to have them sell her house and her office in downtown Boston with no sales signs or Multiple Listing Service (MLS) numbers.

***

Deric was debating whether to tell Lesha what Angel told him when she said, "Listen, honey, how long are we going sit and wait for Ms. Murphy to call us. She may never do so. I wish I never met that child. All I can hear now is her voice. I'm dying of guilt for abandoning her. I lied to her, Deric, I lied to her!"

Deric believed in telling people news corresponding to the mood they were in. Otherwise, he imagined would create emotional roller-coasters. So, he said, "Baby, I'm sorry, but I have a rather sobering news about the child. I called Angel earlier today, and he told me that Ms. Murphy might be moving to Paris for good."

"I knew that woman would make it hard for us to see the child. What made her think that we can't move to Paris? At least we can travel there frequently."

"Baby, even though the child is not accepting it now, Ava is her mom both legally and biologically. Also, she is safe with her, at least physically. Therefore, it is time for us to let go. We are not new to living with the memories of Sandy. To be honest, it is not Ava, it was the car accident that took her away from us. Let's not forget that by losing her physical self, she has given life to Teena. We need to rejoice that while moving on."

"Honey, I have never known a situation where hearing could be more powerful than seeing. I heard with my own ears my Sandy talking. And she told me to bring her home, to never abandon her, but I lied to her out of respect for that rude woman. Now, she took her way far from my hearing distance. Are you telling me to just forget about her? I'm sorry, but no! I can't! My mind is too powerful to forget that easily."

"What are you suggesting we do?"

"First, let's not talk about forgetting her. Second let's pursue a legal means of establishing closeness in proximity to her. We should be able to spend time with her. She should be able to come home for a visit."

"I don't know, baby. To tell you the truth, my heart is bleeding for her, and I can hear her voice and feel her caressing my head, but considering the complexity of her situation, I feel like we should leave her to adopt her new life. And hopefully she forgets about us sooner."

"No, honey, no! We shouldn't desert her. It is too late now. I wish she hadn't known that we existed. Believe me, she will never forget us—she will live feeling unwanted and miserable. I think neither of us want that for her."

"So, are you saying we should move to Paris?"

"If that is what it takes, yes! But we should go there for a few weeks and study our options."

***

After six weeks of extended stay past her return day to the US, Ava convinced herself that there were a few but very important things that she needed to go back and take care of. She halfheartedly left Teena with her sister and headed to Boston. She talked herself into believing that leaving Teena in Paris was much safer than bringing her along.

***

Deric called Todd's friend, Toni Mann, a correspondent for the Associative Press in Paris. "Hi, Toni, this is Deric, Deric Johns. ..."

"Hi, Deric, yes, Todd told me that you will be calling. What a fascinating story you're working on! The first article was mesmerizing enough, now the same girl thinks you are her dad! I read many stories of medical miracles, but none of them were as captivating as this one."

"Now, it has become my personal endeavor more than a simple news article."

"Yeah. I wouldn't know what I would have done if I was in your position. What kind of accommodations have you arranged here in Paris?"

"For the first two weeks, Airbnb in the suburb of Paris. We won't be there more than a month. However, we will be needing help with finding the subject. What is the best way to track individuals back there?"

"The methods are pretty much the same as in the US. Your subject, however, might be hard to locate because she hasn't been here long."

"True! She is in the process of moving. She might be staying close to her sister, Jen Dubois, a wife of local designer, Michel Dubois."

"Oh, yeah, I know the Dubois. Before we moved to the suburb, my daughter and their twins used to go to the same school."

"Wow! I never imagined that you would be holding the key to the first entrance, so to speak."

"Well, I wouldn't put all my hopes on this clue. I don't even know if the kids are still going to the same school, and most importantly I don't know where the Dubois live."

"I learned that Mr. Dubois is a local celebrity there, but still, I didn't expect that you would know them with such familiarity."

"I'm sure I will have more info about them before you come. In a couple of days, my daughter and I will stop by the school and check if the twins are still attending there."

"That would be wonderful! My wife has been dying to see the child, she will never have a normal life without some kind of closure."

"Your wife has met her too?"

"Oh, yes! At first, she was skeptical, she thought I was going crazy for saying that I met a child who believes that she is our daughter Sandy. But she met her, then she started driving me and herself insane."

"Interesting! It seems that it is becoming the most bizarre case of identity. I can't wait to see how it unfolds. Anyway, let me know if there's any change on your flight, otherwise, I will meet you and your wife at the airport."

"Sure! Thank you, Toni! Hey, by the way, we have taken a crash course on French so we won't bother you to translate regular interactions."

"Great! I was worried to death about that, ha, ha, ha..."

Chapter Seven

The airplane left the US airspace. It was flying over the Atlantic Ocean through the usual route to Europe.

The airline, Ethiopian, had made a name for itself in Africa, and it was earning recognition on the other continents. After fueling and changing crews in London, this flight would head to Million's city of birth, Addis Ababa. He was both excited and nervous about going home.

Million remembered his flight to the US. It wasn't long and boring because he'd been talking and laughing with Amin. They'd met on the airplane and later had become roommates and good friends. Situated in the airplane, he tried to imagine Amin sitting beside him. Instead, the frame that he saw in the bathroom mirror of the hospital entered into his mind's eyes and startled him. Jittery, he covered his face with both hands.

A young woman with big brown eyes, nicely kempt thick eyebrows, and long hair was sitting in the seat next to his. She noticed his reaction to his own thoughts. She was curious if he had seen anything in the airplane, so she looked around, but there was nothing out of the ordinary that she could spot. She initiated a conversation. Million however, seemed mute, he simply smiled. Seeing an unoccupied seat in the back, she went there and began stretching. Then sat, her neck and back arched.

Million's thoughts didn't seem to have an end. He picked one after another. Most of them addressed his concerns about a very likely strange incident that he would be running into. He started picking and dropping one thought after another, answering one question following another, liking one idea and disliking the other, and supporting one solution and despising the other. His brain needed fuel—unintentionally, he slid into sleep.

The nightmare in the airplane: Million imagined that he was walking alone on one of the streets of Boston. It was around nine pm, the streetlights were dim. Suddenly, he felt unease. He stopped and looked around and realized that he was circled by giant creatures with huge eyes, big noses of sunken deep on the bridges, and big and protruded jaws. He couldn't figure out what they were.

Their blazing look was chilling him down to his bones when they asked him in one echoing thunder sounding voice, "How did you become like this?"

Though he felt it, he couldn't see that there was anything new about him. Apparently, the scary things were after him for the change he wasn't able to see. He was shaking, and his knees were about to give up on him. He could tell that it was unlikely that they would leave him alone. He said, "It…ttttt's n…ooo…t me." Stammering, and winded.

"Who was it then?" burst one of them. He seemed to be their leader. His fiery red eyes were scarier than the others'. He continued, "You know, we won't leave you alone unless you tell and show us."

"Eeeet was th… th… th… the pro… fe…fe… ssor," he said, his heart pounding fast, as if wanting to leave his chest.

They said in one voice, "Show us, let's go." They picked him up by his shoulder cuff. In a few seconds, they were already in the research center. They kept pushing him forward, saying, "Show us, show us, show us…" in a repetitive, aggressive, and marching rhythm.

Million didn't sense the strangeness of how the creatures knew the center to bring him to. As if he was there, he simply walked to the professor's office with the anxious desire to point him out to them and vanish from that place, away from those creatures.

He started devising ways he could hide and disappear from the creatures. He sensed that they were remotely watching his every move—even worse, they knew what he was planning. He figured the only way out of that mess was finding the professor.

When it came to Million's knowledge, it was more advanced in the dream world than in the real one. As much as the creatures knew his thoughts, he knew what and how much they knew about him. On the other hand, they were fully powered and energized to go somewhere and do something, while his willpower for anything was drained.

He didn't hesitate to do anything and go anywhere for them. His every move was orchestrated by them. And that started to worry him.

Million was sure that he was in a world with its own rules and regulations—he just couldn't name the world.

In the creatures' world, the speed of light was relatively slow. They could imagine of a place and be there at the same time. Their speed was equal to the speed of thought. On the contrary, when Million tried to run and moved his feet forward one after the other, his feet remained in the same area—as if he was running on a treadmill. He saw people around him and yelled for help. But no one could hear him because his voice didn't have enough functional vibration. It was as if he was muted.

Million understood that the only chance he had was finding the professor. He walked fast to get to the area where the buildings for the different research centers were located. He went into the building where the professor's office was and pushed open the door. He was sure that the professor would be there, but he didn't find things as he expected. Rather, everything was out of place, new, and strange. He felt like a stranger at a strange place. The further he went into the office, the eerier the place became. People were drinking, dancing to a song he never heard before, laughing and having fun. Million felt his body soaking in sweat and his head spinning.

He tried to get out of the strange place, but he couldn't. He stood in one place and kept looking at the people who were sitting and those who were dancing or simply moving around. He could sense what they were thinking. They were all his enemies and would not hesitate to destroy him. He felt that his fear was increasing with each lapsing minute.

He couldn't see their faces because all of them had turned their back. Though they didn't see him when he came in, they could sense his presence. For the second time, he planned escape methods, but they read his thoughts and decided to suck his internal energy just so he would be stuck until their action time. Before he decided on his plan of escape, they started to encircle him. They had intimidating looks. More than that, the aggressive and horrifying thought he read from their minds booted his anxiety to the next level.

Before they closed the circle, leaving him in the middle, he saw a shoulder-width strip that could be an escape route. He determined to try his chance and followed that route without knowing where it would take him. For a while, he had to run sideways, because the width of the corridor was too narrow. Then, the corridor started to get wider where he could run with his whole body turned forward.

The creatures followed him at a relaxed speed. When he turned forward from checking back to see how far behind, they were, his eyes met a huge and scary thing that blocked his way. Again, he looked back behind him and found that the creatures were closing in. He charged ahead toward them to fight his way out, but the huge and scary thing held him on his right shoulder tightly.

When he woke-up screaming, the flight attendant was tapping on his shoulder to ask him if he needed food. He startled her to a point of throwing what she was holding.

His fellow travelers, those who were sitting not too far from him were shocked and turned around to look at him. He bashfully blushed for disturbing them. But he didn't dwell on it for very long because the stress from his dream kept coming up. "Sir, I didn't mean to alarm you. I apologize," said the flight attendant, looking up at Million while her hands were searching under the seat for a spoon and fork that fell during the commotion.

He said, "It wasn't you who scared me. I was having a nightmare in which a strange thing was holding me tight on the shoulder."

"Can I get you something caffeinated?" asked the attendant.

He smiled.

She took it as "yes," so went to bring him coffee.

While still sitting, he stretched out a bit. Then, he got up and went to the bathroom. Washing his face, he looked at the mirror and saw a face that he couldn't get used to. That triggered more emotional tension.

***

Returning from the restroom, he looked around, and noticed that a few people were peering at him. They reminded him that he had yelled so loud to scare them off from their thoughts. A minute or two later, he glanced at the people whom he startled. This time, everyone was doing his or her own thing, except for one East Asian man. He caught him again staring at him. Million wondered what and how the Asian man felt when he screamed.

He was still very tired. He peeked through the window to see anything interesting. Rather, the endless Atlantic Ocean made him more staled. Through the reflection in the window, he looked at the people, and saw that almost all of them were busy reading.

***

The East Asian man was sleeping. After staring at him, he thought, *Assuming this man is Chinese, if I had received his body, or if I was installed in his body, which country's citizen would I be? Which embassy would I go to? If I say I'm Ethiopian, even though I speak the language fluently, it would be difficult for the embassy employees to believe me. They may assume that I'm a Chinese man who had lived and worked in Ethiopia for a very long and had learned the language, and so speaks it very well. They wouldn't consider anything else. My passport would have said Chinese.*

They would have said, 'This Insane Chinese man believes he is Ethiopian,' because I don't look Ethiopian, I would have to explain my situation for them to consider me. What if I go to a Chinese Embassy? With what language would I explain my identity to them? Where would I say was born, and from whom?

I would have been in a more complex problem than the one I'm in. I would have been someone with no family and no country. Wow! There are worst scenarios than my current life. Well, at the very least, no one will doubt that I'm Ethiopian, he thought and smiled at the strangeness of the idea.

***

Back in the research center, no one noticed that Million had gone missing. It helped that all his medications were self-administered and that his physical therapy was only twice a week, Tuesday and Friday. As they had planned in their meeting, on Sunday, around 6 am, one of the doctors who used to care for him went to his room. In the doctors left chest pocket was a slow acting lethal injection. At first, the doctor wasn't concerned that Million wasn't in the room.

He knocked on the bathroom door, but there was no answer. After walking around the room for a couple of minutes, contemplating, he called the lead nurse and learned that no one among the nurses had seen him that morning. One of the nurses suggested to check the cafeteria or the track behind the building, where he had been doing his morning walk since he was able to do it on his own.

As recommended, the doctor called the cafeteria, but it wasn't open yet. He went to the track, walking slowly and looking around as far as he could see, he dialed Professor Woods.

"Did you say you checked in the bathroom? Keep looking around, he can't be any further from the center this early," said the professor after listening to the doctor's report.

"Oh, shoot! I didn't open and check the bathroom. I knocked and there was no answer. I'm sorry, I just remember that he was a moderate suicidal risk," he said, heading back to the room.

"Could he have done the work for us? That would be

great! Hey, that reminds me, if you find him alive, make it look like suicide—a biopsy won't be done," said the professor.

"You got it, boss!" "Knock, knock, hey, sir, are you in the bathroom?" asked the doctor, but there was no response from inside. He gently twisted the door handle and entered. Let alone a person, an ant wasn't there. He checked the bathtub and learned that there was no recent use, it was all dry. To be sure, he looked under the bed and inside the closet. Deciding not to waste any more time, he called the professor.

"Where could he be? Why and how did he leave his room this early in the day?" asked the professor crossly. "Check the cafeteria again. Does he have friends in the hospital or the center that he could be with?"

"I'm not sure, boss! Let me check in the cafeteria and get back to you."

It was now, seven am. The doctor walked to the cafeteria and asked one of the employees. "Normally he is among the first ones here. But lately, he has been infrequent. In fact, I didn't see him the last few days. Does he have family around? he might have left for the Christmas holiday," commented one of the cafeteria employees.

The doctor thanked the employee and left the cafeteria, dialing the professor's number.

The professor was furious. "Do you understand what this means?" he asked. He sighed and said, "He is missing. It means, we are lost. His disappearance is our headache. Someone among us might have done the malicious act of whispering at him to escape. Meet me in the conference room in half an hour and tell Art and Kim as well. But first, tell the security officers to review all recordings of the security cameras beginning Thursday," he said, screaming.

***

In the conference room, the team members were listening to the doctor's report and waiting for the security footage. "Also, I checked on my way here that all his personal belongings are gone. We can all agree that this is a calculated move. Let's just hope that no one who knew the plan helped him escape," said the doctor in conclusion of his report.

"This could be just a coincidence. Everyone in here is aware of the legal and social issues that are hanging over each one of us' head. So, who among us would take that risk by conspiring to help the guy vanish? Whoever told him about the plan and helped him escape must be someone who is not in the team and will not be affected by the matter," said Professor Art with the intent of redirecting the professor's perception.

"Do you guys sense the severity of the predicament we are in? The courts' decision has complicated the little girl's case even more. Unless the circuit court reverses the judgement and return the child to Ava and her family, they will be the first with the lawsuit against us. So, unless we quickly find and take-care of him, his case puts us on the hot seat," said Professor Woods, wondering what was to be done next.

His leaving the facility with all his belongings and without telling anyone created the suspicion that he might have gone to his country. They talked over the questions, where and how could he have left? Wherever he went, they all agreed that he would be using Amin's passport for identification.

Professor Kim called Ethiopian Airlines and learned that a couple of days ago, a passenger named Amin Mustafa had traveled from DC to Ethiopia.

***

Finally! The airplane landed in Bole International Airport.

Looking at the people who were getting off the plain, Million thought, *Most of these people are here to see their loved ones. A family member, two or more are probably waiting for them outside.*

He continued, *Let's see, my wife, my kids, my mother and father, my brother and sister—I would have had at least seven people waiting for me at the family area. But now, not even my brother who works here would know who I am. Thank God for Abigail! If it was not for her, whom would I talk to?*

The people in front of him had already left. He decided to be the last one to leave.

I'm nearly a tourist in my own country. I could be like a foreign-born Ethiopian who had never been to the country and don't have any family here, except that I speak the language and Amin's family or people who knew him might assume I'm him.

He felt loneliness caressing him.

He continued his thoughts. *I wish this face was a mask. I would have surprised my family and be the husband, the father, the son, and the brother that they thought they had buried.*

He remembered an old Ethiopian saying, "Don't believe and accept the death of a person until his or her corpse is buried beneath the ground."

He smiled. *My corpse was buried. I guess that saying doesn't apply to me. When the research that created the new me receives the recognition, that saying will have to be changed to: don't trust a person's death, until you make sure that his or her brain is not in someone else's body.* He smiled again.

He started a different trail of thought, but he stopped it because he was the only passenger left on the airplane. The flight attendant who woke him up from his horrible dream was by the exit with another crew member saying goodbye to all who flew with them. When it was Million's turn, she held his hand, asking him if he was going to be okay. He assured her he would—but he wasn't sure.

***

At the baggage claim area, Million's luggage was put away with unclaimed ones because it had rotated on the conveyer belt a couple of times and no one picked it up. He waited there, and other people's bags came, but not his. Everyone who was in his flight had left. Realizing that he was a little late, he tried not to panic. He asked one of the employees.

The employee, looking around the conveyor said, "I thought all the luggage was out—are you sure if it came in the same flight with you?"

Hearing that, Million felt a slight panic kicking in. He thought, *If the research center employees had reported me missing and my items were held, the authorities here will take me for questioning. Maybe I'm considered a fugitive and they have my luggage. Could they be waiting for me to show up?* his fear escalated. Whomever seemed to be staring at him, as far as he was concerned, was a person looking to catch him. He couldn't think of himself as anything but a criminal. Traveling in someone's body and with that person's documents, he thought was a serious crime. He whimpered. His chin tacked, kept looking over his shoulders for someone who may be coming to drag him to jail.

He cursed the day when he was born.

Then he changed his mind, *No, no, no! the day the researchers decided to make me this way should be cursed. I never had these problems before that. Now, I'm stranger to those who hear me and an alien to those who see me—therefore, my existence has no use to anyone. For me it is purgatory. Unless I'm disassembled back, I will remain to be a headache to my family,* he thought, trying to make a point to himself.

He hated the new him to death. But he found death to be something he hated more than himself. Though he thought he hadn't had interest to live, he was mesmerized by the fact that he didn't want to die.

He thought, *Even if a person wants to die, he or she still has unreasonable fear of death. Some people, therefore, may choose living over dying despite headaches that life would surely bring them.*

***

Abigail was waiting outside, and she knew that the airplane arrived on time. She walked around the parking lot, but Million didn't show up. She went to the security and asked, "Can I peek inside really quick?"

The security informed her that it was not permitted for non-travelers to go past the security area. She begged and begged; the security had noticed that she was waiting for a while, so he peeked through the glass and saw only one person inside. He asked, "could it be that man?" inviting her to look through, as he did.

"Yes, yes!" she replied.

"Don't go anywhere other than where he is. Go meet him and come back quickly," said the security guy.

She thanked and strode in.

***

Million was sinking deeper and deeper into his thought world, when suddenly, from the back, someone said, "Can you hear me?" in a loud and low-pitched voice. He turned quickly to be surprised by a guy pushing a cart with his luggage in it. Noticing that all the self-created angst was nothing but just that, he felt relief.

The guy took Million's boarding pass, and began comparing the info from the pass to that of the tags on the bags.

Abigail, while still fifteen feet away, yelled, "Welcome home, Million!" The guy looked but there was no one around other than himself and Million. And he was sure the name he had seen on both the boarding pass and the tags read Amin.

The employee, himself being a Muslim, he found it odd for a Muslim person to be called by a none Muslim name. So, looking toward them, he yelled, "Amin," twice, but Million didn't turn around. Not only was he busy talking to Abigail, but also, he had forgotten that he was traveling as Amin.

The guy's curiosity grew to suspicion. Authoritatively, he yelled, "Million!" and that drew Million's attention. Still alarmed, he turned around and said, "Yes!" staring at the guy.

Oh, gosh! I'm supposed to be Amin, he thought. *How does this guy know, my actual name?* he wondered and started to worry. "Sir, why are you yelling?" asked Million, frowning.

"When I called you by the name on your boarding pass, you didn't respond. You responded rather immediately when I yelled Million. I'm curious, why so?" said the guy.

Looking down, Million said, "Sorry, I was just busy, talking to this lady."

"Which one is your name? Because you can't be both Amin and Million. I noticed you are not very familiar with the name Amin, despite being the name you traveled under. I can tell your real name is Million. Why are you traveling by the name Amin?"

"How is that your business?" asked Million, his eyebrows coming closer.

The guy drew the attention of a safety officer who was standing about a hundred feet from them by waving his hand. "If you judge I don't have a business in that, the guy who does is coming," said the guy.

"Brother, please, I need to go home and see my family whom I have missed so much. I have been gone for a while," said Million, lifting his hands up to his chest with the palms up and looking at the guy with narrowed eyes.

The involvement of the safety officer started to worry him. His brother who works there had enough authority to save him from the situation he was getting into. However, he didn't know who he would have explained himself as. He knew his identity would be more puzzling to his brother than it would to his interrogators. *This is problematic*! he thought.

Abigail couldn't hear where the conversation was heading, but she sensed it was not heading anywhere good. She was afraid anything she said might complicate things more, so she decided to stand there quietly. Even then, she didn't know that calling him Million was what started the issue.

The guy took the officer aside, pointing at Million, said softly, "That man says his name is Amin. However, not only did I hear the white woman calling him Million, but also, when I called him Amin loudly, a couple of times, he didn't respond. So, I yelled 'Million' and he answered immediately. He also seems uneasy about something. I'm not sure what to make of it, so you might want to check him out."

***

The officer turned toward Million, "Brother, what is your name?" he asked, calmly.

"Amin," he replied, trying to look confident and

comfortable.

"Amin, can you show me your passport?" asked the officer.

The officer inspected the passport and learned that it was legitimate. He matched the photo on the passport and the face of the passport holder and it matched. While returning the passport to him, "So, who is Million?" he asked.

"Because I know some Americans and Europeans assume all Muslims are terrorists, when that lady and I met, I introduced myself to her as Million—I didn't want to take a chance, you know. Look at her, she is beautiful!" said Million, pointing to Abigail and laughing spuriously.

"My apologies, for the sake of everyone's safety, we have to check any suspicious situations, things, or people. That was why I asked you," he said and started walking away waving goodbye.

"It is okay, it happens," said Million and started to head out pushing his cart quickly. Abigail had to increase her pace to catch up to him.

She had noticed Million's interaction with the two guys was serious. As soon as they walked far enough, she asked, "What were they saying to you?"

"Wow! that was some serious incident that could have gone sour. Apparently, while I was talking to you, the first guy had called me by Amin. Forgetting that it is my legal name, I kept quiet, assuming he was calling someone else.

Because he heard you calling me Million when you came

in, suspiciously, he yelled Million, and I answered right away. So, he called the second guy, who was the safety officer of the airport."

"How did they let you go, then?"

"He verified that I'm Amin from looking at the passport. And I told him that when the first guy called me, I didn't hear because I was busy talking to you. As for the name Million, I told him that I introduced myself to you with that name because most white people consider all Muslims terrorists, therefore I didn't want to miss my chance with you. And he bought it. In fact, he laughed about it."

"How were you able to make up a story like that in such a short and critical moment? It was as if you were prepared for the situation. It sure was a very challenging deadlock. I had been noticing that you don't get a slight confusion to come up satisfactory solutions in crisis."

"Amazingly, the second guy didn't scrutinize me. The first one, however, was suspicious enough to get very close to the Million in Amin. He just didn't know what to say."

***

The conversation had slowed them from the escape-walk that they had when they were leaving the luggage claim area. Abigail had her left hand on one of the main doors ready to push it open, but she hadn't done so because Million was still telling her more about the incident. "Excuse me, brother, could you let me through?" asked a young man whom they had trapped-in behind them by blocking the exit.

The young man's voice shocked Million, he was about to turn around and hug him, but he controlled his urge and moved toward Abigail for the man to leave.

The young man didn't know who Million was but noticed his reaction toward him.

He thought, *Maybe he knew someone who sounded like me. Man, I have never seen such a surprised look. What if he hugged me, and he realized he didn't know me, he would be abashed forever?*

He looked back and noticed that Million was looking at him. He continued his thought, *Dude, he is still looking at me like his long-lost brother or friend. I don't think we know each other. Why don't I just ask him?* He hesitated to go back and ask Million.

Anguish stricken, Million didn't know what to do. He had missed this young man, but he could neither tell him nor just simply leave. He cried inside. His eyes turned red, and he felt that his tears were about to tumble down his face. He turned his face away.

The young man walked to Million, and asked him, "Excuse me, brother, do you know me from somewhere?"

Million felt his head spinning. He didn't know what to do or say. He covered both ears and said, "I heard you and I looked at you. You are my brother. But I'm not your brother. That is why I'm shocked—otherwise I don't know you." He was getting emotional, and his tears were falling down his face.

The young man, seeing Million crying, felt creepy. He said, "Sorry to remind you of something that you didn't want to," and left. While walking, he remembered what Million said and didn't know what to make of it. *He said you are my brother, instead of saying that you look and sound like my brother. I can't wait to tell my diaspora friends, they need to know how sometimes they are so confusing,* he said to himself and smiled.

When Million and the young man were talking, Abigail had left to load the luggage into the car.

Sensing his ach from the tears rolling on his face, Abigail asked, "Million, you look bothered. Who was that man? What did he say to you?"

"Abigail, death could be preferred in some situations. They should have let me die. What did I do to them that they saved my life when they didn't have to? Now, I'm the loneliest man on Earth. It doesn't matter how rich and popular a person is if his or her loved ones do not know him or her, he or she is lonely. Of course, I'm neither popular nor rich, but it would not have mattered to me," he said, crying, his head leaned onto the car.

He continued between his sobbing, "In this world, there are so many pitiful and atrocious things. But, as long as we didn't hear about or see them, they are nothing. It is better to die than to live and hear about and see those things."

"What did you hear? Million, what happened to you?

Relax, don't allow everything to bother you. Try to take things easy. Otherwise, you will hurt yourself."

"I would rather die. What life do I have to live for?"

She opened the back door and prompt him to get in, wanting to take him away from the scene. Sitting beside him, she instructed the driver to take them to Helton Hotel.

***

Million was still sobbing tears of pain. He was a stranger to everybody. He knew them, but they didn't know him. He was keenly waiting to see them, but they didn't even know he existed. Though he was alive, they believed he passed. He was walking as a stranger in a city where he was born and raised. So, how was he to interpret all those things?

The hotel had nice trees and huge backyard. They got out of the car and sat down under a shady tree. "Million, who did you run into? You have to tell me. At least temporarily, I'm the one who could understand and help you. Others wouldn't know you. Who was the guy?"

"He was my brother, whom I love and have missed. These feelings are nothing to him because he judges I'm a stranger. This is almost death to me. I don't see any value in being alive," he said.

"Million, please be patient. There is always potential in fortitude. By enduring your current living conditions, your chances of living a better life increases and it is around the corner. Don't forget that things always have beginning and end—speeding or delaying the end is up to you. Therefore, control your emotions, then we will patiently march to our goal," said Abigail, in a serious but calm manner.

An insightfulness, understanding, sincerity, and mental strength were among the most important riches that Abigail possessed.

***

Chapter Eight

The search for Million's whereabouts stretched to Ethiopia. A man who called from the States reached out to Million's wife, Saba. He claimed that he was a friend of Million from the university and tried to speak words of consolation for her loss. Saba thought she found a genuine comforting person and started talking to him openly.

Then the man transitioned to the actual reason for his call. "We had sent one student from this university to visit you. Has he arrived yet?" he asked.

She told him that no one from America has visited her.

The man concluded that Million didn't go to his wife and said "Maybe he lost your address. Can you give me the address to where you live and work just so I can call and give it to him?"

Judging that there were people in America who consider her and that they had sent someone to visit her gave her a sense of satisfaction. She said, "You know, it is not necessary for you guys to go through any trouble."

He said, "This is the least we could do for Million's family; he was someone who deserves better."

"Thank you very much! But we are doing fine, please don't go through any inconvenience for us."

"No worries, the student is just bringing you a condolence gift. I'm sure he is already in Ethiopia. It will be inconvenient only if he doesn't meet you. Please give me your address, and I will pass it to him," said the man speaking gently but firmly.

After taking the address of her house and the her place of work, he told her that he would call some other time and hung up.

***

After visiting the Eiffel Tower, the Johns sat for coffee in Tour Eiffel Café. "Honey, I have been thinking about our decision of coming here, are we acting like teenagers who are driven by their emotions? We didn't discuss or develop plans of what we will do if Ms. Murphy makes it harder for us to see the child."

"I agree to an extent. We have been following a natural process of reaction to an action. The steps are simple, first locate the mom and the child, then approach the mom and ask if we could see the child."

"What if she refuses, then what?"

"Then, find a good lawyer."

"That is mainly what I'm wondering about. What are we going to tell the law? The child is our daughter? What kind of lawyer, let alone, a judge would believe us?"

"The belief has to start with us. Even if we don't directly claim that she is our daughter, when the child says we are her parents, we need to accept her. Why? Because we know she has our daughter's brain."

"You might have a point there. The child is the plaintiff, and we are witnesses."

"Another way to put it. I love that you are smart like that."

"Don't forget that I'm pretty too, ha…ha… ha. Now, if the child acts the same way she did when we saw her at her mom's place, we definitely have to find a lawyer who can see past her pretty Caucasian frame."

"Yes, ma'am!"

"Wow! It is almost time; can you drop me off at the Hair Salon? When I'm done, we will go to Rue Du Commerce, I saw a nice dress in one of the stores there."

"Sure. Call me when you're finished. I will park somewhere and walk down on Avenue Winston Churchill."

***

Sitting under the hair dryer hood, Lesha imagined Deric and her in a courtroom, testifying, alleging the little girl was their daughter. She thought, *What if the girl changes sides in the middle of the trial and says that the people whom she looks like are her family? That would kill Deric,* she shivered.

***

Walking on Avenue Winston Churchill, the constantly appearing mental image of the girl seemed to remind Deric that there was no way he would confidently stand in a courtroom and defend the girl saying, "She is my daughter." While trying to question his judgement, the girl's voice "Baba, I want to come home and feed my bird. Please take me to my new school," started to echo in his head. "Ava is my pretend mom—you and mommy are my real parents," continued the echo. Could a witness testify based on gut-feeling? His eyes saw someone else's daughter, his ears on the other hand heard his own daughter, what kind of witness would he be in a court of law?

In his head, the case was being squabbled over in a courtroom, except, he was the judge, the lawyers of both sides, the witnesses, the juries, and the spectators. He felt as though his head was about to explode, so, he decided to have a recess. With the hope of taking his mind off the case, he debated whether to check out a popular looking bar on his right.

The bar was a lot bigger inside than it looked from the outside. He observed that there were too many people of all origins and walks of life. From where he could see, there wasn't an unoccupied table. So, he joined the crowded bunch who were looking for seats.

It could be the alcohol's fault, but some of the drinkers were talking louder than they could hear. In fact, it appeared as if occupants of most of the tables were having some kind of bickering.

His phone rang, he answered it with his hand cupped just below his nose, “Good timing! Are you done?”

“Yes.”

“I was about to check out this populated bar. Okay, I’m a little further from the car, so it might take me twenty to thirty minutes to get to you.”

“Okay, there is a store on the second floor, I will visit that. Call me when you get here.”

***

“Here is the school where the twins are still attending. It is highly secured. There are cameras everywhere,” said Toni, pointing with his chin toward a fenced three-story gray building, then glanced at Deric.

“Is there a coffee place around here that we can sit and chat while enjoying the sight?”

“Yes, there is one around the corner. In fact, if we find a seat outside, we will have better view on the entrance of the school.”

Deric and Toni, sitting at the balcony of the second floor of the cafeteria, discussed many topics. Toni had been growing fond of the story about the little girl with brain transplant. He proposed to Deric that he would do his own investigation and write a book. Deric agreed to the plan.

***

Deric and Lesha, equipped with photos of the Dubois family, began hanging out by the school in their rented vehicle. They also became the newly, repeated customers to the cafeteria on the left corner of the school.

They went there every day, but at different times, including on late evenings.

On one particular day, they went to the cafeteria a half hour prior to end of school for the day and secured a table with nice view to the school and surrounding streets. After enjoying their macchiato and cake, they started taking pictures of each other with their back to the school and all-around areas,

The minute students began exiting the building, two men with cameras hanging from their necks and held in their hands appeared from the northern corner of the school and stood about one hundred feet from the main gate of the school. They seemed to be looking for someone in particular. Three little girls, almost the same height, all wearing the same design but different color dresses, exited. Immediately, the two men started clicking their cameras. They might have captured a couple of photos before a black and tinted SUV came and blocked their lenses and swept the girls and sped.

The Johns couldn't clearly ID the girls, but two of them they suspected were the Dubois twins, and the third could possibly be Teena. After a little discussion, they concluded that the camera men were paparazzi and the girls were whom they surmised.

***

Toni had taken the assignment to find the Dubois'

residence. He called while the Johns were summarizing what their next move should be and said, "I found out where they live, but it is impossible to see them getting in or out of the car because their house is in gated community."

"Toni, nothing is impossible!" said Deric.

"Well, except with a helicopter or a drone. Other than that, there is no way to go past the gate. Don't ask about deliveries. There is a delivery area on the left side of the gate both for small and large items."

"I think our girl might be going to the same school, where the twins go to. Looking down from the cafe, we saw three girls in similar dresses, two the same height and one taller. We couldn't tell whether they were the kids in the picture you give us. However, paparazzi were photographing them until a black SUV took them away. We now believe the two girls are the twins while the third one is Teena."

"Your best bet is to stand by the school gate tomorrow at two thirty pm and find out if the girls are whom you conjectured."

"That is another idea. Hopefully we won't be accused of trying to take the child. That is if one of the girls is Teena."

"All that is risky, we should, instead, find Ms. Murphy and ask her a favor to let us spend a few minutes with her daughter," said Lesha.

"I wish my daughter was still going to that school, we would have known their scheduled field trips."

"Toni, you might be up to something now. Are you

friends or in good terms with one of the teachers there?" asked Lesha.

"No, but there's one congenial teacher whom I feel comfortable with. She always approaches me as her friend whom she hasn't seen for a while."

"I wonder if she would share that info with you?"

"She knows my daughter was friends with the twins, so I can tell her that she wants to join them at their next field trip."

"Thank you, Toni! I don't know what we would have done without you, other than going around Paris, hoping for the best?" said Lesha.

***

When the first-grade teacher gave the list of scheduled field trips of the girls' class to Toni, she had no idea one of the trips in the list would shake some people's lives to the core.

***

A few days later, the Johns were in the first animals' station of Vincennes Zoo, seemingly enjoying the scenery, when a bunch of kids accompanied by adults entered, giggling and chatting in French.

"Oh! Shoot! Honey, don't look back, let's just go, let's go to the next station," whispered Lesha into Deric's left ear.

"What? Are they here?" he asked trying to look back.

"Ms. Murphy is here with the kids!" said Lesha, putting her arm on his shoulder and walking fast. Despite their best efforts, they couldn't walk fast to the next station because a group of tourists were standing by the transit door waiting for their guide to finish explaining about the next scenes.

"Let's blend in with the tourists," said Deric.

"We might as well—we will be the second set of black couple," said Lesha smiling nervously. She continued, "Obviously, the third girl from the other day was Teena. Can I take a peek?"

"Please, don't. The plan is for her to see us, not the other way around. In the next room, we should shake our nervousness and act like other tourists."

"We have to make ourselves visible to her. But, how do we do that without knowing where she is?"

"Baby, relax! She will find us. The child is too smart to miss what she wants. Besides, I'm wearing the shirt that Sandy used to like on me," he said, trying to get smile from his anxious wife.

"Why didn't you tell me to wear any of her favorite clothes of mine?"

"Sorry, I didn't know which one it is."

"You could have reminded me when you remembered yours."

"You are right, I'm sorry! Can we just move on? Please concentrate on what we came for."

"Oh, my Gosh! Here they come, what do we do now?"

"Let's just keep staring at the hyena cubs, and hope for the..."

Deric didn't finish his sentence, when Teena, followed by a man in a suit and tie, came running and jumped to his chest and hugged him tightly. "Baba, I knew you and mommy would come to take me home. Can we wait until my graduation? Please! I even speak French now," said Teena, looking up into Deric's eyes and turning to Lesha. Deric and Lesha didn't say a word. They sandwiched the child and began sobbing.

"Excuse me sir, madam, please come this way with the child," said the man after talking over the phone to another security personal, who was outside by the bathroom.

He made another phone call and said, "I'm taking them outside, you stay with the rest of them and tell the teacher and the parents that everything is okay, the child knows the couple."

Teena jumped to Lesha's chest and the three of them followed the man outside.

Ava was coming out of the bathroom, and the twins were following her. When she saw Deric, her stomach fluttered, her heart began racing, her hands and lips started shaking.

Then, she spotted Lesha holding Teena close to her chest, a rush of anger washed over her. "Put my daughter down," she cried with a shaky voice, her hands continued trembling. "Security, are you going to stand there and do nothing while these people are stealing my daughter? If you don't know anything else, call for help, call the police," she screamed and startled the two men, who were observed by the child's interaction with the black couple. Even the one who was detailing outside for Ava and the twins had forgotten all about them.

Staggering, she went past Deric and stood three feet from Lesha, and said, "Didn't I tell you to let go of my daughter?" she said, staring at her with rage.

"Go ahead, my dear, go to your mom, we don't want to upset her," said Lesha, kneeling with her right knee to lower the child.

"No! You are my mom. Please don't make me go!" said Teena, tightening her hug of Lesha.

The guard who took the twins inside to join their peers returned to the scene and began whispering to his partner what the twins had told him. He said, "The twins told me that Teena, when she was staying with them, she kept saying that she is black and that Ava is not her mom," both guards chuckled.

More visitors were coming, some stood staring at the child and the black lady, and the visibly enraged Ava.

Deric weak-kneed, noticed his wife shrinking from embarrassment, he wished that they could leave the area.

"Teena, please stay with the gentlemen while we speak with your mom," said Deric, trying to grab her from his wife.

Teena looked at him with teary eyes and said, "Daddy, why you don't call me Sandy anymore? But it is the doctor—I don't want to look like Teena."

Hearing that, Lesha felt her heart melting, and held the

child tighter.

Teena's statements infuriated and inflamed Ava. She thought, *She never said this before and had stopped talking about them until these idiots show up.*

Then, she turned to Deric and said, "You have nothing to talk to me about. The police are on their way, speak with them. You were stalking me in Boston, and now you followed us to torture me and my daughter. We moved here seeking peace, but you, lawless criminals are still shadowing us."

"Ms. Murphy, please don't insult us. If you listen to the child and you let us spend a few minutes with her, things wouldn't have come this far," said Lesha.

"Don't tell me what to do with my daughter. Neither of us want to see you people ever again. I will have my lawyers prosecute you here and in the US."

"Now, stop being rude. You call us criminals for trying to listen and understand the child, and trying to reason with you? Maybe you don't know that holding a child against her will is a crime," said Lesha.

Security guards of the zoo, after taking reports from the school guards, instructed the Johns to walk with them to the office. Teena, however, refused to let go of Lesha.

Her mom tried to trick her, then tried to forcefully remove her, but the child wouldn't budge.

The Johns implored, they even told her that the police could take them to jail if she didn't go to her mom, but she kept shaking her head and tightening her hold of Lesha.

The securities' assumption was that the child might have some mental health issue for her to believe that the black couple were her parents.

After asking a permission from Ava, they forcefully removed her from Lesha.

The child, however seemed determined. She fought and wiggled out from Ava and ran and hugged Deric's right leg.

Ava, her face turning red and her jaws clenched, ran after Teena and said to her, "You, ungrateful brat, let go of that man. Right now! Or else, I will call Dr. Bruce."

"Okay, okay, don't call him. I don't want to get shocked," she said and started crying.

Deric felt her shaking hands while letting go of his legs. His heart ached. He picked her up. His tears rolled down to her forehead. He lifted her up to kiss and hug her tight before he sent her to her mom. When his lips were to meet her forehead, Ava pulled her from him.

***

Million and Abigail, while heading to his house from the airport, engaged in an intense discussion on how he should approach his wife and kids, and his parents and siblings. Then they finally came up with one idea.

They parked their car by the fence of the house and went out. "Now, instead of Million, I'm Biniam, and the house, instead of mine, it is my friend's," said Million, turning and looking at Abigail with narrowed eyes.

Noticing his sadness, Abigail said, "Million, this is only strategically true, but technically it's the contrary. Facts remain facts no matter what."

Out of excitement to see his wife and kids, Million rang the doorbell repeatedly. While waiting, he anticipated, "Who will answer the door? the maid, one of my kids, or my wife?"

"Million, I want to remind you again, be careful of forgetting your name. It shouldn't become a problem, as it was at the airport. Right?" said Abigail.

"I already told you my name is Biniam. Instead of Million; you can call me Bini."

A girl opened the door and said, "Yes?" timidly.

Million quickly said, "This is Mr. Million and Mrs. Saba's house, right?"

"It is," replied the girl.

"Is Mrs. Saba home?"

"She just stepped out. She said that she would be back soon."

The moment he opened his mouth to inquire about the availability of the kids, his son came running from the hallway. An urge of running, lifting, and kissing his son flooded into him, then he remembered his situation. Looking at the kid, he asked the girl, "He must be Rui?" he said with the intent of creating the impression that he knew a thing or two about the family he was visiting. "And you are Mulu, Saba's cousin, yes?" he added.

"Yes," she replied with a smile, raising her eyebrows.

"Is Mica inside?"

"Yes, she is doing her homework."

"So, can we chat with the kids while waiting for Mrs. Saba?"

"Come in, that shouldn't be a problem," said Mulu.

***

Million felt less anxious. His wife not being home when they arrived gave him time to calm the nerves. Walking fast toward his son, he wished, somehow, the child would recognize him. However, the boy moved back, running timidly. That elevated Million's sorrow.

He saw their dog leashed by the door. Remembering how he liked that dog and how he used to play with it and the kids when he got home from work, he stretched his hand to pet it. The dog growled and bit him.

"Shouldn't the dog I raised recognize me?" asked Million frustrated, looking at his bitten right hand.

Abigail approached him saying, "Are you all right? Did it get you bad?" She rolled his sleeve to check the bitten area.

"I'm alright," he replied. Getting close to her, he whispered, "Even my dog bit me. If my dog doesn't recognize me, how could people?"

"A dog knows a person by sniffing that person's bodily scent or trace. What makes you think that it would read a mind. Only humans can read a brain's imprint," said Abigail.

Because he was anxious to see his kids and chat with them, he tried to forget the dog bite. "I'm okay," he said and walked into the house, and Abigail followed him. Toward the right of the living room, a family picture in a nice frame hung. There were also multiple pictures of each family member and a pair of them on the other side of the wall. Pointing to a slightly larger picture, Million asked Abigail, "Who do you think is that?"

"I don't know what you looked like before, but I can imagine that person was you,"

"Am I more handsome now?" asked smiling.

"You are not too far from your previous look."

"Even though it may be unnoticeable to foreigners, there is a striking difference in looks within our race. For instance, in the past, my skin was slightly lighter, now it is darker. I'm taller and skinnier in this body than I was in my own."

"I see!"

"How can I make them get rid of the Million in the photo from their heart and replace him with the new me? This seems a difficult undertaking," he said while plopping down to the sofa, forgetting that he was supposed to act as a guest.

After both of them sat and talked for a few minutes, Million turned his head toward Mulu and said, "Sorry to bother you, can you tell the children to come?"

She nodded and went to get the children. She came back followed by them. The girl was his eight-year-old, she was growing to look like her mom. The boy was six and had taken Million's old look.

It was easy to tell that they were properly cared for.

Though everything in the house seemed to be going well, Million imagined that they felt something was missing.

***

Bini's heart sank when he saw the kids. It had been two years since he'd last seen them up close. Realizing that he could see them but they couldn't see that he was their father and that he knew them, but they didn't know him, he wished he was dreaming. He felt like screaming, then he bit the back of his hand.

Mulu encouraged the kids to say hi. Looking at the white woman and the strange Afro man with narrow eyes, they walked toward them, dragging their feet.

Bini kissed and hugged them tightly, but he sensed their empty heart for him. They were as cold as they would be toward a stranger whom they had never met before. That began to kill him inside. Abigail noticed the odd interaction between the children and their father. And she got worried that they might leave. She started to act humorous, crossing her eyes, popping her cheeks and wrinkling her nose. As she hoped, they began laughing and sat between them.

He offered the kids various sweets that he brought for them. And they started eating. He remembered how shy they were and that it took them long time to be themselves around strangers. Now, that he was the stranger to them, he wasn't surprise by their timidness.

***

Back to the drama in Vincennes Zoo in Paris, France, in the security office, one of the guards was interrogating the Johns, while another one was talking to the police outside.

Deric pictured some doctor putting something on the child's head and shocking her. The sound of her saying, "No, I don't want to be shocked," kept echoing in his mind.

He got up with clenched hands and said, "Are we done here? We need to leave now."

"Sir, please sit down, the police are outside, taking notes from my associate," said the security personnel.

"Why don't they come and talk to us? Baby, let's go. We have to hire a very good lawyer. They are putting her through electro-compulsions to make her forget about us. We can't sit and watch that woman abusing our child," he said, his veins popping with each word.

Lesha never saw Deric this upset. Her concern grew that they might consider him violent. Softly rubbing his arm and gently pulling him to sit down, she said, "Honey, we will leave when they tell us we can do so. We don't want to be accused of refusing to cooperate with the law."

The police came inside and asked the Johns for ID. They gave them their passports. One of the cops scanned the profile pages of both passports and handed them to his partner. Then he said, "You two are accused of luring a mentally disabled six-year-old child. The parent of the child has filed a restraining order against both of you. Therefore, you will be staying in custody and expedited to the US. Your case will be seen by a court there."

Lesha felt her blood boiling. She wanted to tear her clothes out. Luckily, Deric was calmer. He said to her, "Baby, we knew this could happen. So, stay strong." He turned to the cop and said, "Do we not have the right for an attorney?"

"Yes sir, you do. But it has no use in Paris. As I mentioned, your case will be expedited to a court in the US, there you can use your lawyer to defend you."

"How long are we going to be in jail here for?"

"It is hard to say. As soon as a court in your country picks up your cases, you will be flying accompanied by police."

"Can we at least make a phone call?" asked Lesha, still the veins on her forehead popped.

"Yes, ma'am," replied the deputy.

"Honey, why haven't you told them that you are a reporter? Sir, my husband is a reporter. He was working on a case that involved the child," said Lesha, looking at her husband and at the officers.

"Baby, you know, I'm not on official business for any of my clients. Hence, my being a reporter has no purpose here."

"Sir, we had no idea that you are a reporter. Which media do you work for?" asked one of the officers.

"I'm independent investigative reporter. I do freelance with a couple of major news media, but the case about the child is more of personal than a news project," he replied clenching his teeth.

***

In Saba's house, Million, the current Bini was playing with his kids when the doorbell rang and startled him. He suspected that it was his wife who buzzed the bell. He felt mother nature calling him, but his thought of wanting to see his wife won. He had missed her so much, and wished he could embrace her tightly as soon as she came in, but he imagined the serious consequence his act would have.

He came to his sense that he could only talk to his wife as the guest and stranger that he was to her. Even if temporarily hiding his feelings, he knew it was a tool to make his plan work. He also wanted to be careful about how a stranger were to act around her. He knew she didn't like arrogant guys and those who are easily excited. Thinking through the whole thing, he felt like he was playing her, and that upset him. What a drama—a lie to him, but a truth to her.

There was no limit to how much he loved her. So, how was he to hide his feelings? He had missed her very much. So, how was he to hold back his desire to express his longing? On their wedding day, her beauty was the talk of the neighborhood. He was a hunk too—though he gained some weight later. Now he was in a skinnier and taller frame. The problem was that he was no longer Million to the people he knew and loved, rather some stranger named Bini.

She pushed the door open and entered. Her beauty was still breathtaking. After saying hi to them, she sat across from Bini. The more he tried to convince himself that she was not his and couldn't get close to her, the more her beauty shined like a precious thing. As if his lovely wife was taken from him, he felt extreme jealousy and started to worry that he might not control his feelings much longer.

Poor Saba didn't know that her husband was inside the stranger's frame sitting across from her. He was hidden from her sight. Unless he came out from his hiding, she could never find him.

At least he could peep at her through the two openings called eyes. Quite impressive! The loss of his spousal rights to his wife had become unbearable pain he couldn't get help for. He didn't know how long he could be patient.

Saba was suffering from grief and loss of her husband. Similarly, because he was an invisible husband, he was suffering from the yearning of his wife. However, his was worse because his situation was the first of its kind. Her problem, on the other hand was more common. Also, while his support system was only Abigail, hers could be any understanding person.

He said, “My name is Biniam Yemane. I don’t know if Million ever told you about me. I live in Frankfurt, Germany.” He couldn’t believe he looked her in the eye while saying so. He immediately started to feel guilty for lying to his wife. However, he didn’t think he had any other choice, so he continued. A careful listener could pick up that he was not talking from within.

He continued, “I was Million’s close friend. We were friends since kindergarten. I was already living in Germany when you two got married. I haven’t had a chance to introduce myself to you. I heard how good the two of you were together and that you had brought up two kids.

“Let alone to come to Ethiopia, I was very busy even to call family and friends. I just got a short break and decided to come and see my parents while they are alive. And you were the first on my list of family and friends whom I had planned to visit during my stay here.

“She is Doctor Abigail Muzik, my friend and coworker. She came to see our country.” He looked at Abigail and smiled.

Saba, addressing both said, “Welcome!” then she asked him, “Did you find your parents well?”

“Yes, they are doing great! They are getting tired; it could be part of aging. What about you? How are you doing?” he asked, making himself comfortable on his seat.

***

Saba, sobbingly narrated the story about how her loving husband had died in America and was buried at a cemetery not too far from the house.

He said, “I had heard all about it. It was sad. A great sorrow had fallen on you. However, too much grief could hurt you both physically and mentally. For the sake of your kids, try to ease on the mourning.” Inside, he was fighting a nagging feeling that was pushing him to hug her and tell her that he was alive.

He thought, *She would forget all her sorrow if she knew that I’m not dead. The problem is how to make her realize that I’m alive.*

She asked, “Do you have siblings?”

“I have two brothers and one sister. I am the eldest, and my sister is the youngest of us.” He replied.

“Wow! The same as my husband. He also is the first child to his parents and has two brothers and one sister,” she said and slipped into thinking her sad thoughts.

Returning from her thought journey, she said, “Since you said you had been gone for a long time, I could imagine how happy your parents are to see you.”

"Yes, but it was after I told them who I am."

"Oh! How sad! Are they having trouble identifying people due to age?"

"No, not like that. I'm not sure whether the trouble is seeing or remembering. But they couldn't recognize me. Also, it could be that I'm changed in many ways."

"What do you mean by changed? Were you very young, when you left?" she asked. Then she thought, *If he left when he was young, he couldn't be my husband's close friend.* She wanted to be fully convinced that he was Million's old friend. *Million never told me that he had a friend who lives in Germany*, she judged.

"It may be exaggerating to say that I had been gone for a while. However, because of an auto accident, I had an extensive surgery of repair and replacement of my entire face. That could be why they are not able to recognize me."

As soon as he said that, he wanted to change the subject, so he turned to Abigail and said something in whispering voice, he got up, and Abigail followed him.

"Please, stay, have dinner with us. At least have a snack," said Saba, confused by their abrupt move to leave.

"We are not leaving. We are just going to get some stuff from the car. We will be back," said Bini and went to the car with Abigail.

Saba started to wonder if Million had mentioned Bini. *I don't remember Million telling me having a friend in Germany. Maybe they had lost contact long before we got married. Or he told me, but my memory is not serving me well. Is it weird that his parents couldn't identify him? Hmm... Would Million have spotted the change on him? I just have to talk to him more...* before she finished her train of thought, they came back, pulling two small and one big bag and sat back down. Bini put one of the small bags on the coffee table and opened it. It was full of goodies.

The kids stood left and right, leaning forward with their eyes opened wide. "Come take a look at what I brought you," said Bini to Mica. She apprehensively walked a couple of steps closer, then stood.

"You can come closer, it is okay, I'm your uncle,"

She looked at her mom then at him, and again at her mom with narrowing eyes, looking sideways and tilting her head.

Abigail, smiling, she opened her arms wide, inviting the kids with her chin.

"Go ahead, it is alright," said their mom, looking at both of them.

The shoes and clothes he brought her were so pretty, and they were the same as what she'd asked her dad to bring her. When she saw them, her eyes lit up with joy. "I told my dad to bring me this kind of clothes and shoes, but he didn't," said Mica. That tested her mom's emotion and hurt her dad's feeling.

Bini would have been happy to tell her the truth. Since he couldn't, he said, "I guess I think like your dad, that is why I brought you these."

"Our father went to America and died there, so, we don't have a father. While other kids go on vacation with their daddy, we don't have anyone to take us," said Mica holding her presents tightly close to her chest.

"Come here, Mica, you are very expressive. You are making your mom and I sad. Though I'm your uncle, I love you, and I care for you and your brother as much as your dad did. So, I'm almost your father. I mean, your dad is not dead," he said and took out the clothes and shoes he brought for Rui.

"A few days before my husband passed, we talked about shoes and clothes similar to those, and he was going to send them to us. The chance of such things happening is an impressive coincidence," said Saba feeling goose bump.

"Yes, it is an impressive coincidence. Let me show you what I have brought you," he said, and when he was about to open the larger bag, Million's sister, said "Hello guys!" coming into the living room through the back door.

Hearing her voice, Bini, accidently, muttered, "Machid," and turned around to embrace her. Machida and Saba stood there confused and stared at each other.

***

Million retreated, looking at his wife then at his sister. He clearly called the name, and he didn't have the answer handy for the question of how he knew Machida.

Both ladies were entertaining two unanswered questions in their minds. Saba seemed more puzzled by the situation. She was at loss of words. She wanted to introduce them, but she figured they knew each other. *Good, Machid knows him! Then Million might have told me about him. I don't understand why I can't place this guy*, she thought. She didn't stop it there. Her desire to know more about the stranger in her house seemed to grow. So, she asked, "Machid, you know Bini? How come you or Million never made mention of him before?"

Machida looked at him as if to be sure, and said, "I don't think I know him. Unless I forgot or something."

"Bini, I think you know her, right? She is Million's sister, Machida. She doesn't think she knows you. Please remind her. I'm trying to remember myself whether Million had told me about you or not," said Saba hoping that he would say something that would prompt her memory.

"I understand that she is Million's sister, but she and I have never met. Anyway, I'm Million's friend, and my name is Biniam or Bini," he said and put out his hand to shake hers.

She said, "Well you already know my name." And shook his hand. The questions, *How did he know my name and my voice?* were still in her head.

Million opened the bag he brought for Saba and handed her clothes, shoes, and a neckless.

Saba screamed holding her head, "I can't believe! How could this be? How can this be just a coincidence?" she said, feeling confused.

A few years back, Million and she had attended a neighbor's wedding. There was a woman who was wearing a nice dress, matching shoes, and neckless. Saba commented to Million on the loveliness of what the woman was wearing. That was when Million promised her that if he went abroad, he would bring her the dress, the shoes, and the neckless. It was creepy to her that someone other than her husband would know about it and had brought her those things.

She said, "I'm sorry, but this seems more than coincidence to me. Please tell me that Million bought all of these before the accident and someone sent you to bring them to us. Was that what happened?" she asked, baffled by everything that she was seeing.

"The important thing is that what you received is similar to what you want. People are happier when they find what they want and need," he said, speaking softly.

"Bini, how are you able to bring us all these? How long before the accident did my husband tell you all about these?" she asked believing that it had something to do with her husband.

Talking in a manner that seemed a joke, he replied, "Maybe I'm able to read what people's wishes are."

"Are you telling me all these are your selections?" she asked. Then she remembered something, "Aha, are you Million's friend whom they sent from America? They called and asked me if I had received an item that they sent with some guy."

When Million heard that, he startled. He knew he didn't have a school friend who could send anything. "Who did they say they are?" he asked with a wrinkled face.

"He didn't tell me his name."

"Then, what did he say?"

"First he asked me if anyone who came from the US was staying with us. I told him that no one had come. When I asked him who he was and why he was calling me, he said they were Million's friends from school, and had sent a friend to bring us something, they were just wondering if he has met us, yet. And I told them that no one had come."

"Then, what did they say?"

"He asked for my work and house address, that way they would pass it to the guy, and I gave them."

"I'm not whom they said. As I mentioned earlier, I'm from Germany."

"I'm sure all these cost a fortune, are we not hurting you?" said Saba, Still wondering how all this had happened.

"This is nothing. Please put them on and let us see if they fit you so that we can enjoy ourselves seeing how good you look in them."

Abigail, even though she couldn't understand most of what was being said, was happy seeing the kids giggling and running around joyously. Bini translated some of the conversation so she was not bored.

"Okay, kids, let us go to the bedroom and put on the clothes and shoes that your uncle has brought us," said Saba and all three of them went to the bedroom.

While going to the bedroom, she told the maid to serve the guests their dinner.

Interestingly, that day was her third day since she quit wearing grieving clothes. It was a custom to the Orthodox Christians in Ethiopia to dress up in black, head to toe, when grieving a passing of loved one. Saba wore grieving clothes until family and friends did an intervention, consulted, begged, and nagged her to start wearing regular clothes. Now, her favorite clothes, shoes, and necklace have arrived at the right time, as if a comforting and condolence gift.

***

When Mulu put the food on the table and turned around, Bini was leading Abigail to the restroom to wash their hands. She wondered how he knew where the bathroom was. Machida, who was sitting on one of the sofas, thought the same thing. Earlier, he recognized her voice and called her by her name, and now he was walking in the house as if he knew every corner of it. She thought, *He is a man with some hidden secret.*

Sitting around the dining table, they started eating the pizza. Abigail liked the atmosphere in the house. Bini was joyous to the point of feeling as if he was still the old Million, enjoying life with his wife and kids.

"I'm very happy! This by itself is half success. How do you feel?" Abigail whispered to him.

"Compared to the past few months, this day is multiple days—this day is unique. I sense high hope. At the same time, I smell a dreadful thing coming my way."

Abigail's heart dropped, "What? What scary thing is that?" she asked.

He heard Saba and the kids coming, so he said, "I will tell you later," and took another bite of his pizza.

A few seconds later, Saba and the kids came looking great in their new clothes and shoes. Saba was fascinated by the coincidence of everything. She felt the presence of her husband. The thought of it gave her goosebumps.

In the middle of every conversation, she kept saying, "This is remarkable!" Not only had she and her husband talk about the exact clothes and shoes, but also, they were the perfect sizes. *How could the neckless be the exact match of the one my husband and I saw at the wedding? How would Bini know what I wanted without talking to someone?* she asked herself.

When she couldn't find the answer, she made up a temporary answer, *Maybe it is God's way of comforting me.*

Since the day that they were informed about Million's death, this was the first time that Saba and her kids felt alive. Abigail and Bini were also very happy to see the house filled with joy.

***

In France, the Johns were taken to the prison, Maison d'Arrêt in Nanterre, western suburb of Paris, where people with pre-trial cases were housed. There, in a gender specific buildings, to wait their extradition to the US.

***

"You three look fantastic!" said Bini, revealing his ecstasy with an ear to ear smile. Likewise, Abigail expressed her amusement through huge smiles and words. Machida and Mulu's jaws dropped too. They looked at Saba and her kids with wow and excitement.

"I'm bewildered! All the clothes and shoes fit us perfectly, thank you so much for spending a fortune and your valuable time to makes us happy!" said Saba looking at Bini.

Then, she thought “He can’t be lying. After all, a person lies to take, not to give. There is nothing that could make him lie. This is just the unbelievably unique thing.”

He opened the bag again, took out and handed to Saba a picture of a natural scenic place in a frame that was decorated with a bronze of grapes hanging from its vine. When she saw that, she frowned, her eyes teared up, and she stood frozen. Then, as if each drop of her tears were waiting for its turn to come out, they started to flow down pushing one another.

The picture was a wedding gift from her late brother whom she loved dearly. Because the picture reminded her of him, she valued it tremendously. She felt she had honored her brother when she cared for and looked at it. One day, while cleaning a spider web with an extendable broom, Million accidently hit and smashed it to a point where the frame couldn’t be repaired.

Million always remembered how Saba was upset that day and how badly she’d cried. She cried as if her brother had just died. Million tried hard to comfort her, but she wouldn’t stop crying. He felt guilty for being the reason for her sadness. He couldn’t find the same frame anywhere in town.

When he found the picture in the same frame in the US, he bought it, thinking that it would make her happy and give her satisfaction. However, when he gave it to her, her tears flooded down her face as much as it did when the frame broke.

Bini was stunned. Her reaction was contrary to what he

had imagined. It was justifiable that she cried during the loss of the picture because she had associated it with her brother. But now, she was supposed to be happy, considering that a replacement for her brother's memorabilia was found.

She was crying because she felt guilty of how she reacted toward her husband when he broke the frame. She'd ignored him for days. She thought he had bought it to make her happy, but he died before he could give it to her. So, his friend brought it instead.

The fact that Saba didn't understand what he was trying to convey by bringing her the picture made him mad. Her crying didn't make him feel sorry for her. Instead, it drove him crazy. That he couldn't express his feeling made it worse. Somehow, fighting with his emotion tried to calm her down. But she wouldn't stop crying.

Abigail kept asking Bini, "What is the matter?" And she tried to comfort Saba. But to no avail. This disturbed, everyone in the house.

Except for Bini, occasionally trying to calm her, everyone sat down quietly. So, her sobbing was echoing. A little while later, Bini, Machida, and Abigail begged her to stop crying, and she did.

***

Bini and Abigail whispered at each other to leave.

Saba begged them to stay. "We need to go; we have to be somewhere soon. At least one of us will be back some other time," said Bini. He kissed the kids and began to leave.

"I'm sorry to disturb you guys, the picture reminded me both my late brother and husband," said Saba, wiping her face.

Saba's extreme sorrow and nonstop cry for her supposedly dead husband reminded Million that she loved him so much. And he thought "If she knew that I'm alive, how happy would she be?"

***

Chapter Nine

In the chow-hall of the prison, Deric felt that the line was moving one foot per hour. The rich aroma of the food seemed to awaken his salivary glands and the hungry lion in his stomach. The thought of his stomach was so strong that he felt the urge to run to the front of the longest line he had ever seen.

A man, three places ahead of him moved to the edge leaving only the left side of his body in the line and turned facing the end of the line. Then began starting at Deric. However, Deric didn't seem to notice—let alone a man he never met, even if God, whom he had heard a great deal about was standing in front of him, he wouldn't have noticed. He had urgent messages, rumbling of the stomach, irritation, and weakening, to attend to.

The man walked to Deric and said, "Are you the American who got caught with his wife while trying to loot a child? My cousin posted a video about you on her Facebook page."

"We didn't try to abduct any kid. We know the child and she knows us too. Her mom, however, doesn't want us to meet her," said Deric struggling to control his irritation.

"Hey, dick, you are already in, admit it. You are a child molester, right?"

"Jacopo, leave the man alone," said another man in French.

"You must be out of your freaking mind to accuse me of such thing, now get out of my fucking face before I kill you," said Deric feeling his blood pressure rising. The thought of his stomach had disappeared.

Jacopo pulled a four-knuckles ring out of his pocket, and said, "Maybe I should kill you first. I don't like child molesters," and punched Deric on the back of his right ear twice and once on the back of the neck, just below the head.

***

While traveling in their car, "She has a serious mourner's depression. She couldn't help but to cry remembering her brother and her husband," said Abigail.

"If introducing myself wasn't a matter of concern, I would have held my lovely wife tightly and tell her that I'm alive. I'm dying for my wife to know me as her husband, and for my kids, as their father. I'm hurting inside that I'm a guest in my own house and to my own family," said Bini clenching his hand and jaws.

"There isn't any other choice now. She saw her husband's body in a box and said goodbye when he was buried. This fact will remain with her for a while. You and I know that Million is still alive. So, as of now, between her and us, Million is dead, and Million is alive are both true, but opposite facts. We can't destroy any of them in a hurry. Eventually, one of them needs to be made old. Once old, it is easier to destroy," said Abigail insightfully.

"What do you mean by making old?" he asked.

"By continuing what you started today, slowly make her understand that yesterday's Million is still alive. Look, there are many things that the two of you together did, saw, and ate. Bit by bit, remind her those things and that you were once part of her life. For instance, the shoes and clothes that you brought her are great stimulators. Adding the picture, however, was too much for her. If somebody carefully put a hundred pounds on you, you could easily carry it.

"But, if that someone throws the hundred pounds at you from a distance, you will fall holding it. Throwing multiple facts at her at once could become more than she could handle. Just step by step, show her that there is Million in Bini. It may take time, but she will recognize that fact. Eventually, as she comes closer to the living you, the dead you will become old to her."

"What about the issue that you made me promise you."

"That was a temporary issue. I have high hopes that it will have a legal conclusion soon.

***

When Lesha arrived at the hospital accompanied by a prison guard, Deric's bed was being wheeled from the emergency department to the surgical unit. A portable breathing machine was exchanging gas to and from his lungs through a tube that was inserted into his trachea. Seeing her husband's seemingly lifeless body hooked up to multiple medical devices, Lesha fainted. The prison guard and a couple of nurses pulled her to the side. After assessing that she was breathing okay, the nurses left. Before they did, they told the guard that post surgery Deric would be taken to ICU.

Sitting at the waiting area of the ICU, Lesha felt lost; the scene of her husband's lifeless body came to her mind and she began sobbing. *Is he really dead, or I'm being negative?* she thought.

She got up to go to the bathroom, and the guard stood up with her. "I'm just going there, I don't think you need to come with me," she told the guard pointing to the bathroom with her chin.

In the restroom, looking at her reflection in the mirror, she began reflecting on her predicament. "What am I going to do now? Deric, why did you get into a fight? You know I have no one here; even back home. I can't afford to lose you…"

"Are you okay in there?" asked the guard in French.

Lesha, swing opened the bathroom door wide. Then without saying a word, she went and sat on the couch. "What now? Deric, what now? You know I'm not going to abandon the child. Are you leaving me alone to deal with the ungrateful woman? …" she stopped talking to herself because she saw a nurse and a doctor coming toward her.

Both of them sat in front of Lesha quietly for about ten seconds. "Is my husband gone? Please say no. Please tell me he is alive, even with some kind of disability. Please don't tell me he is dead," said Lesha, the tears in her eyes fighting to break loose.

"Mrs. Johns, we are really sorry, we lost your husband," said the doctor in French and the nurse handed a box of tissues.

Lesha began howling.

"Is there anyone local whom you need to call? If so, the phone is on the corner," said the nurse in English.

“Thank you!” said Lesha between her sobbing and headed to the phone.

***

The next morning, associated press had the news of assassination of an American man in a prison in Paris, France, both in French and English. The reporter, Toni Mann described in great details why Mr. Johns and his wife came to France and how both of them were sent to prison. The article summarized with recommendation on the need for further investigation to the killer’s true motive.

***

In the US, CNN picked up the news and began reporting about the child with brain transplant. The channel invited Toni Mann for an in-person interview after he briefed them about the child’s identity crisis.

***

Three days after Deric passed, Lesha and Deric’s body were extradited to the US accompanied by a police officer from the France prison systems. Also, Toni arranged his interview date to fly with Lesha.

As soon as she sat in the airplane, Lesha cried her heart out staring at the empty seat next to hers. The thought that her best friend was no longer going to sit beside her ached her heart. While crying she decided to make the best of the close to eight hours flight.

She texted herself, "The only way to prove that Deric didn't die in vain is to seek justice for the child. After the funeral, hire the best lawyer in town to represent your family and the child. This is worthy investment of every penny of our saving."

Seeing Lesha had stopped crying, Toni offered to sit with her, but she said, "Toni, I really appreciate your offer to sit beside me in my moments of grief, but I want to feel Deric's sprit in this seat. It might look empty but it is not. Don't worry! I'm not going crazy; I'm just feeling his presence," and sniffled with big smile.

***

The crowed outside of Boston International Airport was overwhelming. Lesha expected that her and Deric's families would be waiting for them. But what she saw was beyond her wildest dream. The multitude of clicking cameras, and pointed mics gave the airport exit a resemblance of the supreme court building after a decision on a highly polarized social issue.

Apparently, CNN had aired a breaking news of the controversial case of identity of the child with brain transplant. Some people in social medias picked up the news and took it further and said that a black couple went to France to claim the child as their daughter.

There were some among the crowed, including a few reporters who expected to see the child with Lesha.

***

Bini and Abigail were heading to their hotel from Saba's house, when she asked, "Bini, earlier you said that you felt something scary was following you; what was it?"

"Someone is following me."

"Who is that?"

"An assassin who is sent by the professor and his team."

"What makes you believe that?"

"Saba told me earlier that someone called her and said that they are friends of Million from school and wanted to know if recently a guy came from America to see her."

Abigail felt a lump in her stomach; she bit her bottom lip. "So, what did she say to the caller?" she asked in weak voice.

"She told him that nobody came to see her."

"She did great!"

"She said that because the call came before she met us."

"Why didn't you tell her not to tell anyone about us."

"What is the use of telling her?"

"Why wouldn't it be any use?"

"They tricked her to give them both her residence and work address. Which means they will send someone up to the door."

***

Abigail was driving their rental car on the main road. Bini noticed that after he told her about the possibility that someone was following them, she had started driving faster and glancing back, through the rearview mirror frequently. To direct her focus elsewhere, Bini came up with the idea that might cheer her up.

"Abigail, we are going to put my case on hold for a little while. It is your turn now; let me take you to a resort and swimming park that has natural hot water springs. We will come back after a couple of days of swimming and relaxing. Then, we will discuss and have strategies in place before we get back here."

She agreed with him, and said, "Where is the park?"

"It is called Soderea, about sixty-nine miles from here. It has lots of natural attraction, forests, wild animals, birds, rivers, mountains, and valleys."

"Sure; let's check it out! I love natural scenery."

***

They ate lunch at around 1 pm; then packed everything they needed for the Journey and by 3:30 pm they headed east.

With the sun reflecting behind them, the scene in the road looked a beautiful picture.

Around 5 pm, they arrived in Sodere, the swimming and recreational village. Though the surrounding area was warm with scattered trees. The actual relaxation spot, however, was close to the river, with dense trees count.

Because the day was Sunday, the area seemed a small town crowded with people. Multiple groups were eating and drinking in different spots. Kids were being kids.

Given the amount and intensity of the noise, Sodere insinuated a very crowded market, rather than a place where people come to relax and unwind.

The scene of monkeys jumping from one tree to another, from trees to the ground and after grabbing people's food, back to the trees, added fun to the place.

Million and Abigail went to the reception desk to claim the rooms they reserved over the phone. A helper took them to two rooms next to each other. They both liked their respective room. After putting away their stuff, they put on swimming clothes and headed to the pools.

They both jumped into the deepest side of one of the pools. Abigail loved swimming. She was enjoying her time.

She swam under water from one end to the other end of the pool.

Million was a man who never cared about any sport except swimming. He loved to swim. He was a fast and tireless swimmer. When he jumped in with Abigail, he was thinking of impressing her with his swimming skill and speed. However, the skill he thought he had, let alone to impress anyone, it was not enough to save his life. Despite his arms paddling and his legs kicking, he couldn't swim right. It seemed he was not able to coordinate his arms and legs. He felt his body getting tired and weak; so, he slowly returned to the edge.

He couldn't figure out why he was having a demanding time of swimming. After resting for a bit, he went in through the steps and tried to swim, but he just couldn't. A bystander who noticed Million struggling to swim said, "Why are you risking your life, you should go and swim in the shallow area of the pool, that is where new swimmers swim." That comment pissed Million off, but he didn't say anything to the commenter. Headstrongly, he tried to swim a short distance, but his body felt weak. He struggled, but he couldn't swim.

Abigail, while squeezing her hair to dry, searched for Million with her eyes. She saw him struggling. She ran and jumped in and pulled him with his hands out to the edge. Holding the railing, he fought to catch his breath. Because he couldn't swim, the effort he invested to save his life wore him out. He was exhausted; too exhausted even to talk.

Still trying to catch his breath, he said, "I don't understand why I'm unable to swim. I never get tired like this even after twenty laps. I'm worried, I might have some problem that weakens my body."

"Right now, it is better if you sit and rest. Don't worry about it; your body will do self-correction in a timely fashion. I will do a whole-body exam, to see if there is any change since the last check. By the way, have you taken your medication that you are supposed to take today?"

"Yes, I have been taking all my meds as ordered."

"All the health assessments I made on you since your arrival indicate that you are doing well. Anyway, you should get some rest."

"You enjoy your swimming while I go lay down in my room for a little bit. When you're done, we will go out for dinner."

"We have to go together so I can examine you." Abigail brought her examining tools to Million's room and assessed him. "I don't think you have the health issue that I suspected. Everything is working as it is supposed to, so, you shouldn't be worrying about anything. Now, take a break, and I will come back in an hour for us to go to dinner. I'd like to think that they have nice food here."

***

When the spy arrived at Saba's neighborhood, around five pm Sunday local time, Million and Abigail were unwinding in Soderea. He hung out close to Saba's place, but no one came in or out of the house. He waited there until midnight.

The next day, he stayed in the vicinity from six am until eleven pm, however, let alone Million, no human male came to the house, as if the place was a women's monastery that was forbidden for male visitors. Worried that hanging out around that area any longer might trigger suspicion from the residents, he reported his findings to his boss in the US.

Back in the States, those who were given the homework sat down for discussion. One of them said, "I had suspicion that he would not go to his wife and kids because he knows that they would think of him a stranger."

"Maybe he went to Amin's family because he looks like Amin," said another participant.

A third input from another team member surfaced, "Though it is possible that Amin's family might accept him, assuming that they believed the news of Amin's death was fabricated, this guy doesn't know any of them. They are strangers to him. Therefore, he will never go to them."

Finally, everyone accepted the idea that he may be in hiding because he was informed or suspected that someone was after him. Hence, new strategies of hunting and getting rid of him developed.

Million/Amin needed to be searched in every hotel and motel in town—the surveillance of Saba's house to continue with new agents assigned daily.

Also, Amin’s family and friends should be recruited to inform local reps if they see Amin or someone who looks like him. And a close contact to be started with Amin’s wife.

Before the close of the meeting, one of them took the assignment of establishing the contact with Amin's wife by calling directly from Boston.

***

Back in France, Ava, who was shaken by the news of Mr. Johns death had decided to drop the charges she had filed in criminal courts. Instead, after consulting with her attorneys, she determined to file a civil case requesting a restraining order against Mrs. Johns.

***

The restaurant in Soderea was thronged by diners, and the aroma of different foods was attracting more eaters. Million and Abigail found a table for two on the back right of the dining area. Million noticed the hosts were serving orders of roasted chicken with other side dishes to neighboring tables. Seeing that, he lusted for chicken. When their host came, Million ordered roasted chicken and lamb.

Abigail, after looking through the menu, ordered pasta and vegetables. They also ordered drinks.

While they were eating their appetizers, Abigail thought about Million’s order, and said, “I think the meat you ordered is not going to be fully cooked. It could have some serious health issues. So, it is best if you don’t eat it.”

"Doctor, thank you for your advice, but in our culture, we have a unique way of eating meat. Look at the table at three o'clock from you and notice what and how they are eating," he said pointing with his chin.

She looked to the table and saw a group of people eating something that they cut with a knife holding one end with their teeth and the other end with their free hand. They were a little further, so, she couldn't tell what they were eating. She asked, "Are they eating meat?"

"Not any kind of meat, they are eating straight raw meat."

"Wow! I got to see that close up. Would it bother them, if I go see and take a picture?"

"Ask them, they may give you permission."

Fascinated, she went and looked closer and confirmed what they were eating was raw meat. Impressed by what and how they were eating it, she asked their permission to take a photo of them in action, cutting and eating the meat that they stretched between their teeth and their left hands. She thanked them for allowing her to take the picture and went back to Million.

"Million, I do not doubt that these people will catch some serious disease. Because there could be different disease hosts in the meat," said Abigail, feeling that she had a professional obligation for health education anywhere and anytime.

"Abigail, the meat is fresh. Also, raw meat is one of the cultural foods of Ethiopians. So far, there haven't been any issue related to eating raw meat compared to cooked."

"How can they feed on raw meat? It is carnivorous."

"How come you eat foliage?" he asked, looking at the salad on her plate. "It is a matter of preference," he added.

Still puzzled by what she saw, she started looking around for another odd thing. She saw some people rolling and eating an orange, creamy stuff in a piece of a cloth looking thing. She asked, "What is that creamy stuff that they are rolling and eating in the cloth looking thing?"

"It is not cream. It is one of the prominent traditional sauces of the country, it is called "shiro wot." The stuff in which they are rolling the shiro with is not a piece of cloth, rather it is the spongy bread that I told you about, Injera, it is made of the unique grain called teff."

"Is it properly cooked? Your diets seem rather peculiar. And it differs in many ways from that of other countries. I wonder if they received coverage in food and travel channels," she wondered, impressed by the uniqueness.

***

Bini and Abigail were halfway through their dinner when Million decided to share what was on his mind. "Abigail, how do you suggest I approach my family? I still miss my parents, even though I'm happy that I have seen both my brother and sister, it hurts me that I can't express brotherly love to them and that they don't know I'm their brother to reciprocate."

"Yes, that is one of the issues we haven't addressed yet.

Your wife and your parents frequently meet, right?"

"Yes, they do."

"Well, she might have already told them about Million's best friend, Bini. After all, your sister knows you now as Biniam. Therefore, that is who you are to your parents too. But it is very important that you control your emotions when acting as Biniam. Even though it will take a little time, they will eventually know you as Million."

"I'm someone they saw dead and buried. How could they dismiss that? This is the question I haven't found an answer for," said Million, imagining the perplexing nature of the matter.

"Of course, it is a complicated. Remember, the two true but opposite facts we talked about last time? They apply equally to your parents and siblings as they do to your wife and kids. They apply to everyone who knew you before and attended the burial of your dead body. The two true but opposite facts are about one person, you.

"However, these facts won't remain opposite. It will take your patience and hard work to create the illusion of your aliveness. Then, only then, as much as you struggle to introduce yourself to them, they will start looking for Million in Bini."

"Also, you might need to show them the story about brain transplant and its results, and the media coverage about it. Show or explain to them the child's chance of living in someone else's body. When they realize that the child could live in another girl's body, they will start to understand your story or situation. I'm sure there is a video of the story about the child on YouTube.

"You could also get your old body exhumed. Though it might already be disintegrated, the skull will still have the opening that was cracked to take your brain out. The other evidence is the big fracture and repair on the back of your skull, which is made to replace Amin's brain with yours. But before you get to that evidence, by bringing old memories, help them develop the question, "Could Biniam be Million?" She took a couple of sips from her wine and continued.

"We both know, the case is inherently a mess and sensitive, so, you have a lot of work ahead of you to steer it clean.

"Another thing, as soon as the research center receives its permit, the work will become legal. You, as the first result of a brain transplant, I will work with the center to make sure that you receive the worldwide recognition that you deserve. After that, it will be easy for you to explain your situation to anyone. In the meantime, you will need to be patient, and mentally and emotionally strong."

***

When Lesha received a call from her attorney with the

news of Ms. Murphy dropping the criminal charge that were filed both in France and the US, she was preparing for two court dates, one as a defendant for harassment and child abduction charge, and another one as plaintiff to establish kinship with the child whom the researchers called TS Harvard.

***

They were quietly walking back from the restaurant to their rooms, when Abigail decided to touch base on a topic that was in the back of her head. "Don't you think our hunters are close to us? What do you suggest we do? I think going back to your wife's place is exposing oneself to danger."

"You are right, we need to stay low for a while. In fact, I'm thinking if we should split. I don't want the bullet fired at me to hit you."

"No, we are not separating, we should stay together and watch each other's back."

***

The next day, Sodere was a lot sedated. There weren't as many people as there were the day before. At 6 am Million and Abigail headed to the swimming area. Though the sun hadn't come out, it wasn't cold. A warm breeze was blowing.

The crowded and noisy place of yesterday was very quiet and tranquil. Abigail felt as if tranquility had some physical presence. "It would be great if every dawn was like this," she said, staring fixated as far as she could see.

They arrived at the farthest swimming area from their rooms. The calmness of the surroundings could awaken a childhood joyfulness of jumping and running. The evaporating steam from the warm water made the pool look like a saucepan filled with boiling water. There were only two people in the pool. Looking from a few meters through the steam, they looked like natural decorations of that beautiful place. Monkeys were jumping from tree to tree.

Melodies of birds and the sound uttered by other animals simulated a pleasing orchestra conducted by nature.

"This is exactly how getting away from the intrusive noise of a city feels like," said Bini after quietly enjoying the beautiful view and sounds of daybreak.

The sun started to come out, the light from the sun penetrating the morning fog of the hot spring water created a beautiful light prism and rainbow. The scene looked like the astonishing work of a talented artist rather than a natural phenomenon.

Below the swimming area, Awash river ran through the rift. Looking down, one could see trees that had grown on the banks of the river. Half of their branches rested on the moving water, they looked as if they were bowing to the river. Awash river moved calmly with grace, therefore, at a glance, it looked as if it was standing still. In the morning, lack of reflection from the sun gave it a resemblance of a well-constructed new asphalt road.

***

While enjoying the sound of nature, Abigail started stretching by the pool. Bini noticed that she was preparing to run. He hated running. He used to joke, "The only time I would run is if I see something scary coming toward me. Otherwise, I get exhausted just from seeing others run."

"The reason you got tired when swimming yesterday could be because your body parts, especially your muscles weren't moving as they were supposed to. Maybe you should run a short distance at a moderate speed, then we will do some strengthening exercises followed by a shower. After that, you might swim better," said Abigail sounding self-assured.

He said, "There is nothing that I hate and that exhausts me as much as running. So, please allow me to stretch through walking."

"For sure, walking is good too. However, unless you walk for a long time, it doesn't replace a good run of a couple of laps. Also, running awakens each and every individual part of your body and forces it to engage."

"I understand its benefits, the only problem is that I get tired as soon as I run just a little bit," he said, and started jogging with her.

They started slow and gradually sped up. Impressed by his tolerance of the first round, he kept with her for another three rounds. On the fourth round, they sprinted to race. She beat him by a few seconds. However, she was winded and breathless, while he was still strong and ready to go for more.

He didn't know what to make of his sudden strength and appetite for running.

Seeing how great he ran with her, Abigail thought he was joking when he told her about his dislike and lack of tenacity of running. She said, "I almost believed you when you said you don't like running."

"I wasn't lying about that. This is amazing! I have no explanation how, yesterday, I had trouble swimming, an activity I love, and I know I'm good at, and today I'm running the best I could have imagined. I know the two activities use different muscles, but the strength and tolerance needed should be similar, right?" said Bini, truly puzzled.

"I have an idea, let's take a shower, then go swimming and see how you do. Maybe you were tired yesterday."

***

Swimming back from the other end of the pool, Abigail saw Million struggling to get out of the water. She swam fast and pulled him to the rail.

"Million, are you pulling my leg? Or you really are having hard time swimming?"

"No, Abigail, I almost drowned. I don't know what is going on with me. I swam all my life and I was good at it," he said after catching his breath.

"Sorry Bini! I'm not sure what is going on either, but if I were to guess, it has to do with your new body. To be sure, I have to examine you more and you should probably run a little bit and see how you do," she said walking with him to the rinsing station.

After they both rinsed, he started running. He stopped after two laps at a sprint pace around the pool. "Abigail, I think you are right. Now that I think of it, Amin had told me that he used to be a professional runner. Maybe he wasn't a good swimmer," said Bini smiling big.

"That makes a total sense."

"But, isn't it my brain that instructs this or my old body. It should have made it swim to save my life."

"I understand your point, but remember if a right-handed person loses that hand, he or she has to train the left to do what the right did and it might take years for the left to gain the skills. It is not because the brain couldn't instruct the left hand, it is because it takes longer to train a body or its part to adopt new dexterity."

***

Amin's brother, Ahmed picked up a phone and said "Hello, who is this?" with extra emphasis on the question.

"My name is Eyob, and I'm calling from America. Amin was my friend here at the school. The reason for my call is to express my condolences to his family, may I please speak with his widow?"

"It is for you," said Ahmed and gave the phone to Barakat. "Hello, who is this?" she inquired.

"My name is Eyob, Amin's friend from America. I'm very sorry for your loss. We are all saddened by his death. I meant to call sooner, but we have been very busy with school work. I wish we could come in person, but the distance and the school work have made it impossible. My condolences!"

"Thank you! Did you happen to attend his funeral?"

"No, sorry! I wasn't able to. By the way, in the last few days, did someone from America visit you?"

"Like who?" Asked Barakat, sounding confused.

"No one came from here?"

"No one has come to me from America. Was someone supposed to come?"

"Yes, another student, he has come to see his family in Addis, so we sent you a little condolence gift with him."

"No, no one has come," she said.

"I'm sure he will be coming soon. Again, sorry for your loss. May Allah grant you comfort."

"Thank you so much!"

"I will call you during my next school break, which is not too far. In the meantime, take care of yourself."

"Okay, you as well!"

After he hung up the phone, he thought, *A diaspora from the States, who recently moved to Ethiopia should go visit her, then collect all the information that could help track Million.*

***

A couple of days later, a tall man, who looked in his late thirties came to see Barakat. He introduced himself as Brook. Sitting on the couch not far from her, he started to narrate how he knew Amin, and everything he heard about the accident. He showed her a picture of him with Amin, Eyob and a couple of other friends.

Barakat, looking at the picture sobbed. Then she stopped and started to tell the guest everything without holding back. She told him how much she loved Amin, that their marriage was great, and now how her kids became fatherless. Then she continued crying.

While Brook was trying to comfort her, Ahmed entered the house without knocking on the door. Seeing Brook, he frowned. Looking at Barakat and the guest with narrowed eyes, he sat on the sofa.

“Hello sir, my name is Brook,” said the stranger.

Ahmed said nothing.

Barakat, tried to cheer the guest up, thinking that his feelings would be hurt. She was also worried that the jealous and suspicious Ahmed would harass her after Brook left. She was stressed out judging Ahmed’s animosity toward Brook.

Brook, realizing Ahmed’s discomfort with his presence, said, “goodbye!” and got up to leave. Barakat got up with him and as if to close the gate, she followed him. Outside, she gave him the address to her store and told him that he could come there.

***

Brook came to Barakat’s store on the day and time of their appointment. There, they talked without apprehension. Barakat, without suspicion that the man could have a hidden agenda, she poured her heart out to him.

"By the way, sorry I left abruptly the other day. I could tell the elderly man wasn't comfortable with my presence. Is he your dad?"

Sad and ashamed of being a wife of a man who was twice her age, she said, "No, he is my husband."

"Come again? Why would a young and beautiful girl like you marry such an old man? It is not like you couldn't find a man of your age."

She sighed and said nothing for a few seconds, then she began her narration, "There is more to it. It is long and more complicated story. He is Amin's brother."

"This is crazy! You are married to a man who could be your father, he also the brother of your dead husband. I don't believe you chose to marry him—you must have been forced," said Brook, analyzing the strangeness of the story.

"Maybe it has to do with the freak side of life. It is like winning the lottery of something you hate, except you didn't play the game. I'm just living the rest of my life for the sake of my kids," she said and sighed long and deep.

"Sorry, I don't mean to stress you out by asking questions that are not my business. Now, let's leave that there and talk about some other topic." He waited to get her attention and said, "From our conversation the other day, I gathered that you loved Amin dearly. How would you feel, if somebody would tell you he is in town?"

"I would have to be lucky for such a thing to happen. His case is like spilled water. What I want to know is, did you guys bury his body?" she said, remembering her other heartbreak, not be able to say goodbye to her husband's body when it was put to its resting place.

"How do you happen to ask me such a question? Is there anything that you have heard?" He asked to dig to see if she might have recently heard about Amin.

"No, I didn't hear anything. I was just hoping that you would tell me how his funeral went, if you were present."

"I wish I could have been present and told you something about it. In America, unlike in our country, most funerals are performed only by individuals who are trained and are experienced in doing that," he said hoping she wouldn't ask a difficult follow up question.

After they chatted for another half hour on other topics, he left, promising that he would come some other time.

That night, the spy, who named himself Brook, called Boston and reported what he learned from speaking to Barakat.

"She is married to Amin's brother, he is an elderly man, more than twice her age. He is a jealous and suspicious man who is insecure. My take on him is that if he saw Amin in the vicinity, he would not hesitate to kill him."

The man who introduced himself as Eyob received the report and concluded that Ahmed was the best weapon whose trigger could be pulled from Boston to kill Million.

Chapter Ten

The team of researchers of the center gathered together to hear an update and discuss the status of the search for Million/Amin. After he fled to his country, where did he disappear to? No one could tell. If his case went public, the center and the researchers would fall into the swamp that they could never came out of. Thus, they were sitting and discussing the matter. Different ideas came from around the table.

After hearing an updates from Eyob, the team developed new strategy of killing Million and that involved Ahmed and possibly other Amin's family.

***

Other, current and reporting worthy news were overshadowing the once hot news about the research on brain transplants, and the first beneficiary of such a trial. Then the report about the homicide of an American man in Paris, and the association of the deceased with the girl who received brain transplant surfaced.

***

CNN's news man was back on the air. He said, "As we promised to our viewers, we are back with details of the little girl's case. These two questions: is she Caucasian or African-American? and whose daughter is she? are related, but different. As far as the court is concerned, it is the second, not the first question that matters. In the next few minutes, you will have a better understanding of why. YB firm is the proud sponsor of this episode of the show."

After a couple of commercials, the host came to the screen and said, "The Caucasian family has presented documents, such as birth certificate, vaccination, and hospital records to prove that the girl is their biological daughter. They also have personal witnesses who know that the child is theirs.

However, the little girl has expressed that the African-American couple are her parents. Also, people close to the case have reported that she has been heard talking in great details about her alleged grandparents from both sides of the couple. No, she wasn't stolen after birth and raised by the African-American family, as some of you are commenting on social media."

***

The question, "Is the little girl Sandra or Teena or a different person?" had become a topic of discussion both in a courtroom and all forms of media. Different media outlets were covering the court proceeding live.

Besides the court case, media began to report about the scientific breakthrough that the girl was the result of. Then the controversy around the research concentrated immediately.

***

One Wednesday, around 6:30 pm, Bini and Abigail went to his parents' place. They knocked on the gate, and his sister, Machida, opened it. Considering they had met a few days back; he couldn't be any happier that she answered the gate. He addressed her by name and hugged her.

To Machida, he was still a stranger, she was still confused by how he reacted when he saw her in Saba's house. She sensed that he knew her from somewhere, but she couldn't recall where she knew him or if she even knew him at all. She admitted that his demeanor had some form of familiarity. She'd thought about him multiple times since the day of their awkward meeting. This man knew her, but she didn't know him—how could it be? She had been confused since.

"Is the family available?" he asked.

"Who? Mom and Dad? Do you know them too? Bini, you are strange. Come in anyway, they are here. Abigail, come in. How do you like Ethiopia, so far?" she said smiling at him, then locking eyes with Abigail.

Though he knew she didn't know him, he was very happy to see his sister. Despite his excitement and eagerness to see his parents, he felt uncomfortable and anxious about actually seeing them. His anxiety started to rise with each step of walking closer to them.

The puzzle that their son, whose body they buried with tears and heartbreak was alive and had come to see them was something his parents couldn't imagine solving. Only Million knew the puzzle, and he was hopeful that the key to its solution would come to him soon.

His parents were in the living room having coffee. He kissed them both, and they kissed him back, except their awareness was confused, and their approaches were cold. When they saw Abigail, they guessed the guests were from some other country. After saying hi to Abigail, they invited them both to have seats.

Following a short eye contact, he said, "Father, how are you? What about you, Mother, how have you been?" still with the sense of belongingness of a son enquiring his parents about their wellbeing.

They replied that they were doing well. His mom sat quietly with her head down.

He noticed both of them looked much older than he saw them last. Their eye sights seemed weaker, they had lost weight, and his dad was having watery eyes. Everything about them screamed to him that they had been enduring grief.

His tears rolled down his face. He wanted to stop, so as not to make them cry, but he couldn't hold it together. They began to flow down as a water from a dam burst. That followed with intense sobbing and mourning. As he had feared, the whole family joined him, and his parents began to cry bitterly.

The thought of his parents' suffering grieving his death, added to his own vivid feeling of loneliness, intensified his sorrow. He continued to sob unconsolably. Abigail knew most of the reasons for his sadness. She found her sympathy for him growing, so her tears started to roll down her face.

He continued to cry his heart out. His family's mourning exacerbated and kept crying with him. They were crying because of his death—he was crying because his physical nonexistence hurt his family and because of the deep loneliness that had left him with. Then Abigail whispered in his ear, "Bini, by crying, you are making your family sadder. Please stop crying now. Everything will be all right, and the sad things will be forgotten soon."

His dad said, "Let's not cry anymore. If tears were to bring my son back, we have been shedding it since the news of his passing. Tomorrow, we are all like him, so please stop crying."

Slowly, everyone calmed down and tranquility rose in the house.

His dad, "My son, I do not recognize you, I suspect my wife doesn't either, who are you? Etabeba, do you know this young man?" he asked looking at Bini, then turning toward his wife.

"No, I don't," replied the mother after a glance at Biniam.

"Sir, yes, I just came from Germany. My name is Biniam. I'm a very close friend of Million. This lady is my coworker. She is visiting our country."

"So, how is life in foreign land?" he asked sighing lengthily.

"Life in Germany is rushed. People are busy with work, so they don't have enough time to relax. Other than that, it is all right," he said, looking down. He was feeling slightly comforted by crying out his built-up pain.

Biniam got up and fetched a bag he had brought with him. He knew his family's choices, so, he was confident that they would be satisfied with the gifts in it.

Their happiness was his satisfaction. This time, again, as with his wife and kids, he was curious to know how they felt.

Someone knocked on the door, and the father said, "Come in."

It was Million's brother, Aman. As soon as they saw each other, both of them began thinking about their interaction at the airport. Bini, fighting the urge of going and hugging him tightly, stood and shook his hand.

Seeing the strange man from the airport in his house, startled Aman. At the time of their interaction at the airport, this guy had concluded Million had mistaken him for someone and didn't think of it since. However, seeing him in his house, he thought, "I'm sure he knew me."

Looking at his brother, the memory of them playing together as kids and helping each other as adults rushed to his mind. Consumed by lust for brotherly love and fighting to control his emotions, he said, "You must be Million's brother. My name is Bini, a close friend of your brother."

"Hi, Bini, actually, we met before," said Aman, looking at Bini in the eye.

"Oh! Really? Where?" asked Bini raising his eyebrows.

Abigail, impressed by her friend's ability to act surprised, smiled big.

"A few days ago, at the airport. You two were standing by the door," said Aman, looking at Abigail, then back at Bini.

"I guess, it is possible," said Bini.

Another round of coffee was made for the guests, and they were all chatting. Bini opened the luggage and handed clothes and shoes to each one of his family members. Despite their satisfaction with the gifts, they all had unanswered questions. *How did he know everyone's size of both the clothes and shoes?*

They stared at each other. But none of them felt courageous enough to ask the question. Instead, they all thanked him with a smile.

Seeing, all who were crying earlier smiling, Bini felt alive. Their happiness gave him pleasure.

Abigail was taking pictures and recording videos of his family's interaction with Million as she'd done when he met his wife and kids.

***

After the guests left, the family started to talk about the gifts Bini brought them. Aman raised the question that was on everyone's mind. "How did he know what size fits each of us?"

"Maybe your brother told him about it," said his dad.

Machida considered Bini some kind of mystery man. So, she said, "Father, this guy is special."

"How do you mean?" asked her dad.

"He did the same thing with Saba and the kids' clothes and shoes."

"So, what is surprising about it? He could have asked and learned," argued the father.

"Dad, it is more than that." She decided to explain herself more, "You see, a while ago, Million and Saba went to a wedding party. At the party, there was a woman who came from abroad, and she wore a nice dress and shoes and a nice neckless on. Saba told Million her admiration of what the woman wore. Million promised her that he would bring her from abroad if he ended up going. So, how did this man know all that?"

"Daughter, that is not surprising either," said the father again.

"But, father, I'm not sure if you understand it. He did something unique," said Machida, sounding slightly frustrated.

"I also noticed something that impressed me. When he and the white woman were leaving the airport, I asked them to let me through the door that they stood blocking. He didn't see me; he only heard my voice from the back. He turned around and tried to embrace me, then he stopped as if he realized that I'm not the person he thought I was. Then he said to me something that I didn't understand," said Aman.

"Since you brought it up, he called me Machid, when I entered Saba's house. He didn't see me; he only heard my voice. How did he know who I was? I have never seen the man before, how did he know my name. Another interesting thing he did, when he and his friend were served food, they got up to wash their hands, he went straight to the bathroom with his friend following him. He didn't ask where it was, he just knew where to go. As you know, Saba's bathroom is not easy to find for someone new to the house."

"Well, I too have observed something strange in that man," said their mother. "Have any of you noticed the clothes and shoes he wore? They look exactly Million's. Even the bleach mark on Million's pants was there."

***

Meanwhile, the court proceedings about the identity of the little girl continued with lawyers of each family presenting their cases and evidence for an argument.

The attorney of the black family conferred, "Your honor, before we proceed with the case of requesting for parental right to Ms. Sandra Johns, we would like to remind the court that the child is under coercive electroconvulsive and brain wash therapy that compromises her mental and physical health. Therefore, we implore the court to place her with a court assigned custody effective immediately, until the decision for parental right is reached. Thank you!"

"Your honor, we would like to straighten the record, we do not know who the plaintiff is speaking in regard to. My client's daughter's name is Ms. Teena Soprano and there is no apparent reason for her to be removed from her biological mom, Ms. Murphy, temporarily or permanently. Thus, we request the court to dismiss the case all together," contended the attorney for the White family.

"Your honor, my clients were approached by a child who claimed that she is their daughter. After a serious deliberation, they discovered that the child is recipient of their late daughter's brain, which was removed, then transplanted into her head without their consent. After they learned the fact, my clients asked permission from the defendant to spend some quality time with the child.

"However, the defendant had my clients thrown to prison in foreign land. As the result, Mr. Johns died. This case is under investigation, thus I can't go in to details. Going back to the case in this court, my client would like to establish parenthood of the child, and be given custody. Your honor, we would still like to stress the need for removal and placement of the child with a court assigned custody. At the moment, as shown on the evidence we presented, the physical and mental wellbeing of the child is at risk. Basically, there is an urgent safety risk that needs to be addressed before anything else."

"Your honor, my client, Ms. Murphy acknowledges that her daughter had an organ transplant, a brain, and she paid over one and half million dollars. Nowadays, it is a common knowledge that all donated organs take time to adjust to the recipients' body. Miss. Soprano's donated brain has been going through a similar process. Unlike other organs, the brain came with both good and bad memories that the donor had accumulated, and Miss. Soprano has been suffering from the bad ones.

"To put it lightly, her old memories have been getting her into multiple innocent troubles. The plaintiffs are not the first and won't be the last victims of her approaching with accurate familiarity. Unfortunately, the position they were at due to the loss of their daughter, made them more susceptible. We understand the plaintiff's suffering as the consequence and we hereby formally apologize. Also, we are willing to settle any monitory compensations in a civil court. Hence, we respectfully request this court to dismiss this case."

"Let's cut to the chase—we are not here for sympathy, apology, or money. We are here to seek justice for the child who has been forced to live with people whom she is not familiar with. We are here to seek justice for Miss. Sandra Johns, who has been forced to answer to names she doesn't want to be called by. We are here to seek justice of stopping the violent electroconvulsive and brain wash therapy she is being subjected to. We are here to seek justice for Mr. Johns, who was send to prison only because he asked to spend a few minutes with a child who has his daughter's brain. We are here to ask the court to award custody of little Miss. Johns to her mom, Ms. Lesha Johns."

"Your honor, even if we entertain the hypothesis that Miss. Soprano's transplanted brain once belonged to the late daughter of the plaintiff, and they want it back, they should ask the hospital they donated to, not my client. It happened to be that particular brain that matched better to Miss. Soprano's body, otherwise, any other brain could have been and would be transplanted into her. Please instruct the plaintiff to deal with the hospital and leave my client out of it."

After hearing both sides' arguments, the court scheduled

another hearing and adjourned.

***

Two friends, a man and woman, came in to a restaurant where Million and Abigail just had lunch. The friends sat down, chatting, on the left side of the entrance. Million and Abigail were enjoying their coffee at three o'clock to the man. After sitting comfortably, he casually glanced toward Million and Abigail.

He tried to immerse back to the conversation he was having with his companion, but he couldn't because his attention shifted to deciding whether he saw whom he thought or not. Without totally ignoring his friend, he looked toward who drew his attention. However, this time, he didn't glance back—he stared at Million.

Million noticed the man staring at him, but he didn't make of it anything, he turned his full attention to Abigail and the topic they were discussing. A few seconds later, Million glanced to find the man still staring at him. He started to become vigilant but not nervous.

The man went on to talk with his companion about who he saw. Then they both looked at him. Million started to get annoyed by the man.

Abigail noticed the slight unease on her friend and that his attention was being drawn by something. She followed his direction of sight and tried to check what he saw, but she didn't see anything new. "Million, what is up? You seem anxious."

He turned toward her. Acting as if nothing happened, he said, “Oh, nothing! I’m all right!”

The man, after whispering something with the woman, came toward Million.

Million’s caution escalated to protection. Mentally, he started preparing a plan of stopping the man before he hurt Abigail or himself. However, the man’s smile grew the closer he got to Million.

Then Million’s nerves began to calm down. He didn’t know him, but he assured himself that he didn’t come to hurt him. Million stretched his hand for a handshake as soon as the man came close to them. The man seemed to have realized that Million didn’t recognize him. So, he said, “Do you not recognize me? I’m Awet.”

“I’m sorry, but I don’t remember where I know you,” said Million, still trying to remember where he knew the man.

“Amin! I hope you’re kidding! You could never forget me, even if you tried to,” said the man confidently.

This time, spooked, Million replied, “No, no sir, you are mistaken, I’m not who you said.”

“Yes! Of course, you are Amin. How could you say you are not? I’m Awet—we used to run together. I know it has been a while since we have seen each other. When I heard you went to America for higher education, I couldn’t be any happier for you. Anyway, do you not still remember me?

“You know me very well unless you want to say you

forgot me," said the man, wondering why Amin denied him.

Million understood where the man was coming from, but he didn't know what to say. "Again, I'm sorry, but I'm not the person, who you suppose I'm. My name is Million," he said.

The man stood erect and said, "Come on, how could it be? Why are you kidding me?"

"Could it be a coincidence that I look like your friend? Either way, I'm not whom you are referring to," said Million firmly.

"But you are. When are you going to stop joking? Oh, brother! Did going abroad make you forget your old friends. Or, you married a white girl, and you decided to ignore us? That is ridiculous! It shouldn't be that way," said the man, snooping at Abigail.

"I'm not joking, brother! In fact, I have never been in any formal training of any sport. Also, I'm new to this country. There are so many look-alikes in the world. It is not surprising that I look like your friend. If I knew you, I would have liked to call you by your name. If I were a runner, I would have been proud of it. I wish I had the tenacity to become a runner. I'm just a guest in this country," said Million, hoping that he would leave him alone.

"It is hard for me to believe this. How could my mind accept it?" murmured the man.

Million knew Amin's ethnicity. "Did you say your name is Awet?"

"Do you not know my name that you are asking me?" he said with a difficulty accepting the difference between what he was seeing, and was hearing.

"Brother, I'm not playing. I want to make it clear that you don't know me. Therefore, it helps if you just answer me. Because I might help you accept that we don't know each other."

"I'm Awet. Okay, let's see how you are going to make me believe that the person whom I know like the back of my hand would have confused him with some look-alike. I'm still sure you are Amin."

"Do you speak Tigrigna?" asked Million.

Awet didn't like the question, but he answered anyway; "Yes!"

"Does your friend, Amin, speak Tigrigna?"

"No, he does not, he speaks only Amharic and Afaan-Oromo."

"Then, this is a good opportunity that will convince you that I'm not him," he said, feeling a relief that he found a point to convince the man. He continued, but this time in Tigrigna, rather than in Amharic. "I speak Tigrigna. You could ask me any question in Tigrigna."

Awet, confused by the fluent Tigrigna he heard from Million, he asked, "How could this be?" He didn't know what to say. He just mumbled "Sorry!" and left to his seat.

Million sighed deep and long.

Abigail seemed more relieved because the man left. She

was annoyed by the guy's argument that she didn't even understand. She asked, "What was he saying to you?"

"He is an old friend of Amin. He argued that I'm Amin and that I shouldn't act like I don't know him."

"Then, what did you say to him?"

"I told him that I don't know him. That it could be a matter of similarity. But he insisted that I'm Amin and that I could never be anybody else but him."

"That is crazy! How did you stop the argument then?"

"From hearing his name, I figured out that he is from my ethnic group. I also knew that Amin was from another ethnic group. After confirming that Amin didn't speak the language that our ethnic group speaks, which is Tigrigna, I spoke to him in that language. That did it! He said sorry and left."

"If you didn't come up with such a brilliant idea, it is safe to say that, he wouldn't have left," said Abigail, impressed by his creativeness. She continued, "You see, what I told you at the swimming place is correct."

"What did you tell me?"

"I told you that your current body is that of a runner's."

"Oh that! You are right."

***

Awet, as soon as he sat down, "Have you ever been forced to choose between believing what you are seeing or what you are hearing about one thing?" he asked his lady companion. Before, she answered. He told her everything about the incident. "I still don't know what to make of this. I see my old friend Amin. But then he tells me he is not, in fluent Tigrigna. The Amin I know spoke only Afaan-Oromo and Amharic. How could he have learned to speak Tigrigna fluently within such a short time? Learning to speak fluent Tigrigna in two years is rather impossible. Despite what I heard, whom I saw is a hundred percent, Amin."

His friend found everything he told her to be a bit strange. "How could it be?" she asked impressed. But then, she wondered why he wouldn't let it go. At the same instant, she decided to see the matter from his perspective.

Awet couldn't stop thinking about Amin's pretension. While ruminating his believes, one idea came to his mind.

***

Except Abigail, no one in Ethiopia knew that Amin was the physical manifestation of Million. Even those who were hired to kill him didn't know the person they were IDing from the photo their recruiter sent them was not the ultimate game.

Million believed, for him to be considered alive, he had to play at two theatres simultaneously, but with different stage names.

At home and around family, he acted as the childhood friend of himself, named Biniam. On official and legal entities, he trouped as Amin. He accepted both dramaturgy painfully but with the hope, one day, they would help him reveal his hidden stage, where he would play as Million. He realized, truth obliged to be handled carefully, because, if not revealed at the right time and place, its unintended impacts could be devastating.

***

It had been a little while since Million started playing as the lead character of his life's drama with the stage name, Biniam, and his parents accepted him as the beloved friend of their beloved son. He loved his family. Especially his sister. She was his only sister and he knew how she used to love him. He liked to spend time with her.

Machida too, loved to spend time with Bini. The mystery of him speaking and doing things the way her brother used to intensified her love for him. Her curiosity about him continued to grow with each passing hour. She was worried that he was becoming a puzzle whose number of pieces increased every day.

She believed no one understood her as much as he did. In fact, she was convinced that he possessed all qualities she required from a man, and began imagining spending the rest of her life with him.

Machida's family noticed and honored their daughter's flourishing relationship with Bini. They believed Bini dominated all the criteria they expected from a son in-law and started entertaining the idea of the two of them getting married.

Machida's love for Bini was blocking the sense of her brother Million she was perceiving from him when they first started hanging out. Actually, him suiting her brother's personality soothed her belief.

Million was getting frustrated noticing Machida's confusion and misinterpretation of his brotherly gestures. He thwarted more and more, imagining the lack of a specific day when he could disclose the truth.

***

Chapter Eleven

The complexity and the uniqueness of the case seemed to weigh on lawyers from both sides. Each argument revealed the case's innate perplexity and began to reflect its sophistication. With the hope of getting a scientific explanation, the court instructed the researchers to testify. However, they refused, reasoning that the point of argument was out of their expertise.

The court listened the counselors assert their relative case for a long time. Then, the day when the judges would decide came. On that day, the courtroom was packed with people who came to be part of history in such a perpetuated court case. The security in and outside the courtroom was tight.

The courtroom aisle that divided plaintiffs and defendants' seats looked wider than usual. In the hallway and outside of the courthouse, people had formed lines.

The little girl was sitting to the left of the judge with her court assigned custodian. Until the judge took his bench and along the way drew the audiences' attention, everyone's eyes were on her.

The judge hit the sound block twice with his gavel. Everyone in the courthouse and the hallway hushed and began to wait on what the judge would say. "I have to admit—throughout my career of thirty years as a judge, this is the most complex case I have had the privilege to sit for. This case is the first of its kind. There are no references and no rules that govern this kind of case. Either way, the rights of parent and child should be established. The court, therefore, has listened to arguments from both sides, testimony from witnesses, and interviewed this young girl who is the center of the case. Despite the difficulty and complexity of the case, the court has made a decision."

At that moment, the courtroom was so quiet that it seemed everyone could hear the sound of his or her heart beating. The clock ticked, and the judge shuffled a few papers as he gathered his thoughts and will.

The judge continued, "The child could walk and talk due to the combination of the two body parts that came one from each family. Her brain used to be that of the defendants' daughter, Sandra, and her body used to be that of the plaintiff's daughter, Teena. However, defendants acquired the brain from the hopital. Therefore, this girl's whole body, torso plus brain belongs to the defendant."

Hearing the judge's last sentence, Ava almost passed out from excitement. Her face glowed, adding beauty to her incredible elegance. She looked at those around her on the counsels' table and the gallery behind her with a smile. Her fans and supporters gave her congratulatory looks.

Families and friends of the Johns couldn't believe what they heard. They all gave Lesha a sad look. Lesha's tears began to roll down her face. She looked up to the ceiling and mumbled something.

The noise from the winning team, the losing team, and the neutral team gave the courtroom resemblance of an indoor stadium. The judge called for attention and started reading the next page, "Her intangible part, moral being, personhood, idea, and most of all her self-awareness is assessed by professionals in the fields of psychology and philosophy. She also stood in this courtroom as a witness and was cross-examined by attorneys of both the plaintiff and the defendants.

"When she was asked what her desire is, she said that she would want to go live with her parents. To a follow-up question of who her parents were, she specified that they are the Johns."

Everyone's attention was toward the judge. Again, the courtroom was quiet, except a clicking sound of computer keyboards.

The judge continued, "I told you this case is complicated and one of its kind! Even though the court recognizes that this girl's body and the brain inside it belongs to the defendant, her identity was found to be distinct from the body that you see. And because her rights and wishes need to be respected, the court has determined that this girl's name is Sandra, and she is the daughter of the plaintiff of this case. Therefore, she should immediately join the parents of her choosing. It is so ordered."

Ava, who just heard the most difficult news of her life stood up and stared at the child, and said to herself, *The freaking judge knows nothing, that girl is my daughter.*

She sat and put her head down. The judge's final decision kept playing in her head. She tried to ignore it, but she couldn't. Her attorney and her family were trying to console her, but all she could hear was the sound, "This girl's name is Sandra … it is so ordered, it is so ordered…!"

She covered both her ears and sprang from her seat saying, "No! No! No!" at the top of her lungs. People in the courtroom, including those who were leaving turned around toward her to see what was going on. Her head had started spinning when she got up.

The spinning got worst, and she couldn't keep her balance, her whole body fell to the ground. A second before she hit the ground, blood gushed from a gash that her head sustained in an uppercut from the corner of the table in front of her.

***

Grandma Meme was in the hospital, being treated for pneumonia. When she heard the judge's final decision. She didn't believe what she heard until one family member jumped with joy, saying, "Meme, did you hear? the judge decided that the girl is Sandra! I wish you and I were there with Lesha and the rest of our family instead of the darn hospital," and reached out to hug her.

"Child! Don't come near me! I mean it! What in God's name got in to y'al? How could that white girl be my sweet Sandy? Sandy is long gone, even worse, she took her dad, my only son with her. I just can't wait until the Lord takes me to be with them," said Meme, the humidity from her tears fogging up her glasses.

"Meme, I know you believe this is just some people playing God, but you can't ignore the fact that people could do God's work on Earth. Why do you think Deric died? He believed that this child has Sandy's brain, therefore she is Sandy. She is the reason for my brother's death. White or not, I happily accept her as my niece! I'm sure Deric is looking down from heaven and rejoicing the judge's decision," said Deric's sister, her eyes still planted on the TV where CNN was showing a replay of the final court proceeding, her hands cleaning her mom's glasses.

***

To Ava's families, relatives, and supporters, it was impossible to accept the face-value of the court's judgement. They read and reread the court statement, but they didn't find that they could rationalize with the decision, except for a single sentence that said they have the right to appeal.

These people couldn't believe that a girl who was the exact copy of her mom, Ava, was considered black and sent to live with a black family. When they looked at her, everything about her screamed that she was their own. Her pale skin, blond hair, and blue eyes did not show any indication of blackness. So, they promised that they would never abandon her.

When cancer threatened her life, they stood with her mom, mourning and crying with her. Providently, time brought a solution, the combination of great talent, technology, and her mom's money saved her life. When they thought she was all well and would grow up to be like her mom, the law made her another family's daughter—it made her black.

Though the cloud of death cleared from her daughter like a morning fog would, the sun briefly shined and started to hide from Ava. When pride clouded her family and supporter's view, they wished that death had taken Teena instead of a black family. Her life became a puzzle to them. She was alive, she was not, then she was alive; she was white, then she was black.

As if one blow of misfortune was not enough, death started threatening to make Ava its victim. Since her injury in the courtroom, the powerful and creepy angel of death kept giving her a quick visit to leave her scared and freaked out. Despite, the state-of-the-art medical assistance that she was receiving, her health wasn't improving.

***

When Million woke up from his sleep, he found a piece of paper under the door of his room. Reading the note, he learned that Abigail had gone somewhere.

He expected her to come back soon, but she didn't. He dialed her number, but she didn't answer.

He thought, *Oh man, I can't stand this loneliness. I miss Sab and the kids.*

He read the rest of the note again, "The huntsmen are looking for you everywhere. I'm sure they are expecting you to go home or to your parents' house. Please, don't go near there. I will be back soon."

"So, now, my wife and kids, and the rest of my family are targets? I need to go! I didn't come here for my family to get hurt as a consequence. They have suffered enough," he said, crumpling the paper. He went in and out of the shower hastily, and headed out.

He left through the back gate of the hotel and contracted a taxi.

***

Unlike when it first started, operation HAKMA (Hunt and Kill Million/Amin) had become more organized. Million's chasers rented a house about six-hundred-feet from Saba's place. The house faced the opposite direction. Sitting inside, they had a 360-degree view of the area. At the same time, three agents were taking turns to walk at close proximity from their target's house.

***

"Not, this one. The next house please," said Million to the taxi driver pointing to his house.

While getting out of the cab, Abigail's warning echoed in his head. Nervously, he looked both ways and headed to the gate. When he was about to knock, the gate opened. Shaking, he peeped just his head.

***

"Hello, Bega, where the hell are you? You're not in the zone. I think it's our man, he just got off a taxi. Run! Fat ass! Now, he is getting inside. You just let him barricade. I still can't see you. You are not in any of the cameras sight. I hope you have a good explanation for the boss."

"I was in the corner store getting a chewing gum. Fuck! I see the gate being closed. I'm going to knock; he should be the one who will answer. Stay with me in case I need backup."

“What if the maid or his wife, even worse, one of the kids open it for you? Forget it, you’re going to blow our cover. Just stay around there until he comes out. Your other option is to go inside and send everyone to heaven or hell, no testimony left. However, last time I checked, his wife and kids are not on the target list, just him.”

“I know the maid is not there. She left about ten minutes ago. But you are right, his wife or kids could open for me. I will just wait here until he gets out and end this project tonight. Can you not tell the boss what just happened, please?”

“I won’t, but DD might tell him. He’s listening, tell him you owe him one.”

“DD, bro, I owe you one.”

“Don’t worry, dude, I’ll keep my mouth shut. Let’s just hope that he doesn’t come and review the recording for the day. You know what, Bega, if I were you, I would just go in and take out the entire family.”

“Both of you are blood thirsty dicks! I have no desire to do that. It is already indicated in the memo that he is the only chess piece, why would you suggest otherwise? Anyway, we’ll wait for him till he gets out, no matter how long he stays there. In an hour, one of you need to give me a break. In fact, I prefer you, Red, DD can keep an eye on the Cams.”

“Why are you bossing us around? Oh, I remember now. You’re in charge today. Man, you’re doing shitty work for a man who is in charge of the project.”

"Shut the fuck up, Red! I was only gone for one minute. We all make mistakes. Wait a second, were you guys listening to his wife's phone conversations? Did he not call to tell her that he was coming? Or could she have a phone that we haven't tapped?"

"It was only her female friend who called her this morning. I don't think she would have another phone. I like your idea, though. You always consider all possibilities. No wonder you are almost the boss, ha, ha, ha! See you in an hour. I will bring my pistol with a silencer. You know, we won't get a penny before this work is completed, and I need money asap."

"Dude, did you consider that you might not receive a dime unless the job is done right?"

"Says who? They want me to kill their target and I will make that happen. But things happen. People other than the prey might get hurt along the way."

***

Noticing no one was by the gate, Million entered and locked it. Then rushed into the living room.

Saba was helping Rui with his homework. "Oh, Bini, you startled me," she said.

"Thank God!" he sighed! "Sorry, I don't mean to scare you. How come the gate was not locked? Any bad intentioned person could come in like this," he said, feeling a heavy weight slide off his shoulders.

"Mulu, might have left it cracked. She went to the store to get something."

In his lifetime, he'd never been worried as much as he'd been right before he went inside and saw everyone in the house safe. After kissing his wife and kids, he sat down on the sofa with Mica, then Rui joined them.

Saba got up and started preparing for a traditional coffee ceremony.

***

Saba heard a knock on the gate. While getting up to unlock it, she thought, "It is about time, how long does it take to pick up a couple of items?"

Bini thought he heard a knock, but he wasn't sure. He was waiting for a repeat. When he saw Saba getting up, he said, "Sab, wait, I got it. It was only knocked once. You think it is a person, not a wind?"

"I believe I heard twice. That is how Mulu knocks. Sometimes I couldn't hear her follow up knock to the first. The weird thing is, she has a set of keys, but she rarely uses them."

He had just stepped out of the door, when Saba said, "Bini, wait, she should use her key. I don't know why she wouldn't. She either leaves the gate cracked open when she leaves or knock and stand there forever. I think we should leave her to use the key."

"You don't think she might have left it at home?"

"I hope she didn't go to the store without her wallet, that is where she keeps the keys too."

"I guess we can give her a chance to use it or to knock again. It has only been, what, a minute?" said Bini smiling and going back to sit between his kids.

A few minutes had passed before Saba thought about Mulu not using her key to came in.

"I guess who knocked on the gate wasn't the girl," said Bini, as if he read his wife's thoughts.

"Bini, I'm starting to worry now. What could have happened to her? The store she went to is not that far. She either couldn't find what she wanted to buy there and went to different shop that is far, or something has happened to her."

"Or she could be visiting with a friend. Does she have friends in the area?" said Bini, wondering who could have knocked if it wasn't Mulu.

***

"Hey, Red, what the heck are you waiting for? Did you chicken out? You know, if we wait for Bega, this mission will never end anytime soon."

"No, dude I'm just careful. Don't your fucken cameras show you how busy this zone has been? A few minutes after Bega left, I knocked, but they didn't answer. I guess they are enjoying themselves in there. I will knock again in a little bit.

I hope no one else answers it but him. I don't want to wipe out the whole family, unless I have to."

"Whatever, man! You only have twenty minutes before Bega gets back."

***

"I hope it is her," she thought. And wondered, who could have knocked earlier.

Bini knew why Saba stopped talking, so he got up and went to open the gate.

When she heeded the gate open, Saba was deciding how to approach her cousin for taking so long and not using her key to open the bar.

***

When she heard someone groan and the door slammed shut, Saba was still trying to determine whether to reprimand or tell Mulu nicely about her action that has both worried and upset her. Startled, she ran outside. Bini was walking back to the house pressing his blood drenched left upper arm.

"What happened Bini? Who did that to you? They can still be outside. I need to call the police," said Saba talking fast with a shaky voice and touching his shoulder with her trembling hand.

"Sab, I'm okay! I think he was a burglar or something. If I didn't see his gun, he was aiming to shoot me in the chest. I quickly slammed the door on him, it might have gotten his face," said Bini, trying recover from his shock. "Don't call the police. He barely got my arm," he added.

Both of them were still in shock, when they noticed the gate opening. Bini stood erect, leaving Saba kneeled, holding a long cotton strip of clothe that she was going to tie onto his wounded arm. He marched outside with what seemed a determination to keep the danger far and away from his wife and kids. Saba followed him, despite closing the door behind him.

He saw Mulu coming in, but it took him a couple of seconds to come out of the fight mode he was in.

"Oh, Mulu! Thank God! I'd like to know what took you forever. But first, I need to attend to Bini's bleeding arm," said Saba, looking at Mulu. She returned her attention to Bini and said, "Bini, you're still bleeding, should I call an Ambulance?"

"I will be alright! Let's fold half of the clothe multiple times and the other half tear it into two, lengthwise, then we will have a bandage and a tourniquet. My dad thought me that. He was a medic during the Korean war," said Bini grimacing.

***

"Red, you look upset, what's wrong?"

"Nothing. The sucker might not leave the house today. Anyway, do you mind if I go home after giving DD a break? I want take a nap and come back to help the night shift."

“Dude, calm down, you’re acting and talking weird. First, how do you know the man won’t be leaving the house, and second why do you want to come at night? I’d also like to know why the fuck are you far away from the belt? Earlier, you guys were ripping me off because I went to the store for a second.”

“Just like you, I was getting a chewing gum.”

“Where are you going? You didn’t answer my questions. Did anything happen while I was gone?”

“Nothing happened. I’m just tired. Forget about me helping night shift, but I still want to go home.”

***

“Hello, Boss?”

“Bega, what’s up?”

“Red is acting strange and won’t tell me why. I think he should be pulled off this mission.”

“Is he nervous or over acting? If so, it could be because he is newbie.”

“No sir! He is upset for a reason that he doesn’t want say. He has been talking about going inside and wiping the target with his family. He also said that he needed to go home and take a nap, and come back at night. The night shift is covered, and to keep low profile, we don’t need any more people than what we have.”

“We don’t have authorization to shoot anyone but the man. So, the reason he wanted to come at night is to jump in and wipe them out?”

“That might be his plan, but he didn’t want to tell me. Also, I don’t know how he knew, but he believes that the game won’t get out of the house for the rest of the day.”

“Is he armed at the moment?”

“Yes!”

“Don’t start an argument. Tell him to go home and let me know when he leaves. I will send a cleaning team to his place. Another guy will replace him there.”

“Yes sir! Thank you!”

***

“DD, go take your break, I have to go home when you come back.”

“Hey, you didn’t try to walk in, did you? I was hoping that you would finish the mission today. Dude, the lunch you brought us has given me an upset stomach. I have been in the bathroom for the last half an hour or so. Anyway, is Bega okay with you going home? We need a third person here.”

“I think he is okay with that. Just take your freaking break or tell me I can leave now,” said Red staring at the security monitors. Then he thought, *Good, he didn’t see that I missed, wow! I can delete the video and no one will know.*

“Okay, okay, I need to take twenty,” said DD.

***

“How long have you been here? I didn’t see or hear you returning.”

"Long enough to see you trying to delete your embarrassing video. I already know you missed the target. Quit trying to delete it, the boss knows when recordings are deleted or blocked."

"Please, DD, help me! Can't we tell him that no videos were recoded today? I will make it up to you."

"Dude, I can't help you with that. He checks every recording remotely. He probably already has seen both Bega and your cases. Why are you making a big deal about it, anyway? Everybody misses a shot. I saw that he slammed the metal door on your face. You're lucky that he wasn't armed."

"I'm going to come back tonight and finish them all. Hold on, Bega is calling, what's up, man? Thanks! You can call one of the night shift guys to come early and work until midnight because I will arrive at that time to replace him."

"Will do! Enjoy your nap! I hope you won't oversleep," said Bega and hung up the phone, imaging what would happen to Red.

"DD, can you at least not tell Bega about what happened, also, leave the boss to discover for himself," said Red, getting up to leave.

***

In one nursing home, two elderly gentlemen, Geo and Jeri had been following the news about the court case on TV, they saw a reporter's analysis of Ava's suffering for her daughter.

Geo said, “Why do they try to change life’s natural process by creating unnecessary and complicated issues of putting two or more separate things together? They should let nature take its course in leaving this planet. Nowadays, for the sake of applying their philosophy, they are working sleeplessly to bugle by mixing human beginning.

“Botching is easy, but reversing might be impossible. This makes me long the old times when a man had all the time he or she needed. Back then there was less stress. Now the young ones are stressed out about everything. They run and run with no resting time and place. If somehow, they halt their run, they don’t relax because their minds are always moving.”

“I don’t understand why she wants to go through all this. We did love our kids back then too. Parents of these days seem to assume obligation, pressure, or are driven by some form of self-created value to love their kids. Do you remember when this case first was shown on TV? Ava was talking about how beautiful her daughter is, how an exact copy of her she is, and how she would grow up to be a model. So, it makes you wonder whether she loved her daughter or what her daughter could be when she grows up. Or the challenge of raising a model,” said Jeri sounding annoyed.

"I read in the Sunday paper that Ava's daughter was fighting brain cancer when she volunteered for the child to be a guinea-pig of the experiment that led to this bumble. Ava paid a boat load of money for the brain and the experiment with the hope of saving her daughter's life. What kind of love, other than motherly would prompt her to go through all that trouble?" asked Geo and got up and walked to a table where three ladies were drinking tea.

***

"Sab, Abigail is waiting for me, I have to go. Also, my arm is starting to hurt, and I have pain medications in the hotel."

"No! Bini! Whoever tried to kill you might still be outside. Instead, let me go the pharmacy and get you something for pain."

"I must go. The criminal would not be still standing there. He should have fled for fear of getting caught."

"Okay, if you must leave, use the back door. Even for the future, use that door to come and go. Here is a spare key, that way you don't have to wait for someone to let you in."

Million had forgotten all about the back door. It led to a crowded neighborhood and a few feet away there was a corner, a shortcut to his parents' place. He realized, in addition to his wife and himself, only Machida knew that the door existed.

"Sab, no one should know about what happened. Including the police and Abigail. Especially her. When she thought of coming here, I told her that we don't have this kind of issue in our country. So, if she knows about it, she will be disappointed in me."

He felt bad and sad that he lied to his wife and that he couldn't tell her everything, including why he was almost killed. He said goodbye and sneaked out through the backdoor.

***

CHAPTER TWELVE

"Hello!"

"Hello! Who this?"

"My name is Awet, is this Amin's residence?"

"Yes, it is."

"Who am I speaking with?"

"This is Barakat."

"I'm Awet, Amin's old friend. I'm not sure if you know me, but he and I used to work together before he joined the new hospital. We were also running mates. We worked and ran together for many years. I heard he went to America for school." He stopped as if to gather his thoughts, then continued.

"Today, I met him at the hotel and tried talking to him, but he said he doesn't know me. In fact, he said that he is not Amin, but Million. I know Amin very well! So, when he told me he is someone else, I couldn't believe what I heard, and my head wouldn't let me move on. Do you know what is wrong with him? Has he been acting normal at home?"

Barakat sank into despair, and struggling not to cry, she said, "Maybe you saw someone who looks like him. It has been over a year since Amin died in a vehicle accident in America."

"Barakat, Amin and I were trained and running for one company since a young age. So, I know him! If whom I met is not Amin, it would have to be a miracle. Or else I'm going crazy," said Awet, surely.

"I wish whom you saw is Amin. But he is dead," said Barakat with grief.

"I'm sorry to be a burden to you in your tough time. I still don't know what to believe," he said and hung up.

While Barakat was sitting depressed and sad, and crying, Amin's mom came in. "What happened? Why so sad?"

"Some guy called and said, he met Amin at a hotel. But when he tried to talk to him, he told him that he is not Amin, but Million."

"What kind of insane man is he? Why wouldn't he leave us to our grief? Please do not hurt yourself listening to some psycho," said Amin's mom with mixed emotion of anger and sorrow.

As time went by, more and more people reported seeing Amin at different locations in Addis-Ababa. Considering that they didn't get to bury his body, his family started to suspect the possibility of what they heard from different people. Thus, his older brother decided to find out for himself.

***

"Hello!"

"Hello! Who this?"

"My name is Ahmed; I'm calling from Ethiopia."

"Okay, how can I help you?" Asked Eyob.

"When you called the other day, you said that you are Amin's friend from school. I'm his oldest brother, and I have a few questions about him. I was wondering if you could help me by answering what you know."

"Sure! Not only am I his friend, I also work for the school. So, I may be able to answer your questions, at least I'm able to find out for you."

"Let me start with the most pressing one. Is Amin dead or not? You see, his wife and kids need a man in their lives. And there is someone who she is preparing to marry. But before everything is set in stone, we would like to know if for sure Amin has died. If he is alive and ends up coming back, it is easy to imagine how sour things will go. So, we need to know the truth now," said Ahmed, knowingly mixing his true concern with deceit.

"Sir, it is a matter of fact. Amin is dead," said Eyob, excited that his weapon reached out to him. He suspected that Ahmed was worried that Amin might come and take his wife from him. Eyob and his team were convinced that Ahmed would be less hesitant to kill someone who looks like his brother than his actual brother. Therefore, they did not want to change the story about Amin's death.

"So, can you tell me how he died?" Asked Ahmed.

"While heading out of town for vacation, his car slid and rolled over. Emergency responders brought him to the hospital close to our school. There are many well-known doctors in that hospital. Those doctors tried to save his life, but because of the severity of his injury, they couldn't."

"His old friends claim to have seen him at different locations here in Addis. When we tell them that they must have seen someone who looks likes him, they argue that it is not a matter of resemblance. I wonder who the man, whom they consider my brother is?" said Ahmed, processing the assurance that Amin had passed.

"Who did the look alike say he is? Have you met him in person?" Asked Eyob.

"Sorry, I don't remember what the name was, and no, I haven't met him myself."

Eyob knew that the man in question was Million/Amin. He said, "We would like to know about this person. Can you find out more about him and let me know? Find out where he lives. In the meantime, get me the contact info to the people who thought they saw Amin."

Ahmed remembered what he'd heard Amin's friends had said. "I'm still not sure why his old friends insist who they saw was him."

"I don't know why, but if that person is Amin, he would have come home," said Eyob, sensing the complication of the matter. But he couldn't be sure that Ahmed would kill his own brother.

Ahmed felt his stress coming back. He didn't hear any fact that proved the death of his brother. The logical analysis rather than concrete facts he heard from Eyob seemed to upset him. Trying to calm himself down, he said, "Sir, I sense that there is more you haven't, or you don't want to tell me about how my brother died. Let me tell you the truth why I want to confirm his death, that way you will understand where I'm coming from."

"No worries! I'm willing to help you with anything you want."

"After we heard about the death of my brother, we were concerned how his wife and kids would be cared for. As it is in our custom, I was instructed to marry his wife and raise his kids like my own. Now, she and I are married. If the man in town is him, there will be a big problem in our house. Thus, I need you to tell me the truth."

He thought, *Poor man, he doesn't know that I know a lot more about him.* Then he said, "I understand your problem. However, the man you are talking about is not Amin. If you want, I can send you pictures that affirm your brother's death. As for the look alike man, I recommend that you educate your family, especially your wife, not to mistake him for Amin and be taken advantage of. Another thing, if not more, we would like to know as much as you do who he is. Hence, please find his address and call me. As soon as we are done with this phone call, I'm going to go wire you one thousand dollars to help you with expenses of finding that man's whereabouts and communicating with me."

"If you would do me a big favor and send me those pictures, I will appreciate it so much. His wife is agitated and confused by the news of him being seen in town. So, showing her the pictures may help her put things to rest. Please send me the pictures as urgently as you can, and I will gather all the information you need about the man."

"Don't worry about it! I will send them in priority mail right away. By the way, I will send you a thousand dollars more if you find the exact address of the lookalike man for me."

With the newly discovered support system who backed his idea and financial needs, Ahmed's confidence went through the roof. Then he started preparing for the fight of his life, to save his marriage.

Ahmed was older and on the heavy side. His education level never went past reading and writing. However, he knew how to make money and swore by frugality. He seemed not to care about other people's feelings, yet, he would go to any length to satisfy his own.

***

A couple of days after the incident, Saba and her friend Maron were chatting in the house over coffee. Bini sneaked in through his special entry and caught Maron by surprise. Even Saba would not have known to warn her, because he never told her when he might be coming. Luckily, she had told her about Bini, that he was Million's childhood friend and lived in Germany. So, despite her startle, she didn't make it a big deal that a man came from one of the bedrooms, she believed.

He joined them for coffee and started enjoying their conversation on different timely topics of the country. About twenty minutes later, the phone rang. It was from the kids' school. The secretary told Saba that their daughter got hit by a bicycle and sent to the closest hospital. When Saba told both Bini and Maron what she heard over the phone, Million panicked. He couldn't sit still. He became restless and told her that he needed to go to the hospital right away. Maron heard his voice choking with tears.

Maron was impressed by Biniam's worry for the kids more than Saba. She couldn't understand why he was like that. While she was wondering about Bini, Saba came to the living room ready to go.

"Saba, I noticed this Bini guy loves your children tremendously. He couldn't even wait until you get ready. He already took off," said Maron picturing how he was acting before he left.

"Gosh, yes! He loves them so much. He cares about every minute thing about them. Let alone an accident like this, he wouldn't allow even a fly to stop on them. Their father was like that too," said Saba fascinated by his love for the kids.

"I'm surprised he is shaken by what he heard more than you. That kind of reaction is expected from a mother or a father of a child in a serious accident, not from the best friend of the father," said Maron.

"Just because I didn't show it, doesn't mean I didn't panic," murmured Saba.

"I don't mean you are not terrified by what you heard. His being like that is unexpected. He is worried to death. Even if you panicked, you held yourself together. You didn't react the way he did," said Maron, trying not to disappoint her friend.

The child suffered a laceration on her forehead. When Saba and Maron arrived at the hospital, she was sitting on Bini's lap, her forehead bandaged. Bini kept kissing and caressing her ear. He said, "Thank God! She is okay!" looking at her then at her mom.

To those who knew the fact of the matter, Abigail and himself, there was nothing surprising about the way he was treating the child. To bystanders, however, Bini seemed the father of the child.

Because he took the child's case as his business, Saba couldn't say much, except, "I'm glad she wasn't hurt seriously," and heaved. He was holding the child as a Wide Receiver would grip the ball he or she just caught. Seeing how he was caring for the child, she remembered what her friend, Maron said and felt bad for him. She thought, *He could have been a loving father to his children. Why wouldn't he marry someone and have children instead of trying to be like a father to his friend's?*

Bini didn't want Maron to know about his different entry. So, after he whispered something to Saba, he said, "You guys go without me, I'm going to stop by the grocery to grab some fruits," loudly, making sure Maron could hear him.

The adults were glad that the child didn't suffer severe injury. The child, however, had forgotten about the accident, she was playing with her brother. After Maron, and other visitors left, Saba embraced her daughter and started stroking her head in search of unnoticed injury. "My darling, you are lucky, you could have suffered worse injuries," said Saba, still stroking her daughter's scalp.

"If my dad was alive, he would have hurt the guy who pushed me, right mommy?" said Mica.

There was nothing more that bothered and annoyed Million than hearing his kids talking about their dead father and seeing them in a sad mood. He wanted a fatherhood recognition both from the children and their mom.

Saba knew that Bini was sensitive when it came to the children talking about their dead father. When she realized that he heard what Mica said, she startled. Though he was facing away, she noticed he was crying. She felt bad for him and her eyes filled with tears. She said to the children, "Didn't I tell you not to say such things? Never say anything like that again."

Mica and Rui knew that Bini loved them so much. Mica, realizing that she hurt his feelings, she said, "Bini sorry, I said that, but I still miss my daddy." And started crying.

Looking up to the celling, he thought, *Oh, God! Are you there?* Then, looking at Mica, he said, "Sweet child, what am I to say now?" his jaw and fist clenched, tears rolling from his eyes, he knelt and held her tight to his chest.

Saba was mesmerized by how great the man was with her kids, he made everything about them his concern. She, however, didn't know anything about his everyday life in Addis. She felt guilty for not bothered to know. So, she decided to ask more and get to know him more.

She thought, *Is he not able to have his own kids that he is trying to be a father figure to his best friend's?*

***

When they got home from the hospital, it was almost bedtime for the kids. Bini tucked them in. Mulu was already a sleep. Bini and Saba sat across from each other. Remembering the promise, she made to herself of getting to know Bini, Saba thought, *This is the perfect moment*, and started asking him different questions.

"Bini, do you know that I know nothing about you, except that you came from Germany to visit your parents and that you are my late husband's childhood friend?"

"What would like to know?"

"Okay, let's get this out of the way, I have been dying to know. Were you ever married? If you don't want to tell me, it's okay. We can just talk about something else."

"Oh, no, it doesn't bother me. In fact, I'm happy to tell you that I'm married and have one girl and a boy."

"I'm guessing they are in Germany; they couldn't come with you? The kids would have met or seen their grandparents."

"No, they are here with me. It is just that, I know them but they don't …"

Mica came out crying and strolled into her mom's bosom. "Mica, what happen?" Saba asked, trying look the girl in the eyes.

"What is wrong, baby? Did you have a nightmare?" asked Bini.

"Yes, I'm scared. Mommy, can I sleep with you?"

"Go ahead, Sab, you guys go to sleep. I will lock both doors when I leave. We will talk more some other time."

Saba didn't know what to make of what Bini said. Confused and crossed, she thought, *What the heck are you doing here, then?* She wanted him to finish what he was saying, however, he insisted that she and the child went to bed and that he would leave to his hotel. The normally reserved Saba fought with herself from saying, *If you have your own family, why don't you spend your quality time with them? And most of all why do you get emotional and I end up scolding my kids, whenever they speak about their dead father?*

But she held back her comment and said good night and went to bed with Mica.

Million's eyes followed his wife while she walked to their bedroom carrying Mica. That reminded him the old days, when she used to tease him and make him wait on the sofa while she went and slipped into a pajama that accentuated her curves and nipples, straighten her long and silky hear down, and come back, sat on his lap and start caressing and kissing him.

Tormented by nostalgia and suffering from his present condition, he laid his head back on the sofa and covered his eyes.

Though Mica fall fast to sleep and rolled to the other side of the bed, Saba couldn't sleep. She realized that she didn't hear the doors open or close. She got up and went to the living room. *This is what I don't understand—why hasn't he left? This guy is weird*, she thought, *Could he have quarreled with his wife*?

"Bini, should I get you a sheet and blanket?"

He was asleep.

She brought a light blanket and covered him and went back to bed. And kept rolling and tossing until three in the morning.

Million woke up around three thirty to find himself still sitting on the sofa covered with a blanket from the chest down. He felt mad and annoyed that he was a stranger in his own house and to his wife. Sleeping on a sofa in a living room as a guest while his wife was sleeping in their bedroom induced a test of his patience. His masculinity, and libido began to challenge him. Then, he involved his reasoning mind to the situation.

***

Despite reaching closer to the height of his career goal in politics by becoming adviser to state representative, Marc Soprano was never happy until the day Ava called and told him about the success in Teena's brain implant. He visited the child a few times while she was still in recovery and later when she was in therapy. Even though she didn't recognize him or show him any reaction that he expected from Teena, he was ecstatic to see his daughter progressing well with her new brain.

Before his second marriage, he believed that he was robbed of joy for over three and half years by his first marriage to Ava, and later by their ugly divorce, then, most of all, by his daughter's diagnosis with brain cancer and lack of treatment. Those who knew him commented on his politician's-smile being the best. He was talented both in hiding his emotions and faking his grins.

Unfortunately, his real beam that came after seeing his daughter triumph death, twice, was short lived, it faded, then disappeared when he heard the court's final decision. Reflecting on how he took the news, he started to worry, wondering if he could fake his smile any longer.

He was resentful of Ava, because when she decided for Teena to go through the experimental procedure, she didn't seek his advice or ask for his opinion. It was only after the fact that she told him. He believed she might not have told him at all, if he hadn't called to check on Teena. That day, he regretted that he allowed her to have full custody of their daughter.

However, when he'd seen the child in the hospital, recovering from the procedure, he'd been glad that Ava didn't ask for his opinion—he was sure that he wouldn't have agreed. Seeing the child, he didn't have any doubt that she was his Teena. Despite frequent reflections that reminded him of her brain being other child's, he was self-indoctrinated that getting a brain implant was similar to getting a heart, lung, or kidney transplant, except more complex.

Fast forward, Marc was saddened by the court's decision. With Ava being sick, families and friends kept calling him to step up on the fight not to abandon the child. So, he hired a high-profile attorney with a track record of winning family-related court cases.

***

The new attorney took the case to the circuit court.

He opened his oral argument by saying, "Your honor, thank you for the opportunity to present our appeal. The district court awarded parents' right to individuals who once owned the small organ that was placed in Teena's body. The court failed to recognize the parents who gave birth to the girl's whole body, head to toe, including internal organs, except the brain. Disregarding an arranged parent and child relation, isn't a child always the child of who gave birth?

"The parenthood of the girl should have been awarded to

her parents from whom she had taken her looks including her skin color, and who are capable of loving and caring for her. When her mom heard the unbelievable decision of the lower court, that violated her motherhood rights, she passed out and fell inside the courtroom. She suffered a serious head injury and as it has been seen on news outlets, she remains hospitalized. If a judgment of a court of law doesn't defeat the person's consciousness or at least challenge his or her, how could it be considered fair? The lower court's judgement, made my clients feel like they have been robbed of their child and left them crying for justice.

"Even though making such a decision based on the cognition of a child who lacks life experience for the obvious reason may momentarily excite the child, it could affect her future negatively. Unless we, the adults, help her now to be with the people who love and understand her, and whom she looks like and belongs to, she will one day wake up lonely in the middle of crowded avenue. As life experience has taught us, who you walk with matters.

"Your honor, again, for the obvious reason, the child lacks the experience to deduce about the prospect of her future, it is up to us to set her up in the right path. Therefore, I respectfully ask this court to thoroughly review this case. Thank you!"

The attorney of the black family took his turn to present his oral argument, looking at the panel of judges, he said, "Your honor, there is no new substance on the appellant's oral argument. It is all the same that the district court reviewed and decided on. Thus, I respectfully request this court to uphold the district court's decision and dismiss this appeal."

"Counselors of both parties know that this case is unique and unparalleled. There has never been a case from which we can refer a substance or two to relate to it. Thus, the court will review the case in great details. Now, the hearing is adjourned, but we recommend that the appellee prepare a response for a later day," said the middle judge.

***

When Million didn't show up for a couple of days since the night he slept on the sofa, Saba started to get worried and wondered if she had said something that offended him. She realized that she missed his company.

Million, on the other hand was entertaining the idea of revealing himself to his wife. However, the thought of the promise he made to Abigail held him at bay. He was also worried about how Saba would react if he told her.

Though he felt guilty for breaking his promise to Abigail on a couple of occasions. He justified his action considering, in both incidents, his conscience was challenged, and he was unable to live with himself otherwise. However, he didn't believe divulging was worth breaking his promise for the third time, therefore, he determined to be patient.

He hoped that she would, one day, understand him. Until then, he decided to travel with her by a train called time to a mountain called the future. The day she recognized him as her husband was when they would reach the top of that mountain. However, because he was anxious for them to get to the top sooner, the mountain was becoming steeper to him.

After all, telling her could have dire consequences of her reacting negatively. She may tell him to go away and that she never wanted to see him ever again. It was a truth beyond the truth of things that she was familiar with. She would consider it as if some stranger was telling her that he was her husband. Furthermore, she might view him as some scary and mysterious person. So far, whenever he attempted to tell her something serious and deep about himself, she stopped him, claiming that he was scaring her. Then how was he to reveal the real him to her? He believed only time would tell.

Saba was always happy with Bini. She believed that he seemed to understand her better than Million did. She was always amazed by how he knew everything she desired. Especially when he surprised her with his knowledge of secrets that she and her husband knew. Bini was a mysterious puzzle that she was not able to understand. Sometimes, all of a sudden, the thought of him would give her goosebumps.

More than the great and wonderful things that Bini did for and said to Saba, she was impressed by and admired how he cared for and loved the kids. She wondered if the exceptional love for Million's children was a pretense just to buy her love. But when she realized he went above and beyond what a father would do for his kids, she began questioning her doubt. However, she still couldn't answer why he loved and cared for someone's children beyond any father would for his own.

As part of her plan of getting to know him better, she said, "Bini, when are you going to get married and have your own children to care and love for as you are doing mine? Whoever marries you will be lucky. Because, more than anything, you can read human emotion. You will know and do what your wife wants without her telling you." Knowing that she had asked him before.

"Saba, I guess you forgot—I told you that I'm married and have two children like you."

"Then, where are they?"

"If I tell you now, you won't understand me just like last time. So, it will remain as a puzzle as it has been, until the right time."

"Do you mean they are not around?"

"They are. However, I know them, but they don't know me; I can see them, but they can't see me; I can hear them, but they can't hear me; they are close to me, but I'm not the same to them; in general, because I'm not in their life zone, though I understand them, they don't understand me. The best scenario that describes the situation would be someone in a sound-proofed booth made of one-way viewing glasses. The person in the booth can see everyone, but no one can see him."

"Sorry, but I don't understand what you are trying to say. What do you mean by that?"

"For now, that is all I'm able to tell you. The whole situation is a skeleton in the closet, and I'm the one who can keep it there. It is a secret that you could hardly bear to discover. If I disclose it to you, it might disturb your peace, at least for a little while."

"Bini, why do you scare me talking like that? Let alone with that kind of talk, sometimes, I get nervous thinking how full of mystery you are. I'm not willing to have that kind of scary conversation."

"At a time when I need a close friend and confidant with whom to share my deepest secret, people are creeped out by me, as if I'm some scary creature. This is saddening! Am I supposed to keep quiet, for fear of repulsing people by my story? If I continue this way with no one willing to listen and help me, one day, the burden of the secret I'm carrying will kill me. Then, you will hear the secret about the poor man. By then, it will be too late even to regret," said Million, wailing his heart out.

Hearing what he said and seeing his tears dripping to the floor, Saba felt sorry for him. She started crying and went to where he sat with his head bent, his face covered with his hands, and his elbows anchored on his laps. She stood at a right angle to him and tried to lift his head by gently propping his forehead.

She said, "Bini, please don't cry because of what I said. I have so much respect for you. I don't think there is anyone who cares about me and supports me as much as you do. However, I could never say the same about me for you. To be honest, my late husband was a good man, but he never understood or supported me as much as you do. You have been so great and wonderful to me, and it hurts me to imagine that I could never pay you back in my lifetime," said Saba, still sobbing.

His sorrow softened her heart. Her sorrow made him perceive that she cared about him. Since his new body, this was the first time his wife had touched him. Her soft hand and calming voice started to melt his heart. He felt as if he was being comforted by his wife.

"Then why did you say that you don't want to hear me?" he said between his sobbing.

"When you talk like that, I don't know why, but fear overwhelms me. Maybe it is because I'm a coward. It is more of my weakness. So, if you believe I can withstand hearing it, you have all my attention. Though, I'm not sure how much of a help I could be to you. There was a poetry book that Million liked to read. I guess he took it to America—I couldn't find it anywhere. Anyway, it used to make him laugh to tears. I, on the other hand, let alone to laugh, couldn't understand what was funny in it. When I think about that, I wonder to myself, maybe I'm a wimp who doesn't understand human emotion."

He asked, "Do you want me to bring you that poetry book?" and he went to one of the drawers. He opened the drawer and lifted a couple of other books and brought the book back to her.

"You found it!" she said in amazement. She wondered how Biniam knew where the book has been? On one occasion, she searched everywhere in the house but couldn't find it. She gave up looking for it because she thought Million had taken it.

"That is how you scare the Bejesus out of me. I don't assume there is anything that you don't know about this house. I have no idea how you know it, though."

"I guess, I was born with the knowledge about everything."

"Seriously; how do you know everything?"

"I have no idea why and how I know it."

"Are you a psychic?"

"My grandma once told me a story related to this. She said, when she was a young girl, a boy went missing from their village. There was no phone, no radio, obviously no social media. So, after searching where they could, they concluded that he was dead. They grieved and moved on. One day, out of nowhere, the man came to the village. The residents were both surprised and rejoiced at his return. Most of all, they were fascinated, and some of them scared, by the radio he brought with him. Some thought there were tiny people inside it; others thought it was the Devil that lived in it and is, therefore, talking to them."

"Please tell me how the story is related to my question of whether you are a psychic."

"The point I'm trying to make is that the villagers didn't know that the radio was the result of technology."

"Yes, that I understand. I just can't put together psychic and technology. I guess some of us need more explanation to get the message behind a message."

"Here is what I'm trying to say. I'm not a psychic or magician, but Million has been placed inside me through technology. Otherwise, how would have I known all your previous histories and secrets that only the two of you knew? You know that I don't know anything about the future, including what could happen in the next minute. As far as the past, I only know what Million knew. Just imagine the spirit of Million living in me. Million's sprit is placed in me with the help of technology."

"I don't know what you are saying, and it is scaring me. Maybe you are more than human. You are too complex for me to understand you. I think a lot about how mysterious you are, but I could never figure you out. The more I realized about how much I don't know you, the more I get petrified."

"One day, I will explain everything to you in detail. In the meantime, consider me a man who knows everything about you, who loves you and your kids dearly, who will never hurt you. Especially in relation to the kids, I'm not just a father figure, but their father."

"Yes, I could consider you like that, except the father of my kids. How could I say this man is their father?"

"As you have seen me so far, I have been acting as a father or father figure. I have been performing the duty of fatherhood."

"Don't you think that it is a little weird, if I recognize you as their father, not as their father figure, then you are my husband, Million."

"That is what it means!" said Million with satisfaction.

She said, "Bini, I could never understand what you say and do. You are a strange man." She walked to the kitchen.

***

CNN had set aside airtime around three in the afternoon to cover the little girl's case, new findings, court proceedings, and most of all, discussion with experts. "Today's topic of discussion is the law of human identity. Our guest is Dr. Simon. He is a professor of law at Harvard university school of law. And I'm your host Suzan Banani. I'd like to thank you, Dr. Simon for coming over, on behalf of myself and our viewers. Why don't we start with you introducing yourself to our audience?" said Suzan looking at Dr. Simon.

"I received my Ph.D. from Harvard University in 1999. I'm now a professor of law there. My wife Bella and I have a daughter and one dog."

"Great! I imagine you may be viewing the case not only in respect to the law but also in terms of your life as a father. How much do you love your daughter?"

"More than myself!"

"What if both parents in each side of the case, have as much love for their respective daughter as you have for yours?"

"I would say it is a very difficult thing."

"How?"

"Even though both sides are arguing for kinship of this child, no matter who wins the case, she could never be the same child whom they had for either of them."

"Can you tell us in detail what you mean by that?"

"It is an uncomfortable and inconvenient matter to both families. For example, if she is given to the Caucasian family, they will have a child who doesn't accept them, and they will try to teach her to like them. Which means they will be staging a parent and child relationship in their real-life drama. If she ends up with the African American family, she may behave like a child from that family, but her physical makeup will always make her look like a stranger in the family. It may create distorted self-image and problems in her social life when she grows up."

"Based on your expertise of the law, with respect to the law, which family or race do you say this child belongs to?"

"The law has its own way of identifying a person. To help me explain what I mean by that, I will use a scenario. Let's say a child was stolen from a house and there were multiple suspects who could have taken the child. The law enforcement team who has the case therefore will use at least three main factors to get closer to identifying who the perpetrator is.

“The three factors are: eye witnesses, finger prints, and the suspect’s uninfluenced statement of admission or denial. The witnesses will testify to what they saw, heard, and sometimes, what they touched and smelled. All those factors are, therefore, what the law uses to determine the who was who in this example or other real-world cases. DNA tests and medical reports have also been used on applicable situations.” He stopped to drink water, then continued.

“Especially in maternity-related questions, the law has been using DNA tests as a reliable means of proof. The law, therefore, could apply all the tools I mentioned to surely say which family the girl belongs to. Her fingerprints show she is of the Caucasian family. Eye witnesses, who see her skin color and facial features, could testify that she is white, and most of all, DNA tests could undoubtedly establish her maternal relationship with the Caucasian parents.

“However, her testimony, which is one of the legal factors I mentioned, must be used to determine who she belongs to. And she swears that she is black, and that her parents are the African American family. Because of that, the case is challenging the court from applying traditional methodologies to decide on it.

"If this was a criminal case and she was an adult suspect, her statement would have been considered a denial because it contradicts the other evidences; and the court, then would decide based on the proved factors only. But this is a civil case and she is a child. Speaking of a child, the law requires that courts decide on behalf of children and people with mental disabilities. However, this case is much more complicated and has other socially charged issues, hence, I can imagine why it could be a headache to the court."

"Indeed! This is a complicated case. Dr. Simon, thank you for being here and giving us insightful discussion."

***

Million's sister had fallen head over heels in love with Bini. If he skipped a day to come to her parents' house, she would get unhinged, agitated and angry. Then, with him, her joyous, enthusiastic, and blissful moments would return.

Every time she noticed his concern for her wellbeing, she would hope that he confessed his love soon. Despite her anxious expectation, that day didn't come. Though she was frustrated by that, she was never aggravated until he started insistently talking about Saba and her children. She didn't recognize it, but his intent of doing so was for her, even for a second, to assume the possibility that he could be her brother, Million. Contrary to the intent, it enhanced her hatred and jealousy toward Saba.

At times, the realization that Bini never asked her out. made her wonder whether he loved her, and she doubted that he did. And that in turn aggravated her hatred toward Saba.

Other times, she asked herself, "If he doesn't love me, who and what am I to him that he greatly cares for me and that he does everything I want?"

She wondered when, if ever, she would find an answer to that question. *I guess it is a matter of time,* she thought, *I hate to rely on time. The current and the future never communicate. Decisions that could affect the far future are made based on the information that is acquired at the moment. The worst part is when the future becomes current and the particular decision is discovered to be wrong. The other oddness of time is the difference between the past, the current, and the future is only Planck-time. And that much time makes a difference between the right and not so right decision a person makes.*

While she was ironing her father's shirt, Bini was talking to her about different things that he thought would interest her. However, Machida barely listened to what he said. She was having a private conversation in her head. The argument with herself was more pressing than anything or anyone around her.

No, I'm not going to wait until he tells me he loves me. When would that be? What if that time never comes? Let me take matters into my own hands and ask him what the heck he is thinking about me, she argued.

She suspected that he knew that she loved him. Either way, she was ready to come clean by telling him upfront.

She stopped ironing and turned toward him and said, “Bini, out of curiosity, why are you not married?”

“I’m married and the father of two children.”

What she heard startled her. Her ears started ringing as if someone slapped them. She purposely forgot what she was going to say and began pulling herself from the sad mood threatening to swallow her. But she didn’t want to ignore her disappointment of him leading her into falling in love with him.

So, she thought for a second and said, “How come you never said anything about it until now? You’ve never uttered a word about them. Where are they, when are you going to introduce us?” she said, trying to hide her furiousness.

Bini thought for a second and said, “Let alone to introduce you, I need someone to introduce me to them. There is a complex matter that couldn’t be solved by man. Only time can solve it. There has never been a day that I didn’t talk about them, the problem is that I have been out of luck to find anyone who could understand me.”

“Are you serious? I’m unable to make sense of what you are saying.”

“Definitely! Why would I lie? For what reason would I lie? But I understand where you are coming from,” said Bini with conviction.

"Then, where are they?" she asked sounding as serious as he did.

"They live around here."

Now she was more upset, she could hardly hide it any longer. She assumed he was playing her.

"Why are you lying to me? Why don't you tell the truth?" she pleaded. She hoped that he was playing with her.

"You know my wife and kids. However, you don't know that I'm her husband and the father of the kids."

"Oh, my, gosh!" said Machida, confused, "I thought I was smart, but this is incomprehensible. If I know them, who are they?" she added, still hoping that he would say, "just, kidding!"

"I can't tell you now, because they don't know me. But I'm sure that the day that we all introduc to each other will come."

"Why do I always have a tough time understanding what you are saying?"

"It is only because you assume that you don't know me."

"Aren't you Bini?"

"Yes, I'm."

"Why did you tell me that I don't know you then?"

"You just don't know my internal identity."

"If I know that you are Bini, what does it mean by internal identity?"

"Because you don't know my exact identity, you wouldn't understand me. However, the time you and I will get to know each other should be coming."

"Hey, man, I don't know what you are talking about."

"Can I ask you a quick question?"

"Sure! What is it?"

"Am I different than anybody else or not?"

"In what context?"

"For example, I told you a lot of things that you did when you were a kid. I even told you your old secrets. Wouldn't consideration of that I know all those make me special?"

"In that framework, yes—you are very special. My family and I talked a lot about how you knew all those things about each of us. But we couldn't come up with an answer. It's a mystery to us."

"Therefore, at least you know that I have something exceptional that is mysterious to everybody. A day when the conundrum will be revealed is coming. By then, you will be glad that I'm someone who you know very well."

"What are you saying? By then, will I know you as a different person or will I just remember that I used to know you?" she asked, knowing that she couldn't explain her questions.

"I know you, as I have known you before. You, on the other hand, will know that I'm someone you used to know before."

“Please don’t go around, just tell me who you are,” she said mockingly. But still sensing the enigma about him.

“Time will answer that question,” he replied with a serious tone.

“Do you understand what you are saying? Right now, I’m looking at you, and I’m sure that I didn’t know you before. How could some other time in the future could I have an aha! moment about you? There are two conditions that I may have moments of discovery like that. One, if you mysteriously become someone whom I knew before. Two, if you and I go our separate ways and meet again in the future, I will remember you as Bini and that you have been a mystery man to my family and I.”

“You brought up two great conditions. But, no! I won’t be mysteriously changed or not because we will separate now and meet in the future.”

“This is something I can’t swallow,” she argued.

“Don’t forget that I’m special. You sure will say aha!”

“You are talking strongly of that. I’m starting to get nervous. Who knows? If neither of those conditions is applicable, the only possible condition left is that you may change me, so I know what I don’t know.”

“Ha, ha, ha…! Funny! Though I wish I had the power to make people magically know who I am, the only condition needed for you to know is the right time. Without involving a change in either of us, a moment of realization will come, and you will say aha!”

"So, will you be someone I know very well?"

"Yes! Yes! You will have an insight that I'm someone you know very well, love and reminds you of someone you thought you lost."

"Okay, okay, let's leave it there! I think you might be a spirit. You are scaring me," said Machida feeling a chill. She grabbed her shirt on each of her shoulders with her crossed arms. What he told her added to the darkness of the night, reminding her of a story about Demons she heard when she was younger. Sometimes, even though she tried to, she could never understand what Bini talked about. Even worse, it freaked her out.

She said, "Please let's change the subject and talk about something else because I'm getting nervous."

After he left, she started to analyze everything he told her. Especially, the story about his wife and kids. She thought about it more and more. She wondered which woman and two children in the area could be his wife and kids. She thought about all the single women whom she knew who had two children.

With her mind's eye, she looked inside every such household, then she added certain criteria that could place Bini in that house. There were only a couple. One of them was Million's house. *There she found a household where Bini could fit in.*

Aha! It is Saba! What, a fool I have been? He is almost straight-forward. There it is the aha moment he told me about. Why didn't I understand it? He is always with her, and when he is not, he likes to talk about her, she said to herself, biting the inside of her lower lip. She assured herself that, that was her aha moment about Bini and Saba. Every time she thought of it, fire raged within her. Her muscles would get visibly tense.

Her friend who noticed the change said, "What's up, Machid? You are unusually tense and irritated."

She moaned with frustration and said, "It is not surprising that a person who is hurt to behave differently."

Alarmed by what she heard, her friend asked, "What hurt are you talking about? Who hurt you?"

"I used to be very patient and tolerant, now I heard something that hurts me badly. I can't stand it. It is driving me crazy. Unless I find some solution, I might end up in an asylum," said Million's sister.

"Your family is worried about you. Why are you putting them in so much anguish? Don't you care about them? When you are tense, they can read it on your face, and that makes them uncomfortable."

Machida's mom had been worried about her daughter and had begged her friend to find out what was going.

"You're right—I'm emotionally wounded. Until my wound heals and I get back to my old self, they should be patient with me. After all, they are healthy."

"What exactly happened to you? Why don't you tell me? I'm your friend. You can talk to me about whatever is bothering you. Sometimes that could be a relief and comfort. The more you keep things to yourself the more bitter it could become and that may be hard to wash down."

"No worries! I covered my eyes and took it in bravely."

"Even if you have swallowed it bravely, sooner or later, it will start to bother you. Why are you hiding things from me? Do you have closer friend than me?"

"I'm sorry, but I have been trying to fight it myself. My dead brother's wife and his self-claimed friend have been taking my family and I for a ride. They are both traitors. He used my brother's name to get to us and to be with his wife and kids. It hasn't been long since my brother died, but this person couldn't wait until we wipe our tears," said Machida, picturing Bini whispering into Saba's ears, and her giggling. She felt her blood boiling.

The friend didn't want to come out and say it, but she recognized that Hellen was afflicted of the self-created disease known as Jealousy, and that her friend had the antidote.

From personal experience, the friend knew that time was the potent elixir to her buddy's malady, and hoped that it ticked faster to the rescue.

***

CHAPTER THIRTEEN

Amin's younger brother, Nuraan was heading to Mosque when he was stopped by a neighbor.

"Congratulations!" said the neighbor.

"Thank you! But for what?" asked Nuraan.

"Hasn't Amin come home? I saw him by the post office in a white Land Cruiser," said thc witness with certainty.

"Where did you see him? Are you sure?" he asked, mesmerized by what he just heard.

"At a traffic light, but I saw him very well. Also, when I yelled his name, he turned around, though he said nothing. I'm guessing he didn't recognize me because of the way I'm dressed today."

Nuraan, considering that was not the first time he'd heard the news, imagined some bizarre and scary secret revolving around his family.

"You are the third person to tell me of seeing my brother in town. The other two knew Amin very well, just like you. They said that when they met him at hotels and approached him, he told them that he is Million, not Amin. It is confusing," he grumbled. Continuing, he said, "After all, we never saw his body. They told us about his death, and we took that at face value. They sent us his money and belongings, so why would we doubt. Also, there hasn't been any clue to assume otherwise, because you don't imagine someone would say, out of the blue, that your loved one has died. Anyway, the news of him seen in town but him not coming home has become a headache to my family and I."

Nuraan wanted to believe that his brother was in town, however, the question, *If the man is Amin, why wouldn't he come home*? kept bothering him. He believed he had an idea why, but was not sure.

Amin's family was disturbed by what they were hearing. Disagreement rose in the household. Ahmed's anger and agitation, Barakat's ignoring everyone and being shut down, and everyone else's uncomfortableness decimated the peaceful life of the whole family.

Amin's father, Haji Mustafa, knowing his son's personality, couldn't believe that Amin was in town and didn't bother to come home.

"Come on! How could you consider that Amin would do that? You know, he was a peaceful and humble young man, he was not some pitiless man who forgets his family. My son is not wicked or savage. I believe, as Ahmed said, the person in town could be some low life criminal who came from America."

When Barakat refused to marry Ahmed, Amin's mom, Amina, stood by her side and encouraged her to say no. However, Ahmed made her felt bad by saying, "It is only because I'm your step-son that you are against my marriage to your widowed daughter in-law." So, she withdrew her rcfusal. Now, she regretted that she fell for Ahmed's querulous attempt to make her feel bad.

"To begin with, I was against the idea of Ahmed marrying his brother's wife. However, you guys insisted. My son must be vexed by what we have done. Otherwise he would have come home. I wish I could see him and ask his forgiveness," said Amina, feeling depressed.

"So, you think the reason he has vanished is to avenge us?" Amin's dad asked his wife.

"Why do you not get it? His disappointment in us has turned him into an unkind and hardhearted person. There is no question that he hates his wife, kids, family, and the religion. I fear that Ahmed and Amin may try to kill each other because of Barakat."

"Oh, Allah! What a bizarre thing are we subjected to? Where possibly is he going to be found now?" said his father, sighing deeply out of confusion and frustration.

While the parents were talking about their worry and regrets regarding Amin, Ahmed and his brother Nuraan joined them. Shortly after the brothers' arrival, Barakat came in and went straight to her bedroom. The bump in her belly was noticeable.

A few days after they were told about Amin's death, his father advised Barakat that she could move in with them. Moving in with them not only was economical, but it also had both social and safety advantages.

As a widow with two young kids, Barakat was not ambitious enough to attempt living alone in a rental house. So, she moved in with them.

The house was huge. The father built it ten years back. It had multiple bedrooms, an oversized salon, nice kitchen, and dining area. The only inconvenient thing about it was that there was no separate access to the bedrooms. Even when all the household members were uncomfortable to see eye to eye, everyone had to stop by the salon before retreating to his or her bedroom.

A few days passed; Amin's father thought the news about his son being seen in town was a fools' drone. However, as the source of the news grew, he was forced to consider the possibility. Every time he lay down in bed, he started to measure the credibility of the news of his son's death and that of him being in town.

The people who reported to have seen or met Amin were his friends who either had grown or worked with him for a long time. But then he denied being Amin.

So, what was his father to make of that? He suspected Amin was alive. He thought, "But due to some kind of conspiracy, that I can't explain at the moment, my son's identity is changed to Million." However, he decided to set his conspiracy theory aside for a while.

Even though Amin's family sat around in the Salon and tried to discuss the guy in town, they kept departing from each other both physically and emotionally after a few minutes of argument.

"I wish I was dead rather than to hear my Amin's case become a joking matter. Unless Allah fixes it soon, it is embarrassing to this family," said Amin's mom, consumed with regret and grief.

"What is humiliating about it?" asked his father, disagreeing with her.

"We rushed into allowing his brother to marry his wife. Neighbors and friends may consider that the reason why he has changed his religion and why he doesn't want to see his kids, let alone his wife and us. I doubt that there is anything more humiliating than this," replied Amina, speaking her mind bravely.

Ahmed was irritated by what his step-mother said.

He said, "Who told you that he is alive? How do you think Barakat will feel about such false claims? Just because you don't like me, you have been trying to destroy my marriage. The time when I will find the man and show you that he is not Amin, and when the haters and the jealous will be put to shame is not too far from today. I showed you pictures of Amin's dead body with opened and hollow head that I received from America.

"However, because you don't consider me family, you prefer to believe what bystanders are telling you. Even though the man has said that he is not Amin, you and your reporters are insisting in being him. We can't force the man to become who he is not. If that person was Amin, he would have come home," said Ahmed, veins popping on his forehead.

Barakat, who came from her bedroom unexpectedly, happened to hear what Ahmed was saying.

She stood with crossed arms, and said, "Don't you have shame to criminalize your mother? You are an opportunist who preys on the grim. You didn't even give me a chance to confirm the death of my husband. Now I'm living a life of regret. What do I do now?"

"Barakat, you are ungrateful. I'm taking care of you and your kids, and I'm happily doing everything you ask. What are you missing in this marriage that you had in the previous one? Say it now, in front of the family,"

"I know you measure a marriage in terms of how much money you spend in it. But I'm missing a whole lot more. I miss the love of my life. My kids are missing a loving father. However, I'm responsible for all this—I should have been decisive enough."

"Instead of dreaming about the dead, why don't you contently live with the living and raise your kids nicely as a responsible mother would do? What is the use of all this regret and aggression? If you assume Amin is alive, you are nothing but a fool. Instead of lamenting about the past, enjoy the living and the life you have now."

The father interrupted and annoyedly said, "Guys, I brought my concern to you for discussion, not for private argument."

Nuraan looked at his dad and said, "In my opinion, what we are hearing is true. The individuals who met Amin are all his close friends, so, they won't mistake him for some look alike. Also, they have no motive to lie about meeting him. The most important questions should be why hasn't he come home? Why did he change his name and live in hiding? Why hasn't he started work?"

He stopped to see if everyone was listening.

Then he continued, "Now, I am wondering If he has started work, and if so, which name is he using there? I'm fretted thinking whether he is in his right mind. It is unlike him to stay away from his kids. I remember how he used to run home from work to see his children. Now, sitting here in town, not even attempting to reach out to them makes me believe that he is extremely mad at us. I assume that, because he loves his wife dearly, he hid to avenge us for what has happened. So, we have to seek and make peace with him actively."

"How could you believe he is alive? I called to America and confirmed his death and showed to all of you the pictures I received from them. So, how isn't that credible?" said Ahmed, crossly.

"Ahmed, let me ask you a question. If you see me somewhere, would you mistake me for somebody else? And if I tell you my name was not Nuraan, instead tell you some other name, would you just think you are wrong and move on?

"It is a similar situation for those who met him. Even though they are not his brothers, at least three of them were his very close friends. For example, Emanuel understood him more than you and I did. Also, as I said, they don't have any hidden agenda to lie. The other thing is that they are all different, but they all reported that he told them the same name."

"What do you consider we should do now?" asked the father, agreeing with his son's analysis and hoping that he had a suggestion for a solution.

"The first step is for us to make peace with him. Among all his friends, Emanuel was the closest and who knew him the longest. He has been confused and sad ever since he met him at a café and told him he was not he. So, I'm confident that he is willing to help us with our mission.

"The mission is for the three of us to go to the café and the other places where other friends had met him. While you and I hide somewhere around the place, Emanuel should approach him. Then we meet him and tell him that we are sorry. Before that, you and I should go to his work place and talk to the human resources manager and ask if they have rehired him or what they know about his current situation," said Nuraan.

Haji Mustafa thought for a moment before responding, "This is a great idea! I'm available in the morning. We could go to his workplace around nine."

"Sure!"

***

The TV station was crowded with multiple programs—especially, the timely hot topic, a politician's sexual harassment scandal had taken most of the station's airtime. Around three in the evening, Suzan appeared on the screen sitting across a table from a man in a gray suit.

"As part of our coverage on the controversial case regarding the little girl, we have been speaking with experts in different walks of life. Our guest of the day is Doctor Mark Powel. He is a Doctor of Theology. We have invited him to help us discuss the case of brain transplants in perspective to religion.

"First of all, I would like to thank you, Doctor Powell, on behalf of our viewers and myself for accepting our invitation. I believe you are aware of the most controversial court case about the little girl. Before we immerse ourselves into the discussion of the case, allow me to ask you one question that you could answer as a religious scholar," said Suzan.

"Sure!"

"Looking through glasses of religion, is brain transplants a permitted or forbidden act?"

"Human beings have the right to do anything that they are able to. Basically, they are not prohibited from doing anything at all. It is indicated in the Bible that people are to be taught what is right and wrong. Then they could choose to do either or, or both."

"So, did I hear you say that human beings have the right to do anything? No limit?"

"Yes, again, in the Bible, it is written that both the righteous and the sinners have unsolicited right to do righteous or sinning things. It is up to us to decide what to do or not to do. However, it is indicated that there is a price to be paid for the choice that is made. We are given the right to choose between going to heaven or hell."

"Okay, Doctor Powel, theologically speaking, what makes a person, a person? Is it his or her brain? His or her body? Or the combination of the two? Or do you have any other idea?"

"A person is neither his or her body, nor his or her brain. They are tools that enable him or her to live in this tangible world. When a person loses both, he or she ceases to exist in the tangible world. A person's personhood is intricate, and it is called soul. Matthew chapter 10 verse 28, teaches that we should not be afraid of those who can kill the body for they cannot kill the soul. This explains that a man is mainly a soul, and even if the human body passes, his or her soul doesn't."

"Based on what you just said, if his or her soul is what makes a person, a person, is the soul of the child in our discussion that of the African American or the Caucasian family?"

"Neither. A person's relationship with his or her parents, and other familial relationships for that matter, are based on the flesh. Soul, on the other hand, has been passing from male to male through generations beginning from the creation of mankind. In different areas of the Bible, we see that man is of body, soul, and Spirit. Therefore, if they are arguing about her flesh, they are considering her body and brain. Because, their parenthood is limited to the flesh. They can't reach and limit the soul—it is not their child. A question about ownership of a soul may arise between God and the Devil, but if the person had lived as God wanted him or her to, his or her soul is God's."

"Doctor Paul, thank you again for coming! I hope to see you in some other discussions."

***

Mr. Ermias was in his office since 7 am, working on his new projects. When his phone rang, it startled him. It was his secretary. She told him that two gentlemen wanted to see him. He told her to let them in.

Nuraan and his father walked in quietly and stood in front of Mr. Ermias' conference table. He stood up smiling and invited them to sit in any of the chairs by the table. Then, inquired how he could help them.

After introducing themselves, Haji Mustafa asked what and how much the office knew about Amin's death.

"We don't know anything more than you know. The last thing I knew about Amin before we heard the news of his death, was that he was accepted to a prestigious university in America. He came and told me about the opportunity he had received after multiple attempts," said Mr. Ermias.

"That is what we are wondering about. The news about his death, was it sent to this office from America? If so, what are the details on that?" Asked Nuraan, hoping that they may find the key to the mystery of his brother's news of death with Mr. Ermias.

"We heard the news from one of his colleagues, who heard it from your neighbor. When the news was announced in this facility, everyone felt bad for Amin, and a bunch of us were preparing to come to his funeral.

"But, since there wasn't one, we sent a couple of his coworkers and friends with the letter of condolence and a gift we all put together to your house," said Mr. Ermias expecting more question to come.

"Are you saying, you didn't receive a letter about his death from America?" Asked Haji Mustafa.

"No, we didn't. As I tried to explain, we didn't send him for the higher education. We didn't sponsor him, not even a penny. He pursued the specialization out of his desire, and he spent a lot of money and time to secure it.

"He must have been paying out of pocket. He told me that he worked hard for that chance. Anyway, because we didn't send him or sponsor him for that education, the school he went to didn't recognize us. That means they wouldn't send any letter to us informing anything about him," said Mr. Ermias.

"Well! That is a bummer!" Exclaimed Nuraan, looking at his dad. Then, he continued, "Let me ask you a different question. Did you hear about him within the last couple of months?"

"That is odd! However, to answer your question directly, no. Were we supposed to?" said Mr. Ermias, wondering where the question was coming from.

"Mr. Ermias, more than four people told us they saw him here in Addis. Three of these people are his closest friends, so they knew him very well. They all said that they approached him, but he told them that he is not Amin. Instead, he said that he is Million. So, has Amin or this Million guy come asking for his job back?" Explained Haji Mustafa.

"No, nobody has come. His position is still vacant. Do you think it is a look alike? The man told them he is Million. I'm not sure how you guys believe that it is remotely possible that he could be Amin," said Mr. Ermias, wondering why they would assume a dead person was walking in the streets of Addis.

"All his friends insist that it is him. We don't know what to think of it. Because if this man is Amin, why hasn't he come to his house at least to see his kids? One thing that makes us believe in the remote possibility, as you put it, is that we never saw his dead body. We were told that he died in a vehicle accident.

"So, we came to you to see if you and your agency has better information about his death. We thought the letter about his death and his belongings that came to us were sent through this office. Anyway, thank you for your time. However, if he comes looking for his job, please let us know, here is my phone number," said Nuraan, handing him a piece of paper with his phone number.

"I shall do that. Matter of fact, we will be in touch with his widow soon to disburse his employee benefits that she is supposed to receive," Mr. Ermias said and accompanied them to his secretary for her to help them exit.

Walking back to his office, Mr. Ermias thought about the hard time this family was having and said to himself, "But, every look alike in town shouldn't steer them."

***

At around 6 pm, Million went to Addis Mercato shopping mall to buy some lighter clothes. There, he visited one store after another, and he bought two V-neck shirts in one, an open-toed-shoes in another, and nothing in others.

Doing so, he arrived at a nicely stocked store. Inside, a young pregnant woman was on a ladder, pulling a pair of pants from a neatly arranged stack to show to perspective buyers. Also, inside, two boys of seven and five were standing and looking at a book of animal pictures.

Casually, Million went in and started looking for clothes of his choice from hanged bunches. After locating one shirt that he wanted, and went to check-out, he looked down toward the back of the sales desk. The older boy, Amin, was staring at him with surprise and a grin on his face, so, their eyes met. Immediately, the kid shouted, "ba-ba" and ran into Million. And then the younger one, Nur, followed his brother shouting, "baba, baba."

Their mom startled greatly by the kids screaming and running. Even though she stood up on the ladder, her view was blocked by products that were hanging, so, she couldn't identify the person to whom the kids ran toward. She suspected they ran to Haji Mustafa and tried to return her attention to picking a pair of jeans for a customer. But she couldn't. Though not sure, she thought, she heard her kids scream "baba."

She knew the only person whom they call baba was their dad. She felt and heard her heart beating overwhelmingly fast. A cold sweat began rolling down the back of her neck. Her legs started shaking. She stood on the ladder for what seemed an hour to her, but twenty seconds on the clock. She wanted to quickly get down the ladder, but the fear added to her pregnancy slowed her down.

For the first few weeks, after she heard about his death, Barakat didn't give up imagining that her husband would call and tell her that the news of his death was a lie and the money and belongings that came in his name was a scam. Then reality sank into her. When, in addition to Awet, Amin's other friends reported of meeting or seeing him in town, she began exploring the possibility of her earlier imagination.

Her vision grew and started picturing him coming when she was not expecting, to surprise her, but leaving with anger and sadness after seeing her pregnant. She wanted to hide her pregnancy, but there was no way she could because it was over six months.

The news of him being in town was true. As I thought, he was here to surprise me. Oh, Allah! What do I do with my big belly now? thought Barakat. Her yearning of hugging and kissing him increased with each step of the ladder. However, her fear of him seeing her the way she was started to defeat her.

Million was stunned seeing two kids running toward him screaming “baba” and laughing joyously. He immediately realized the kids were Amin’s sons. They looked so too.

Especially Amin—he had the same look as the current Million. He picked the older

son up and kissed him on the forehead and the cheek and did the same with the younger.

The kids were cheerful, and one of them said, “Baba, you are back, you are not dead. Let’s go home.” Million was devastated.

They both put their heads on each side of his chest, and they had their hand on his back through his shoulders. They held him very tight, as if for him not to leave them again.

“Mama is over there,” said Nur, pointing toward his mom. Million turned around and saw the pretty woman Amin had shown him in a picture. He was afraid that she would come running, but she didn’t.

Shocked to see her husband, she felt her knees giving up on her. Cold sweat rolling throughout her body, she started trembling.

Million kissed the kids and lowered them to the ground. But they kept tightening their embrace.

Trying to free himself, he said, “Let me go get my bags, I will be right back.” Then started rushing out.

“Okay, don’t take long, we will all go home with mammy,” said Amin. Nur started crying, then Amin joined him.

Hearing them cry devastated Million. As he went further, the sound of the kids' crying began to fade, but the self-criticism and regret in his head grew louder. The sound of cries of the kids kept echoing in his head and stared to crush his spirit. Because there was nothing he could do, his feet kept marching forward while his mind swam in guilt.

His peace was disturbed, thinking about the poor kids, the worst part was that he couldn't get them off his mind, even if he tried hard.

He thought, *These kids have a bizarre phenomenon to grow up remembering. They probably think their dad has risen from the dead and came to see them—then, he left to get his baggage but never came back.* "They don't deserve this!" he screamed. He was also worried about Amin's wife. He thought, *She saw her husband for seconds, then he vanished without saying hi to her. This experience may have some sort of negative effect on her emotional well-being.*

Million was distressed, recalling the encounter with Amin's wife and kids. While walking, he was talking to himself, "Without their consent and permission, I'm living in a body of a man who was dear to these people. If that wasn't enough, I just disarrayed their peace. Am I a man who is created for no reason than to tousle everything?"

***

Barakat's shaking knees finally gave up, and her legs started crumpling. Before she collapsed to the ground, a couple of shoppers rushed and supported her down to the floor. Million was at the door, leaving. Hence, he didn't witness her falling.

The kids, however, were walking back toward their mom when she fell. Amin was scared. Nur didn't seem to know how to react. Amin, while supporting his mom's head and asking her what happened, told his brother to call home.

Shortly after the kid made the phone call, Amin's parents came running. The mother reached down to Barakat, her hands nervously shaking, touched her, and started calling her name. But Barakat neither responded nor opened her eyes.

One of the shoppers said, "We should call an ambulance right away."

"Can anyone please tell me, what exactly happened to her?" asked the mother without taking her eye off Barakat.

"I'm not sure but I noticed a guy came in and these kids ran into him, yelling baba, and she stood here with a look of surprise on her face. A pair of shoes she was holding to hand them to me fell from her hand. Then, she was about to fall, and my friend, he and I supported her down," said the shopper whom she was helping right before falling.

The kids said at the same time, "Mamina, baba was here! He went to get his bags."

The grandparents looked at the kids with confusion, and the grandpa asked, "Was Ahmed here?"

"No, our father, Amin," said Amin.

"Kids, didn't we all tell you that you should leave the dead alone. Not to say anything about him again. Stop the silliness!" said Amin's father, sounding irritated.

"No silliness—baba was here. You will see him soon," said Amin.

The Ambulance arrived. They gently laid her on the stretcher and took her to the hospital. Since one family member was allowed to ride with the patient to the hospital, her mother in-law went with her.

When the doctor came into her room, the otherwise healthy looking pregnant young woman was lying on her right side with her eyes covered. He asked what happened to her, but he didn't get a satisfactory answer from the mother. So, he did his assessment and concluded that she had passed out but wasn't hurt and that she didn't have a history of any diseases that could have caused fainting.

The doctor asked her mother in-law if she knew why Barakat passed out. The mother didn't believe she should narrate what she learned from the shopper, so, she said, "I'm not sure, she simply passed out."

He sensed from the elderly's response that she might be hiding something. So, he pressed, "Don't you want her to be better? We won't be able to find the best solution for her unless we know what the cause of her problem is. Please tell us why exactly she passed out so that we could prescribe her the right medication and treatment," he said firmly.

"Doctor, it is complicated. It has no use for you," said Amina with sad voice.

Still firmly, he said; "Please, ma'am! Every information could be useful in treating her."

"She is my daughter in-law. My son and her have two sons together. My son went to America for higher education, and they told us that he died there. Losing him was hard on everyone in the family, especially on her and the kids. Reasoning that the kids would receive a continuation in fatherly care, we had her marry his brother.

"She didn't want to, but, after pressure from us and religious leaders, she gave in, and then she got pregnant. She seemed to have accepted everything for the sake of her kids, until she heard a rumor that her supposedly dead husband is in town.

"Today, the kids were with her when she passed out, they said that their father, again, who is supposed to be dead, came and saw her. That is when all this happened. We didn't see him. It is something the children imagined and talked about," said Amina.

Doctor Desta, fascinated by what he heard said, "How old is the child who saw him?"

"They are two, seven and five."

"So, was it their father whom they said they saw?"

"Yes!"

The doctor was dazzled by the complexity of the story. He understood Barakat's cause of mental stress and fainting. He ordered an extended period of resting and glucose. He reminded the nurse that her pregnancy should be considered in the planning of all her treatments.

He turned to Amin's mom and told her that Barakat was doing okay, and she may wake up within an hour or two. "In the meantime, go get the children."

As soon as the mother left, he told the nurses manager to have her moved to different room. He said, "She is dealing with a very complicated family affair. We need to keep an eye on her when she wakes up. She will need one on one care. Otherwise, she might try to hurt herself."

One of the nurses asked, "Doctor Desta, what happened to her?"

"Her husband went abroad for school. Several months later, she and his family were told that he died from a car accident. Her in-laws, considering for the good of her kids, forced her to marry his brother; and now she is pregnant. But then again, the supposedly dead husband came back."

"Why would they force her to marry his brother? How could they?" asked the nurse.

"According to her mother in-law, their religion permits it," said Doctor Desta.

Another nurse, "What about his brother? How can he comfortably sleep with his dead brother's wife? He must have been wishing to have her even when his brother was alive," said the nurse, saddened by the story.

"She is in the worst family issue that any can be at. The father of her children must have despised his family, especially his brother. You know she was at fault too. She could have used the law to stop them from forcing her," commented a third nurse.

While the nurses were conversing in Barakat's old room, Amina opened the door without knocking and entered with a man.

The man seemed annoyed and irritated. He went straight to the doctor's office. Slightly hyper ventilating, he asked, "Where is the girl, we are here to see her?"

"She hasn't woken up. We have given her everything she needs to recover. She will wake up in a little while," said Doctor Desta, and turned around to Amina and said, "The children…" before he could finish, Ahmed interrupted him.

"No, they have nothing to do with this. I'm her husband, if you have any questions, ask me," he said aggressively.

"My whole point is this, knowing the cause of her problem is half the solution. Therefore, interviewing the people who witnessed the incident will help greatly. Because her treatments could be tailored based on the cause of her problem."

"I don't want you to ask too many unnecessary questions. If you don't know her disease, just say so, and I will take her to another hospital."

"Sorry you feel that way, but my questions are necessary to save your wife as well as your unborn baby's lives. Please, understand that I'm a doctor, not a police officer. Even if I sound like a police officer when I ask questions, the responses I receive are used to find the right solution to these two lives, not to prosecute anyone.

"We can always treat your wife even without knowing the cause of her problem, but the treatment could harm the pregnancy. However, if we know the problem, we can come up with a care plan that addresses the mother and the pregnancy. So, if you understand me, my questions are intended to make sure that we give the right medication both to the mother and the unborn baby."

The last explanation had softened Ahmed's rigid and defensive approach. It addressed his worries and plans. He asked nicely, "Doctor, do you think the baby is affected?" He believed the birth of the child will secure the status that he was Barakat's husband.

He was worried that Amin might find her before she had the baby and had her get rid of the pregnancy. And he assumed that if she had the opportunity, she wouldn't hesitate doing so. Therefore, he decided that as soon as she got better, he would take and hide her some place where anyone from the family couldn't find her, until she had the baby.

"You see, the only way we can assure that the fetus is safe is by carefully selecting the medication we give to your wife. If we don't know the cause of her problem, we could give her all kinds of medications that we know could help her, but might harm the unborn baby."

Ahmed's anger disappeared and he started pleading, "Please doctor, save the child too."

"We will do everything to save both, but your help is important. We still have to determine the cause of her problem."

"I was told that she passed out because she heard her ex-husband came to our store," said Ahmed, trying not to go into much detail.

Doctor Desta wanted to ask more questions, but he didn't want to upset the man, so he said, "No worries, we are doing our best, and we will continue to do so to protect the unborn child from being harmed. Now, the nurse will show you where she is."

Hearing the doctor's willingness to help, Ahmed felt relief.

***

Barakat woke up from her faint. She looked around the room and wondered where she was and how she got there. A few seconds later, she realized that she was in a hospital and remembered how she ended up there. It was because her husband, Amin, saw that she was pregnant and left without even saying hi.

Her nurse noticed that she was waking up, "Hi there, my name is Tigist, I'm your nurse. Your doctor would like to see that you are doing better, so let me go get him," said Nurse Tigist and dashed out.

"It is great to see you doing better," said Doctor Desta, smiling big.

She said, "thank you!" softly and quietly.

He pulled up a chair and sat by her bed, and said, "Are you able to tell me what happened, or should I come back later?"

"I would like to go home to my kids," said Barakat, her eyes tearing up.

"I understand, but first we need to discuss your situation. Your mother in-law told me about why you passed out. I gathered you are dealing with a complicated family issue. I'm both a medical doctor and psychologist. You can talk to me, or I can refer you to a specialist. What do you think?" said Doctor Desta.

While the doctor was talking, Barakat thought about how her life had turned upside down and how she lost her irreplaceable loving husband who was alive and well. Her tears started to run down her face. Then, she broke out and said, "Doctor, there is no end to my misery. My life is broken beyond repair. And it has become too knotty to untangle. Many people are getting hurt because of my poor decision. especially my kids—they lost their dad. When they know that I'm to blame, they will hate me forever."

"Can you tell me about the decision you made that you think is poor?"

"I shouldn't have married his brother. I should have gone to the streets with my kids."

"Your mother in-law told me that you were pressured by religious leaders to marry him. Is that not accurate?"

"Yes, but still, I'm responsible."

"But you didn't know that the father of your children was still alive."

"I didn't know. But I should have listened to my gut."

"I'm noticing that you are taking sole responsibility to what happened. However, I want to remind you that it was never your idea to marry your current husband, you and everyone else thought your ex-husband was dead, and most of all, when you finally accepted the proposal, you were thinking of the wellbeing of your children. So, I think you're being too hard on yourself."

"I don't know. I have no idea how I can live with myself knowing that my loving husband is alive. And my children, they don't deserve what they are going through. They love their dad."

"You can arrange for the kids to see their dad. Do you know where he is staying? Is he in contact with anyone that you know of?"

"No, I don't."

"We need to set up an appointment for you and I to meet in a couple of days. Are you going to be okay if we send you home today? Let me ask you directly, do you feel like hurting yourself or others?"

"No, I'm okay. But I don't know for how long."

"Try to take it one day at time. Let's meet two days from today, the nurse will help you chose the right time to come to my office. I need to go now; I have another patient to see."

***

Abigail called her workplace and tried to learn from unsuspecting coworkers what was on the agenda regarding Million. A colleague, who was in the meeting, told her about the different webs that were being woven to catch Million.

She was not surprised by what she heard; however, it gave her perspective on how much trouble Million was in, and herself if seen or caught with him.

When they met in the bar of the hotel they were staying at, she noticed he was sad and uncomfortable. He headed toward her with slumped shoulders and bowed head.

Concerned by what she saw, she said, "Million, what is wrong? I can see it in your face that something is bothering you."

"I ran into Amin's wife and kids."

"Oh! Man! What did they say?"

"The kids came running and latched on to me."

"Then?"

"I told them that I had to go get my bags. And they let me go."

"That was good, for now, you escaped easily. We will talk about this later, there is a more pressing issue that I have been waiting to tell you about. You should probably sit comfortably."

"What is more important than that?"

"The hunt for you has increased both in technique and complexity. Your enemies are using both names, Million and Amin, to their advantage. So, maybe you should divorce those names. They suspect that you would be either with your wife and kids, your family, or Amin's family.

"So, unless you have a better idea, I suggest that we stay low for a bit. In fact, we should go someplace where they wouldn't suspect you have gone to. Nobody should know where we are going. Also, since my departure to the States is coming soon, I need to visit the historical places.

We should see the obelisk, relics, and rock churches in North Ethiopia. When I go home, I will know any other plan that they may have, and I will keep you informed."

Million thought, *Poor Abigail, you have no idea that I had run in to all the troubles you are warning me against, and more.*

Knowing how much she cared for him, he felt guilty for not telling her that he went out behind her back and almost got killed.

He hesitated whether to tell her or not, then he said, "I used Amin's passport to register for all the hotels we have been staying at, including this one. They always ask for ID, so I don't think I have any other option even in the future."

"When we get back, we will figure something out. If anything, we could rent a house in a quiet and nice neighborhood," she said.

Being nagged by one guilt and another, he mumbled, "Courage, where are you?"

***

Among the nurses who were caring for Barakat, Fatuma seemed to have taken her case to heart. Without mentioning her name, she brought up the case into multiple discussions. Especially at home, that was all she talked about. Even her husband, Jemal, who normally was conservative about getting involved other people's issues, agreed with her when she consulted him about bringing the woman home for a moral support.

A couple of days later, when Barakat didn't come for her follow up appointment with Dr. Desta, Fatuma began to worry and felt guilty for not intervening when Barakat said, "Only if I'm still alive then," when talking about showing up for her appointment.

Though freaking out, she waited half an hour, before she called Dr. Desta, and said, "Doc. Barakat is a no show, I wonder if she is okay."

"Do we have her contact? Did you try to call her?"

"Yes, some guy answered the phone and told me that she is not available to talk."

"Maybe you should call back to see if she wanted to reschedule."

She called and said, "Hello, my name is Fatuma, I'm a nurse at Yemane and Desta Hospital, may I speak with Barakat please?"

"Didn't you call earlier? I told you! she is not available."

"She missed her appointment; I was just checking if she wants to reschedule?"

"SHE DOESN'T."

"Can, I at least... hello, hello?"

Fatuma's fear started to change to anger. She went to the nurses' manager's office and said, "Hi Martha, sorry, but I don't feel well, can you please have someone cover for me?"

"What is wrong? Does your Migraine started to bother you, again? Go ahead, get some rest, if anything, I will cover for you."

"Thank you, Martha! Again, sorry for the abrupt request," said Fatuma. As soon as she left her boss's office, she called her husband and told him to meet her at a cafe close to Barakat's house.

"Jemal, I'm about to explode from guilt!" said Fatuma, sitting on a chair across the table from her husband.

"What guilt?"

"Not only moral, I have a professional obligation to intervene when someone is hinting of suicide. The girl told me, she might not be alive to come to the appointment, but I did nothing. What kind of idiot am I?"

"I see!"

"She didn't show up for her appointment and when I called her house, some rude guy told me that she is not available to talk and hung up on me. I think he is her husband."

"Okay?"

"Well, her house is a block from here. First and foremost, I want to know if she is okay. And we can check if she needs any help."

"How do you suggest we do that?"

"I don't have a well thought out plan, I'm just hoping that we find someone from her neighbors, who knows what is going on in her house."

"I have a couple of ideas! Let's see which one you like the most. But first, do you know what her husband looks like?"

"Yes, he came to take her home while she was still sick. He was arguing with Doctor Desta, until he learned that if he didn't cooperate in providing information why she fainted, his unborn child might be endangered."

"Okay, the first idea is this, we knock on the door, and if he opens it, we will tell him that we are from Bureau of Health Management and we need to check on the pregnant woman in the house. The other idea is whoever opens the door, we impersonate agents from the Statistics Bureau, and ask to see household members. Which one do you like better?"

"Jemal, you are genius! Both are fraudulent, but regardless, you are brilliant! I'm glad you are mine and only mine! I have a good hunch that the first one will work," said Fatuma and kissed her husband on the cheek.

When they were a couple of hundred feet away from where Barakat lived, they noticed a young girl of about twenty-two-years-old come out of the house and started walking their direction.

"Perfect! This is what you hoped would happen, your wish has come through. Ask her—that might save us from pretending," said Jemal, smiling at his wife.

"WOW!" whispered Fatima. The girl was nearing. She stopped her, and said, "Excuse me, dear! We are from Bureau of Health Management, visiting pregnant moms in the area. Do you know if Barakat is at home?"

"Yes, she is," answered the girl.

"Who else is at home, with her?"

"Father Ahmed, and her sons."

"Do you mind going and have her come out to talk to us? We don't want to bother father Ahmed."

"Sorry, I have to go to that store over there. Father Ahmed has sent me to buy Chat, I should've been back by now. He gets upset if I take longer. But, if you wait here or by the door, I can help you when I come back."

"Yes, we will wait for you."

Fatuma and Jemal began waiting for her where she left them. To their surprise, she went running and a came back in less than eight minutes.

"Don't you want to wait by the gate? I will tell Barakat that you guys are outside," she said, and sprinted to the house.

"This Ahmed guy must be very impatient and aggressive. Did you see how she ran not to be late?" said Jemal.

"I have interacted with him twice, once at the hospital and today on the phone, and I noticed he is the angriest man I have dealt with. I feel bad for Barakat. I'm just glad she is doing okay, so far. I wouldn't have lived with myself if something had happened to her before today," said Fatuma.

"So, if you do see her, what are you planning on telling her?"

"I want to tell her that she has an option. And that I'm, we, are willing to help her flee if she doesn't feel safe where she is."

"Hopefully we get a chance to talk to her alone."

"Please pray for that! But, if anything, I can give her our number to call us."

"I don't think I know how to pray anymore. Thanks to you, the last time I had been to Mosque was when I was fifteen."

"How am I to blame in all that?"

"Well, if I didn't fall in love with you, I wouldn't have abandoned my dream of becoming a Caliph."

***

Jemal and Fatima were non practicing Muslims. Fatima thought of herself a modernized Muslim. Early on, she picked and chose rules from the Quran that she believed would work for her. Though she first met Jemal at a Mosque, she hadn't been to one ever since the day they met.

They started seeing each other despite their parents' dismay. At age seventeen, they got married without the knowledge of each ones' parents.

***

Inside the house, Ahmed was preparing to sit for Chat, so didn't even notice if the girl was late. After handing him the Chat, the girl ran to Barakat's bedroom. A few minutes later, Barakat, her kids, and the girl came out of the bedroom and were walking across the living room.

"Where the heck are you going?" asked Ahmed getting up from his comfortable seat.

"Agents from the Bureau of Health want to talk to me about my pregnancy, they are outside."

"They have no business to come to my house and talk to you without my permission. Now, sit down! I will go talk to them."

Ahmed opened the gate to find the young couple standing to the side. "Who are you, and what do you want?"

They were both startled to see him, Jemal, pulled himself quickly up and said, "We are from the health bureau. We received a report that your wife had an emergency and the unborn baby could particularly be at risk. This is a normal procedure of checking on pregnant moms who have been to the emergency department."

"She was already seen by a doctor and they didn't find any issue. Thank you for checking, good bye!" said Ahmed trying to close the gate.

"Sorry, sir! But we have to hear it from the mom. Sometimes it takes a few days or weeks before any issue is discovered. The moms are the one who feel the change and report. So, we are required to speak the pregnant mom before we report back that there is no issue or otherwise," said Fatuma gently, adjourning the door from closing them out.

"Stay here! When she comes, don't ask anything else other than what brought you here," he said, sounding extremely annoyed.

"Yes, sir! We are here to check on the health of the unborn child and the mom, that and that only," said Fatima, trying to control her excitement.

As soon as Ahmed closed the gate, she pulled her husband a few steps away from the house and whispered, "He is going to come back with her, do you have any idea how we can distract him, and isolate her, at least until I give her my phone number?"

"I don't know, maybe I can talk to him about something that will upset him and draw his attention to me."

"I think that will ..."

The gate swung open and Ahmed said, "Come in and ask her, and leave quickly."

When they walked in, they were noticeably nervous. Fatima shook Barakat's hand with her shaking one. She held the hand shake longer until Barakat recognized the piece of paper that she was given her. She looked her in the eye and slowly loosened her grip.

"Excuse me, sir, you seem upset. We are just doing our job," said Jemal looking at Ahmed.

As the couple hoped, Ahmed completely forgot the interaction his wife was having with Fatima and turned his attention to Jemal and said, "I understand that, but some of you are too intrusive. You ask questions that have nothing to do with what you came for." When he said that, he was trying to return his attention to his wife.

"Is there anything in particular that you don't want us to ask your wife about? "asked Jemal, attempting to block Ahmed's view.

"Just do what you came to do and leave," said Ahmed, staring at the man who was slightly taller than himself.

By then, Barakat had understood who Fatima was and what she came to do. She said, "I didn't feel the baby moving since about ten, this morning. But I was reluctant to tell anyone, assuming he might just be sleeping. Do you think that is a concern?" She spoke loudly, making sure that Ahmed could hear her.

"Yes, it is a concern. What time is it now?" said Jemal purposely returning his awareness to the pregnant mom.

Ahmed looked at his gold watch and said, "It is 1 pm. Why didn't you tell me? Had it been about something those rude sons of yours, you would have been nagging me and my family already."

Barakat ignored him and asked the pretending agents, "What do I do now?"

"Our record shows that you are just entering your third-trimester. That means, the baby should have been kicking more than twenty times every hour. I'm very concerned," said Fatima, looking at Barakat. Then she turned to Ahmed and said, "You need to call the ambulance and take her to the hospital. NOW!"

Ahmed started to freak out. Aimlessly, he ran into the house. He came out in flip-flops, carrying his coat. He went back in and changed his shoes. Then he called the ambulance from the house phone.

While Ahmed was going crazy, Barakat told the couple that she had been meaning to kill herself. They assured her that they will help her through her difficult time and that she shouldn't hesitate to call them. She agreed that she would call them if she needed help.

When Ahmed joined his wife and the "agents," he was perspiring. With a nervous sound, he asked, looking at Jemal "Is the baby going to be okay?"

"Sometimes, the baby could be just sleeping. But we are not doctors, so, no matter the case might be, she should be seen by a doctor. At the hospital, they have ways to monitor the baby's current condition," replied Jemal. He added, "I'm just glad we came to check on her and that you let us interview her. Thank you! We need to leave, and you two head to the hospital. My associate will be calling to check how your visit went, so please, let her talk to your wife."

***

"So, if she decided to flee, have you thought about where she will hide until you meet and talk to her supposedly dead husband?" asked Jemal to his wife, while they were heading to their car.

"I have been planning on sending her to one of my aunts in Jima. I don't think it is smart idea to have her stay in our house for more than a couple of nights. Do you have any other ideas?"

"No, that is perfect!"

"Speaking of perfect…" she hesitated. She had been struggling whether to tell him her other agenda of why she wanted to help Barakat, but she wasn't sure how he would react. So, decided to wait until Barakat gave birth.

Instead she said, "I already talked to aunt Tumi, she would be glad to help."

Finding Barakat alive and being able to make plans with her made Fatima ecstatic. She was also feeling grateful to her husband for his priceless support. Smiling, she looked at him and grabbed his left hand and kissed it, then put it on her shoulder, and wrapped her right arm around his waist.

"So, you want her to go to Jima. That is a great idea. Hopefully, she doesn't already have relatives there that her husband would suspect she went to them."

"I don't think she has. During our conversation, when she was at the hospital, she told me that her parents are from Mekelle, and she was born and raised in Addis," said Fatima, smiling with excitement that her plan to rescue Barakat was taking shape. She added, "You want to hear something impressive about her?"

"Definitely!"

"She speaks four languages, Amharic, Tigrigna, Afaan-Oromo, and Arabic. What is more interesting is that she learned Afaan-Oromo after she married to Amin, whose native tongue is that."

"Man, she is smart! I'm having a hard time speaking the only language I know, Amharic, correctly, she is communicating with three more," said Jemal smiling ear to ear.

***

Chapter Fourteen

Per the court's schedule, everyone was sitting and ready to hear the response of the appellees' attorney on the case.

"Your honor, the child knows her parents, and she has told the district court on her own words. She was a character witness to the parenthood of her parents. She recognized her parents, because she was raised by them. The appellant family didn't raise her, so, she doesn't know them. And it was impractical to make a couple whom she doesn't know and accept her parents. As she put it, these parents are the pretend parents to her. Basically, she doesn't accept them as her parents because they are not."

The appellants' attorney argued, "I haven't received an appropriate response to my questions—let me repeat the questions again: what does a parent mean? And, how could a mother who didn't recognize her supposed child be considered the mother to that child? No baby is born with the inherent ability to recognize who its parents are. Any child acquires that knowledge slowly, overtime.

"A mom of a particular child, however, knew that the child is hers, from the time of her pregnancy of that child. The supposed mom in this case didn't give birth to the child, hence she didn't know her. A mom couldn't be a mom to a child whom she didn't know even if the child says that assumed mom is her mom."

He paused, then continued, "In my opinion, a parent is who gave birth not who just nurtured. And a child is offspring to a parent who gave birth to that child not to who he or she claims as his or her parent. My clients gave birth to the child's full body except the brain. The appellees' daughter on the other hand, except for her brain, which they donated to the hospital, her body is buried somewhere they definitely know. Which means, except for her brain, the child that they gave birth to is long gone.

"Even if the court judges that each party should have what belongs to it, there is no practical way to make that happen without killing the child. And that is illegal and inhumane. Therefore, I respectfully appeal to this court to reverse the district court's decision and that the child be returned to the parents who gave birth to her and are eager to hug and hold their daughter," said the appellant's attorney.

"The previous ruling was made based on analysis of the case from different angles. It took the rights of both the child and her parents into consideration and it also accounted for the child's knowledge and understanding. Therefore, looking at a human-being in terms of its body parts, as if he or she is a cow that is butchered for cuts, is inhumane and uncivilized. Such mentality doesn't discern humans from animals, and it lacks consideration to human dignity. Thus, I respectfully ask the court to put a limit on corresponding talk," said the black family's lawyer.

"Your honor, I would like to address a couple of points that the appellee had presented and close with questions for everyone in here to ponder on. The appellee's counsel mentioned that the previous judgement had taken knowledge into account. But the familiarities of the supposed mother and that of the child were conflicted. One of them must be true. Is it the child who should recognize that the woman is her birth mom, or the mother who should know that she had given birth to the child?"

The three judges whispered among themselves and the middle judge said, "As court put it previously, this case is the first of its kind therefor it needs a thoroughly investigated. Therefore, we would like to discuss it further."

***

The road was full of hillsides, and twists and turns, but neither their rental Toyota Landcruiser, nor the people in it seemed to be bothered by it. Especially Abigail, trilled by the scary edge of the road, kept laughing and clapping throughout the zigzag road. She was also consumed by the scenery alongside and across the road.

Seeing houses that looked like they were from a different time in the past, and village residents living a lifestyle that she never imagined, she felt as if she was on another planet. She imagined them being from a dream world, where real world experiences would never come to spoil the custom they were living.

She loved Bahir-Dar, she said, “It is a small but beautiful city. Impressively green and has nice lakes around it.” They spent one night there, the next day, they told their driver to wait in Gorgora, and they traveled on a sailboat through Lake Tana.

They checked out some islands. Everything that she saw added fascination to her impression. The islands had kept their natural look. The all-natural presence of everything in the islands created a unique love for nature in Abigail’s mind. She believed the territory, its trees, birds, and other animals were all genuine.

“Million, this is the best time of my life.”

“How?”

"I can't imagine where in my country I could have seen such unaltered and untouched beauty of nature. Everything in here is nature in its originality."

"What makes you say that?"

"In my country, even if you search, you won't find anything that human technology hasn't interrupted. Here, you don't have to search, the majority of things are contained and maintained by nature as it put them. They are unaffected."

"I agree with you! This country is gifted that way. If you are impressed by this, I wonder how dazzled you would be to see the oldest human bones in the world?"

"Where are they? Million, I want to see those."

"They are in Addis Ababa Museum. I didn't think about them until now. I will take you when we get back to Addis."

"Please do so."

"As much as you enjoy seeing ancient things, how come you never heard about the oldest of all bones?"

"I have no idea why. It is interesting, there are many things that don't exist anywhere else but here."

"The skeletons are that of women. Their names are Lucy and Ardi. They are well known fossils."

Talking about that and this, they finished their on-boat travel, and they joined their driver to Gondar, another Ethiopian city with great signature marks of ancient civilization. When they were visiting an ancient emperors' fortress and palace compound, and churches, a tour guide was explaining to them when and by who the buildings were built.

Abigail couldn't find an explanation to how and why people who once were able to build those kinds of buildings went backward instead of forward in civilization.

"Million, on our way here, we saw people living in houses that looked like caves. Why didn't the skillsets that enabled to build these wonders or architectures transfer from the generation of that period to the next, and then after to todays?"

"Maybe it was destroyed in one of the wars. Ethiopia's history revolves around war. It starts with war, continues with war, and ends in war. Maybe we are cursed. Instead of agreeing and working together on a common good, it is easier for us to kill each other and destroy things that benefit all of us.

"I hope that the curse is washed away now by the blood of the innocents who died in a war created by a few leaders' inabilities to compromise. Also, this country has lived through different self-defense wars against invaders and aggressors from all four directions."

"Use your imagination and start at a time when these architectures were designed. If you remove all the wars and add technological development to the math, can you believe how advanced this country would have been now?"

"Oh, yes, I can imagine that! Because leaders in previous generations spent their time destroying one another and the country, and the people of this naturally rich nation never got a break from poverty. If the current and the upcoming generation learn from history and correct what didn't work—such as the time spent in civil war—there is still a chance that my country will reach the development status that your country has reached," said Million with conviction.

From Gondar, they headed to the North Mountains Park. After enjoying scenes of mountains, valleys, rivers, forests, and wild animals, they started their journey to Axum. While on the road, Million wanted to tell her the incidence where he was almost killed, and free himself from the guilt of hiding

things from her. But he thought that would make her worry more, so, he decided not to.

Abigail pictured, in Axum, there would be rows of ancient building from one area to another. When they arrived there, she was disappointed to find nothing that fit her imagination. She wondered, other than being peculiarly tall, what else about the obelisks made them special. While heading to see them, from a distance, they looked like pieces of rocks put together with cement. Even when they arrived where the monuments were located, she was still disenchanted.

As if to find some proof, she began carefully studying what materials were used to make such a towering stele. She noticed one of them was made out of a rock. Just rock, nothing else! She looked closely at the rest of the stelae—they each were made from single rock. That got her attention.

She wondered, how each one of them was carved from a single rock? She was astonished by the possibility of finding such a huge rock from which the tall stele could be cut out. If that wasn't amazing enough, the question, *how this humongous obelisk was erected without a crane?* surfaced in her mind.

She asked their tour guide, "There is no indication that the pillars were made here. Where were they brought from?"

"Each one of these stelae is a monolithic boulder, cut and then carved. They were brought from a couple of places called Dura and Child of Dura, those areas are located a few miles away from the city limit. The largest stelae weigh over 500 tons, and they are estimated to be about two thousand years old," said the guide.

Abigail wondered what kind of technology could there have been that enabled transporting those gigantic markers.

"Is there any evidence that they came from the places you just mentioned?" She asked the guide.

She was finding it hard to believe these huge things were transported from miles away to their current location without the support from some form of technology. She tried but couldn't deem any primitive technology, other than dragging with a bunch of horses.

"Definitely! We can go there and see the boulder from which these stelae are made out of. On those mountains, there also are multiple unfinished monuments that we could see," said the guide.

"They were brought from mountains? Fascinating! This country is rich in mesmerizing treasures of the ancients. This must be the most puzzling part of our planet," said Abigail, captivated by the conundrum the ancients and their works.

"At the time when this part of the world was making these thrilling things, America was just a forest land. Now, it is the opposite. What a reversed scenario! Though their ancestors were civilized and modernized, the current generations are primitives.

"How did this country's technologies go backward? Those who do not know that these people were once civilized before it somehow collapsed, may consider them archaic," said Abigail recognizing the poor beggar she saw on the streets of Addis had descended from rich and civilized ancestors.

The more she thought about the monuments, the more questions popped to her mind. Abigail didn't believe the stelae were an ordinary work of history. She imagined the brainteaser behind them.

"Million, what do you think are the tales of these stelae?"

"I'm not sure."

"Let rephrase my question—why do you believe they were made?"

"I have no idea."

"I presume they are letters on a rock written to the modern-day man."

"What do you think is the message on them?"

"You know what it says? It is saying—you could build a nine-story building in this design that has steps in the bottom, doors, windows, floors, and ceilings. If they had cement, they would have built it themselves. They are owners of an amazing design of a skyscraper. The design for high rise buildings was hidden for thousands of years."

"I see what you mean! It is amazing! They are narrating something? I never saw them this way before. Thank you for opening my eyes. Modern-man had a message on a rock to interpret and implement," Million said, wondering why he never imagined the monuments that way.

Seeing underground burial rooms, Abigail said, "You guys have a rich history in so many ways. Treasures of history that are found in other parts of the world do not tell what the upcoming generation could do."

Her amazement skyrocketed when she saw a monolithic rock of an ancient church designed as a cross in Lalibela. That and the other treasures in the area seemed to communicate with the curious of the archaic Abigail beyond astonishment.

"Where are the beautiful minded and skilled individuals who were able to do this? They are impressive people of the past with modern-day's knowledge. Where did they disappear to? People like them need to be found," said Abigail, captivated by what she was seeing.

"It is enchanting!" said Million, hoping he could describe how he felt about the magnificent work of art.

"You know what, Million, I believe poverty in your country started when you guys lost those people." She understood the technology that made those markers of civilization had collapsed for a long time.

Million traveled back in time in his imagination and saw those brilliant people working on those unique architectures that have never been attempted by mankind, since, and said "enchanting!" for the second time.

"Before the work started, the idea was in the designer's mind. Therefore, there were designers, architects, and engineers. Checkout the steps, the walls, the doors, windows, and the other decorative carvings and tell me how impressed you are. Have you noticed that this building's design is the same as the obelisks of Axum? But this is built in Lalibela.

"If the builders who built this had a much bigger rock, they would have built a nine-story skyscraper. I don't assume people of this era know why the obelisks were carved and erected. People of the Lalibela period, however, knew and transcribed the design of the stele of Axum to this monolithic-rock church.

"Look at the similarity between the windows, doors, and steps of this church with that of the designs on the obelisks of Axum," said Abigail with fascination driven enthusiasm, standing in front of Lalibela church and comparatively looking at it with a closeup picture she took of the obelisks.

"In school, we were taught Ethiopian history which included most of the historical places you and I visited, but no one understood and explained in detail as you have," said Million.

***

As anticipated by the court, the respondent's lawyer came with his response to the appellant's lawyer's questions. "Maternal parent of a specific child means a parent who gave birth to that child, regardless of whether the parent recognizes the child or not. Maternity is not ascertained based on whom the child looks like, or in terms of percentage of body parts shared.

"It is only determined by giving birth. If you look into

what Sandra is made of, the brain and the body, the brain is obviously more important and valuable than the body. It is like comparing a gram of a diamond to a one kilogram of cotton. Even though the size ratio between the two is one to one thousand, the one gram of diamond is more expensive than the one thousand grams of cotton because of its demand.

"Similarly, despite being one small organ in the whole body, the brain is far more important than the rest of the body it is in. Since all other body parts are made to be instructed by a brain, let alone to be superior, they could never be equal to it. That is why a person remains to be the same person after an organ, or any body part is replaced. However, if a brain is placed in a body, as in the case of little Miss. Johns, the body becomes part of the person and functions with the brain just bestowed.

"When conjoined with a body, it is the brain that comes to the body with the knowledge, understanding, belief, culture, behavior, personality, attitude, and most of all, emotion and the ability to reason that make a person, a person," he paused for a few seconds with the attempt of letting his point sink into everyone's mind.

Then he continued, "The once crawling and cylinder insect, caterpillar, becomes a flying and beautiful insect, butterfly. In this scenario, we see that the same sprit living in two different insects for the continuation of life. This is a complex and mesmerizing work of nature. Though complex and controversial work of mankind through science, Sandra's case is similar to the above plot of the caterpillar and butterfly. She was once Sandra in her own body and she is still Sandra in Teena's body," he concluded and went back to his seat.

The appellant took the stage, "Your honor, for what it's worth, the parents of Teena's body are maternal parents of that body. This body came out of the womb, not made in a factory. When it comes to the brain on the other hand, it is one organ of the body. Therefore, other than playing its role in the body, it doesn't have any superiority. It could neither replace any of the other organs nor survive without them.

"Hence, each organ in a body is needed to make a person. That being said, I would like to speak about the independence of knowledge and thought from the body and brain. Since knowledge and thought are not born, neither party could claim parenthood to it. Knowledge and thought are not a person or a person's identity. Knowledge is richness that people accumulate over time through the sense organs, sense of sight, hearing, smell, and touch; which everyone knows that they are parts of the body.

"Thought, on the other hand, is a combination of different knowledge. This doesn't mean knowledge and thought are a person. Therefore, I respectfully request a careful evaluation of these points to determine who the parents of the child are."

"Your honor, man's ability to analyze is what differentiates him from other animals. Through sight, hearing, and other senses, man obtains knowledge and thoughts. He knows; therefore, he reasons; he reasons therefore he knows. Animals do see and hear, but they can't cognize or reason as much as human beings. Therefore, knowledge and intelligence are faculties of the mind, which is part of the brain. This is uniquely human; and it is human. The other party's argument is based on ordinary philosophy on humanity and their ideas ignore that man and his thought are inseparable," said the black family's lawyer, calmly.

"Your honor, may I have the court's permission to perhaps more clearly present my argument using a hypothetical scenario?" asked the appellants' lawyer.

The judge gave him permission to proceed.

"If the late Miss. Johns was deaf and blind since birth, what would she have recognized and reasoned? When the brain was donated, it would have been a blank slate, as it had been since birth. If that same brain was placed in Teena's body with its hearing and sight senses intact, with no doubt, we wouldn't have been in here. The child, by looking at her similarity with Ava, she wouldn't have questioned that she was her mom. She would have been a witness who claims that her mother was Ava.

"The knowledge that the child has accumulated might have served its purpose at one time, but now it has expired and has no benefit to her. Hence, it should be erased from her memory. If she is left with this old and useless knowledge, it will hinder her from being with her actual family, and her future will be in jeopardy. It is up to this respected court to set this child's future in the right path by helping her join her maternal parents," said the appellant.

One of the judges was confused by what he heard from the appellant's lawyer; after whispering with the other two judges, he asked the lawyer, "Are you saying, the girl that is speaking now is not her?"

"It is her. But the knowledge from which she is speaking is wrong. May I again use a scenario to explain my point?"

"Continue," said the judge.

"If a six-month-old girl was abducted by a couple who did not have their own child, and they raised her with love and care, all she knows is that they are her parents. Then, if three and a half years later, the truth that they had stolen the child was discovered. Both the biological and the abductor parents then were summoned to the court and on their respective podium.

"If the four-year-old child was asked which couple are her parents, undoubtedly, she will answer that they are the abductors. Because, even though that is not the truth, that is her knowledge. Obviously, the verdict of the court in such case would be to send the suspects to prison and the child to her maternal parents.

"The child then would be helped to erase the knowledge that is related to her deceptive parents and install a new knowledge about her biological parents. The case on hand should end in the same manner. Because knowledge is not identity, rather, it is riches that people accumulate over time.

As time goes by, knowledge could improve, change, fade or be lost, or it could end up being proven that it is an erroneous."

He paused, then continued, "Your honor, Teena's mother, Ava, is suffering from the loss of her daughter, therefore, I respectfully request that the child be returned to her. Because she could never forget a piece of her who looks like her in many ways. Instead of hoping that this mother would forgo or forget her motherhood and about her daughter, it is easier to help the child edit the knowledge she has about her mom. Doing so will benefit both the child and the mother.

"The child's future will for sure be free of identity crises that could rise from being the only white in a black family. I also want to add that, the old knowledge that accumulated in the brain because of the African American child, the motherly love and care that her mom gives her will erase and be replaced with new knowledge about her real family. Whoever sees her will tell her whose child she is by noticing her looks and skin color. She will develop that same understanding with time and accept and believe the mother whom she looks like is actually her mom."

One of the judges asked, "Is doing so not manipulation by influencing her way of reasoning?"

"If an otherwise healthy man loses both his legs from an auto accident, he will have a challenging time to accept his loss. Since the man is walking and running with those legs up until the accident, the photographic memories he would have about his legs are what he used to do with them. If there isn't any way to replace those legs, he will accept his luck of losing them, as bitter as it may be.

"For the successful adaptation of his new life, he will need every rehabilitation and support he can get, mostly from his family and relatives. Otherwise, he may be subjected to and suffer from depression and despondence, and he could become suicidal. Once he develops the awareness about his current life, he would understand how to live the rest of it. If he tries to live in the past, reasoning with his old knowledge, he would be unhappy with himself."

After stopping to read his audiences' emotion, he continued, "The probable effect of influencing the child's thought process is not long lasting. The various kinds of crisis and discomforts that come with being white and at the same time a daughter of black family, however, is forever. The issue is always with her; therefore, she will often be fighting and unhappy with herself.

"This will be a result of her lack of understanding and ability to analyze her decision, and our lack of care for her future. This case not only answers the question who the maternal parent is, it should also clarify her racial background. Hence, we respectfully request that the court orders a DNA test to be conducted. Because that is the only test that will accurately display her identity," concluded the appellants' lawyer.

***

The time for Million and Abigail to say goodbye to each other was coming close. Sitting in their car at the airport parking lot, the fair minded, and warmhearted Abigail was giving Million candid, and honest advice of what he needed to do. And she was assuring him that keeping him up to date and sending money was her responsibility.

Million has been impressed by Abigail's kindness and her willingness to make his case hers. He felt that hiding anything from her was destroying her trust, therefore, he didn't think he could live with that kind of scar.

He said, "Abigail, I neither have a standard to measure you with nor someone to compare you to. You are immeasurable and incomparable to me. That is all I can say about you. Having said that, there is one secret that I have hidden from you. Letting you go without telling you would be staining the great person that you are, and that will bother me forever. Therefore, I have finally decided to tell you and ask for your forgiveness.

"A couple of weeks ago, despite your advice not to go to Saba's house, I went behind your back, and I was almost killed from gunshots fired by some man. Until now, I kept it a secret because I didn't want you to get mad at me and worry about me more."

"Oh, Million! How are you going to keep yourself away from them then? Please take care of yourself. I will be happy if you don't go anywhere else other than where I told you, at least for a little while. To avoid going from one hotel to another, you have rented a secluded unit in a reportedly safe neighborhood, and your landlord seems a very nice man. Please take advantage of that."

"Saba has given me a key to a clandestine door in the back of the house, and I will be using that without fear of calamity. So, please don't worry."

"That is good, but be careful at all times. Don't forget that you are dealing with sleepless research and outcome maniacs."

"So, have you forgiven me?"

"Your decision of trying not to hide the issue from me shows your love and respect for me. And the only thing I need from you is your love. We don't necessarily have to have blood or a romantic relationship for us to love one another. As an only child to my parents, I always wanted to have a brother. Now, I'm happy to say that I have adopted you as one. When I think of you, I feel like a proud sister of a man who is learning to live a brand new and complicated life. Even though we are parting now…" She choked on her tears.

Saying goodbye to his brave, zealous, and intelligent sister became unbearable to him, so, he started crying.

***

Sami, Million's childhood friend, had been visiting Saba and the kids whenever he was in town. On one of those occasions, Saba left them alone in the house and went to buy something from the corner store by her house. Ermi had noticed Bini getting agitated every time he hugged Saba tightly and they whispered something holding hands.

"Bini, you seemed to be a good person, but I still want to know more about you. You suddenly appeared from nowhere and are trying to immerse yourself into my best friend's family, why don't we grub a beer sometime this weekend and you tell me more about yourself. To tell you the truth, in addition to protecting my best friend's family, I have a professional duty to know about your identity," said Ermi.

Bini was heartbroken and upset seeing his beloved friend hugging tightly and holding his wife in what seemed a romantic manner. He was planning on confronting them both, but separately.

"Sami, I agree with you, we need to sit and chat. However, we should do it at a quieter place. Well, I have a lot to tell you and bars are too loud for that."

"Sure, anywhere you want, man."

***

Back in the Amin's family, Ahmed had been confused and agitated about his brother. He was starting to doubt whether the information he received from America had any truth.

"Unless it was his ghost, my wife and his sons have said they saw him in person. The kids said they touched him, and he carried and kissed them. Well, that wasn't a ghost. No! It was him! Anyway, why does his self-claimed friend wanted me to believe it was not him?" said Ahmed, conversing with his angry self.

Million's appearance in the store and vanishing again seemed to support Amin's mom's and his brother Nuraan's analysis that he was pissed at them for giving away his wife to Ahmed. Even Ahmed joined the rest of the adult family members in believing that Amin showed up at the store and left when he saw Barakat being pregnant.

Amin's father was remorseful of allowing Ahmed to marry Barakat. He urged Nuraan for them to find Amin and ask for his forgiveness. So, they started visiting all the places where his friends reportedly had met him. However, they could find neither him nor anyone who looked like him.

Nuraan, showing the most recent picture of Amin that they had at home, asked about him to a few of the waitresses of the two hotels where they heard he was frequenting. The waitresses replied that he used to come but haven't seen him recently.

Haji and Nuraan started wondering if he went back to where he came from. They began doubting those who said they had physical contact with him, and began considering whoever was seen was Amin's spirit.

Saddened and more confused, Amin's family went back to the drawing board. Ahmed, however, continued his search for the "so-called Amin" more aggressively.

***

"Boss, the guy in the video I sent you has been coming to the house a lot. Thanks to the dumb, Red, our subject is still alive, and we don't know how badly he is injured. I don't know how long we have to wait for him to get out of the house. What do you want us to do?"

"DD said that he studied the guest and he is an old friend of the family, his name is Ermias, or Sami. He lives in a house not too far from the zone. Now, about our guy, tonight, I will call my contact in America and find out if we can go inside and finish him."

***

They met at a different part of town. Sami chose a table close to the window on the quieter side of the café. Five minutes later, Million arrived. After exchanging greetings and talking about how busy the traffic was, Million jumped into the heart of the reason for their meeting.

"Sami, let me ask you one thing, weren't you Million's closest friend?"

"Yes, I still am. Why do you ask?"

"Then why are you doing that?"

"What is that? What did I do?"

"Now, you are acting innocent."

"I don't understand what you are trying to say. Either way, whatever it was I did, how is that your business?"

"He who turns a blind's eye to treachery is deceptive. At least I have to let you know that you are committing an act of betrayal," he said getting upset.

"I don't understand what betrayal you are talking about?" asked Sami looking at him with squinted eyes.

"Let alone seeing, even hearing about how you are acting with your friend Million's wife shows that you are shameless."

"How come you sound like a man whose wife is taken from him? I don't think you are concerned about Million. It is none of your business how she and I interact. I would appreciate it if you stay away from something that you don't know about."

"What do you know if my wife is taken from me? If you know how a man reacts if he believes his wife is taken from him, why would you do something that is hurtful?"

"Let me guess—you like Saba. First of all, Million and I were very close friends for over seventeen years, and he never told me that he had a friend, let alone a childhood friend, in Germany. So, I'm not buying who you say you are. Either way, don't talk to me as if you are advocating for Million, because you are not."

"Just because he never told you, doesn't mean he didn't have friends in Germany or anywhere else. More importantly, accepting me or buying it or not, I can say I'm his friend and am doing what a best friend of the departed should do—which is looking after his loved ones and advocating for him. Above all, there is a hidden and sensitive thing that you don't know about. So, don't try to misdirect."

"Listen, I don't know you! As I said, it is none of your business how she and I interact. If you have a beef with her, talk to her. Otherwise, leave me alone."

"The time when I will clear things up with her will come. In the meantime, I want to remind you that you are destroying the trust your friend had on you because you broke one of your promises. Whether you understand or not, what I'm telling you now are his words. Don't suppose Million is dead and gone. He is alive as he once was; therefore, he can see and hear you."

"Don't try to scare me, because I wouldn't," he bluffed, but he was terrified inside.

"If I'm going to tell you Million's words, instead of as Bini, I might as well talk to you as himself—he, who knew you from your head to your toes."

"Still, don't try to scare me. You know nothing about Million and I," said Sami, his heart pounding from fear.

"To the contrary, I know a lot. Do you remember that you invited him for dinner at Lalibela Hotel on the eve of Million's departure to America?"

"Yes, I do. So?"

"He said to you. 'I love my wife dearly! Let alone while I'm alive, even when I die, I don't want anyone to touch her.' And you said, 'I promise you; Saba won't be with anyone even if you leave not to return. I'm sure the love between the two of you could resist death, let alone a person.'

“The love you have for one another will travel beyond your graves. Rather, pray for me to find that kind of love. Then, when he said take care of Saba and the children, you promised you would. So, do you still think I don’t know?” said Million, looking at Sami in the eye.

“Bini! Who did you hear all this from? There was no one with us that evening. I’m having trouble understanding everything about you. Until now, I wasn’t sure if I should believe when Saba told me that there is something strange about you. This was a private conversation between my friend and I, how do you know of it?” said Sami, sensing the weirdness of the guy in front of him.

“I was there with you when you said all that. The proper question, therefore, would be to ask who I am, instead of who I heard it from.”

“Unless you were invisible, there wasn’t anyone around us when Million and I had that visit. I still wonder how you know everything we talked about. I could never believe that Million might have told you because I knew him as I know myself and he wouldn’t do that. Are you psychic or something?”

“Either way, why did you break your promise and start a relationship with Saba? Aren’t you a moral being?” he said, his eyes filling up with tears.

"Don't ask me what I did and did not do. You don't know the nature of my relationship with Saba. If for any reason you should know the truth, I haven't and will never break the promise I made to Million. He was an unreplaceable friend of mine."

"How could you say this to Bini. You are an apostate! I don't need a witness to prove something I saw with my own eyes," he said loudly.

"What is she to you that you are getting so frustrated anyway?" said Sami. He had been observing Bini, and his reaction consistently has been that of someone who is hurt by the situation.

Could she have had more than a platonic relationship with this man that I have yet to learn? he asked himself.

"Doesn't my approach to the case say something to you about how it concerns me? Let me tell you—it concerns me one hundred percent. Sami, even though nobody cares about me and I have become like…" he choked back tears. "An abandoned and forgotten orphan, I care about everyone. It is sad when you know a lot about a person, but that person doesn't know even that you exist. Let me tell you a secret from long ago that your mom told you and you shared only with Million." As if every fight had to have a winner, the tears that he had fought to hold back won and started sliding down his face.

He cleaned his tears and continued, "Your mom told you that the man you had grown up believing to be your dad is a father to all your siblings but not to you. Your mom had an affair while married, and you are the result of that affair. Neither your siblings nor their father knew this fact.

"As for your biological father, he joined the army, and your mom never heard from him. She didn't know whether he was alive or not. You shared this highly confidential story with Million. And he had kept it to himself since, and he will keep it to his grave. You on the other hand, because you assume, he is dead, you are fooling around with his wife. Dead or not, you should have kept the words you gave to your best friend."

"Oh, Million! I never imagined he would do such a thing. Why are you talking about keeping it to grave? Even you know about it. What about Saba, does she know? Who else knows?" he said, looking to the sky. He was shocked and embarrassed.

"Please, take it easy! I'm just telling you what I heard from no one else but you. The only reason it seems otherwise is only because you believe Million is dead."

"Except my mom, myself and him, no one on earth knew about it. And you! Are you some kind of weird creature? I have only known you, how long? A week and a half, and you are telling me you heard it from me? Also, why the heck do you keep telling me that I believe Million is dead? Why wouldn't I?

"You seem to know everything—why don't you tell me what I should consider? He died, and we buried him. What else could I accept? I have to go, now! I don't even know why I'm putting up with this," said Ermi, shouting and getting more furious with each question that he uttered and stormed off his seat.

"Sami, I know I'm agitating you. But so am I. I'm upset at myself, and at the people I trusted the most. You are one of those people," said Million, getting up with his friend.

"This is more unnerving! Though you keep saying you know me, I don't know you! What trust are you talking about?" said Sami, sitting back down as if deliberately to hear more.

Million sat back and said, "Sami, I didn't call you here to intentionally get you cross. I called you to tell you that what you are doing with Saba is a breach of the bond between friends. That being said, I didn't hear the secret you told to Million from anyone else but yourself.

"Let me give you more evidence to show that I received that info from you. It was Sunday evening, on the way back from the stadium, sitting and eating dinner on the rooftop-deck of Shebelle Hotel. If you need me to, I can tell you the color and type clothes you were wearing, the meal you had, the drink you had, and how you were sitting."

Sami was more curious than furious, he wanted to know how the creepy guy who was sitting in front of him knew all that?

Struggling to remain calm, he said, "You have told me enough! I just don't know what to make of you. I have a hard time accepting that you are a human being. Are you a phantom? I admit everything you said about the event was on the dot, but how do you know? It is okay if you don't tell me. I'm a grown man, I will get over it. To begin with, I should have recognized that a secret was no longer confidential as soon as a third party knew about it. Anyway, let me tell you this, I'm a man of my word, I haven't and won't break what I promised to Million. The interaction you noticed between Saba and me isn't maudlin. It is a little trick we are playing. And it involves you."

"What is the trick? Can you tell me?"

"Yes, I can tell you. But, first, you have to tell me exactly how you know all about me. Or disclose to me who or what you are."

"There are two conditions under which I will reveal myself to you—one, swear to me that you never slept with Saba, and two, promise me that you will guard my private matter that I will tell you."

"I swear in the name of God that I never sexually touched Saba! I also swear to keep your secret safe!"

"If you mean it, vow the way you used to, the living God is my witness."

"The living God is my witness!" said Sami, with astonishment.

"Then, how come you two are hugging and whispering at each other's ears, it seems to me that you guys have something going on. What exactly is the secret that the two of you have anyways?"

"As I said, if you want me to tell you the secret between the two of us, first you have to tell me who you are."

"I'm Million."

"So, your name is Million, not Biniam. Great! Though I don't have any problem with either name, I like to know why you want us to call you Biniam or Bini. My main concern, however, is who you really are, and how you know that story, and what you are up to."

"Sami! I'm Million Bayou! Not just my name—but everything else that you are not able to see of me. I'm your best friend, Million!"

"Don't joke, tell me the truth. The only reason I'm sitting here is to find out who you are, otherwise, you can tell that I don't like you. However, this is your chance to spit the truth out and make me change my mind before it is too late."

"I'm serious!"

"But, my best friend Million is dead! I was among the ones who put Million Bayou's body into his grave and buried it with rock and soil. Now, the top is nicely built, and a headstone is placed on it. We can go now to the grave site, if you want to see for yourself," said Sami getting confused more than ever.

"Sami! what you know is half-truth! If you want to know the whole truth, set aside the knowledge you gain through seeing, at least for a while. I will explain to you that I'm Million and you will understand that here with you is the invisible Million. But, before I reveal everything about me and why I'm imperceptible to you, you have to tell me about the secret between you and Saba."

"Do you promise that you won't tell her that I told you?"

"You know how good Million is in keeping secrets, so, until I make you understand that I'm him, trust me as you would him."

"Here is the thing, because, Machida, Million's sister, is in love with you, she has been giving Saba hell. She thought they have some special relationship. Therefore, Saba is trying to get rid of you by making you believe that she and I are dating."

"Machida is in love with me! Because of me, she is angry at Saba? What a disgraceful thing? My sister loves me romantically and wants to take me away from my wife? What is happening here? is this some dream?" said Million, pronouncing the pain he was sensing.

What Million just said added more bewilderment to Ermias. *Am I dreaming? My ears couldn't be deceiving me. If I'm not dreaming, yes, Machida is Million's sister, and Saba is Million's wife, well, his widow, to be exact. He has been saying he is Million, and I just heard him say, my sister Machida and my wife Saba,* thought Sami, getting more disoriented.

"Brother, seeing you mournful and crying makes me worry. Who really should I know and address you as?"

"Sami, I understand that it is hard to believe, but, I'm your old friend, Million."

"Yes, it is impossible to believe. I know Million from head to toe, and you are not him. Also, I saw his body with my naked eyes and buried it with my own hands. So, how do you expect me to accept what you are saying?"

"Yes, you knew the body that Million was living in, but not Million himself. In other words, you know the cover that I was in and enabled me to interact with this world. People, including myself, by the way, I'm not a phantom, could only describe what we can see and hear. Even if we create something that never existed, we have to give it physical description through the mental picture that we draw using our eyes and ears. That is how limited we are."

"What are you talking about Mr.? Isn't Million, just like any human being? A total of his body? How could he live without his body?"

"Let me give you a scenario. Let's say you were in a horrible vehicle accident and you lost both your eyes, arms, and legs, wouldn't you still be Sami?"

"I would probably be miserable, at least until I learn to live with my loss, but yes I will still be Sami."

"Great! What if your doctors were able to carefully remove each part of your body and replace it with someone else's abled body? Wouldn't you still be Sami?"

"I'm listening! but let's get back to your case."

"As in the scenario, Million's body, that you saw and buried was carefully removed and replaced with another person's body. Million, therefore, is alive, except in a borrowed body. Hence, he may look like someone else, but he is still alive."

"Brother, what you are telling me is puzzling! I'm trying to understand it, in fact, at some point, I thought I understood what you meant by loss and replacement of body parts, but I still don't get how the whole body could be replaced and the person lives?"

"Okay, give me your full attention, and I will explain the secret behind it. Earlier, I told you everything that you revealed to Million. I was able to do that only because I was with you then and that is because I'm Million, not Bini.

"Understandably, because you never knew or thought about the possibility of a person losing his or her whole body and living in someone else's, it is incomprehensible to you that I'm your friend, Million, wearing another person's body." Million was about to continue explaining, but Sami interrupted.

"I'm having difficulty believing everything you are saying. How is that possible?" Yelled Sami.

"My good friend, I don't blame you. Just give me a chance to explain how it happened. My body that you buried, as you saw it, was mutilated in the vehicle accident. My brain, however, wasn't affected and had remained intact, so it didn't die. My friend from school, who was in the accident with me, his head was hit, and he died. But his body was still okay.

"The doctors then took my brain from my body and put it in to my friend's body after they took out his damaged brain. Long story short, as you see, I have become Million who lives in another person's frame," said Million feeling relieved by telling his friend the mystery behind his invisibility.

Hearing the story, Sami felt eerie and started to get disgusted. He could hardly look at Million.

Million misinterpreted Sami's silence for expectation of more explanation.

"You guys buried my body that became useless because of the accident. As I said, my brain is put in this body, now I'm about to show you the incision of the procedure," he said. Then he put his forehead on the table and exposed the back of his head and neck.

Sami, who was already disgusted picturing the procedure from the story, when he saw the incision, his head started spinning, he felt nauseated and began throwing up.

Million, seeing the change in his friend's health condition, wished he didn't tell him. He was worried. He paced back and forth by their table. He offered to help him, but Sami pushed him away saying, "I don't need your help."

Sami couldn't believe what he saw, he was disgusted, annoyed and scared. Let alone to accept Million as Million, he doubted that the man was a human being. He didn't have the guts to look at him, much less to touch him. He imagined him as some unknown and scary creature that looked human.

He said, "I got to go! Don't follow me!" and left.

Million thought, *Am I some freak, or a revolting and scary creature to him? In this case, what would I be to my wife? If I tell and show her how I came about to be the way I am, she would probably be screaming and running in no time. What then, makes me human?* and he cried bitterly.

***

Chapter Fifteen

Meanwhile, in the US, people were attuned to the "Teena or Sandra" case. The federal court was back in session again. After many arguments, the appellant's lawyer summoned Mrs. John to witness stand.

"Mrs. John, where was the first time you met Teena?"

Her lawyer intervened by saying, "Your honor, the question is not relevant to the case."

"Your honor, I'm in the rim of the case and this is an introductory question."

"Proceed," said the judge.

"At Ms. Murphy's place." she replied.

"how old did you think she was?"

"Five or six."

"Did you ever meet the child before that day?"

"No."

"Can you please identify, for the court, the child whom you met at Ms. Murphy's house?"

Mrs. Johns pointed at the child who was playing on a phone, sitting with her court assigned custodian on a bench, to the left of the judges.

"Mrs. Johns, can you tell the court who that child is?"

"That child is Sandra Johns in Teena's body. As long as she believes that she is Sandra, that is who she is. Yes, at first there was no way for my husband or I to know that this child is so special to us…"

Her attorney interrupted, "Mrs. Johns you don't need to elaborate any further."

"Your honor, the counselor Mrs. Johns is my sworn witness." off topic," said the appellants' attorney.

"Your honor, I'm only advising my client."

"Proceed," said the judge to the appellants' lawyer.

"Mrs. Johns, you and the late Mr. Johns had a daughter whom you named Sandra. As soon as she turned six, Sandra died from a car accident. You donated her brain and her other organs to the hospital. And the rest of her body is or was in resting place. Is all what I described correct? Please answer yes or no"

"Yes."

"How did you and the late Mr. Johns feel when you learned the death of your daughter?"

"Devastated, to say the least."

"Now, as a parent who once experienced the loss of her daughter, how do you think the parents of little Ms. Soprano are feeling?"

"I'm sure they are heart broken. But it wouldn't have come to this point and most importantly, my dear husband wouldn't have been murdered, if Ms. Murphy had listened to the child and let us spent a few minutes with her."

"Mrs. Johns, you are right, Teena's parents are heart broken and they would like their daughter back. If you have a sense of humanity and know the law of giving and taking allow us to use the brain you donated to the hospital and we paid money to have it implanted into our child, Teena's living and healthy body. If you are not willing to do that, pay to get the procedure reversed and take the brain. We could afford to buy another brain and get it transplanted," concluded the appellant's lawyer.

Mrs. John surprised by the change in the attorney's tone, she felt like saying, "go ahead I will find a body for my daughter's brain." But reality pinched her, and mixture of fear and anger began to overwhelm her. Now, she had to worry. She said, "No!" as if she was talking to herself. She looked at the lawyer in the eye and added, "Can you think for a bit, how could our daughter live without a body? That is impossible. It is not fair to her," she said clutching her hand.

"It is your idea, not ours. You are telling us to consider all options, and that is one of them. If you want the brain to stay or reside in our daughter, Teena, we accept. No one has a legal reason to order us to give our daughter to anyone, and we won't do it.

“And if you would rather take your daughter’s brain, we could have it removed from Teena’s body and give it back to you. If it comes down to it, we all have to take our shares; fair is fair! So, we want you to know that we can’t and won’t give what is ours. If anything, we are capable of buying another brain,” said the lawyer, sensing pride in inducing the affected sensitivity he intended in Mrs. Johns.

Mrs. Johns imagined getting her daughter’s brain in a box. She pictured her daughter, who she considered was in the brain, suffocated and strained because she couldn’t see and hear. She pictured her fighting to stay alive and struggling from lack of oxygen. Then, she thought, she heard her saying, “Mom, please put me back into a body.” She felt guilty for her daughter’s suffering, and tears began falling from her eyes.

***

When Million walked to the office, Mr. Ermias was speaking with his secretary about an upcoming meeting with union representatives. He glanced to see who just walked in. Whom he saw startled him. He turned around to check if his eyes did not deceive him. He realized they weren’t. He saw who he thought was seeing. He felt a shock, and a cold sweat started to roll down his back and underarms.

He tried to collect his composure and wanted to say, "Hey, Amin, is it you?" but the only word he uttered was "Hi!" The secretary didn't know Amin because she was newer, so, as far she was concerned, Million was another guest who probably wanted to see her boss.

"Come in," said Mr. Ermias leading the way to his office. He was careful to hide his nervousness.

Million suspected what the personnel manager was judging. "Another person who assumes I'm Amin," he thought.

Million wanted to clear the air by making sure that he introduced himself to the man he had put high hopes on. He said, "Sir, is it fair to say that you are assuming I'm Amin?"

"Come again?" said Mr. Ermias, because he wasn't sure if he heard him right.

"I have been stopped by many people who want to greet me as Amin and expected me to know their names and some part of their life histories, especially, the ones who had something to do with Amin. So, based on that and your reaction earlier, also considering how you invited me in without asking who I am and the reason for my visit, I'm comfortable to say that you judge I'm Amin. Sir, please understand that I'm not questioning your intelligence, in fact, I'm here to put myself at the mercy of your brilliance," said Million confidently but tenderly.

"Sir, if I understand you correctly, you are telling me that your name is not Amin. Am I right?" said Mr. Ermias, confused and looking at Million as much as his eyes could see and his brain could recognize.

"Yes, sir, my name is Million. Million Bayou."

"It doesn't matter to me as long as you bring the proper documentation. Just out of curiosity, why did you change your name to Million?" said the manager, and thought, *Forget about your name; aren't you supposed to be dead*?

"No sir, my name was never Amin. My given name throughout my life has been Million. Sorry for the confusion," said Million, waiting for the request for more explanation to come from the gentleman sitting in front of him in a very comfy looking chair.

"Then why were you called Doctor Amin Mustafa when you worked here for over six years? I saw all your documents during hiring and you were cleared as Amin Mustafa. A few months back, I was reviewing your file for compensation and benefit distribution to your wife because we were told you had passed. I will come back to that can of worms later, but now let's talk about who you say you are. If your given name is Million, why were you being called Amin?"

"Sir, we seem to be hanging up on the name alone. As I mentioned earlier, as a person, I'm not Amin, instead, I'm Million," he said with irritation boiling inside but trying not to show it outwardly.

Mr. Ermias remembered what Amin's brother and father had said. He felt bad for judging them. He thought, *No wonder his friends are dead sure. Why does he prefer to be someone else? Could he be suffering from some form of psychosis such as Dissociative Identity Disorder or Schizophrenia? Oh, my! He could have faked his death. This guy needs serious help! I wonder if he is willing to see one of our psychologists.*

Million was waiting quietly for the man in the nice suit to say something. He knew how his case was unique, complicated, and most of all unbelievable. He thought, *I don't blame anyone who thinks I'm Amin. If I find Sami somewhere and he tells me he is someone else, I would have thought that he was either having some mental health problem or he was stubborn or being difficult.*

Then, he calmed himself and said, "Sir, I understand how you feel. This is a difficult matter to process. If someone I knew very well comes to me and told me he was not who I thought he was, I would think he was having some sort of mental health issue or he no longer wanted to associate with me. Anyway…"

Mr. Ermias, interrupted and said the following with conviction, “Look, some people, instead of finding the root cause of any problem that they may have and solving it once for all, they like to go along with the issue until it gets them into a tight situation that they could hardly get out of. You know, some of us want to fight alone even the most difficult problem that life brings us. Let me ask you this, are you willing to talk to one of our psychologists? It is free and confidential. Remember, there is nothing wrong in seeking help.”

Million teared up from frustration.

He thought, *I came to this schooled man hoping for understanding and help, rather, he perceives I’m crazy. Getting emotional won’t get me anywhere. Let me reveal everything to him, and he will eventually understand this thing.*

He said, “Sir, I’m not shy to ask for help, that is why I’m here. Except the help I need is not what you think. Before I go about detailing my situation, let me show you something.”

Mr. Ermias was expecting Million to take out some document from his pocket. Million however, walked closer to the man and bent over, cleared his hair to each side of his head divulging the long incision in the middle of his skull, crossing incision from the back of one ear to the other, and the back of his neck.

"I see, you had full brain surgery. I could only imagine how intensive the recovery and rehabilitation processes were. Why did you have this operation? Was there a tumor or you had an accident?" asked Mr. Ermias with genuine curiosity.

"Yes, I had an accident, though the surgery was not directly related to that. My brain was very healthy, and it still is. I was involved in a serious vehicle accident that damaged all my body except my brain. In other words, only my brain remained functional."

Mr. Ermias glanced at his office for an escape route. He thought Million might have been institutionalized for mental health and behavioral issues.

He said, "According to you, what was affected was your body except for your head, but the incision was on your head. What took the doctors up to your skull? Were they insane?" he asked mockingly. He told himself, *Maybe, this is the time to abscond.*

"Sir, there is more to it. Amin and I met in the airplane when we both were flying to the US for a higher education. So, we were …"

Mr. Ermias interrupted and exclaimed his fear by saying, "Oh, Oh!" unintentionally.

"I sound crazy—right? I'm not. If you let me finish, you will have a better understanding of where I'm coming from," said Million, noticing that the story had become hard to swallow for the man in front of him.

"I think you can understand. I'm just confused! But I didn't interject your talk on purpose. Please, proceed," said Mr. Ermias trying to justify his reaction.

"As I was saying, we were friends and roommates. And at the time of the accident, I was the driver. To make a long story short, my whole body except my brain was damaged beyond repair. Amin's on the contrary, while his body remained intact except for some treatable injuries, his brain became useless and started to die.

"As soon as they realized that his brain would not make it, they took out my able brain from my head and his defaced brain from his head and put mine in his head. The incision I showed you earlier is from that," said Million, checking out Mr. Ermias reaction.

"What are you talking about? How could one brain be replaced for another?" Mr. Ermias was incredulous. His prior knowledge could not allow him to imagine the possibility of such things as a brain transplant.

Million ignored the questions and continued his explanation. "Replacing one brain in place of another means a new person takes the place of the previous one—Amin moved out then Million moved in. Just for the sake of this explanation, think of the human body as a house or a temple as it is assumed in the Bible. Therefore, everyone who knew Amin thinks I'm him because he or she knew this house as his. But now someone else is residing in it. That someone is me, Million."

"I need time to process this. I've never heard about brain transplantation. Interesting! You are Million! then, why are you here?"

"I'm here to talk to you about Amin's family. If you understand me that I'm not Amin, please help me clear this issue with them."

"I don't know how, but before I promise to even try, I need to do some research about what you told me. You understand, right? Your situation is so peculiar."

"If an educated person such as yourself can't process my situation, who in this world is going to understand me? I don't know how long I have to live like this with no help, alone, and a mystery to everyone?" said Million, losing his hope on Mr. Ermias .

He continued, "If a human being cannot hear and understand me, I will have to tell you, earth and sky, please lend me your ears, I'm living alone in a prison that man built just for me. Never-mind who could help, I'm unable to find a person who may understand me," yelled Million in frustration with his hands opened to the sky, looking up and slowly down.

"Mr. Ermias, I tried to get my family to know me, but my sister loves me romantically. Our parents wish that I marry her. Just the thought of that gives me a headache. I told her that I'm her brother, but she, as the rest of my family have concluded my dead body that they buried was me. How do I get them to reopen the file about me that they seem to have closed forever?" His tears started to flow down to his face.

Mr. Ermias' fear vanished and began to be replaced by sympathy for the man who was making him confused and wonder whether to believe his sight or his hearing.

Million continued, "I'm a stranger to my wife and kids. All they know is that I'm dead and gone not to return. If it is up to me, I believe and I know, I'm alive. I miss and love them so much. I'm not a spirit because they can see and touch me, but again, I can't for sure say they are able to see me because they don't know that I'm alive.

"Though I know them, they don't know me. This is the same as trying to clap with one hand—my knowledge of that they are my kids has no meaning if they don't know I'm their father. I have a burning desire to be recognized by my wife as husband and by my kids as a father, but I'm unable to procure that. I'm not better than the dead ones. Mr. Ermias, I hope you understand my problem," said Million, sniffling and with noticeable frustration.

Mr. Ermias felt bad for Million. He said, “I understand! The source of your life has complicated your living. Take it one day at a time, otherwise, sadness will destroy you. One of these days, the solution to your problem will surface.”

“Shouldn’t today be the first day when the solutions to my problems begin taking shape?”

“You never know—maybe it has started.”

“Sir, I wish my problem was limited to my family. I would like to put mine and my family’s case on hold. The reason I came to you is because of Amin’s wife and kids.”

“Yes, Amin’s family! His dad and brother came the other day and told me that Amin is in town except he changed his name. They were talking about you. I had imagined that they had a case of a look-alike, so, I didn’t give it any attention,” said Mr. Ermias wondering how some things look simple to the unaffected party.

“Let me tell you what happened. A few weeks back, I ran into Amin’s kids at a store. They came running, embraced, and started to kiss me, saying, ‘Baba, you are here, you are not dead.’ I kissed and hugged them, I didn’t know what else to do and say. A minute or two later I disappeared from them claiming to get my luggage.

"Those poor kids were so excited believing their dad had come. I felt terrible for creating a lingering image and false impression of their dead father. Since that day, I might have become neither a dream nor reality to them. They would probably, anxiously anticipate my return with each passing day. Isn't that sad?

"They probably are nagging their mom to produce my whereabouts. When she and other people tell them that their dad is dead, should they believe that or their eyes? I'm suffering from guilt for creating an illusion of a living father in their mind after they may have believed his death. I can't forget and ignore these kids knowing that I ruined their peace about the death of their father and creating a false hope of eagerly awaiting to see him. My being alive has benefited no one, including myself. What am I to do now?" he said and started sobbing irrepressibly.

Hearing what Million said, Mr. Ermias' empathy for him escalated. His heart ached to imagine Amin's kids' yearning to see their dad who they believed is alive. He pictured them mistaking every man who is dressed as Million. His eyes filled with tears.

He turned to Million and said, "No worries, I understand what you said, and I will do my best to help you with everything I can. Don't feel like you are alone any longer."

***

"Hello, who is this?"

"Professor Woods, it is me, Ava."

"How are you doing, Ava?"

"To tell you the truth, I'm not doing well. The case about my daughter is killing me."

"Sorry, I have been very busy to keep up on that. What is the status now?"

"It doesn't look good. If it continues the way it is now, I may end up losing yet again for the second time and not see my daughter forever."

"What are they saying?"

"I have no idea! They are talking about some science gibberish."

"Are they saying there is a scientific explanation to the case?"

"If you care about me and the promises you made about my daughter, no one else but you could explain it to them." Ever since she recovered from her accident in the courtroom, she had been nagging the professor on the phone and in person about keeping his promise of giving her daughter another life with a new brain.

"What made you assume that I have a say in a case that is being seen by a judge? Please, give me a break," he said with frustration believing that she was trying to pressure him in the name of promise.

"Please put yourself in my shoes, just for five seconds. How could your mind accept and not go nuts, when someone is taking your loving daughter? So long as you are alive, everything about her will haunt you day and night."

"The case is out of my hands; it is in the courts. What is that you consider that I could do about it?"

"If you appear in the court and testify that she is my daughter, it would be additional evidence for me."

"If I testify, it won't be to support you but to tell the truth based on what I know and what the scientific implication of the research's outcome."

"So, you don't believe that she is my daughter either? If you knew that she was not going to be my daughter after the transplant, why did you put me through all that trouble? Just for me to suffer mental anguish and monetary loss? If I should be frunk about it, it is you, who got me into all this

mess. Please give me an answer that could convince my mind that she is not my daughter, then I might try to move on with my life. Better yet, find me a new brain, or help me forget about her, then I won't have to go insane, if I lose her."

By then, he had the phone away from his ear. When she stopped, he said, calmly, "I didn't say that she is not your daughter. What I meant is that I will testify not because I must support you, but because I have a responsibility to do so,"

"I'm sorry, now, I understand what you mean," said Ava trying to collect herself. She started to gain hope from what he said. "In whatever way you view it, if your testimony addresses your research, the procedures and outcomes, I know what to do after that."

"I will notify the court that I'm ready to give my testimony."

"Thank you so much, Professor Woods," said Ava, bouncing back to excitement with the prospect of his testimony straightening out the matter in the court. She was confident that he would convince the court that the child was her daughter.

***

After thinking the matter of Million and Amin thoroughly, Mr. Ermias decided to tell Nuraan that the man whom Amin's friends met was Million, not Amin. He thought that it was easier to talk to Nuraan first, then to Amin's wife with Nuraan's help. So, he invited him to his office.

Mr. Ermias was worried about how Nuraan would react when he told him why he called him to his office. They both were having coffee. While finding ways to slide into the main point of their meeting, he was doing unrelated small talk.

He cleared his throat and said, “Nuraan, there is something I need to tell you. Sorry, I couldn’t tell you over the phone. By the way, has anyone from the family met the man believed to be Amin?”

“He went to his wife’s store. He hugged and kissed his kids and gave his wife an angry look and left without saying hi.”

“I had found that matter worrisome, until, I met the man himself and spoke with him for a lengthy time.”

Nuraan was a thirty-two-year-old, ambitious man. He had been eager to restore peace in the family by finding and brining over his brother to the house. So, he was anxiously awaiting to hear what Mr. Ermias was about to say next.

“Nuraan, before I tell you the matter, I need you to promise me that you won’t tell anyone before you and I discuss and reach an agreement.”

“If it needs to be kept confidential, I promise you in Allah’s name that I won’t tell anyone without your consent.”

Mr. Ermias cleared his throat and said, “The man in question’s name is Million. According to him, that is his given name since birth. Which means he is not Amin.”

“You are telling me that Amin’s wife and kids were wrong. His friends were wrong. How could they all identify him erroneously?” said Nuraan in disbelief and disagreeing with what he heard.

He replied, “No, that is not what I mean.” He felt lost and confused about how to explain it to him. “They all had seen Amin’s face and possibly heard his voice too.”

“Then how come you are saying it is not him, and that it is someone else?”

“But the man is Million, not Amin.”

“Mr. Ermias, I understand you are having difficulty explaining to me why he changed his name to Million. I had my suspicions. But, please, tell me why he said he did so?”

“Nuraan, don’t get hung up on the name change. I did the same thing when he told me the story that I’m about to tell you. At first, I didn’t understand what he was saying, then I tried to comprehend it, but my mind wouldn’t let me accept it.” He took a sip of his coffee and continued, “Here is where the confusion is coming from, the man is inside your brother’s body. So, everyone who reported seeing Amin was right, except the person in that body is Million.”

Nuraan froze for a second with his mouth open wide. Then he said, “I hope you are joking! Otherwise, what you are telling me is unbelievable.”

“I’m telling you what happened. Listen to me carefully, and I will explain how the unbelievable thing happened,” said Mr. Ermias, still debating on ways how to explain to him. He continued, “Here is how it all took place, your brother and this guy, Million, not only were they college friends, but they were also roommates. I would assume Amin had told his wife or his parents about his friend and roommate. So, on one of their school breaks, they decided to rent a car and drive from Boston to New York to visit. As soon as they drove a few miles, they had a serious accident. During the casualty, Amin’s head impacted, and Million’s whole body was injured beyond repair.” He paused.

Then he continued, “Both of them were taken to the hospital. The medical center that they were taken to, apparently, is a well-known research hospital, and it is part of the school where both of them were attending.

“When they examined them both, they learned that Amin’s brain was destroyed by the head injury he suffered, and despite Million’s brain still being okay, his body was shattered. Their medical exam reflected that they both would die in a few hours. That when the researchers decided to try to save one life out of the two.

“So, they took out Amin’s damaged brain and replaced it with Million’s working brain. When he woke up from the induced coma, even though his whole body was Amin’s, because the brain in that body is Million’s, he was thinking as Million. Therefore, the man became Million. That is why I am trying to tell you that he didn’t change his name, instead, this man is Million.”

Nuraan heard enough, he felt as if any word after that would burst his head. He didn’t want to say anything, instead, he wanted to leave, just run, or fly from that place. Then everything went dark on him, and his head started spinning. He got up to leave, but he wobbled and fell back into the chair. He felt nauseated and started sweating from the head and forehead. He fainted.

Mr. Ermias saw Nuraan losing his balance and about to fall from his seat. He quickly got up and supported him to remain in the seat. With his other hand, he pressed a button repeatedly.

Mr. Ermias’ secretary, hearing the alarm going off, ran into his office. When she arrived, she saw the guest had fainted and her boss, keeping him from falling, urged her, “Hurry and get me the driver and a couple of people to help us carry him into the car, we need to take him to the hospital.”

With the help of the driver and a couple of other helpers, they carried him into the car and transported him to the hospital.

Mr. Ermias was confused by what just happened. He couldn't figure out what to say when the doctor asked him why Nuraan fainted.

***

Poor Amin's family haven't had peace for a while. Since the day when they heard that he was in town, they had been arguing and fighting with each other, they couldn't come up with any solution.

After seeing her purportedly dead but beloved husband in her store, Barakat had been distancing herself from Ahmed, both physically and emotionally. Ahmed had concluded that the reason she was avoiding him was because of the incident. Hence, his animosity toward his brother continued to upsurge with each passing day.

Barakat judged, if it weren't for Ahmed, her life would have been back to normal with Amin. She knew that Amin loved her very much. Most of all, her kids' eagerness and anxiety to see their dad was killing her inside. Disrespecting each other and altercations had risen in Ahmed's household. He began to get upset at everything the kids did.

Sitting in the living room for coffee, Amin's family didn't seem to have anything to talk about. Until, Haji Mustafa said, "I understand that he is mad at us, what about his kids? How could he give up on them? And why exactly would he change his religion?"

"He already saw his kids, and he probably would go to their school and see them again. The change in his religion, however, is you guys' fault. He must have been furious seeing her like that. No wonder he left without saying a word," said the mother.

"This is absurd! How did we make him change his religion?" Asked Haji staring at his wife with his mouth halfway opened and his one eye squinted.

"Well! If somebody has to speak the truth, when his wife refused to marry his brother, you brought elders and put a burden through religious guilt-trips. Amin must have heard that and counted the religion as one factor for the breakup of his marriage. He is angry. A person who is upset could do more than change a religion. We should fear that he might kill all of us," argued the mother.

"Why do you always believe your imagination is right?" said Haji to his wife. But inside, he considered that she might have a point. *He might try to take revenge on us,* he thought.

Ahmed took the opportunity to express his deep hate for Amin and said, "He is a son of hell who renegaded against his family and his religion."

They all turned toward him with anger and gave him intense stares.

Nevertheless, Ahmed added, "How could he abandon our prophet's teaching and became a Christian? This kind of traitor will go to hell."

He believed killing his brother was justified because he was an apostate of Islam. He considered himself the guardian of the religion. He felt standing for his religion would absolve him of any guilty feeling he would endure from killing his brother.

Everybody seemed to have ignored him, but he continued, “I swear in the name of Allah and our prophet, if I find him, I will butcher him.”

Barakat had enough of his judgmental and hateful tone, so, began to tell him as he should hear from her. “You are an animal. Isn’t it enough that you have held his family a hostage? Oh, don’t act like you are advocating for the religion. You are saying that out of jealousy. He can do whatever he wants. You are not in a position to criticize him. If Allah wants, he will judge him himself.”

“You be quiet. If not, I will cut out your tongue. I suspect you may deal with him to get me killed. Don’t think you would destroy my life and walk freely. I will kill both of you, then, what will happen will happen. Think about that thoroughly,” exploded Ahmed, staring at Barakat.

“If you hurt me, don’t imagine that you will be alive for another day,” said Barakat furiously.

The fight with words between the couple kept escalating. So, the parents intervened and told them both to stop.

While the family was in a mini recess, the phone rang, and the caller told Haji that his son, Nuraan, was hospitalized.

They were all taken aback by the news. Barakat just got out of the hospital, and now Nuraan went in, each one of them began to worry and felt as if he or she could see or sense the shadow of death was around him or her.

Except for Barakat, all of them rushed to the hospital. She didn't want to see Ahmed's face. All the things he said began echoing in her mind again and again.

***

Walking to her bedroom, she said to herself, "That is it! I don't want to spend another day in this place with this man." In the bedroom, she noticed Ahmed had forgotten his keys hooked on the safe. She opened the safe, inside a bunch of money was arranged untidily. She felt as if everything was conspiring for her to run away.

She picked up her phone from the table and dialed. "Hello, Fatuma, this is Barakat. If I'm going to get out of this house alive, today would be the best day. Can you meet somewhere in a few hours?"

"Hi Barakat, I'm so glad you called. How are you doing?"

"I'm doing okay! Right now, my in-laws are out. They went to the hospital to check on my brother in-law who just got admitted…"

"Where is easier for you, for us to meet?"

"Anywhere should be okay, tell me a place and time, and I will be there."

"Okay then, my husband is out of town, so, it will just be me. Do you know where Ibex hotel is?"

"Yes, I know where it is."

"Wait for me there. Tonight, you will stay at our place. Then, early morning, you will catch the cross-country bus to Jima."

"But I don't have a bus ticket to travel in the morning."

"Leave that to me. There are other options. You might find a bus that still has empty seats, if not, we will pay double to buy one from a person who is not in a hurry to leave, still, if anything, you will travel some of the distance on one bus and the rest on another. Otherwise, when he knows you have run-away, he will search for you in every terminal."

"You are right! Thank you and see you at Ibex hotel."

***

The thought of staying in that house a moment longer began to exasperate Barakat. She tried to stop and think about the decision she was about to make, but all she could picture in her mind was sitting by herself in a meadow, staring at Amin's shadow.

She went to the living room and sat on the couch, and began to internalize the tranquility. She abruptly got up and walked to the kitchen, pulled a knife from the drawer. She stood there holding it with the pointer down on the counter. She thought about her kids, and exclaimed, "I'm nothing to them!" A few seconds later, she put the knife back in the drawer and started sobbing.

She sat back on the couch and continued wailing loudly. Still crying, she went to her bedroom and began writing letters, one to her mom, and another one to her ex-husband to be delivered through her mom.

Dear Mom,

The scent of your motherhood is the everyday feast that I would never get enough of. I wish I could stay close to you and enjoy your motherly love. Unfortunately, a bad day has come to take us apart.

The moment I'm writing you this letter, I'm in deep grief, my tears are running down my face. If tears could have been an ink, I would have written multiple pages with what was coming out of my eyes. I don't believe anyone had encountered or experienced what I'm going through. I can't accept and live the shameful relationship that I'm forced to be tied into and be a burden to others, so, I have decided to vanish. There isn't anything else that could be done. I guess I was born unlucky.

I know I will never forgive myself for leaving my babies, but it might be for the better. Though I don't know where I'm going, I sense, it is far away, and I won't be seeing my kids again. I don't know how my life will be without them or theirs without me—only Allah knows! Please, don't stop praying for me.

The kids, by losing me, will gain their dad. it was because of me that he never came to see them since that day. So, at least they would feel better by having their dad back. Mom, I haven't the slightest idea how I could and will endure being away from my lovely kids. May Allah help me!

My disappearance may bring peace into the household. At the very least, Amin will come to his beloved kids and that way he will join his family. He shouldn't live a lonely life at no mistake of his. I'm the one to blame for replacing him with his brother. Oh, what a mental torment? Mom, I wish the Earth had swallowed me when I caved in to the pressure, or I had disappeared when just the idea came in.

Mom, I need you to know that I'm leaving for good and hiding, not to be found. So, there is no use looking for me. Remember what Dad used to say, "He, who acts asleep, could not be awakened."

I love you, mom! I always will!

Your loving daughter, Barik

P.S., please hand the second letter to Amin. No one else other than him should ever see it. Thank you!

***

Dear Amin,

I'm anything but naïve. You have seen me; being in that position, I could never have the confidence to say to you my loving husband. But still, nothing will change my love for you. I love you, and I miss you so much! Unfortunately, my luck stood in the way of my desire to be with you. As much as

I want to be with the people I love, I can't bear being the reason for my kids not being able to see their dad. So, I decided to depart with my scarlet letter, the one you saw and repelled you from me.

Since you probably don't want to hear me talk, please, read my last letter. This is the last thing I'm bothering you with; because you will never hear from me again.

I'm aware of that it was because you saw me being pregnant that you didn't return to see your kids who are yearning to see you.

Despite the degree of your disappointment in me, you shouldn't forsake these poor children. What crime did they commit that you would leave them with the thirst and hunger for spending a couple of minutes with you? Since the last time they saw you, they have been constantly peeping through the door, expecting you to show up any minute. The enquiry, "Why wouldn't our daddy come?" has become the most asked question since that day. And I have no answer. They once thought you were dead, and then they saw you among the living. If you don't come for them again, they may believe you are a zombie. Nobody could tell them when you will come to see them, so, they are anxiously longing for you.

In all fairness, I'm the one who broke the bridge and built a huge wall instead, between you and your kids. So, if I just get out of the way, all that will change. Then, not only will their question be answered, but also, you will live with them serenely. If the loss of one promotes the availability of the other, my receding out of the way makes more sense. Even if they lose me, having you around will solace them.

As far as marrying your brother, I want you to know that I did it neither out of interest nor desire. You know that he is a lot older than me, but I'm not sure that you know that he and I differ so much in rationalization. Despite that, I was forced by the pressure that was put on me from your dad and other religious leaders.

I explained to them that I desire just to raise my kids and never to marry again; rather live as Amin's widow. However, they said that marrying his brother is close to living with him, and it is permitted in the Quran for him to marry me. And they told me that it is my religious ethic that I need to do it, and that he is required to raise his nephews. They made it sound like, if I don't do it, I'm defying Allah. Most of all, I didn't know you were alive.

Amin, please know that I'm writing you this letter not to bother you with considering of forgiving me so that we can get back together. I'm doing it only because I believe you deserve an explanation from me. As for the next chapter of my life, I don't know what is written, but I know that I'm leaving to endure what is on each page.

My beloved Amin, if there is one thing that I want to bother you with is this, since my departure, leaving my precious and delicate babies is not in search of a good life, please take excellent care of them.

Instead of remaining the blockage between you and your kids, along with your family, I have removed myself. Though doing so may cost me my life, since it will bring you closer to our kids and your family, I don't mind paying for it.

Your brother did what he did because he thought you were dead, and because his religion permits him. One of the reasons for my disappearance is to put an end to the quarrel between the two of you. Since I'm paying a lot for that, please don't ignore my request and beseech to forgive him.

Wherever we may be, may Allah keep us all safe for the rest of our lives!

Your ex-wife, Barakat

She put both letters in one envelop and sealed it. Then she called her maid, who just got back from the grocery, and instructed her, "Please leave everything you are doing and take this mail to my mother."

Barakat snooped through her bedroom window and saw the maid leaving the premises. She quickly packed her clothes and her family album. As soon as she made sure that she had everything she needed and was able to fit everything into the bag, she picked up a piece of paper and wrote, "Don't look for me because you won't find me alive." And put it on the neatly made bed.

She stood for a moment quietly, covered her eyes and imagined her kids were in front of her, without saying a word, she hugged and kissed them. She opened her eyes, and quickly went to the safe and grabbed enough cash, and she dashed out before anyone came back. She went into a taxi and told the driver to take her to the Ibex hotel.

***

When Ahmed and her in-laws came back from the hospital, Barakat wasn't there; they found the gate half open. Inside, the house was awfully quiet. Because the gate wasn't locked, they believed she went to pick up her kids from her mom's house, which was a few blocks away.

The day had been slightly chilly, Ahmed went to the closet in the bedroom to grab his favorite sweatshirt. As soon as he opened the door, he noticed that some things were out of place. Looking for more changes, he saw a piece of paper on the bed.

He picked it up in a hurry and started reading a one line note and signature, "Don't look for me because you won't find me alive." In the bottom right corner, there was a signature, "Barakat." He glanced at the back of the paper as it might have the address of her destination. He immediately thought about his safe box, so, he headed to check if things were as they should be.

He opened it and looked and learned that lots of money had been gone. That was when he realized that she had fled solemnly. He went nuts and started screaming and yelling, "No! no, no, she ransacked me, my money and my child!"

His parents, and his cousin from his dad's side, Ali, startled by his yelling, came running.

Holding his head with his hands, he yelled, "I'm ruined!"

"What happened?" asked his father.

"She wrecked me and disappeared with my child and my money. Alas! Alas! Oh, Allah! How could she do this to me? I will destroy both her and her husband. I will make her pay for what she has done to me," he yelled angrily.

His dad called, "Please try to calm yourself down. Maybe she went to her mother's house or her relative's place."

"Father, she has stolen my money! Thousands! With that amount of money in her hands, let alone she would go to her relatives who live around here, she won't spend the night in the city. But I will find her wherever she may be hiding.

"I suspected that she would conspire against me with that traitor husband of hers, I just didn't imagine it could be coming this soon. Is this what he was preparing for? He got me! I know I won't have a break until I get rid of this evil," said Ahmed, as if speaking to himself aloud.

"My son was nice and generous to everyone let alone to his family and relatives; he was peaceful too! It seems that he has become cruel and evil, what in the devil got into him?" said Haji, trying to picture Amin as he knew him before.

"They called me from America to tell me that he was a wanted man. I don't know what it is, but he had committed some kind of crime. He is a cancer to those in America and us here," said Ahmed, with the intent of increasing his fan base.

Though the mother couldn't stand hearing that much being said about Amin, she didn't want to defend him. Because she knew better—saying anything would aggravate her step-son.

***

Professor Woods, who led the team of innovative researchers, who introduced break-through research and outcomes to science and humanity, and who miraculously saved the little girl's life by applying his research, was about to testify on the case about the child whom he knew very well.

Those who heard about his decision to appear in the court were eager to listen to what his testimony would be. He and his associates had never been willing to talk to news outlets. Hence, most of their work had been hidden from the media.

The news about the professor's decision to testify drew public attention and restarted public discussions on the case. Some people voiced, despite who testified, the child's right and choice should be respected. Others expected comments that did not address her desire or need. The majority, however, expected to hear something new and impressive from the researcher who made the child.

Media continued to hammer the case with scholars, religious leaders, women's right advocates, children's right advocates, human right advocates, and some members of the LGBT community.

***

Ahmed picked up the phone and dialed Boston. As he hoped, Eyob answered the phone. After a short greeting, "That man robbed me my money and took my wife with him. My wife is expecting. I'm worried, thinking what he will do to my child," said Ahmed.

Eyob had hoped that Ahmed would be a good recruit to get rid of Million. Especially now, hearing what he had encountered, his confidence in him advanced. After listening quietly, "To tell you the truth, I'm not surprised by what he has done to you. It is a matter of time before he kills you. Because he knows that every man goes after someone who killed his child, after taking his wife and his money. No man can get a better night sleep without destroying the life of the person who did such a thing," said Eyob, purposely implanting the idea of revenge in Ahmed.

Hearing what Eyob said, Ahmed's furiousness enhanced, and said, "I will get rid of him. I will never stop going after him. I know I will find him."

To Ahmed's surprise, Eyob said, "If you kill that bastard, you will be rewarded with one hundred thousand dollars. Right now, I will wire you ten thousand dollars to help you with what was stolen from you and for some expenses in searching for him. His death is a relief to all of us," and he gave him addresses to the possible locations where Million/Amin may be found.

"Leave this to me. I won't sleep until I find and take vengeance on him," he said. with anger and a sense of intrepidness.

"The sooner you send me evidence that shows you have gotten rid of him, the faster your ninety thousand dollars will be sent to you," said Eyob. Then he said goodbye and hung up the phone.

I don't believe she fled with anyone else other than with the man she foolishly thought is Amin. They intend to ruin my life. No wonder she has been saying that I destroyed her marriage. How stupid is she to believe that? If it is him, none of us knew he was alive. Now, they have started a war! he said to himself after he got off the phone with Eyob.

"Oh, Allah! Are they going to kill my child?" he wondered aloud.

He continued talking to himself, "They better not! Not while I'm breathing! If they do it, I will make them pay—her for my child, and him for taking her from me. I'm not going to sit in this house until I have my revenge. From now on, hunting them is my fulltime job."

He sat contemplating, “It is true, they can’t live while I’m alive. so, they will have to kill me. One of us has to die. It is a matter of who strikes first. It is interesting that I will be rewarded a hundred thousand dollars for killing my enemy. I wouldn’t have hesitated to put a bullet in his head anyway.” The reward had given him an added confidence.

He imagined the person he was about to hunt would be coming after him. He packed the things he thought would need and his pistol, and left the house not to return until he accomplished his goal.

The unfortunate household was disordered by the assumed and invisible enemy.

***

They chose a table where it was more private and ordered their dinner.

“Barakat, how is your health now?” asked Fatima.

“Alghamdi-Lilah! I’m doing well.”

“What about your kids, how are they holding up?”

“They are okay, except they have many unanswered questions and those have been stressing us all. Day in day out, almost every hour, they ask me why their dad wouldn’t come home, and why I wouldn’t tell their uncle to leave the house. They have also been saying if our uncle stops living with us, our dad will come.”

“Poor kids, they have missed their dad badly. Unless something is done, it will have long-term effects on their mental health.”

"I'm scared that something might happen to them and give my mom a hard time. They are agitated, have become disobedient, and their appetite is poor. Especially when they see their uncle, their refusal and fussiness have been increasing. If they continue this way, I'm worried that they may get sick. I noticed their hatred toward their uncle is getting worse each day. Good thing they won't see him again."

"Oh, I feel sorry for them."

"I pray that they listen to my mom or Allah grants her patience to deal with them."

"I understand that you are having a hard time leaving your sons, but remember, you can't help them unless you help yourself first. Thus, your decision is reasonable."

"So, where do you suggest I go?"

"Okay, here is the plan, tonight you will stay at our place. Tomorrow before dawn, I will take you to the bus station for long distance buses. By the evening, you should arrive in Jima and be with my aunt Tumi—she is expecting you."

***

The next morning, as planned, Fatima and Barakat went to the long-distance bus service station. Barakat stayed in the car until Fatima went to get her a bus ticket.

While walking through the main gate, Fatima saw Ahmed wearing a long coat and a scarf on his neck. He was checking every woman who walked into the station. He didn't see the nurse because his attention was on a couple of other ladies.

Fatima quickly turned her face and dashed to the car. Before she sat comfortably in the driver's seat, she said, "He is standing by the main gate."

"Who?" said Barakat, nervously.

"Ahmed!"

"Please take me away from here. He will kill me. Also, I don't want you to get into any trouble because of me."

"I won't rest until I know that you have left this city safely today," she said. Then another idea popped into her head, and she said, "Alright! Here is another plan, let me get some more fuel, then I will take you a couple of towns away from here. There, you will catch a minibus or regular bus that departs from that town."

"But that is too far for you, Also, what about your work? Don't you have to be in today?"

"Considering the situation you are in, my being half an hour late to work is nothing. The thing is, we don't have any alternative solution."

"I have no idea how I will pay you back for all that you are doing for me. Let me at least pay for the fuel, I have enough money that will last me a couple of years."

They filled up the tank and headed west of Addis. They arrived just in time for her to catch a bus leaving for Jima. "As soon as you arrive at the bus station, give aunt Tumi a buzz, and she will come and get you," said Fatima. They said goodbye, and both headed to their destinations.

***

The nurse was driving fast with the plan of arriving to work on time, when all of a sudden, she heard a blowout of a tire and felt her car wobbling. She pulled to the side to learn that it was the right rear side tire.

Rightfully, she was pissed and grumbling. She grabbed her spare tire and sat it beside the flat. She never changed a tire before, she nervously started looking around for help. It was the beginning of rush hour, everyone seemed to be hurrying to avoid that. Seeing a couple of people coming her direction, her hope went up. Unfortunately, none of the people she had anticipated knew how to replace a tire, they were peasants from the nearby countryside.

She was tempted to call her husband for a how-to-guide, but she didn't. Frustrated, "Are people not helping one another anymore?" she mumbled and went back to the trunk and grabbed the jack. She stood by the flat tire and started wondering how to begin. Then, it hit her that she could refer to her car manual.

***

Chapter Sixteen

The courtroom looked like a segregated stadium where the spectators were divided into supporters of the plaintiff and the defendant. Professor Woods' testimonial was expected to be the breaking point for the case.

There were also those who were following the case as neutrally as possible—they were more interested in the scientific, social and psychological implication of the judgement.

With all what was happening, Boston and its suburbs were under high police surveillance for fear of some sort of fight might breakout following the court's decision.

As all long-awaited occasions come to pass, the day when the professor would testify arrived, and people were flooding to the courthouse. Some people had already camped outside the courthouse to make sure that they found the right seat or at least space to stand inside the courtroom. Reporters from different news media outlets had already started interviewing some spectators.

As soon as counsels of both sides took seats in their respective locations, the two massive doors on the front of the courtroom opened. People began streaming in in a somewhat controlled fashion. After the courtroom filled to capacity, the doors closed. Everyone sat down. Then the waiting game started.

After thirteen minutes, but what seemed an eternity to some, the door of the chamber opened and the three especially assigned district court judges in their gowns and robes came out, commanding grace. The public stood quietly until they reached their bench and were seated. The chief judge called the room to order and said, "Please, be seated."

***

He just finished his macchiato at a fancy hotel and was about to head out to see Saba and the kids, when on the TV across from the balcony, Million heard the announcement, "Coming up next, live coverage of the courtroom proceeding on the identity of the six-year-old child with a brain transplant."

Two weeks back, Abigail had told him about the news of the professor testifying in the "Tina or Sandra" case and that it would be broadcasted live on TV, he was planning on watching the hearing. However, he had forgotten the day and time of the viewing.

Wow! interesting! So, it is today, he said to himself. His eyes fixed on the TV, he pulled the chair he had gotten up from, and sat down. Imagining the professor standing in the witness booth, his heart started beating fast.

He looked around the hotel, there weren't many people, out of those who had tuned to the same channel as his, only a couple of them seem to be interested in what was about to be aired. "No one knows how closely related I am to this case," he murmured without taking his eyes from the TV. He couldn't be happier that he'd stumbled onto the show. He wished Saba, Sami, and Machida were there to watch the show with him.

The program began with a live feed of downtown Boston. Million couldn't believe how large the crowd gathered by the courthouse was. Until courtroom coverage started, the program began discussing topics that were compiled around the research center, the researchers, and about brain transplant and its outcomes. Million, again wished that he was watching the show with his families. *Would this have changed Sami's mind?* he thought. Then he remembered that Abigail had told him that she would record the entire coverage and sent it to him including YouTube videos that showed about the research. *I'm sure he would have preferred evidences like this, than my description of the procedure that transformed me. Well, if he ever wants to talk to me, I will show him this and other testimonies*, he thought, picturing how Sami reacted toward his presentation of how the new Million came about.

After showing portions of previous interviews with families of both the black and the white girl, it was followed by comments that were made from experts of different fields. Some of the comments of the so-called experts made Million chuckle a little bit.

Recognizing that it may cost him dearly to introduce himself to those whom he wanted to belong to, he felt sad. He knew that his families were essentially good people, but they were not in a position where their mind could accept the possibility that Biniam could be Million.

So far, the closer he got to his family and his wife, the stranger they imagined he was. He thought, *The question of identity is a strange thing. Here, I'm trying so hard to establish kinship with my own family, in America, families are fighting for the affinity of the little girl. This kid is a lot luckier than me.*

His eyes were still fixed on the TV—his mind traveled to America, he saw the girl and the two families who were fighting for her kinship, he came back to his house, and then went to his family's house. While his mind was still in the journey, CNN's live coverage of the court proceeding began to show everyone settling down inside the courthouse.

The public was sitting, and the judges had taken their benches. Then, the long awaited-for-witness walked gracefully to the witness booth. The cameraperson seemed to want to cover just that man. Different cameras displayed major areas of the courtroom on multiple windows on the TV screen.

Seeing Professor Woods, Million felt as if he met his archenemy on a corner. Both fear and anger bombarded his mind and body. His heartbeat elevated. He wondered, *This man! Should I praise him for saving my life or disgrace him for ruining my death? He saved my life, but he destroyed my identity.*

Did he assume that it is better to live as a stranger to one's loved ones than to die as the one they loved? Now that his own doing is threatening his exitance, he wants me dead. Who gave him the power to kill or save a person? Then he composed himself and decided to listen to his testimony. *Whatever he says about the girl, he means the same to me. I'm curious, who will he say this girl is?* said Million to himself.

"Our viewers, we have a side note that we believe you should know," said the host, then he continued after pausing for a brief moment, "Since the child's name has to be determined with her identity and it is part of the case that the appeals court is looking at, she might not be called Sandra as the district court determined it.

"Hence, until her identity is determined, we at CNN will regulate calling her by any of the two names she is being called. We may use the name that she is given by social media enthusiasts, or simply call her the girl. Today's testimony by Professor Woods is believed to assist the court's decision greatly."

When the professor walked to the witness booth, everyone in the courtroom, including the judges, start to look at him with great admiration. Could it be because he was a man whose work had challenged any existing law on earth, has taken the standard of knowledge to a new level, and has raised the new question—how a person's identity is determined?

Unlike the people in the courtroom, Million saw the professor not with astonishment or marvel, but with spectacles that have a special color. He was one of only two unique people in the world. Whatever the professor said about the other person, the girl, he meant the same for Million, so he started listening carefully to every word the professor uttered,

***

After the oath procedure, the court asked the professor to set the stage for his testimony. Many were surprised by this unaccustomed court procedure, until they realized that this court was purposely designed not to follow all the norms of a courtroom due to the case being unique and there were no rules and no references to draw from for judgement.

Therefore, this appeals court was organized with district court judges who had ruled some complex cases. These judges set the stage for any party to share his or her knowledge about the case. So, the professor was the best candidate as the source of information about the procedure that made the girl who she was and who could explain why she should be one but not the other.

The professor began his testimony as follows, "Our research center puts the highest emphasis there is in improving the health and wellbeing of humanity. Every year, the center invests over a hundred million dollars for that purpose. It started with the transplantation of organs and other body parts. Now, it has set the stage for another level of scientific advancement by successfully replacing a healthy brain for a dying or unhealthy one."

Some spectators began to jeer. The judge called everyone's attention by hitting the table with his gavel. The courtroom went silent. The professor then continued.

"However, we still have work to do. Momentarily, the issue of identity has shadowed the great work that many will rejoice in taking advantage of its immeasurable benefits. I'm confident that soon, a person's individuality will not be the problem. As for the current case, whomever the child is named, the most important part is that she beat death. Instead of arguing over her identity, which is secondary, we should be exulted that she is alive. Because it was impossible for her to survive otherwise. In fact, hours, not days, were being counted until her death. Then, she died. Now she is alive. How incredible is that. Such a thing was mystical, a story in the Bible, but not in the real world."

He briefly paused, then continued, "Myself and the team of researchers whom I worked with, both in the study and transplantation of the brain, took time and discussed the matter of the child's identity. Based on scientific facts and evidence, we have reached the following conclusion.

"Before I proceed, let me clear this up—our areas of research and expertise is anatomical biology, not psychology. In short, we study the physical, not the mental part of being human and animal. Thus, my testimony is about the anatomy and physiology of what we transplanted and implanted. A physically matured person's brain is two percent of the whole body. The rest of the body, therefore, is ninety eight percent.

"Therefore, our research outcome shows that the two percent from one girl was implanted in the ninety eight percent of another girl's body. Even though the girl speaks in a mindset of the knowledge that the brain came with, her identity is that of the girl who contributed ninety eight percent to her current existence. In summary, this girl's identity is not the thought process in her brain, rather it is her physical representation and looks."

Murmur and noise, and words of anger erupted in the courtroom. Supporters' of the black family despised him for saying that.

"Your honor, may I please be allowed to clarify my point further?" asked the professor.

The judge hammered the table with his gavel and instructed everyone to be quiet. As soon as silence resumed in the room, he told the professor that he could continue.

"Idea and knowledge are codes that stay in a brain. The idea could be edited as necessary. The whole body, however, is the identification of the person who has it until the person dies. We all know, in a person's government issued identification documents, the photo, which is the physical representation of the person is used to authenticate that person's identity," said the professor.

The court set the stage for questions and answers.

"Professor, let me ask you, I believe you are saying all that about this girl because she is too young. What if the person who had the transplant was an adult? Who would you have told her or him to be?

"Do you assume that she or he would change her or his identity just because you told her or him to? Let's take yourself as an example, while you are at your current identity and level of understanding, what if, for some legitimate reason, your brain was placed in someone's body and that someone was a monk. Would you have considered yourself a doctor or a monk?" asked the black families' lawyer.

"My answer is based on biological, not on psychological analyses—because I can only explain what is in my area of expertise. Let me give you an answer to your hypothetical question in which I'm the subject. However, I will use an example that I presume will help me better in getting my points across."

"Professor, I would rather have you answer my question directly. Would you have considered yourself a Monk or a Doctor?" pursued the lawyer.

"It is not that simple, but let me give you a general answer. I might act and think like a doctor, my identity however is that of the monk. "

"What is your biological analysis that explains that this girl is the one, but not the other?" asked the judge.

"Her DNA, which is the unique biological factor that identifies her and matches her to her genetic origins, is found in her body. The other biological factor we should look into is reproduction. When this girl grows up and gives birth, her offspring will be white, not black because eggs which transmit hereditary information to the offspring are produced by ovaries. And ovaries reside in the body, not in the brain."

He paused for a couple of seconds, then continued, "Whether the child is Caucasian or African American is for the court to judge. But I can say one thing with absolute confidence. And that is, that her future children, will acquire heredities of the white race from her. I can provide evidence that, despite the race of the father of the children, their grandparents in their mom's side are Caucasian. Thus, leaving the moral, humanity, and psychological perspective of the case aside, and just looking at it from biological context, I don't see how it is possible that she could be black while her children and their grandparents in her side are white," the professor concluded.

***

Meanwhile, Million was very upset hearing the professor speak with conviction about the great benefits that their research had for humanity.

"He has no idea how much trouble they set me into. I'm living halfway between the living and the dead. Even worse, they are chasing me to undo their work. This killer, standing before people who don't know him well, is talking as if he is concerned for humanity.

"He is a wolf disguised in sheep's skin. He does what he does for fame and money. He and his associates value life in terms of the success of their research," he mumbled with his teeth clenched.

If their work had received acceptance and a permit, they would have regarded me as the precious model of their accomplishment. And used me to accumulate their riches. Now that things didn't go as they had planned, they want to get rid of me. Where is their humanity? They are selfish animals, and they don't care about anyone but themselves, he said to himself, remembering that he was almost killed by the assassin they recruited.

Million became furious and stood up abruptly when he heard the professor's conclusion about the girl's identity.

"Does he know what he is saying? He's telling me, I'm Amin, not Million. He is also saying my wife and kids are not mine! Is he aware of what it implies, a woman I don't know is my wife and the kids whom I never met, but once, are my kids? He must be crazy!" said Million aloud.

Guests of the hotel who were a couple of tables away from him noticed Million was unhinged. They thought that he was unwise to get flustered about some public issue discussed in America. They had no idea how the topic was so personal to him, and that it was a matter of being with loved ones or living a miserable lonely life—or in general, a matter of life and death.

Still raged and discombobulated, he started leaving the hotel, mumbling his pain out. But before he stepped out of the door, he remembered that he didn't pay for his macchiato. So, he went back to the balcony and put fifty Ethiopian birrs and left without saying a word or expecting change.

Those who noticed all his moves thought he was losing it. One of the guests said, "Maybe he is insane." They all agreed and went back to their business.

He didn't seem to be aware that he was walking in high foot traffic areas. He thought out loud. Passersby stared at him with curiosity and confusion, but he didn't register anyone's presence.

He argued with himself, "What kind of knowledge is this? And what kind of justice is this? This guy must be out of his mind. How can he imply that I'm Amin? This is not drama. This is my life. He expected me to be someone that I'm not. How could he say that people whom I don't know are my family, a woman I never met is my wife, and kids who are not born from me are my kids? A house I don't even know is my house? This man must be nuts who needs a psychiatrists' help. Maybe he is intoxicated by his research. Either way, he is not in his right mind!"

He held his head with both of his hands and said, "This is a headache that I can't endure."

"Who knows me more than myself? And who could decide for me? Unbelievable! What is wrong with the professor? Does he not know that I'm still alive? Or is he saying that to drive me crazy by destroying the confidence I have about myself, to kill me from inside out?

"Maybe he is right; my sister wants to marry me; my parents are more than glad for me to marry her. What about my wife? Only I say she is my wife, but she only knows me as some nice stranger. How can I live as myself among people who tell me I am not me? What kind of enigmatic loneliness am I in?" His tears began to roll down his face.

He continued talking to himself. "What kind of madness is this? Are they telling me that they could teach me to be someone, then I would be that someone? JUST LIKE THAT? Is this idea coming from a place where sane and rational people live? How could professors, who got the connection of millions of nerve fibers right and who were able to make one person out of two, have such cuckoo idea? Or, is it me who is the fruitcake?

"If the professor's testimony receives acceptance and the court determines that the child is white, then it implies that the court has judged that I'm not who I'm. Then, in the EYES of the LAW, I DON'T EXIST. But I KNOW I AM

ALIVE! However, the law knows that I don't exist, WHAT AM I TO DO NOW?

"Does it mean I have to go to school to find myself? But before that, I have to repudiate my knowledge and belief about my wife, my kids, my family. After that, I will gain the epiphany that enables me to be with another wife, children, and family? IS THAT RIGHT? This body that I'm in once belonged to a medical doctor. If it is determined for me to be him, then I'm considered a doctor. Are the demented professors going to get me the license to practice, and have me do surgeries without the knowledge of how? Is this how far they are able to analyze? Is this the level of their knowledge? Is this their sense of humanity?"

He tried to draw his mind into thinking something else, but he couldn't. "Thanks to them and their great research, every day, I wake up to live a life of misery and loneliness. The idiot professor didn't know that there is beauty in death. Interrupting life's course is not always the best option. Could he have changed his idea and let life do its own doing, if he knew how a living hale my life has become? Now, to protect his selfish self, he is trying to get me killed. Too late, pal! We all have to live with our deeds.

"Because of their lack of foresight, they locked me in a way that even my own family wouldn't understand me, let alone recognize me. They completely separated me from the outside world, especially from the people whom I love. These jerks! Now, they want to get into my head and destroy my identity. Though my wife, my kids, and my family, will never meet me physically, I want to live with the hope of one day them discovering where I live. However, the professor and his associates are laboring to erase the memory and knowledge of my wife, my kids, and my family from my mind. This is an act of savagery, not that of humanity," he said, and wept, recognizing the torment he was in.

He bumped into a man who was standing on the sidewalk. That brought his attention back to the road he was on.

"Now, crying and feeling sorry for myself will not help me. There are a couple of things I need to do. I will let Abigail know about her coworkers' cruel idea and then write a letter to the court explaining how I'm the result of the professors' research and had been suffering from loneliness and guilt, because my loved ones don't recognize me, and the wife, children and families of the man whose body I'm installed into believe that I'm their loved one and that the professors have been chasing me to get rid of me. I need to stand for truth and expose these heartless, self-centered crooks. I have to hurry before they obliterate the poor child's memory and knowledge from her brain," he concluded.

***

All the researchers were summoned for an urgent meeting by Professor Woods. Despite the success of the actual research, the practicality of its outcome was not as they wished it would be. It had led them into too much trouble, and they suspected a serious challenge was yet to come. Their dream of capturing Million had not become a reality.

They were wondering how he was able to scape from all the traps they had webbed. They started to believe that there was an insider who informed him of all their plans. The top leaders of the center were studying and trying to figure out who the informant could be. So far, no luck.

Professor Woods called for their attention by tapping his pen on his table. “Okay, everyone, let’s talk about the pressing issues we have faced,” he said with an attempt to center their thoughts.

“The purpose of this meeting is to discuss why Million/Amin’s case hasn’t been closed yet, and to develop better plans.

“My understanding is that he is getting a leak of our plans. Whoever helped him escape is still informing him on all the strategies we have been developing. Otherwise, he wouldn’t have escaped all the hooks. Thus, our first step should be finding out who the informant is.

“I touched base with our attorneys, and they believe that, if his case became public and brought to court, we will be in big trouble and they won’t defend us in court. So, finding the insider and finishing Million/Amin are the most pressing issues,” said Professor Woods.

“I don’t suspect,” he continued, “The tipster is here in this room. Because each one of us knows the scale of the predicament, we are in. His case is a timebomb. Unless we disconnect the wires now, it will explode in our hands. If his case becomes public or goes to court, we will be the disgraced fools, including our family. What we built so far will be destroyed."

They all agreed on what had been said. So, they started discussing what the informant's motive could be. Among many suggestions, two possible motives, altruism, and revenge were chosen. They had a long discussion on both motives and concluded that, though it was possible that someone might try to get revenge his or her boss by taking such an extreme action, there were no employees within the center who expressed dissatisfaction toward their supervisors. Therefore, the incentive was narrowed down to altruism.

"Despite the motive, I'm more concerned about the person's ability to recognize the problem behind his or her action. We need to know who this person is," said Professor Art after quietly listening to everyone's opinion.

After agreeing that no one from the research team would be crazy enough to become devious, they went back to the drawing board to figure out who else participated in the first meeting, when the decision to undo the work of Million/Amin was reached. So, the suspicion shifted toward three doctors who took part in the meeting.

The professors, then developed a testing strategy to phish who among the three or if all of them are to be suspected. Professor Clark was elected to lead the examining process.

***

"Hello Barakat, how is life in Jima? Is auntie treating you well?"

"Hi Fatima, Jima is great! Even the baby seems to like it, it is always jumping inside me. In a few days, it will come out and we will know whether it is a boy or a girl. Hey, if it is a girl, I will name her after you. Your aunt, she is an amazingly courageous woman! She is inspirational! If things go as I have planned, I will settle down here and bring my kids and my mom."

"Barakat, come down, you're making me jealous with your enthusiasm! You have no idea how happy I am right now, hearing you excited about life!"

"Yes, thanks to you and your family, I'm seeing the bright side of my situation! Just getting out of that place has changed my perspective and given me hope. I have a couple of things remaining to iron out, then I will move on with my life. As always, I'm going to need your help to take care of my final hiccups."

"No problem, it is my pleasure to be part of the solution! Do you want me to help you moving your kids and your mom to Jima?"

"No, that I will do myself. I have an idea how to sneak them out. Instead, I need your help in legitimately separating from Ahmed and finding Amin. I want to see Amin one last time and apologize to him and move on. I have kept the money that I roped from Ahmed, and I want to give it back. Actually, I have sent a letter with no return address to the elder who got us married explaining about my need for divorce and about returning the money."

"I don't know where or how we can find Amin, but we will try. As far as officially divorcing both men, talk to auntie, she has a friend who knows all about that."

"Okay, thank you! Sorry I have been loading you with my issues. How are you anyways? How is work?"

"I'm doing well! I'm about to start a new job. I got fired from the hospital where we met, because I guess, I was calling-in more frequently. But everything happens for a reason, mostly good. Believe it or not, I always wanted to work in the hospital I just found the job at. They take care of more critical patients. It is a research hospital. I'm really excited to work there."

"I'm sorry that you lost your job! So, have you officially started on the new place?"

"Almost, I'm in training until Friday and will start shift on Tuesday."

“Wow! That’s wonderful! You’re right, things happen for a reason. Look at me, I have never dreamed of visiting Jima, let alone reside here, work, and adopt an amazing family like you, your husband and your aunt. So, your new job should be more rewarding to you!”

“Yes! Hey, now I have two jobs. Finding your ex-husband, Amin seems another fulltime job, but temporary. I will call you in a couple of days with an update. Don’t forget to text me with a lead on where we should look for him.”

“Sure, thank you so much, Fatima, you are the sister I never had!”

***

Chapter Seventeen

Professor Clark had Doctors Muzik, William, and Caleb come to his office for a meeting. While they were discussing a particular patient's case, Professor Kim, holding a piece of paper in his hand walked into the office without knocking on the door.

"Sorry! How rude of me to interrupt your guys' meeting. I didn't even knock, my mind has been elsewhere," said Professor Kim.

"It is okay, do you have something quick that you want to talk to me about?" asked Professor Clark.

"Yes, it is quick. I want to let you know that we have found a reliable man there in Ethiopia who could take care of our guy. He knows where to find him, and he is well informed. Apparently, he has a better team. You need to talk to him ASAP. I have written down his number and our guy's address for you," said Professor Kim and handed the paper to him and left.

Professor Clark placed the paper inside a drawer next to his seat.

He made himself comfortable in his seat and said, “Sorry, where were we?”

Abigail, startled by the info about Million, sensed her heart starting to pound hard. She wanted to leave the room immediately and contact Million. But she knew leaving then would make the professors suspicious or assume that she was being disrespectful. So, despite being uncomfortable, she sat there for a couple of minutes. She could barely sit still, she got up and went to the bathroom. While there, she dialed to Million, but he didn’t answer. She knew it was past midnight in Ethiopia and that he could be sleeping, but she tried a couple of times anyways with no luck. She went back to the meeting and sat there inattentively.

Before they got deep into the meeting, the phone rang. Professor Clark picked up the receiver and said, “Hello.” The doctors sensed from the phone call that he had something urgent that he needed to take care of. He said, “Okay, I’m on my way,” getting up from his chair and grabbing his coat. He hung up quickly. Heading to the door, he said to the doctors, “Sorry, I have to take off, we will reschedule this meeting. Please close the office when you leave.”

The two doctors left right away. Doctor Muzik didn’t. She stayed behind acting as if she had something to write. As soon as her colleagues’ steps faded, she got up and popped her head out of the door and peeked if anyone was in the hallway. Concluding no one was around, she closed herself in the office and went to the drawer where the professor put the piece of paper. She took a picture of what was written on the paper. Then closed the drawer after placing the paper back.

Professor Woods couldn't believe who and what he was seeing on the recording of the hidden camera. After quietly watching the video with Professors Clark, Kim and three others, "I'm shocked! I would never have guessed that this bitch is the traitor. Why did she betray us for bringing her into our circle? She will have to pay, but the terms should be torment for a torment," he said with clenched teeth and the vein on the side of his neck popping.

***

A few months back, Abigail had submitted an abstract of her research paper to Professor Woods' office for review. The topic was about new methods of organ transplants. She wanted to publish it in one of the peer reviewed journals of medicine. But, because she was busy with helping Million, she had abandoned it.

So, when Professor Woods called her and said "Congratulations!" she had forgotten all about it. Never the less, she was surprised and nervous at the same time that a man whom she once admired and respected, and later, equally despised called her out of the blue. She thought that he discovered her work with Million and was mocking her, fear began to creep into her.

"Thank you! I guess—what are you congratulating me for?" said Abigail, sounding confused.

"I read your abstract, and it is very good! I might read your whole paper too."

"Oh that, I didn't think you would have time to look at it. Any suggestions?"

He said, "Matter of fact, I do have some, but I have to go now. If you want, we could talk about it over dinner. I'm available tomorrow at seven. I will call you tomorrow afternoon and let you know where we will be dining." And he hung up without waiting to hear whether she would say okay or not.

"What the heck!" she blurted looking at her phone.

Abigail always liked men who took charge but the professor's action she thought was disrespectful. Until the day he announced the plan of getting rid of Million, she thought of him a man with most qualities she would have liked from a partner. She had even pictured herself in bed with him.

However, when she made the determination to help Million, she thought that she got over seeking powerful men and being attracted to those whom she assumed were dominant. Especially the professor, no matter how attractive she found him, she was appalled by his selfish and egotistical personality that she never noticed until that revelation.

"He is a true genius, but an asshole. I wonder if he has a drop of empathy left in him to leave Million alone. Maybe this is my chance to find out," she thought aloud.

***

It was over two years since she had been out on a real date. But she wasn't sure if she should consider this one a date.

She expected him to call between one and three o'clock to let her know what time and where they would be meeting. But he didn't call. Five passed, no call. She sat down on her sofa and started surfing the web on her laptop, and frequently checking her phone. When the clock said 6:10 she made sure that her phone was not in silent mode and hadn't missed any calls.

Realizing her phone was good to go, she gave up and changed the dress she had chosen for the dinner to a night gown. She took out chocolate ice cream from the freezer and sat back on her sofa. Her legs stretched, her feet on the dining table, annoyed and sad, she started eating her ice cream while staring at the TV.

She thought, *I hate being single! He wouldn't have dared to invite me for dinner, let alone to stood me up.* It was now 6:35; she picked up and pressed the home button of her phone just out of habit. There it was, a text. He texted her ten minutes earlier. They were supposed to meet at 7:00, at some fancy restaurant. "Sure—I may be a few minutes late, though." She texted him back. She quickly freshened up and put on the dress she was wearing earlier.

***

They hugged each other, and while taking their seat, Abigail said, “Professor, I’m very grateful that you took time out of your busy life to read and review my abstract, and your willingness to review my whole paper.”

“No problem! How is it coming along so far?”

“Not too bad. I have been busy with work, so, I didn’t put enough time into it. How bad is it?”

“Speaking of work, I heard from your colleagues that you are a hard worker. Don’t you get annoyed when someone comes along and tries to undo what you planned and did?”

“I try my best. And I understand what you mean by that,” said Abigail, remembering how often such things used to happen to her during her residence.

“Some of us are like bees. Bees don’t like to stop working. They work more than they eat. We are beneficiaries of their hard work. However, we never say thank you. That is sad, isn’t it? The bee, if it didn’t have enemies that consume its work, it would have taken a break, relaxed and enjoyed its fruit of labor for a little while. So how do you think the bee could rest with all the enemies around it?” he said, wondering what her answer would be.

“Professor, I feel like I’m in class now. If we were in chefs’ school, this would be the best class to be at. Anyway, is your question rhetorical, or do you want me to answer it? She said, smiling innocently. She didn’t seem to recognize the message behind the bee and its enemies.

He noticed her beautiful smile and how stunning she looked, but he was annoyed by her naivete.

What is the point? he thought. “No, it is rhetorical,” he said.

“Marg, let’s get it out of the way, how bad is my abstract?”

“Actually, there is a more pressing issue that you and I need to talk about. I don’t know why you did what you did with the Million/Amin guy, but I need you to clean up your mess before it’s too late. Forget about how he got there, just tell me exactly where he is now.”

“So, you lied to bring me here. Why didn’t we discuss this in your office or over the phone?”

“You seem upset that I lied to you. I guess you are not just a traitor, you are a hypocrite too. In fact, you were right, I never had time to look at your stupid abstract. You came dressed up to impress me and hear me talk about your article? You really are naïve! I hate young doctors like you—when you give them an opportunity to grow, they sabotage it and stab you in the back. This is a business meeting, okay? A meeting to save your life and your career, in exchange for cooperating to reverse your course,” barraged the professor, forgetting that he had planned to talk to her nicely.”

"Honestly, I came to check if you have the slightest humanity left in you to let him leave his tormented life that you have set him to live. Evidently, you don't! Why do you want to kill him anyway? If he was as bitter as you are, he would have exposed you and everyone around you, including myself long time ago. He is just living alone among his own family.

"He is a stranger to his wife and kids, and someone who came from the dead to Amin's widow and sons. If it wasn't for me, he had chosen to die the day he realized how he survived death. He hates your guts, not because you are chasing him, but because you interrupted his peaceful death. He is not afraid of death. He would be happy for you to kill him. But I won't let that happen. I will have to be dead before you get to him.

"Also, you are right I'm naïve! But not the way you think. I'm naïve for believing that you have some humanity to do the egotistical work you have been doing. But this naïve girl knows how to protect herself. I have submitted secured documents about your work to the FBI to be revealed only if I die or have gone missing for over 36 hours," exploded Abigail at a controlled rate with a subdued voice so as not to draw other dinner's attention. Before he could say anything, she gently pushed back her seat and erupted and left.

The professor realized he had opened a can of worms. He sat there staring at his wine glass, trying to make sense of what just happened. He was working on collecting his composure, when Abigail startled him. Apparently, she had returned but he didn't know.

She said, "A few words of caution, I need you to stop pursuing Million and never try to threaten me with my career or life. The minute anything happens to any of us, you all are going down."

"Come on, Abigail, please sit back down and let's talk about it. I apologize for being hard on you," said the professor. However, she was already leaving. He followed her and tried to talk to her calmly—she ignored him and walked to her car.

***

"Hi Million, I'm so glad you answered your phone, I have been dying to talk to you. I had the worst evening of my life."

"Sorry to hear that! What happened?"

"They know that I helped you escape, and the professor confronted me this evening."

"I'm really sorry! It was a matter of time before they figured it out, but this is too early. Are you okay, though?"

"Maybe it is good that they know now than latter, but I don't know."

"So, what did he say? Did he hurt you? I mean emotionally?"

"He threatened me with my life, unless I cooperate with them, but I burned him back. I told him that documents about you in relation to them are placed under government protection. And they are not to be revealed unless I've gone missing for over thirty-six hours."

"I'm sure that will get his attention."

"I think it already has. Because I told him if they don't stop chasing you and try to mess with my career, I will have the FBI look into the documents."

"Oh, Abigail! I knew you were my courageous sister! All this time, you didn't even tell me—you have been weaving their web."

"No, I didn't. I was just bluffing to him. But it might have worked."

"Well, can we do it now? Can you actually give the FBI presumptive documents with precondition, for future investigation?"

"Honestly, I don't know. I don't think the professor knows either. His lawyer might. But, now that I know that they know everything, I might need to seek a lawyer's advice."

"Yes, that is a good idea. I was going to talk to you about testifying in court anyway. Did you watch his testimony proceeding? Did you hear how he dismissed my existence? I think he is insane. According to him, I'm Amin. Hearing him say all that about the little girl made me sick. And when I realized its implication, it drove me crazy. I hated talking to anyone. That was why I didn't answer when you called the last couple of days."

"Oh! So, you had a chance to watch the whole show? I hope you made Saba or Machida watch it with you. If you haven't, it is okay. I have it recorded, and I have downloaded more video from YouTube."

"I didn't. It was accidental that I stumbled on the show. I will just show both the girls and Sami when you send me the videos. Anyways, about testifying, what do you think? I'm tempted going to authorities here, but the promise I made you grounded me. Another thing, I have written a letter to him. I will email it to you to read it. Now that he knows you are my hero—you can forward it to him."

"If push comes to shove, I will have you fly back here and testify. For now, we are going to use my bluff and your letter as weapons to try to stop him pursuing us."

"Why are you still protecting them, anyway?"

"For two reasons. One, though not the way it was done on you and the girl, I believe in the research and its outcomes. The whole head and spine could be transplanted with the same process. Now, in your case, you wouldn't have had all the issues you have at the moment. Except your wife, nobody would have known that you have someone else's body from the neck down. I have been writing a paper on transforming the research to the one I just told you. The second reason is that I'm responsible to the process of making you the way you are, as much as they are. Because I was there, I understood what they were planning on doing. But said nothing. In fact, my name is listed on the research paper as the part of the team."

"I see! I believe the first reason is your constraint, not the second. You were just treating me and keeping me alive after they did what they did to me. You were not part of their original decision."

"Still. Anyway, you get the idea. But now, we have to do things faster and in precision to get our point across. If you email me the letter, I will forward it to him right away, and I'm sure I will hear from him soon."

"I'm actually sending it to you as we speak."

"Okay, I will call you with any updates."

***

"Abigail used to adore you, why did she say she did that?" asked Professor Art, after quietly listening Professor Wood's narration of his worst evening with Doctor Muzik and the setup she told him about.

"Obviously, she has been upset that we didn't sit there and wait for things to go sour on us because of him. The problem is that we still couldn't avoid it, in fact, we might have created more enemies, such as her."

"Do you think I should talk to her? Would she listen to me?"

"I don't know what you could say to change her mind. She seems determined to take us down unless we stop pursuing him and harassing her."

"Did you talk to the lawyers? Do you think we should pull back and see where things will go?"

"No lawyer is going to help with this one. We either have to pull back and see where things go, or get rid of both of them and take the heat. Sooner or later, we are going to jail because of the child, anyway."

"Come on! Marg! What is getting into you? We are not criminals. The only crime we committed was conducting the human trial without a permit. But killing anyone to cover it up is not going save us from being responsible. Our research was supposed to save human life not kill. In fact, leave his case for the lawyers of the center to work it out. At the same time, let's be diplomatic with Abigail. Especially you, I don't imagine that she would accept seeing you going to jail. I remember how she used to look at you. Though, she is pissed at you now, she won't allow seeing anything bad happening to you."

"At the restaurant, I apologized and asked her to sit down just so we can discuss the matter, but she walked away. So, what do you call that? Maybe I will try to text or email her tomorrow and see what her response will be. "

"We don't want to complicate things more than it already has. Let me know what she says, and I will take it from there. Diplomacy is the only way that will work without further crisis."

"Alright, alright! I will see you tomorrow at the meeting with the lawyers."

***

Hello professor, receive my greetings from hell!

How is life treating you? Stressful, ha? Compared to what I'm going through, yours is a cakewalk. But being the egoistic that you are, even a papercut would probably make you whimper for days. Let's cut to the chase, I'm Million! Not Amin.

What kind of drug were you on to say that the little girl's memories, hopes, dreams, likes, and dislikes do not matter. Those are what make her who she is. She is nobody or someone else without those. You told her that her identity of choice is not right. You didn't count what is in her mind. You dismissed the knowledge and memory she has in her. I assumed wrongly that you have recognized the complexity behind human nature.

You testified that the girl is white, reasoning ninety eight percent of her body is that of the white girl. In other words, you are saying I'm not Million, but Amin. Isn't that what you implied?

You thought you knew what you were doing, but you have no clue what you did to the little girl and I.

You challenged me to denounce my identity and made me hate my life. If my everyday struggle with loneliness and unfamiliarity to people whom I love is not enough, you added pain to my sorrow by saying that I'm someone else.

Here, I can't find a single individual who understands me. My wife, my kids, and my family believe I'm someone they barely know. If that is not enough, you, who installed my brain into this body seem to forget that you have a moral obligation to stand by me. To make matters worse, you have been chasing me to kill me. Even I know that it is unethical to do such a thing in your profession.

Listen, even if your stupid research was perfected, no one lives forever. For your short life on earth, you should be proud of your accomplishment and stand by your work, no matter what the consequences might be, including imprisonment, and death.

By reversing my journey in life, do you know how much living hell you put me through? Place your only daughter in my shoes and try to sense the pain she would be forced to endure because of it. How could you allow that to happen in the first place, and stand there and watch then after?

What I can't figure out is why your research didn't address the issue of identity crisis that your project will lead to. If a civil engineer doesn't know the effect of the combination of certain materials on the future of a specific building, then that engineer either doesn't know what he or she is doing or lacks the merit of the profession.

My plan of coming to your country was to get higher education and therefore to improve mine and my families' lives. I never dreamed of being somebody other than who I was. Unfortunately, I'm living as someone else. And now, my life is worse than death. Because I died, my loved ones and others who are concerned about me shed tears of love and moved on, recognizing everyone has turns. Now, if I say I'm alive, who could believe me? Especially looking completely like someone else. It is not like I can open my enclosure and show them otherwise. I live as a stranger to my wife and kids. My parents estimate I could be a good husband to my sister.

My sister is amorously in love with me. Parents, a wife, and kids whom I know nothing about concluded that I'm their loved one. I can see, but no one can see me. I can hear, but no one can hear me; I understand, but no one understands me, it is like I'm in a dream world.

If all these misfortunes are not enough, you sentenced me to death. What did I do to you? If I wanted to make a report, I had plenty of time on my hands. So far, no hardship has come to you because of me. However, going forward, I have decided to stand for myself and the little girl. I want you to be aware that I will testify in the same court where you dismissed my exitance, my identity, and the identity of the innocent girl.

Sincerely,

Million Bayou

***

Abigail, after reading Million's letter to the professor, forwarded it to his personal email with the following message of her own.

Professor Woods, so far, I have been protecting you and the person who is the outcome of your research from crisis. Now it is time for you two to face each other's demon. The only difference is that you will use your unmatched resources of money and privilege. However, he has a truth and time on his side.

The attached letter is from him. No one, except your own statement in the court, prompted him to write that or to develop the inclination to testify. You might say to me, "If you didn't help him escape it wouldn't have come to this." But I want remind you that people, especially those in our field, don't like to see people die. Most of us, when we pictured ourselves hanging the stethoscope on our neck, we knew we would use it to save lives. And later, we made the oath to confirm what we knew all along about the profession, saving lives!

Therefore, there were and still are many of us who want to see Million thrive despite the consequences to you, your associates and us. That tells you, even if I didn't do it, someone else would have. The reality is, I'm not the only one who is helping him survive this difficult time he is in. He doesn't have a job; therefore, some are sending him money. Despite being with his loved ones, he is always lonely, because as he put it in the attached letter, his family thinks that he is a good-hearted stranger. I have seen his everyday life and I don't blame him that he has been depressed and has chosen to die than to live. I like to believe that my moral support has kept him going as long he has.

Now, that you know the truth, it's time for you to make a decision of whether to remain a coward and try to kill him and those of us who are helping him, or be courageous and celebrate your accomplishment while facing consequences of your work. The choice is yours. Don't forget, compared to him, you are in a better position to choose.

Speaking of making a choice, Million didn't choose to go through the life he is in now. You, your associates, and I made the decision for him to live. So, it is time for us all to face the truth.

If you need to talk, you know where to find me

Abigail

Chapter Eighteen

The ending of the drama titled "Biniam" was approaching. The lead actor planned to come out from behind the curtain and meet the spectators. Unsteady due to turbulence in the ocean of thought, Million was carefully navigating the decision boat of how to make his wife know the truth about Bini.

When the day came, he started getting nervous and anxious because he didn't know how his wife would react. Remembering his friend, Sami's reaction when he told him about his identity, his fear aggravated. Sami considered Million an ugly and scary freak. He had been avoiding him since.

Million was not sure how to tell Saba. He picked and dropped many options of breaking the news to her.

He thought, *Maybe I should wait until I'm certain.* Then his emotions start to nag him saying, *How could you make it the night without telling her? You should tell her now; go, go…* Remembering the day when she showed him kindness and her desire to get close to him by caressing his hair. Then he imagined her reacting as his friend did.

He badly missed being with his wife. His eagerness to spend alone time with her intensified. His anxiousness for his kids to stop considering him someone else but their father elevated. His sister, who was pissed at Saba and him, needed to know the truth sooner.

***

As if he was not applauded for being the most resourceful and creative by his colleagues and others who had a chance to work with him, Professor Woods couldn't come up with a solution to counter Doctor Muzik's threat. After reading her email and Million's letter he realized that his intransigence wouldn't serve him well.

He was glad that, a couple of days back, he denied the hitman's request to go inside the house and carnage Million and his family. Staring at Million's letter, he felt the urge to terminate the mission.

"Hello, Eyob, any news from your guy?"

"No sir, after you and I talked, I told him that they should wait until they find him alone. I haven't heard from him since."

"Okay, call him immediately and tell him to terminate the mission."

"Entirely?"

"YES!"

"Yes, sir! They are still going to ask me to pay them."

"Go ahead pay them fifty percent of what you agreed for completion."

"I don't think he will accept that. He knows my family, so, I'm not going to mess with him if he refuses to take the offer."

"Do what you got to do," concluded the professor.

***

As soon as he hung up with Eyob, the professor texted Abigail, "Abigail, tell Million that he can take whatever action he feels taking. Most importantly, tell him that I apologize that he has suffered so much because of our work. And that we are no longer pursuing to harm him. In fact, I'm ready to help him with everything I can to make his life easier."

Abigail texted back, "I will—thank you! He will be glad to hear that."

"Do you have time for you and I to sit and talk? We can meet at the lounge," Asked the professor.

"I have a couple of patients to see. I should be done in forty-five minutes," replied Abigail.

"Okay, see you in forty-five."

***

Consumed by the idea that Amin had messed up his life, broke his family, robbed his money, and took away his young and beautiful wife, Ahmed left his house to find and retaliate. He began looking for him everywhere he assumed Amin might be. He pictured his brother armed and prepared. Therefore, he decided to move cautiously but fast.

Ahmed wanted to clear his mind from feeling guilty of killing his own brother. So, he pictured him instructing Barakat to get rid of the unborn child. That in itself drove him crazy and he wished he found Amin on the spot and broke his neck. The money that he would be getting from America for killing him was an extra motive to keep looking for Amin.

He went to all the places where Amin's friends reported having seen him. Disappointed, he returned home to gather more information and recharge himself. Sitting alone, looking at his brother's picture, a new idea popped to his head. He grabbed the picture and went to a photo multiplying place. With multiple photos of Amin in his hand and a pistol on his waist, he went to major intersections and busy taxi stations.

He approached as many contract taxi drivers as he could and he told them that he would reward them ten-thousand Birr, if they helped him find his missing brother, and gave them the picture with his own contact info written on its back. He told them that his brother had a fight with their family, thus, shouldn't know that he was looking for him. Heading home, he thought, "This is my last try to find the traitor. If this doesn't work, I'd rather put the bullet in my head than to sit and wait for him to come and kill me."

The same evening, a taxi driver, by the name of Degu, gave a ride to a young man from Addis Ababa University to an area called Bela. On his way back to Piazza, a dark skinned, fit looking, and well-dressed man stopped him and asked him, “Can you take me to Saris? If so, how much would you charge?”

Degu told the man that he would take him and they agreed on the fair. The whole time when they were talking about fair and destination, Degu was wondering where he had seen the man. Every chance he got, he looked at his passenger through the rearview mirror. But he couldn’t produce where he had seen him. They started a conversation, and he confessed about his dilemma. The man told him that he didn’t think he had ridden with him, so, couldn’t tell where they could have met.

Halfway to their destination, the Cabbie decided to get gas. While getting his wallet from the armrest box of his car, his hand ran into a thick but smooth paper. He looked into the box. There it was, the photo of the man in the backseat. He almost pulled the picture out, but immediately, he remembered the searching man wanted to surprise his brother. Degu, then, folded the photo and held it with his wallet went to the gas station’s store. He borrowed a key to the bathroom, once inside, he dialed the number in the back of the photo.

He said, “I think I found your brother.”

“Where is he?” asked Ahmed excitedly, trying to ignore the fear that started to threaten him.

“He is in my cub, as we speak. He asked me to take him to Saris,” replied Degu.

“Great! Now, I will start heading to Saris, but you have to call me with the exact location where he wants you to take him. Once I’m done with him, you and I will meet just so I can give you your reward money,” said Ahmed.

“Sure! In a few minutes, I will call you with the exact destination.”

“Yes, it is important that you do! thank you!”

***

After reading the professor’s text that Abigail forwarded to him, Million felt a relief. He thought, “Good! One less issue to worry about. Maybe this is the clue from the universe that now is the time when I should tell Saba who I really am.”

***

While in the hospital, Nuraan learned about Barakat’s disappearance and Ahmed’s march to hunt and kill Amin and her. He felt sad and confused. The matter that Mr. Ermias told him previously didn’t help him for an opinion whether to side with Million or with Amin—rather it made him morbid.

Facing too many calamities, his family didn’t know whom and what to worry about anymore. Rather, they were concerned something worse may happen to them.

At some moment of clarity, Nuraan realized what was happening in his family. Then, he pictured the chain of destruction that was trailing in his family. He imagined Ahmed and Million killing each other. He felt guilty of not telling Ahmed or the rest of his family what he knew about Million. *I need to find Ahmed, before it is too late,* he said to himself, and vanished from the hospital without telling anyone.

When his family heard about his disappearance from the hospital, they imagined whatever was destroying the family was around the corner to get each member. They weren't going to sit and wait. Fearfully, they gathered their valuables, locked their house behind them and went to a small town where their extended families lived.

***

Million never met Ahmed and he had no idea who he was. He was also sure that no one would be sent by the research center to kill him. So, he was focused on his single goal, becoming Million to his wife, kids, and family. Still thinking how to break the news to his wife, he paid his fair and stepped out of the taxi. His nervousness started to escalate with each foot to the front gate of his house. *I'm no longer Biniam. From now on, everyone needs to know that I'm Million!* he said to himself to fight off his nervousness. Suddenly, he saw a man coming toward him. For a second, he forgot the professor's promise and thought *the man might be there to kill him*. Then he composed himself and kept walking with confidence. The man, instead of passing by, stood in front of Million fearlessly and with clenched teeth. Million was sure that he had never seen the man before.

***

After tiresomely hunting, Ahmed has found his game. He said to Million, "You took Barakat from me, you killed my child, you robbed my money, and you were planning to kill me. No! You can't take everything from me. This is the time for you to pay for what you did so far." He quickly pulled out his gun and shot him.

For Million, everything went quickly. When the man stood blocking his way, he felt nervous. Then the man started talking, and what he said surprised him. And he thought, *Either this man is crazy, or he has mistaken me for someone. It is okay! I will explain to him. What a strange...* boom! Boom! He slowly fell down, his left hand pressed on his bleeding chest. He looked up to see his shooter, but the man had given him his back. He covered his eyes, tried to bear his pain and process what just happened.

After shooting Million twice in the chest and seeing him fall, Ahmed fled from the area quickly.

***

Million, the man of thought, the dreamer, with his dream in him, began fighting to breathe. He hoped that his wife and kids would come before whomever he was fighting won. He was only twenty feet away from Saba's house. His longing for his wife and kids, and his wish to reveal himself to them intensified. The blood from his chest was streaming between his fingers. His pain deepened. People who saw what was happening hurried toward him and called for the ambulance. The ambulance came and rushed him to the hospital.

***

At the emergency department, His eyes still covered, between his breaths, he managed to say, "I'm Million. But my body is Amin's. Please, tell my wife Saba and my kids."

The doctor quickly inserted a breathing tube down his throat, checked for correct placement with a carbon-dioxide-monitor and connected him to a breathing machine. Then, they inserted a chest tube to drain the blood and other fluid to protect his lungs from collapsing.

His bleeding had been stopped. A ventilator still assisted his breathing. Gradually, his oxygenation, blood pressure, and heart rate began to take shape. They stabilized him somehow, and he was to be sent for surgery then to the ICU. After dressing him in a hospital gown, the nurses began to collect his personal belongings—in the process, they found his passport.

However, the photo on the passport didn't match to the patient. They searched all his pockets for more identification documents, but they couldn't find any other. They notified their finding to the hospital administration along with the report that the patient had suffered a gunshot wound from an unidentified shooter. Consequently, the administration informed the police.

***

Ahmed judged he had killed Amin until he heard people talking that he survived. He thought, *Why did Allah save this traitor? He saw me in daylight shooting him, he knows who I am. Now, what? Before he sends me the police, I need to finish him.*

In the same train of thought, he decided to do whatever it took to go to the hospital and cut Amin's throat with a knife. *Again, I got to beat him before he does*, he said to himself and headed to the hospital.

"A guy, named Amin, who suffered a gunshot wound, which room is he in?" asked to a female receptionist of the hospital.

She told him no one named Amin with such an injury had come to the hospital.

Ahmed challenged the receptionist saying, "No! He is here. He came in an ambulance a few hours ago."

Again, she looked in the computer and said, "A few people have come in an ambulance, but a person named Amin is not one of them. Specifically, there is someone who came in for gunshot wound, however his name is not Amin. Sorry!"

After reading more notes, she said, "Anyway, how are you related to the patient? There is a note here that says, the guy with the gunshot wound is not identified. They were able to find someone named Million's passport in his pocket."

Trying to hide his excitement, he said, "Maybe that is him, can I please go see him? what room is he in?"

The receptionist asked again, "How are you related to him?"

"My name is Ali, and I'm his relative," replied Ahmed.

She took him to Million's room, which was in the Intensive Care Unit, third floor, room ten. After telling Ahmed to wait outside, she washed her hands and went inside and told the doctor and nurse who were doing post-surgery care that someone who said he was his relative was there to see him.

"Oh, good! He will help us identify who this patient is, tell him to come-in but warn him that he could only stay for a couple of minutes and that he needs to wear a mask," said the doctor.

She went out and told him what the doctor said and brought him inside. Ahmed saw that the man in bed was his brother Amin. “Yes, that it is him!” he whispered to the receptionist with shaking voice. Then, even though he had no tears, he took out a handkerchief and started wiping his eyes.

The doctor and the nurses were busy with the patient. Ahmed was glad that Amin couldn’t see or hear him. Nevertheless, his nerves started to get to him, he felt his heart beating fast, so, he sneaked out after looking at the room number and the unit. He promised to himself that he would come back to butcher his brother when the doctor and the nurses left the room.

After the procedure, the nurse went to the receptionist and asked, “The man whom you brought to room ten, how was he related to the patient?”

“He told me that he was his relative,” she replied.

“Great! He will help us establish this guy’s identity. Did he say when he will come back?”

“No, he didn’t say. I think he was sad seeing his relative like that.”

***

When Saba came back home from work, she found Mulu sitting depressed, crying, her eyes red and swollen.

Startled, she asked her, “What is wrong, Mulu? Why have you been crying until your face is swollen?”

“Someone shot Bini,” replied Mulu.

"What…? I can't believe it!" she felt as if her heart split into halves. "Where did they hit him?"

"Out there, close to our house. He shot him and ran."

"He who?"

"I don't know, but bystanders said that they saw one man running."

She couldn't accept it for a fact. She interrogated the poor girl, "Did you see for yourself that it was him?"

"I heard a couple of gunshots and people yelling, so, I went out to check what was going on. There I saw Bini on the ground his blood flooding from his chest."

"Oh, my brother! They killed him?" Her tears began to flow down her face. "Why didn't you call me? HE IS ALMOST A FAMILY. Mulu, you should have called me. Do you know where they took him to?" she said between her sobbing.

"Sorry! I didn't want to scare you. An ambulance came, I think they took him to the hospital where Maron had her Baby."

"Oh my Gosh! I don't even know what to say or do now," she said pulling her phone out of her purse.

She called Million's sister, Machida and told her what she heard from Mulu. Machida was shocked and couldn't say a word for seconds. Then they both began crying over the phone. After they hung up, Machida came running to Saba's house, and they cried on each other's shoulder. Together, they went from one hospital to another, looking for him.

"Have you guys admitted today a gentleman named Biniam who suffered a gunshot wound?" Saba asked the receptionists of the hospital, they all told them that they don't have any patient by that name.

Fortunately, an ambulance driver who brought him to the hospital overheard their back and forth and told them that he had transported a thirty-nine-year-old male with similar condition from Saris.

So, when the receptionist of that hospital told them that they don't have a patient by that name, who came in that day, Machida said, "Please check again, because the ambulance driver who brought him has told us he is here."

He said, "I don't mind checking again. However, we don't have a patient by that name."

"He is not a patient. He is a healthy man who suffered a gunshot wound," said Saba innocently, not knowing the lingo that everyone who needed care in a hospital or clinic was considered a patient.

"Still," said the receptionist while looking at the list of patients. Without looking up, he asked, "Did you say, Million Bayou?"

Saba and Machida stared at each other with surprise. And, Saba said, "No, I said Biniam."

"Sorry, but we don't have Biniam here. How are you related to the patient, anyway?"

Machida felt lost. She didn't know what to answer. The question triggered her old feelings of confusion and she thought, *Good question, what is he to me? I love him, but I don't know what this guy...*

Saba's answer to the question cut Machida's thought trail. "He is like our brother. He is my late husband's childhood friend. He was shot in front of my house, but I was at work at the time. Can you please help us find him?" said Saba slightly tilting her head to the side and looking the receptionist with teary eyes.

"I'm trying to help you. Like I said, there is someone named Million who was admitted for a gunshot wound," said the receptionist.

Could they have made a mistake when they were registering him for admission? the receptionist thought. Then he looked at both Saba and Machida and said, "Here is what I will do, I will ask the nurse if she will allow you to go see the man for yourself." And he dialed the phone to the nurses station. After he hung up, he told them to sit in the waiting area until the nurse came to get them. A few minutes later, a nurse came and took them to the room.

On the way in, the nurse instructed them, "We try not to make too much noise so the patient can rest."

Inside the room, a patient was laying in a bed, a tube in his throat, hooked up to a breathing machine, an IV line hanging from his left arm, and a couple more tubes hanging on each side of the bed.

Nervously, they walked closer to the patient. It was Bini. He seemed at the edge of death. They couldn't believe what they were seeing. They stood there with their hands on their mouths. Then, they started crying quietly and walked out quickly because they couldn't control their sobbing. Outside the room, they hugged each other and wept uncontrollably. Both of them were thinking what a great man he was.

"He was a perfect human being. I wonder who shot this peaceful man?" said Saba still crying. They were heading to the waiting area when the receptionist who helped the man called Ali visit Million approached and asked them how they were related to the patient. Saba told her what she told the other receptionist, except she added, "Bini is one of the most perfect spirited man I have ever met."

"So, you guys call him Bini, what is his actual name?" asked the receptionist.

"His name is Biniam, but he goes by Bini," replied Machida.

"Do you ladies mind waiting here for a little bit? The charge nurse, her name is Abreu, she would love to pick your brains about him," said the receptionist and went to her desk to dial to the charge nurse.

"Are you serious!" exclaimed Abreu.

"Interesting! Right? They seem to know him very well. Do you have a minute to come and chat with them?"

"As I told you earlier, there might be some secret behind this man. I will be there in a minute. Please stay with them, I need you to be there while I talked to them. If this turns into something, you and I are potential witnesses," said Abreu, putting away a chart she was looking at.

"The nurse is on her way to speak to you," said the receptionist, leading them into a conference room by the waiting area.

In the conference room, "I understand that he is like a family to you, doesn't he have an actual family who we can talk to?" asked Abreu, looking to both Saba and Machida.

Saba was saying, "Actually, he recently came from Germany to see his parents. But…"

Abreu's work phone rung and she said, "I have to take this, it is the new nurse, she might need some help… Hello, Fatima, do you need help?"

"No, I just have a question about the guy in room ten. It is not urgent," said Fatima.

"Actually, we are talking with his friends in the conference room, if you are done with what you were doing, and want to learn a thing or two, you are welcome to join us," said Abreu.

"Sorry, please continue, how do we get in touch with his parents? Do you know if he has any siblings?" she directed her question to Saba.

"I was going to say that we don't know where his family lives. At least I don't know. Machida, do you know?" Saba looked at Machida.

Fatima opened the door quietly and sat beside the receptionist.

Machida said, "No, he has been telling me that he is married and has two kids. I could never understand him. He was always talking some weird stuff."

"He told me the same thing. But when I asked him where they are, he said that I will know when the time is right."

Fatima, wasn't there but she learned about the visitor, Ali, who came and identified the patient in room ten as Amin. She read on Million's chart the confusion about his identity and lack of next of kin to tell the medical team about his background and who shot him. She remembered what Barakat told her about Amin, that he converted to Christianity and took the name Million.

Thus, she felt she had a better idea than anyone else about the guy in room ten. She thought, *Wow! He is Amin! Yes, he has a wife and two kids. So, he was staying with these people? How come they don't know him as Million? Maybe he has been telling different names to different people. Who is this Ali guy though?* She couldn't wait to call her husband and tell him that they might have found Amin and seek his advice on whether Barakat should come and see him or not.

Abreu didn't think she was getting the information she needed from the ladies. She said, "Can you please help us get in touch with his parents or siblings, better yet, with his wife. We need to know his background, and the police need to know who shot him. Please leave your phone number with the receptionist, in case we have questions." Then she left with Fatima after shaking their hands and saying goodbye.

"I read on his chart that when he first came to the emergency department, he was able to talk, and that he said his name is Million but he is in Amin's body. I have been wondering what he meant by that. He also told them to tell his wife about his situation," said the receptionist while accompanying them out.

"I don't know, the man is strange. I just hope he gets better soon and introduces us to his wife and kids that he has been speaking so fondly of," said Machida, expecting Saba to act differently or say something.

***

"Jemal, I think we might have found Amin."

"Are you serious? Don't tell me he is in your hospital?"

"Matter of fact, yes! Maybe this is the reason why I lost my old job and got this one just in time for this. What a coincidence is this! The main problem is that he is critically ill. He is on a breathing machine, and sedated. Therefore, even if Barakat comes to see him, he won't be able to talk to her."

"Still, she gets to make her peace. Hopefully, she moves on with her life as she has planned."

"This might not be an issue, but she just had her baby three days ago. Anyway, I will leave the decision to her, I will call her in a few minutes and tell her what is going on."

"If she does decide to come, let me know, I will prepare her transportation. You should never miss work anymore."

"Okay, my love, thank you!"

***

Abigail had been happy and relaxed because the gun that was pointing toward Million all the way from America was withdrawn. Excited about talking to him regarding subjects that are not strategies of how to escape the next web that the researchers had prepared, she called him on his cellphone.

However, it was a different man who answered the phone. After telling him who she was, she asked the whereabouts of Million. It was Million's doctor who answered the phone. The doctor heard the phone ringing from inside the drawer of the night stand, where most of Million's belongings were placed.

"My name is Abigail Muzik, Doctor Muzik. May I speak with Million?"

"Hi, Doctor Muzik, I'm one of the doctors who are caring for Million, we have been trying to find his next of kin; do you know him very well?"

“I thought I set up his care with Doctor Emanuel. Is Million able to speak? Where is Doctor Emanuel?” said Abigail sounding anxious.

“We don’t have a doctor named Emanuel in this hospital. Million is intubated and in a medically induced coma. How are you two related?”

“I’m his friend and his doctor here in the US. I know Million very well. Can you please tell me what happened?”

“He suffered gunshot wounds in the chest. Ultrasound shows that the apex of his left and most of his right lungs are damaged. There are still bullets in his right. Surgery is scheduled for tomorrow to remove the bullets.”

“Oh, my! I can’t believe they did that to him. This sick man played me; does he think he can get away with that? I will make him pay!” thought Abigail aloud.

“You know who shot him?”

“No, I don’t know who shot him, but I know who ordered it. I will get back to you with all that. Do you mind if I call you directly? Also, please keep this out of your report. We don’t have all facts, yet. Million is more than what you see. He a is unique and extraordinary man. Please take good care of him. Let me iron out a couple of things here, then I will come there,” said Abigail, her emotions swinging from nervousness to furiousness.

How could the professor lie to us? she asked herself after she took the doctor’s phone number and hung up.

She was sad and mad. If the professor were in front of her, she would have choked him to death. She believed that he had tricked them to relax and then had him killed.

***

Professor Woods was in his office doing some paper work. He had been there for long hours, so he was tired. Especially, with the sad news he'd just heard, he was ready to call it a day. While putting things away to leave, the phone rang.

"Hello?"

"Hello, it is Abigail."

"Oh, yes, I didn't recognize your voice. How is it going?"

"How dare you, you played me! Did you save him just to see him suffer and then kill him yourself? You must be sick! If you think you can get away with this, you must be fool," said Abigail and hung up on him.

The professor was confused. *Oh, shit! Somebody must have hurt the guy*, he said to himself while calling Abigail back.

She didn't answer. She was wondering if she should notify the FBI to protect herself and further damage to Million and his family. She wasn't sure what to do or where to start. Sitting there staring at her phone, a text came.

"Abigail, please understand that I have no idea what you were talking about. If Million is hurt, I have nothing to do with it. As I promised, I had my guys call Ethiopia and tell the assassin to cancel his assignment. However, I was told that there was another man who was pursuing him because he thought he was Amin. The guys here called that man, but his family told them that he left the house a few days ago and had never been back. I had them call repeatedly, but the family didn't know where he went. If what I think has occurred, I'm deeply sorry! It hurts me to hear that the poor man died because of me. Can you please tell me what is going on?

"If he is dead, I believe he is in a better place than I am. The problem that I'm facing is becoming more than I can withstand. It is shaking my peace and lively hood."

"He is not dead, but he is in critical condition. He got shot twice in the chest. They will open him tomorrow to remove the bullets from his right lung. What proof do I have that your guy didn't shoot him?" she texted him back.

"I was just talking to my contacts here, the man who was pursuing him for his own reason is named Ahmed. Apparently, he is Amin's brother and has been married to Amin's widow. Not surprisingly, the wife left him. She fled. The Ahmed guy assumed Amin has taken her. Thus, he wanted to kill him. But, believe me, I take responsibility to whatever happens to Million because if I didn't do the trial this wouldn't have happened. Well, there would never have been this conversation and most importantly the crisis I'm in."

Abigail wanted to believe the professor, but she was not sure. She thought, *Should I just go to Ethiopia without telling anyone and find out for myself. But then again, what if this is a set up? He might get me kidnapped or killed. Maybe I should talk to a lawyer—Million was right, I should have had one by now. Either way, I need to call Saba and explain to her everything. No one can help Million now, but her. She can tell his family in her own way, and his friend Sami too. Oh, yeah, Sami has something to do with law there. He might even help with finding out about this Ahmed guy, if he is actually who shot Million.*

***

"Hello, Fatima, are you busy?"

"Hi, Barakat, I was planning on calling you in a few minutes. What's up? Is everything okay?"

"Everything is great! Except, little Fatima has been crying, and throwing up a couple of times. Do you think I should take her to the hospital or leave her to fight off whatever bug she has?"

"Good question, I'm adults' nurse. Babies scare me. Let me check with other nurses and get back to you on that. In the meantime, make sure she stays hydrated and her breathing is okay. On another note, I have good news! We found Amin! "

"Fatima! You are my angel! Where is he? I can come early tomorrow and get back to my baby the same day."

"Not so fast! He is in the hospital. He is under a medically induced coma. Thus, he won't be talking to you, but you can still talk to him and make your peace. Do you want to do that?"

"Oh, my Amin! What happened to him? Could that devilish Ahmed have hurt him? Either way, I want see him once and for all and move on with my life."

"He was shot twice in the chest. Yesterday, they took out the bullets. But still, he is not doing well. It is good that you want to come tomorrow. You never know what could happen."

"Again, I suspect this is Ahmed's doing," said Barakat and started crying.

"Barakat, the police are working on finding who shot him. You go ahead prepare for tomorrow and I will call you later when I get off work." Fatima meant to ask Barakat who Ali was, "Hello, Barakat, are you still there? I forgot to ask you."

"Yes, I'm still here," said Barakat cleaning her tears from her face.

"Do you know who Ali is?"

"No, I don't."

"A guy named Ali came to see Amin after he got transferred to the third floor. I wasn't here that day. I'm waiting for him to comeback. Anyway, I was wondering if you knew who he was. Okay, will talk later."

***

When the police came to talk to the hospital administrator about the filed report, the charge nurse, Abreu was in the office discussing about the two ladies.

As soon as they finished interviewing the admin, Abreu suggested that they talk to Saba and Machida too. They took Saba's phone number from the receptionist and called and told her that Machida and herself should come to the police station for an interview.

***

The police began by asking both Saba and Machida where they resided, worked, and other identifying information. Then they asked how and where they knew Biniam. Saba told them that he was her husband's childhood friend and that he came from Frankfurt, Germany.

"Do you know who Amin is?" the police asked.

"I don't know," she replied. Machida shook her head, "no."

"Who is Million Bayou?"

Startled, Saba replied, "He is my late husband."

"Sorry for your loss, how did he die?"

"He died from a car accident in America, where he went for school."

"How did you learn of his death?"

"We were told over the phone, then his body came, and we buried him."

"Do you two have children?"

"Yes, we have two kids."

The police took out a passport from the top pocket of his jacket, showing the photo, asked her, “Do you know this person?”

She said, “That is my late husband. Where did you find his passport?” and she began crying.

“Have you confirmed that the patient is the Biniam whom you know?”

“Yes, I saw him very closely,” she replied between her sobbing.

“You are telling us that he is Biniam, but he told the nurses that he is Million Bayou?”

“This is strange! Yes, my late husband’s name is Million Bayou, and the photo on the passport you showed me is his. The patient, however, is not Million.”

“Thank you for all the information you gave us! We are confident that you will help us when we need further evidence. That is all we need for today.”

***

Million had a very good rapport with his landlord. Though sometimes he graciously refused, the landlord always invited him for morning coffee and occasional dinners. When he didn’t come back to his place for a couple of days or didn’t call about his whereabouts, the landlord began to worry. He wasn’t sure if he had left his unit, so he knocked a couple of mornings to check and invite him for coffee. Obviously, Million wasn’t there to answer the door.

For a moment, the landlord thought about opening the unit with his spare key and looking inside. But he didn't want to face whatever may be in the room by himself. Because his concern escalated, and because he was not the kind of person who could let go and wait to see what happened, he called the police.

So, the police, using the spare key, opened the unit and began searching in the room. If not Million, they were looking for any indicator of his whereabouts. On the top of the dresser, in addition to a couple of photo albums, they found a passport. It was Amin's passport.

The police, after looking at the profile page, gave the passport to the landlord to confirm if the person on the photo was the one who was missing. The landlord saw the photo and confirmed, and handed it back.

The police, then, said, "Okay, sir, we will xerox his information from this passport and send it to our field officers. As soon as we have an update, we will let you know. Please let us know if you hear from him sooner."

"Sure, thank you!" said the landlord and accompanied the officers to the gate.

***

Back at the station, one of the officers made multiple copies of the information page of Amin's passport. After posting one copy on the notice board, he handed a bunch to the receptionists for distribution to field officers and other police stations in the city and took a couple with him to the investigation room.

That afternoon, investigators of Saris area police station received a missing person briefing by their commander. Two of the inspectors were the ones who were assigned the hospital case.

After chatting amongst each other, one of them said to the commander, "Chief, the person in this photo looks like the victim in the shooting case we are assigned to. However, the patient identified himself as Million Bayou, which is the name on the missing person's report, and had a passport with that name, but the photo on that passport is no-match."

"You are right, the name on the report doesn't much to this profile, but the landlord who filed the report identified this guy as the tenant who has been missing. A person with two different passports—it looks like your jobs are cutout for you. Well, add this one into your exhibits, but make sure you get the original from Bella Police Station," said the commander.

The two investigators went to the interrogation room and started discussing the case. The lead detective said, "So, who is this guy? I'm sure the answer to this question is holding the clue to who shot him?"

“He told the nurses and doctors that he is Million. What I don’t understand is what he meant by that his body is Amin’s. Even the doctors and nurses didn’t understand him and don’t seem to have taken it seriously. One of the nurses jokingly brought up the scenario of people claiming a man in woman’s body or vice versa. Also, according to his attending physician, Doctor Absalom, his doctors from America call him Million. Either way, you are right, we need to answer if this guy is Biniam, Million, or Amin? Do you want me to call the Bella Station and ask them if they unearthed any other documents other than the passport?”

“That is what I was going to tell you next, I called them right before we went in for the briefing and they told me that they found Million’s school and employment documents, a photo album that has multiple family photos of him with a woman and two kids. I had the detective there to take a picture of one of the family photos and text it. Here it is. The woman in here is one of the witnesses. This is Saba, right?”

“Wow! Yes, that is her. Once we get all the documents and the album, we should call Saba and ask her if those items have been missing from her house. I believe there is more she hasn’t told us. Did they not find photos or documents of the Amin guy or Biniam’s?”

“Negative, they admitted that nothing other than the passport was related to Amin, also none in Biniam’s name.”

“Well, this is interesting! Did they say when they will send everything to us? If they are not going to send it before the end of the day, I can go get it myself.”

“The guy who has the evidences is a friend of mine. He said he would send them right away—that was an hour ago. While waiting for that, one of us should call the hospital and get more info on the guy who identified the victim as Amin. In fact, you do that, and I will call Saba and set up time for her to come, and ask the chief to get the guy’s phone unlocked. If it wasn’t for the password, we might have gotten some clue from looking at calls or texts he made, or his contacts lists.”

***

“Hello, Saba, it is me, Abigail. How is it going? How are the kids?”

“Hi Abigail, I’m so glad you called. Bini is in the hospital. Somebody shot him,” said Saba and started crying.

“I know, I know, I’m sorry, Saba,” said Abigail and began choking on her tears. She continued, “That is mainly why I called. The name of the guy who shot him is Ahmed Mustafa. I will text you his address, the street, and area names, because I don’t think I can pronounce it correctly. Can you please inform the police about this criminal right away before he causes any more damage?”

“I will! As soon we hang up, I will call them. They have been interrogating Machida and I. They asked me how I know Bini and where his family are. There were many strange and upsetting questions too. They said that they found my late husband's passport in his possession. Abigail, I'm sitting here in the middle of it, feeling like a drowning mouse, but you're calling me all the way from Germany, I mean from America, I forgot that Bini had told me you moved back there, with an answer to the question no investigator in town has able to find? Right now, I'm not going to ask you how, but promise me that you will tell me soon?"

"Dear, Saba, I have more things that I want to tell you that will wow you, but you have a more pressing issue to attend to. Million, I mean Bini, needs you now more than ever. I'm tying a few things here, then I will be there with you. We have to help this extraordinary man of yours. When I come, I will explain why I think he is exceptional and why I said your man."

"Abigail, Bini has always been unique and strange to me. He knows everything about me, but I know nothing about him. To make things worse, he had my late husband's passport in his pocket. I don't know what to make of this guy. To begin with, my husband never told me that he knew a guy named Biniam who live in Germany, let alone that, that person has been his childhood friend. Then he came out of nowhere and tries to fill the vacuum that Million left. To tell you the truth, he has been the greatest man around to me and my children since my husband.

"At the same time, I'm always uneasy around him because he is the most peculiar person I've met. Now the most pressing thing for the medical team is finding his next of kin. Thus, they have asked us to help them find his wife, or his parents or siblings. I know he is married because he told both Machida and myself, and the nurses too that he has a wife and kids.

"The problem is, he never told us where they are. The last time I asked him about that, he told me to wait until the right time. I pray that God grants him more time and that he introduces us to his family soon. But still, I hope you know where they are, at least you should know where his parents and siblings are because he should have taken you to them when you were here. So, can you tell me where they live?"

"Saba, you're right, he did introduce me to his wife and kids, and his family. But you have to wait until I come there to tell you all about them. I'm sorry that I'm not being the help you need, but it is for a good reason. However, there is one thing you can do for this man. Earlier you said that he filled the vacuum left by Million. For now, please fill the temporary vacuum left by his wife. I have explained everything to his primary attending physician, Doctor Absalom, so, he will help you help Bini."

"There is one more thing that I have been trying to ignore but kept coming up. Both the nurses and the police told Machida and I that Bini, when he first went to the ER told them that he is Million but his body is Amin's. I'm assuming he was hallucinating, but the nurses don't seem to believe so. What do you think?"

"Actually, he meant what he said—and it is one of the things I will be explaining to you before he gets out of the hospital. Also, in the meantime, you should know the guy who shot him, Ahmed is Amin's brother. I know my dear, you have many unanswered questions. But be patient, I promise I will explain it all to you, and you will not be disappointed. I need to go now; I have many things to attend to. If you have any question, call me. Have a wonderful day!"

***

"Saba, is everything okay?"

"Yes, everything is fine! I'm calling because I have information about who shot Bini. I wasn't sure if I should have called the police directly or you guys."

"It is perfect that you dialed to us. So, you know who shot him?"

"I learned from a reliable source that the criminal's name is Ahmed Mustafa. He lives in Mercato area in house number 503. Please go get him."

"Can you tell us why this man shot Bini?"

"This is the problem with you detectives. Instead of splitting questions, you should speed to action and get the man before he causes any more damage. LIKE I SAID, MY SOURCE IS RELIABLE!"

"I hear you loud and clear! We are just following the appropriate procedure. We will bring him for an interview, and we will go from there. Thank you for your help. By the way, I was going to call you because we have here some items that belong to you. Can you stop by the station at four o'clock?"

"Yes, I will come. But shouldn't you be busy catching this criminal?"

"No worries! We will work on that before you come in."

***

"Hi, Doctor Absalom, how is Million? Do you think he will wake up anytime soon?"

"His nurse just told me that he was coughing and trying to open his eyes. I haven't been to his room, yet. I have been swamped. If you call back in half an hour, I will give you more info."

"Sure, I will call you back. By the way, like I told you, Saba is his wife. I have been trying to install the truth into her head a bit at a time. She is bombarded by so much info from different sources, I hope she doesn't get upset and shut down. I gave her your info, so she will come to talk to you about him and how she can help. When you have time, please explain to her about brain transplant in general and Million's case in particular. I hope you checked some resources for yourself. I know you were skeptical when I first told you about Million and his background."

"Yes, I read some of the actual research papers you emailed me and watched the videos. To say the least, I found it fascinating. But why didn't they try the whole head and the spinal instead of just the brain? Afterall, what they did is more complex than what I'm thinking. At least in theory the implanting the head and the spinal cord seem much easier. I know the little girl's identity issue wouldn't have been avoided, but Million's would have been. Anyway, let me go check on Million and a couple of other patients. Call me back in an hour."

"Just a heads up, I'm already working on a paper about the head and spinal implant. Okay, I will call—thank you!"

***

Chapter Nineteen

Until the last eleven months, Professor Woods believed performing transplants and implants were the callings of his life. Recently, however, an agonizing question about the purpose of life kept bouncing in his head. "If helping people is not life's purpose, what else could it be?" he asked himself. He locked his room, turned off the light, using the light from his phone, he walked to his reclining chair. After he sat down, he switched off his phone. Pitch blackness grew in the room. "What else is there…" The phone rang and startled him. He thought he had turned it off. "Annoying," he yelled. He sent the call to his voice mail and threw the phone to the other end of the sofa. However, the phone rang again with unknown caller ID. This time he said, "Hello." Sounding miffed.

"Are you Professor Woods?" asked the person on the other line.

"Yes, I'm! Who is asking?" he said, becoming sure that he never heard the voice before.

"Listen to what I'm about to tell you quietly, for the sake of your daughter's safety," said a man with a clear indication of threat.

"Daddy! They are stressing me out and threating…" screamed a girl who had his daughter's voice. He was certain that the girl was his daughter. But he didn't know who was torturing her and why.

The same deep voice, "Have you confirmed that who you just heard is your daughter?" asked.

"Yes, but why?"

"We don't have time to waste, so I'm going to tell you upfront. Someone who is important to our organization is wanted by the US government and is on the no fly list. Thus, we need you to give him a new body. The sooner he travels back to his native land without any security complication, the sooner you will see your daughter. One of your assistants is here with us. We will have everything you need ready. Just stay tuned for my cue."

"Who are you guys? And who is my assistant that is with you?"

"Don't worry about that. All you need to know is when and where you will do what we tell you to do. I will contact you. I advise you not to mention what we talked about to anyone," said the man and hung up.

"What now, Marg? What now? More Troubles! ..." he yelled and sprang from his seat and stood in the dark room. He thought about Professor Art, "But, he is vacationing in

Hawaii. I talked him a couple of days ago," he said to himself.

***

"Fatima, I'm having cold feet about seeing Amin. I'm scared!"

"I understand it could be nerve wracking, but you have come all the way from Jima just for that, so I say you work your nerves to it."

"I don't know if I have the courage to see that man. Especially now that he can't talk, I feel like I'm being sneaky. You know, when he was okay, he didn't want to look at me in the eye. If I go to him at a time when he can't describe how he feels about me, am I not being devious?" said Barakat and started crying.

"You are not going there to insult him. You are going there to ask for his forgiveness. And that is the best quality of a human being. Considering that he is an intelligent man, he will respect that and admire your courage. By the way, he can hear you. However, don't expect him to respond. Just go there with a clear mind," said Fatima, wiping Barakat's tears with a napkin.

"If he opens his eyes, he might even like you in hijab and Kandoora," said Jemal smiling. Both Barakat and Fatima chuckled.

"You couldn't find parking?" asked his wife.

"Man! It is packed around here. I had to go two blocks behind the hospital. Anyways, what are you two doing here? Shouldn't you show her the room and go back to your work? When she is done visiting, I will take her home. You ladies can chat when you get off work and she can leave to Jima in the evening."

"She was just telling me that she is scared to go see him."

"I understand that it is not easy seeing someone you once loved in a sick bed, but he is getting the best care. Remember, by asking for his forgiveness, you are freeing both of you from torment of resentment. Even if he doesn't respond, you have done your part. That is all that matters and that is why you came, leaving your infant daughter."

"Thanks to you guys, I came here to take the burden off my shoulders, I don't know why I'm so nervous now. Which way do we go to his room?"

"His room is number ten, on the third floor. I know who his nurse is today. I will call her to help you visit and leave you alone with him. When you are done, take the same elevator, and Jemal will wait for you and take you home, and I will meet you guys in a couple of hours," said Fatima showing her which elevator to take to the ICU unit.

"Thank you! You have no idea how grateful I'm to you and your family!" said Barakat pressing the "UP" arrow on the elevator station.

"No problem, Barakat, we are happy to be able to help a wonderful person like you! By the way, Jemal is right, you look amazing in hijab and Kandoora."

"I'm actually wearing this to hide from the decadent Ahmed. I have never worn hijab in my life. I like it because I can even cover my face. You never know, he could be anywhere. Just talking about him makes me nervous."

"Don't worry, Allah will protect you! Just go do what you came to do. You got this!" said Fatima and rushed back to work.

"Is this elevator not working?" Barakat spoke to herself. And looking around, she noticed the people who were waiting there, had taken the stairs. *Oh, Allah, how do people in robes walk on stairs?* she thought and began slowly ascending. Then a thought of what she was going to say to Amin began bouncing in her brain. Before she knew it, she arrived at the room.

Slowly, she opened the door with her shaking left hand. Inside the room, the scene of a man hooked up to multiple medical devices, a nurse, and a doctor standing on his right side whispering something, unconscious and seemingly in his deathbed startled her. So not to make a loud cry, she beat her knuckles. Still staring at the patient, she walked closer to him.

"Amin, how did you end up like this? is it the cruel brother of yours who did this to you? I'm sorry, I'm the reason! I wish I were dead before all this," she whispered with a hoarse voice and her tears running down her face.

Million began to cough. He seemed trying to open his eyes. The nurse went and silenced the ventilator alarm while the doctor checked on Million. When he calmed down, the nurse left the room, and Doctor Absalom, quietly went close to Barakat and softly said, "You must be Barakat, I'm his physician, Doctor Absalom. The nurse told me that you were coming, and I was waiting to discuss with you a couple of things about this gentleman. Do you have a few minutes?"

"Yes, but I'm not sure if I can be any help."

"Actually, you do! You being here is a great help. Clearing facts while he is hearing will heal him. I apologize I didn't have a chance to speak with your friend, nurse Fatima. Otherwise, you would have come prepared. Nurse Fatima has mistakenly identified this man as Amin. And you probably think I'm crazy for saying that, because I know that you see him externally that he seems the Amin you knew."

"I don't understand, doctor. This man is Amin. Just because he hated me, he became Christian and changed his name to Million, but that doesn't make him someone else," said Barakat, dropping her chin and with wide eyes.

"I hear what you are saying, and if I was in your position, that is what I would have thought. However, some things are not the way they look. Hence, what I'm going to tell you is very confusing at first, so please give me your fullest attention. Let's pull those chairs and sit down, it might take a few minutes."

"Doctor, I have been through a lot these past twenty months. And I don't think any worse could come. So, let me hear it!"

"When Amin was attending school in America, did he ever tell you that he had a fried by the name Million?"

"Yes, on more than one occasion. In fact, I have talked to him once. They were roommates."

Million started coughing again. This time he opened his eyes and looked around and shut them. The nurse came in and gave him pain medication through his IV line."

Barakat went to Million and began caressing his head. She felt a long line of granulation that started in the middle of his head. She quickly pulled her hand back and went to where the doctor was waiting for her.

"Doctor, what happen to his head? Was he shot in the head too? Fatima told me only about his chest."

"No, he wasn't shot in the head. That is the incision for the procedure that made him who this man is. I will explain that soon. Going back to where we left off, when Amin had the car accident, he and Million were going to another city. According to the medical report I read, they both suffered a serious injury. However, Amin's brain was completely destroyed, and his body was treatable. Million's case was the opposite. While his brain remained intact, his body was damage beyond repair."

"So, they treated Amin's brain, that is why he has that incision in the head. Well, despite what he went through, he seemed healthy when I saw him briefly at the store."

"No, that is not how the story evolved. Let me ask you this, have you ever heard about kidney, lung, heart and other body part transplants?"

"Yes, I even know a man who received a kidney transplant."

"Great! In America, they have been doing research on brain transplants. You know, just like any other body parts. Remember, I said Amin's brain was destroyed by the accident?"

"Yes, are you telling me they replaced it with another healthy brain?"

"Yes, Yes, YES! Thank you! And as you know, a brain is not like other organs. The person with that new brain is completely different than the one with the older one."

"I don't know, I'm trying to understand what you are saying, but I'm not sure if I'm getting it."

"No, Barakat, you got it. In fact, you are the first person who understood more clearly than any one I have talked to about the case. Now, let me tell you why this man is Million, not Amin. When they replaced Amin's brain with a healthy one, the later was Million's. Think of your brain in Fatima's head. Which means Fatima's family would think you are her because what they see is her body. But you wouldn't know everyone that she used to know, you couldn't be a wife to her husband, well, you could if you wanted to, but it would feel weird. But you couldn't work as a nurse as she is doing, unless you go to school and become one."

"I got it! I think, I got it! If she had my brain, my mom, my kids, and everyone who knows me would not know her, even though she knows who they are."

Million opened his eyes and started searching to where the conversing people were. Attempting to talk, he slightly coughed. Then he covered his eyes and began listening to the conversation.

"That is actually, the scenario with Mr. Million Bayou. His brain being in your late husband's body, inserted through the incision you felt earlier. …"

"Sorry to interrupt, doc, Fatima is worried about her friend. I told her that she is with you, and she is wondering if she can join you."

"Yes, yes, please have her come in," said the doc.

"What are you two talking about? Is Amin going to be okay?" Fatima whispered.

"Come here, Fatima, things, sometimes are not the way they look," said Barakat and smiled, looking at the doc.

"Or people, are not who they look like they are," added the doctor, smiling back at Barakat and looking at Fatima.

"My dear sister, this nice doctor has been explaining to me many complicated and unbelievable things, but I'm coming close to believing him," said Barakat looking at Fatima without wiping the smile from her face.

"What exactly is going on here?" asked Fatima, looking at both.

"Before you came in, I was telling Barakat that Mr. Million has become a victim of mistaken identity. Barakat will explain to you the details, with the perfect example that I gave her. What you should know is that this gentleman is Million in Amin's body. He knows his family, his wife and kids, but they don't know him. Instead, Amin's family thought he is theirs. And Ahmed shot him to retaliate."

"Barakat, is this man your husband Amin or not?"

"Fatima, when his family and I heard the news about Amin's death, we were devastated. It was even worse that we didn't get to see his body before he was put to rest. Now I'm learning where his body went. The doctor is telling me, in America, they are now doing brain transplants. So, long story short, after Amin died, they took out his brain and replaced it with Million's. Million and Amin were friends at school and they were together during the accident. I guess Million's brain was okay."

"I'm lost. Do you really believe that? I've never heard of a brain transplant."

"I understand, at first, I was skeptical too. Until I read the study and someone who was part of the research explained it to me. So, I don't blame you at all, just take your time and think it through. And, like I said, Barakat will explain it to you."

"Okay, can we leave now? Jemal has been waiting there forever."

"Sure, let me have my final word with these two men and I will join you at the exit."

***

Ahmed was heading to the patient's room to silence Amin once and for all, when he saw a doctor and a woman in hijab and jilbab leaving the room. "Is that the traitor, impersonating true Muslim?" he thought and stood there until he could be sure.

The doctor said goodbye to Barakat and entered room twelve. She headed toward the stairs, pulling her face cover down. She took her phone and started texting to Fatima. She felt something was blocking her way. When she looked up from her phone, a large framed man stood in front of her. Seeing whom she saw, she melted as butter. Her knees gave up on her. Her heart skipped beats. Her brain, when she needed it the most, froze.

Ahmed looked at Barakat, she was not pregnant nor carrying a baby on her arm. He looked down at her with disgust and anger, his eyes seemed to spit fire all over her. He said, "You traitor, and murderer! Look at you, impersonating True Muslim! You, and your scumbag husband killed my child. Both of you have to pay for what you did."

Somehow, she collected her composure, and said “What are you doing here, you devil! This man is not Amin. You believed he is your brother and still didn’t hesitate to shoot him. As for your child, she is alive, but you will never see her.”

He quickly pulled out a knife from his side and stabbed her in the chest and pulled it back out. It didn’t take her a second to fall forward. Her blood started to flow like a stream.

Suddenly, the quiet and calm healing surrounding filled up with screaming, yelling and terror. People, including Doctor Absalom came out from every patients’ room to see the commotion and horror.

Ahmed, scaring those who stood in his way with his blood-soaked knife, headed to the exit. Two hospital security personnel were coming from his direction. He turned around and began searching for another escape. At one of the corridors, he found a small door that led outside. He pushed it as hard and fast as he could, but it wouldn’t open. He pulled it in, it wouldn’t budge.

Giving up on that route, he turned to the right and saw a clear glass window facing the parking lot. He walked backward, then dashed forward with a determination to escape, breaking the glass. He ended up face down on the asphalt of the parking lot. Pieces of the glass sprinkled on his back and elsewhere around him like petals of flowers.

Meanwhile, Doctor Absalom and a couple of nurses, rolled Barakat on her back and began pressing gauzes on the stabbed wound to stop the bleeding, gave her oxygen via mask, and started putting in IV lines. Then other doctors and nurses, including Fatima came. They picked her up and laid her on a stretcher and took her to surgery, working on the wound and blood transfusion as the primary plan. Fatima followed the stretcher, crying uncontrollably.

***

Following Saba's lead, the police directed their search for a man named Ahmed Mustafa. The leader of the team who was sent to bring Ahmed to the station for questioning reported, "Hello, chief, we are at the suspect's house, but no one is here. Neighbors are telling us that the whole family has moved to an unknown location.

"We just received a radio transmission about criminal activity in the hospital, should we stop our search and head there?"

"Another team is heading to the hospital. You guys continue your search, however, stand by for further instructions," replied the Chief.

***

"Sorry, Abigail, I didn't have a chance to answer your calls. We had an incident in our unit."

"What happened? Are you alright?"

"I'm okay! As soon as I hung up with you, I went out to do rounds with a couple of internists. While in the middle of it, Million's nurse called and told me that Amin's widow, Barakat was coming to see our guy. Apparently, one of our nurses, Fatima, who just joined us from a different hospital, knew Barakat and had told her that Amin is here. When the widow came, Fatima called Million's nurse and told her that Amin's wife is here to see him and asked to assist her. The nurse then told me what is being cooked."

"Man, this is weird! Remember I told you about the day Million ran into her and her kids at her store? He has been feeling guilty about taking their loved one's body ever since. Don't tell me Saba was there?"

"No, she didn't come until everything was over. But the story is more complicated than that."

"Sorry I interrupted you, please go ahead."

"I went to Million's room and Barakat came in a couple of minutes later and started crying kneeled on the side of Million's bed. She began to describe how sorry she was for what happened to him. Before she went further, I approached her and told her that the patient is Million not Amin. She thought I was crazy for saying that, but after half an hour-long explanation of why I said what I said, she began to consider the possibility.

"In fact, to my surprise, before she left the room, she called Million by his name and told him that she hoped he gets better soon. The worst part of her visiting started after her and I said goodbye and I went to see another patient. The Ahmed guy found her while leaving and stabbed her with a knife. She is now on life support. I think she will make it, because we got to her in time and reduced her bleeding and got a transfusion in less than thirty minutes. And Ahmed, he killed himself by jumping from the third floor."

"Oh, my gosh! That is tragic! Just terrible! I wish the police had acted quickly. All this wouldn't have happened had they apprehended Ahmed as soon as Saba informed them. They told her that they have protocols to follow. If their protocol doesn't promote catching of criminals and prevent events like this from happening, they should divorce it. I feel bad for Amin's family. I just hope that this is the last thing that will happen as the result of the poorly implemented research."

"The research has many great implications; it just wasn't implemented wisely. You know, soldiers or anyone who suffered a disfiguration of the face due to gunshot wounds and those who lost the functionality of their bodies for any reason could benefit from the procedure tremendously. Anyway, Million is awake and had been listening to the conversation Barakat and I had. He tried to talk on more than one occasion not realizing that he has a breathing tube."

"I agree with you whole heartedly about the research and its implication. About Million though, you have no idea how excited I'm to hear that he is awake. He is fighting the breathing machine, right? So, what is the plan now?"

"Yes, he is fighting it. And I hate to give him pain meds just to calm him, which will end up numbing him. As I told you, his right and a portion of his left lungs are damaged. If we can find a right lung donor, the left might heal on its own. After discussing his case with the pulmonologist of the hospital, and the surgeons who work on transplants, we all agreed that he should have a tracheostomy, then extubated. Do you have any suggestions or inputs?"

"No, that is a great plan. Considering the many surgeries, he will be having, tracheostomy is well thought," said Abigail. She glanced at her watch and said, "Goodness! It is five in the morning here. I have been on the phone all night. Two of the top researchers seem to be missing. Not even their families know where they went. So, my colleagues and I were discussing about them. Then, I had a long but fruitful conversation with Saba. I told her that you have understood how Million has become the way he is now, and she said she would come to talk to you. Did you say she stopped by?"

"Yes, the receptionist told me she did, but it was when all the commotion was going on and all the gates to the third floor were locked. I guess she will come tomorrow, except I won't be here until after three in the afternoon. So, your flight is today, and you didn't sleep all night, what are you going to do? Do you sleep in flight? Because I don't."

"Yes, it is. Very soon, I will head to the center and grab a few things. After I have all my stuff ready for the flight, I will catch two hours sleep. Then, I will go to my parents to say goodbye. After that I will be at the airport. Though I was never good at sleeping in flight, I might sleep this time. Anyways, we will talk when I get there. You have been a great help! Thank you so much!"

***

Back in the courtroom, despite Ava's big hope, the professor's testimony didn't seem to have effect on the way the case was turning. At the defendant's attorney's request, the judges interviewed the child behind closed doors. Then when the defendant's attorney summoned her as a character witness, Ava and her supporters gave up hope and lost confidence.

The lawyer began his question by asking her name, "Child, what is your name?"

"But I told you last time, you don't remember?" she said and chuckled.

"Not like that, everybody in here wants to know your name. Can you go ahead tell everyone just once? Thank you!"

"Okay, my name is Sandra Johns!"

"But some people say your name is Teena, is that not true?"

"Ava calls me Teena, but I don't like that name."

"Why not?"

The plaintiffs' lawyer contested that the question was leading. But the judge encouraged the child to answer.

"Why do you not like when Ava calls you Teena?" asked the defendants' lawyer.

"Because I like Sandra better. My dad and mom call me Sandy."

"Who are your mom and dad? Can you tell everyone their names?"

"My dad is Deric and my mom is Tesha."

"Are they in here?"

"My mom is over there, but I don't know where my dad is. I really miss my dad!" she said and started tearing up.

"Sandra, I'm sorry your dad couldn't be here! Thank you for answering my questions! You are a brave young lady!" said the attorney. Then pointing with his index fingers to the plaintiffs' attorney, he said, "This gentleman might have some questions for you, so stay there for a few minutes."

The plaintiffs' attorney declined questioning the child.

***

Abigail and Saba were on their way back from visiting Million and a meeting with Doctor Absalom, when Abigail asked, "Saba, if Million was able to talk, what do you think he would have said to you?"

"I don't know, maybe he would tell me some secret Million and I talked about or did before he went to America.

But it is hard to imagine that someone you saw buried beneath the ground would come back and talk to you. Despite the convincing explanations both from you and the doctor, I'm still not confident to believe that Bini is in fact Million.

"First off, there is not a slightest resemblance between my Million and Bini. In my mind, there are pictures of Million when we first met, on our wedding day, baptism of our first child, and even when he was crying at the airport the day he left to America. How can I erase all that memory and replace it with this new Million's mental pictures?

"At home, there are many pictures of my Million, including an album that the police gave me saying they found it in Bini's apartment. I can get rid of all those, but I don't think I can do the same with what is in my head. Abigail, don't get me wrong, whenever Bini talked to me about things my Million and I had talked about and did, I had sensed personalities of Million in him, but all it did was scare the bejesus out of me.

"So, tell me, how do I completely shift my mind and turn it one-hundred-eighty-degrees to replace my Million with this someone who might possibly be that Million? Don't think I'm being inflexible. With yours and Doctor Absalom's explanation and the videos and written materials, I drew a mental picture of the brain transplant procedure. It felt like I was next to the surgery room, looking through the window when the brains were being swapped into the two bodies. Million's brain being placed in his friend's body."

"Wait, wait, Saba, you actually were mentally transported to the place where the procedure was conducted and saw Million's brain residing in Amin's body? That is amazing! You have the greatest visual imagery I have ever heard anyone has. Well with that kind of gift and skill, you can convince your brain, let alone the Million you sensed in Bini, anyone who treated you as Million would could be Million. Believe me, I never underestimate the power of memory. But we all have the capacity to put aside what we have and create a new one. So, I don't expect you and don't recommend to dismiss all previous memories of Million and you, what I beg you to consider is to just add new ones to the existing. Except this time, you will have new physical picture of Million but the same thoughtful, loving, honest, and reliable husband and the father of your children."

"Speaking of children, how would I convince Mica and Rui that the man whom they have known as the best friend of their father for the last nine months is in fact their father, Million? They were at their father's burial, crying their hearts out, and still sometimes they cry, saying that they miss him. It is rather crazy to tell them such alternate reality that I as an adult still working to accept. I think, at least for their sake, we should still call him Bini. Maybe after a while, they will slowly learn the reality. In fact, there is this idea that has been knocking from inside my brain. It was formed when you told me about the sameness of Bini and Million. Do you want to hear it?"

"Please do so, Saba, I love hearing anything you have to say about you and Million. There is a lot of work ahead, but let's take things one step at a time."

"Here is the idea, granted Million is Bini, why wouldn't the new Million and I get married but he keeps the name Bini? That is the only way, I believe, that I will be able to trick my brain and that of my children's. What do you think?"

"Saba, you are genius! That is a brilliant idea! In a couple of days, Million will have tracheostomy. A few hours after that, he will be able to speak just like you and I, except he will be using a device. Then we will run this idea by him. In fact, we should share it with him now—he will be ecstatic!"

"As for Million's sister Machida and the rest of his family, you and Doctor Absalom should have a sit down with them and bring all your proof. First, you guys should talk to his siblings, then in a day or two to his parents. Every one of them has some clue that Bini knew the whole family, and me and my children even before he met us. The only question was, how. We talked about him that he is some kind of psychic and someone with special skill. To tell you the truth, I was once convinced that he has some kind of supernatural power. He used to scare me. Now that I know the truth, I can handle the Bini who knows all about me and Million's family."

"I agree. I will ask Absalom what day works for him, and you and I will coordinate the meeting with both Machida and her brother. Hopefully they will explain to their parents prior to us meeting the elders. Do you have a prediction how Machida will react when we tell her the man she once had dreamed of marring is actually her brother?"

"I'm sure, she will be confused, surprised, and upset, probably in that order. And I don't blame her. Those were my reactions. I think she will be more upset than I was."

"Okay, let's just say we need to stay prepared for whatever comes. Also, we need to take things slow, as in one step at a time. Now, for a change, let's talk about something else. What do you think of Doctor Absalom, don't you think that guy is the cutest man alive?"

“Oh! Mama! my American sister is having a crush on an Ethiopian man! Honestly, he is handsome and intelligent!”

“Well, I’m not going to remain single, you know. I might as well be with someone whom I found attractive. Throughout my adult life, I have been attracted to men with power and who are slightly aggressive. Now, I’m going for the same level as me and who is calm and thoughtful—just like Million.”

“Welcome to the club! I liked Million because unlike his friends at the time, he wasn’t a showoff. He was calm, composed, caring, and loving. Anyway, do you know if the doc crush of yours is single? I didn’t see a ring in his finger, but you never know.”

“I don’t know, but if my assessment serves me well, he spent his days off with us, the way he combs his hair, the deodorant he wears, and his wrinkled shirts tell me that he is single. Either way, I’m not shy to ask. Once the things that brought me here take shape, I will ask him for us to go to Sodere. When Million and I went there, we had a blast. The only problem was that we were just two friends. So, going there with a date would be fantastic! And when Million gets better, the four of us will go again. Also, we should find a date for Machida, that way they can join us.”

“This is the loveliest and the most exciting thing I have heard for a while. How long are you going to be here for?”

"At least three months, but it could be six or twelve, depending how it went with Absalom. But first, I need to take care of Million's business. He is my priority! Saba, I admire and love you for being open and accepting to Million. Accepting him back into yours and his kids' lives, the new version of him, even with the new name means a lot to him. All he wanted was recognition, becoming the husband to his wife, the father to his kids, the son to his parents, and the brother to his siblings. My last work, therefore, with your help, is giving form to the remaining two, and setting him up in life as the new Million. Again, thank you so much for understanding and being the support we all come to!"

-THE END-

Made in the USA
Columbia, SC
14 February 2020